Family

is life

Hallowed Elements
The Dúbailte Chronicles
Book Three

M.A. Kilpatrick

Copyright © 2024 by M.A. Kilpatrick

All rights reserved.

No part of this book may be reproduced in any form or by any electronic or mechanical means, including information storage and retrieval systems, without written permission from the author, except for the use of brief quotations in a book review.

ISBN: 979-8-9907053-3-3 (Paperback)

ISBN: 979-8-9907053-4-0 (Special Edition Hardcover)

Any references to historical events, real people, or real places are used fictitiously. Names, characters, and places are products of the author's imagination.

First printing edition 2024

makilpatrick.com

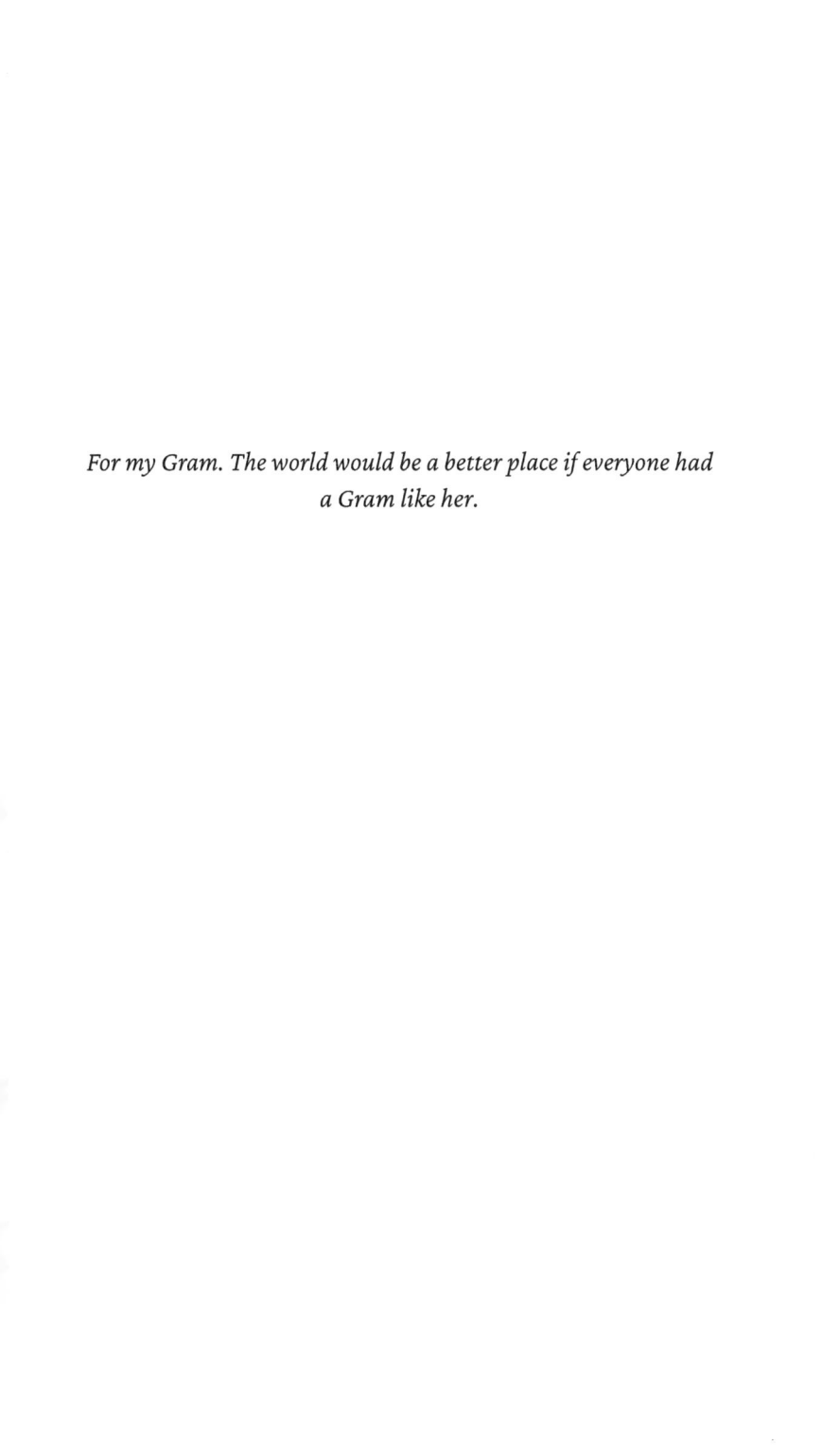

For my Gram. The world would be a better place if everyone had a Gram like her.

TRIGGER WARNINGS

Profanity; violent/battle scenes; blood and gore depiction; loss of limb; death; explicit sexual imagery, including BDSM topics, such as spanking, hair pulling, edging, breath play, and shibari; captivity and confinement; grief and loss depiction; body modification—tattooing

GLOSSARY

All terms are Irish, unless otherwise noted.

> *A chuisle mo chroí (uh-KUSH-luh-muh-C(h)REE)— The beat or pulse of my heart, also a phrase sometimes used to mean "I love you"*
> *A stór (uh-STOR) — Dear, a term of endearment*
> *Aibhleog (AV-lohg) — Ember, also Calder's nickname for Keegan*
> *Aidan (AH-dun)*
> *Ailáine (uh-LONN-uh)*
> *Áine (AWN-yuh)*
> *Aintín (an-T(ch)EEN) — Aunt*
> *Aisling (ASH-ling)*
> *Anamchara (AH-num-CARR-uh) — Soul friend, another term for soulmates*
> *Anfa (ANN-fuh)*
> *Angus (ANN-gus)*
> *Aoife (EE-fa)*

Aos Sí (ES-shee) — Irish Fae
Balor (BAH-lor) — An ancient Fomorian enemy who looked like a hideous, one-eyed monster
Bain sult as (bahn-SULT-as) — Enjoy or have fun
Bháni (VAHN-ee) — Nickname for Siobhán
Brady (BRAY-dee)
Bran (BRANN)
Brennan (BREN-an)
Brian (BREE-an)
Brona (BROH-nuh)
Cailíní (kah-LEEN-ee) — Girls, plural
Cara (CARR-uh)
Carraig (CARR-ig)
Cathal (CA-hull)
Céad míle fáilte (CADE-MEE-luh-FALL-tsuh) — A hundred thousand welcomes, a formal Irish welcome
Céilí (KAY-lee) — Party
Chica (CHEE-kuh) — Girl; Spanish
Clochán (CLOH-(c)hawn) — Stepping stone
Corley (COR-lee)
Cré (CRAY)
Crann (CRANN)
Croía (CREE-ya)
Da (DAH) — Dad
Dáithí (DIE-hee)
Danu (DAN-nuh) — Mother of the gods
Deartháir beag (DREH-har-BEG) — Little brother
Deirdre (DEER-druh)
Desmond (dess-MAWN-d(uh))

Dia duit (DEE-uh (hw)IT) — God to you, a customary Irish greeting
Donn (DAWN) — God of the dead
Doran (duh-RAN)
Dossers (DOSS-ers) — Slackers
Dris (DRISH)
Dúbailte (DOO-ball-tsuh) — Double, also a term used to describe Fae with dual powers
Eejit (EE-jit) — Idiot
Emer (eh-MEER)
Étaín (eh-DEEN)
Fáilte (FALL-tsuh) — Welcome
Falias (FALL-ee-us) — The Earth Clan island
Féirín (FAY-reen)
Feis (FESH) — Clan gathering
Fergal (FAIR-gull)
Fianna (FEE-uh-nuh) — Ancient band of roving warriors/hunters
Findias (FINN-dee-us) — The Fire Clan island
Flannery (FLAWN-er-ee)
Go n-éirí leat (guh-NYIGH-ree-L(y)A) — May you succeed or good luck
Go raibh maith agat (guh ru(v) MAH ah-gut) — Thank you
Gorias (GORE-ee-us) — The Air Clan island
Gorm (GOR-uhm)
Imogen (IMM-uh-guhn)
Iseult (ISH-alt)
Keegan (KEE-gun)
Laoise (LEE-shuh)
Lasair (LOSS-ir)
Litha (LEE-huh)
Lorcan (LOR-ken)

Lughnasa (LOO-nuh-suh) — A Celtic festival marking the beginning of the harvest season
Máire (MOI-ra)
Máthair (MO-hare) – Mother
Máthair Chríona (MO-hare-C(h)REE-uh-na) — Wise Mother, sometimes used as an honorific
Mian (MEE-uhn)
Mo chroí (muh-C(h)REE) — My heart
Mo chuisle (muh-KUSH-LA) — My pulse; the pulse of my heart
Mo leanbh (muh-LAN-uv) — My child
(The) Morrígan (MOR-i-gun) — Shapeshifting, triune war goddess, associated with death and crows, also the name of Siobhán's horse
Muireann (MWEER-in)
Murias (MUR-ee-us) — The Water Clan island
Niall (NIGH-ull)
Niamh (NEEV)
Ó Faoláin (oh-FAY-lin)
Ó Loingsigh (oh-LING-shee)
Oileán na ndéithe (ay-LAWN-na-NYAY-ha) —Island of the Gods
Ómra (OHM-ruh)
Orla (OR-luh)
Osgar (os-GAR)
Púca (POO-ka) — A shapeshifting, mischievous spirit, also Lir's type of familiar
Quinn (KWIN)
Ré (RAY)
Rónán (ROH-nahn)
Rowan (ROH-wahn)

Ruaig (ROO-ig)
Saoirse (SEER-shuh)
Siobhán (shi-VAHN)
Sláine (SLAWN-ya)
Slán (SLAWN) — Goodbye
Spéir (SPARE)
Tá brón orm — *(taw-BROH-n-OR-um)* — I'm sorry or there is sadness on me
Taviseach (TEE-shu(ch)) — High Clan Chief
Tionól (T(s)IN-all) — Assembly, and also the name of the village surrounding the World Tree in Tír na nÓg
Tír na nÓg (TEER-nuh-NOHG) — Land of Youth, the Fae home world
Tonn (TAWN)
Trasa (TRAH-suh)
Tréan (TRAY-uhn)
Treasa (TRESS-uh)
Tuatha Dé Danann (too-AH-(ha)-day-DANN-uhn) — Tribe of Danu
Ula (ULL-uh)
Wanker (WAYN-ker) —Jerk
Wean(s) (WAHN(S)) — Child(ren)

Family

is life

PROLOGUE

"Motherfucker! My turtle is broken!" Lasair extended a dagger-sharp jet-black talon toward the offending reptile, intending to poke some sense, or maybe some speed, into the lethargic creature.

Cré, ever the rule-follower, warned, in his deep, gravelly voice, "Ah, ah, ah! Touch it and you're disqualified!" This stopped her cold—disqualification from one of their contests was a fate worse than death. She pulled her talon back, let out a huff, and replied, "Fine. But I'm not sure why I'm bothering. This stupid turtle is a dud."

"Perhaps we should come up with a new diversion?" Ruaig offered, his lithe, sinuous form floating above them. The setting sun cast shades of vermillion and scarlet across his golden scales, causing them to shimmer when he shifted his position.

Tonn snorted, replying, "Like what? If there's a wager we haven't made, I certainly don't know what it could be." She rolled onto her back as she spoke, stretching like a cat. Well, that is if cats came covered in scales ranging from sky blue to turquoise to indigo with glowing teal eyes. She ran her talons through the long, shaggy scales atop her head, creating a mane cascading down her back. Her turtle had already crawled away, abandoning her and the race she was trying to win.

"Argh!" Lasair exclaimed, "I am so bored, I'm considering asking Cré to read us some of his poetry."

Ruaig, who was lazily spinning through the air slightly above their heads, gasped and jolted to a stop mid-spin. "No! Anything but that!"

A spiky tail covered with metallic scales in all shades of green and bronze snaked up and smacked his companion in the back of the head. "Very funny, dickhead. I'll have you know my poetry is deep and soulful!"

"It's full of something, but soul isn't the first thing that comes to mind," Ruaig snarked, quickly zipping out of range of the poet's tail.

Lasair tilted her scarlet head back and let out a frustrated growl, catching the attention of her three companions. "You're giving me a migraine! Such a highly developed intellect as mine should be nurtured and continuously challenged. Instead, I'm reduced to watching idiotic turtles trying to win a race they don't know they're running." As she spoke, her trailing turtle stepped in a hole and wound up on his back, kicking his stumpy little legs ineffectually in the air. "Just perfect," she groused, rolling her luminescent crimson eyes.

Suddenly, Tonn threw her head back, her eyes rolling back to show only the sclera. Her breath came quick and fast as visions began tumbling through her mind. Her companions, who were quite used to this particular show, waited patiently for the premonition to end.

After a few moments, she lowered her head, her eyes

and breathing returning to normal. "Well, friends, I think the boredom is about to end. Shit is about to hit the fan, and it is blowing in our direction."

Family

is life

I

"Has anyone seen Lir?" Calder asked as he joined Keegan and Áine on his mother's back porch. His beloved, blissfully enjoying the hot tea he'd just prepared for her, shrugged her shoulders and shook her head. The phoenix was perched on the railing, a nondescript black bag clutched in her talon. None of that was suspicious, but she refused to look either Keegan or Calder in the eye.

Keegan's eyes narrowed, and she demanded, "Spill it, Miss Thang. What did you talk Lir into?" Áine made a valiant attempt at righteous indignation but only lasted a few seconds before she couldn't contain her laughter anymore.

"Bwa ha ha, Goat Boy is in here!" she cackled, lifting the bag she was holding. "I double-dog dared him to go inside, and he did! Now he can't get out until I let him." She was inordinately pleased with herself.

Calder crossed his arms and gave her a stern look. "Áine, you know he would never do that to you."

She looked genuinely confused and said, "Of course he

wouldn't. But if he would, he'd be just like me, and we certainly don't need that. I'm as much fabulousness as you lot can handle." Then she sniffed disdainfully as if that should have been perfectly clear from the beginning.

Keegan sat aside her now empty teacup and mumbled something under her breath that sounded suspiciously like "fuck my life," before turning to her familiar. "You know you're being mean, birdbrain. Let the sweet familiar out of the bag and be thankful he's not the vengeful type."

Áine rolled her eyes and said, "Fine. But this is gonna be one long-ass trip if Goat Boy can't take a joke." She dropped the bag onto the porch, and after a few moments, a midnight-black hoof poked its way out, quickly followed by the rest of his leg, and then his entire púca body. It was an eerie sight to see something emerge from a bag that was obviously far too small for it.

Once he was completely out, he looked at the other three, smiled, and exclaimed, "That was bizarre. But I think I liked it."

"See, he's fine. Don't know what everybody's fussin' about," the phoenix mumbled. Keegan started to argue, "That's not really the poi—" but Calder put his hand on her shoulder and said, "It's not worth it, love. Let's just enjoy our time with them before they leave." She sighed but nodded.

"Speaking of leaving, let's get this show on the road," Áine commented, launching herself into the air and circling for a bit as Keegan and Calder pulled themselves onto Lir's back. Then, the púca took off toward the World Tree as the phoenix quickly followed.

As the two Dúbailte and their familiars entered the gardens surrounding the World Tree, several of the colorful, sparkling butterflies Áine found so offensive were leaving glittering trails in their wake as they crossed the path ahead of them. The phoenix refrained from commenting, but a disgusted snort was heard from her general direction.

They made their way to the giant tree in the center of the gardens. Keegan tilted her head back, looking up through the branches and leaves, enjoying the dappled sunlight filtering through. This was one of those places that just felt right to her. She'd struggled her whole life with having to hide the magical side of herself as she grew up on Earth. Being able to embrace her entire being fully was an incredibly freeing sensation, and she intended to protect this place and her people from whatever danger was headed their way.

Áine circled overhead before landing gracefully on Keegan's shoulder. "Come on, sparkle tits, let's get things moving!"

The fiery redhead rolled her silver eyes and snarked, "This is not Portals-R-Us. Keep your panties on." She reached into her back pocket and pulled out a small round artifact with a raised area in the center. "I know Mom gave you the expando-bag, and Deirdre wrote the letter for you, so hopefully, those items will serve you well on your journey. But I also know that my little firebird can only go so long without her tunes. So, I made you a battery." She bent over to set the artifact on the ground, and Áine hopped off her shoulder to inspect it more closely.

"You just step on the button in the center, then place the iPod near it, and it will charge it in just a few minutes. When it's done, it will turn itself off, or you can just push it again to deactivate it, and it will recharge from the ambient magic in the air. You can thank Máire for that part; I'm not that advanced yet." She gave a little shrug as she ended the explanation.

Áine looked at the battery and tentatively pushed the center button with her talon. It began glowing to denote activation. Then she pushed it again to turn it off and fluttered back up to Keegan's shoulder. She flung her wings around Keegan's head in one of her overly dramatic hugs, and said, "Girl, you are a lifesaver. I thought I was gonna have to bone up on my conversation skills once the iPod went dead. I was up for the challenge, but this will be so much better!"

While the girls were having their moment, Calder patted Lir on the side of the neck and said, "You'll watch out for both of you, eh?" The púca leaned into him and said, "You know I will. You just worry about whipping the Fianna, and then the rest of the Aos Sí into shape. We'll bring the reinforcements."

"Good lad," the Dúbailte said, giving him a good scratch behind the ears. "But now I think it's time for you two to be on your way."

Keegan picked up the battery artifact and slipped it into the bag before looping it over Lir's head. Then she and Calder took their places in front of the World Tree, with Áine and Lir waiting a few paces away.

"Are you ready, Aibhleog?" he asked, giving her a sympathetic look as she blinked back tears. This pilgrimage their familiars were undertaking was hitting her harder than she expected, but she was bound and determined to do her part and send them safely on their way.

She nodded and held her hands out to the side, calling fire into one hand and creating a swirl of air around the other. Calder quickly mimicked her, pulling forth water from the air to encircle his wrist and causing a vine to climb up his leg, around his waist, and over his shoulder, snaking its way down to entwine around his other forearm.

"Since you haven't been to Murias, just concentrate on sending the portal wherever I want it to go. I will guide it to the Water Clan island," he explained. Keegan nodded, and they both took a step forward, raising their element-engulfed hands until they touched, and a bright light erupted between their fingertips. They each stepped back, stretching that glowing portal between them until it was large enough for their familiars to fit through, then they flipped it perpendicular to the ground.

A huge tree, similar to the World Tree near Tíonol, could be seen through the glowing shimmery portal. Other trees were nearby, but they were all dwarfed by the Water Clan Tree.

"You're good to go! Be careful and stay safe!" Keegan called as the two familiars stepped through the portal. Once they appeared on the other side and waved to show they had arrived in one piece, Keegan and Calder released the portal. He wrapped his arms around his beloved and pulled her close, offering and receiving comfort in kind. She returned the embrace, squeezing him tightly.

"They'll be all right, love. I'd trust them both with my life," he murmured against her ear, raising one hand to stroke her hair soothingly.

She caressed his cheek, then sighed and pulled back slightly. "I know they will. Now, we need to do our part. It's time to get organized and start training our troops. We've got some monster ass to kick."

Rónán huddled in the alcove, desperately pooling the shadows around him. He kept frantically repeating the mental exercises his sisters had taught him to help ward his mind against intrusion.

This past week had been a waking nightmare for the young Shadow Weaver. He'd been hiding from his twin sisters and their insistence on a clean room. He was twelve after all, but they kept insisting on treating him like a child.

He must've fallen asleep because the next thing he knew, he heard a scream, both mentally and audibly, which startled him awake. He cautiously began wandering the empty halls, searching for somebody—anybody—but finding no one. All the members of the Shadow Faction had disappeared...except for him. He was on his own.

Since then, he'd been scuttling around, avoiding notice at all costs. He didn't know if Cathal was stalking the halls, but he did not intend to find out. So far, the mental exercises had kept him free from Balor's mind control, but he had no illusions that this would be the case indefinitely. He was basically making his mind slippery so that the leader of the Chaos Faction could not truly dig in and take control. If he was able to truly lock on, Rónán would be a goner.

As far as food was concerned, he had found some in the kitchens, but it was almost gone. He was getting very nervous, but he wasn't quite sure what to do about his situation.

Even though he'd never done it before, he thought he should be able to create a shadow portal, if he could make it to the portal room undetected. Then there was the fact that he would need to create the portal quickly, because as soon as he started, Balor would know and send that psychopath after him, or he would just take control of his mind and turn him into a dribbling vegetable. To say he was less than confident would be quite the understatement.

But for now, he would tackle a problem he thought he could solve—food. He had pretty much cleaned out the kitchens and stashed what he found in a few different hidey holes, but now he had his sights set on the gardens. Since they were in a more exposed location, he planned to wait until the middle of the night. He would take any advantage he could get, so for now it was just a waiting game.

A jaw-cracking yawn snuck up on the adolescent—sleep had been hard to come by lately, and he needed to stay sharp, so he decided to risk a nap.

He began shifting his shadows and slowly moving his way down the hall and around the corner until the rooms he had shared with his sisters were in view. The coast appeared to be clear, so he quickly entered the apartment and quietly pulled the door shut.

He had avoided spending too much time in one place, especially his apartment, trying to make it as difficult as possible to find him, just in case somebody was looking. But he needed some rest, and this is where that was most likely to happen. He grabbed his pillow and tossed it in his closet. Then he grabbed a blanket from each of his sisters' beds. He brought them to his face and breathed deeply, catching just a hint of their perfume. He blinked hard, trying to stave off the tears, but he was too tired, and it was all just too hard at the moment. So, he curled up on the floor of his closet, shutting the door in case someone wandered in, and gave in to the fear and loneliness that had been his constant companions as of late. He cried himself to sleep, hoping against hope that tomorrow would be a better day.

It had been almost a week since Cathal's death and the Shadow Faction's escape, and Balor was still seething. Without his pet, he was forced to venture forth from his rooms, needing food as much as any other living creature. But more than that, he needed to make sure his Titans were still contained. His worthless offspring might have handed him a setback, but his plans were merely delayed, not destroyed.

As he ambled slowly through the empty halls of the Fomori Stronghold, he began thinking about the best way to reformulate his strategy. Even with his level of mental control, he still needed some able bodies to care for his Titans. His best option was to delay the transformation of his latest Shadow Faction conscripts and force their compliance. He thought there were a few dozen Shadow Weavers who could handle the job.

As he approached the Titan's cavern, he could hear those conscripts arguing and debating, most likely attempting to break free while things were still chaotic. *Time to put a stop to that and reestablish my control.*

He opened the giant cavern door and unleashed a mental attack so ferocious that every single one of the captive Shadow Weavers dropped to their knees from the pain. He was not screwing around.

Due to unforeseen circumstances, your situation has now changed. Your transformation into Titans has been postponed. You will now be responsible for the other Titans' wellbeing. You will feed them, hose them down when needed, and ensure they remain docile and quiet. Make sure you perform these duties well. Otherwise, you are of no use to me, and your transformation will resume as planned. Choose wisely.

He retreated from the cavern with one final command.
And somebody get me some bloody food.

Family

is life

2

The expanded Council, Fianna, a few of the Shadow Weavers, and a small delegation of familiars were all milling around the Council Hall, speculating about their next steps. Shay amplified his voice and called out, "Would you all please take a seat? We need to get started."

Everyone settled in and turned their attention to the Taoiseach. He ran his gaze over those assembled, took a deep breath, and said, "Well now, I can honestly say this is not the type of gathering to which I am accustomed. So, I would like to open the floor. Who would like to get things rolling?"

Fintan raised two fingers, and Shay nodded at him. "I'd suggest we throw things at the wall and see what sticks. Then we can narrow it down."

Siobhán cleared her throat and said, "The Aos Sí have always had an exceptional cavalry, so that should obviously be listed as one of our strengths."

Calder stood up and moved over to a blank section of wall. He began carving notes in the wood so everyone could keep track of what they discussed. Cara snickered and leaned over to Keegan, whispering, "Someone needs to introduce them to a whiteboard and some dry-erase markers." This made her best friend snort, which, of course, resulted in one of Siobhán's raised eyebrows. Keegan elbowed the instigator, who responded, "Just sayin'."

Liam cleared his throat and offered, "We need to focus on our strengths versus their weaknesses. We know that the Chaos Titans are huge and incredibly strong, correct?" He directed the question to where Lorcan, Nora, and Fergal sat with a few other Shadow Weavers.

"Aye," Fergal replied. "And due to their use of chaos magic, they could also have a variety of powers you may not be expecting. Things like control over chaotic weather—hurricane-force winds and lightning strikes."

Nora added, "Balor can also emit a beam of chaos magic, which has debilitating effects."

Conor piped up with a snarky, "Well, isn't *that* fun?" He hadn't been invited to the war Council, but he couldn't stand the thought of having to wait for his brothers to give him the play-by-play. Siobhán unleashed another eyebrow in his direction, but he was practically immune to them by now.

Liam continued, "All right, that's good. The more information we have, the better we can prepare." He stood and walked over to where Calder was taking notes. "So, let's focus on their weaknesses for a moment. They might be huge, but I'd wager they're also slow. I think we should focus on hit-and-run tactics."

High Druid Deirdre, who was sitting with Nora and her family, perked up at that and said, "I think I may have an idea about that. If I can make it work, I think we could use portals to transport small teams in and out of areas as needed."

Lorcan held up a hand and was recognized by Shay. "What kind of aquatic defenses can you mount?" he asked the room in general.

One of the Water Fae Council members answered hesitantly, "We have a few ships, although they're not really outfitted for battle. But with the time we have to prepare..."

Lorcan looked at him like he'd sprouted a second head. "I'm not talking about ships. Wait, you all do realize how the Titans will be coming, don't you?"

Shay said, "I think we all assumed they would be portaled in. I take it that's an incorrect assumption?"

"The Titans would never fit into the portal room at the stronghold and our shadow portals are constrained by size, so even if they could squeeze into the room, they'd never make it through the actual portal. No, they'll be released into the ocean where they will transform into who-knows-what sort of hideous sea creatures. Then, they will swim toward this island. The monsters will come from the sea. If we want to stand any chance of survival, we need to eliminate as many of them as possible before they get to dry land. Our first line of defense must be in the water." Lorcan wore a perplexed and slightly disturbed look upon realizing this was new information to the rest of them, except for the Shadow Weavers.

Stunned silence greeted that pronouncement. Conor muttered, "This just gets better and better." Riley smacked him in the chest with the back of his hand and said, "Not helping." His twin hissed, rubbed his chest, and said, "I wasn't trying to help. I'm just picking up the snark slack while Áine is gone."

Siobhán drew breath to chastise her twins, but Fintan

beat her to it. He looked at the both of them and said, "Well, thank goodness we've got the snark slack covered. You two dossers need to shut yer yaps and let the grownups talk."

More than one snort could be heard as the old-timer put the pups in their place. Riley just rolled his eyes, but Conor's insouciant grin was still fully intact despite the chastisement.

Lorcan pinched the bridge of his nose and whispered, "Bloody hell, we're doomed." Deirdre chuckled but patted his forearm and said, "Not yet, we aren't."

She turned her attention to the larger group. "I know this is disconcerting news, but we are capable of rising to this challenge." She looked at Nora and asked, "Are all the Shadow Weavers capable of activating the latent Fomori blood in the Aos Sí? Surely, most of us have enough to allow us to morph into merrows."

Nora considered a moment, then glanced at her mate and son, who nodded. "Yes, I would guess the vast majority of the Aos Sí could transform. And all the Shadow Weavers should be capable of triggering the change."

The High Druid flashed an ethereal smile as she said, "Perfect. I hope you're all ready for some swim lessons."

Conor couldn't help himself. "Nothing like swimming with the sharks. Big, lumpy mutant sharks." Siobhán gave that comment a pass. Even the normally unperturbed matriarch was a bit unsettled by the idea of an underwater battle with huge, monstrous sea creatures.

Calder raised his hand, and Shay nodded for him to speak. "I've been discussing something with the healers that might help with casualties. According to my da and the other healers, it should be possible for all of us to learn at least basic healing skills. Being able to get injured fighters back into the battle quickly could make all the difference. And keeping more of us alive is a plus as well."

Morgan, who was sitting with Siobhán, Muireann, and Sláine, stood and continued, "As my son mentioned, it shouldn't be difficult to teach everyone at least basic first aid. If they have an affinity for it, we could even go a bit further and get them to field medic status. Not only will that keep more Aos Sí alive by facilitating quicker response times for injuries in the field, but it will also free up the more experienced healers for the more complicated cases. It's a fantastic idea." He looked over at Calder, eyes shining with pride. Siobhán smiled at their son, causing him to blush slightly, uncomfortable being the center of so much praise.

Keegan, whose pride was also evident, raised her hand to be heard. Her father nodded at her, and she stood, saying, "My cousin and I also have a suggestion. You know how those of us who have spent a lot of time on Earth have enhanced levels of power? I think if we could get as many Aos Sí as possible to spend time there, it might increase their strength as well, at least somewhat. Every little bit helps, doesn't it?" She shrugged and sat back down.

This time it was Shay's turn for a proud dad moment. "I think that's an excellent idea, a stór. Siobhán, will you and your lads look into arranging for lands and training facilities we could use? Ireland or Kansas City, probably both, would be fine. We'll have to have all properties glamoured at all times. Better not to have the humans seeing things we don't want to explain."

"My family can help with that. It's a simple thing to create artifacts that will keep a glamour perpetually engaged. No need for someone to be focused on that when we have tools to do it for us," Máire volunteered.

"Outstanding, Máire, thank you," Shay replied. "I have another thought to add as well. If we are planning a hit-and-run attack style, combined with portaling, I think we should throw in an aerial assault. Many of our Air Fae are capable of keeping themselves as well as others airborne for a fair bit of time. We know that some of the Titans will undoubtedly reach land, where they will tower over us, giving them a distinct advantage." The Taoiseach began gesturing more animatedly as he grew more excited by the possibilities. "However, if at least some, if not most, of our soldiers on land are able to go airborne at will, that advantage is severely mitigated. And we need all the mitigation we can get."

Deirdre's eyes lit up at that suggestion. "That plays into my portaling strategy extremely well. I might even be able to figure out how to let us cast portals through the air so our soldiers can transport themselves from one aerial position to another."

Liam added, "That could make all the difference. But we will have to choreograph this battle almost as we would a dance. We will need to keep the monsters off-balance and totally confused." He glanced at Lorcan, "What level of intelligence can we expect from these creatures?"

"The chaos magic warps their minds until they're capable of little more than animalistic rage. The one exception could be their leader, Balor. For whatever reason, he has been able to maintain at least some level of cognitive function, even while the rest of his body has been warped just as savagely as the rest of them. However, I was able to deal him a fairly substantial blow when I killed Cathal, so we're hopeful that might have enraged him enough to push him over the edge into true madness. Time will tell."

Máire added, "I saw how much Balor relied on his pet

psychopath. When Lorcan killed Cathal, it might very well have sent him off the cliff."

Corley said, somewhat dismissively, "Do you really think it will have made that much of a difference?"

Máire opened her mouth to answer, but Lorcan cut her off with a clipped, "I think I would know better than you how that would affect Balor. While you were writing songs and drinking with your lads, I was living with the threat of that monster. So, forgive me if I feel a bit more qualified to conjecture as to the likely response to me saving your girlfriend's life."

Corley narrowed his eyes, Máire and Muireann rolled theirs, and Conor barely kept from laughing aloud. *Maybe I should've agreed to join the Council a long time ago. This is far more entertaining than I thought it would be.*

Siobhán's eyebrow nearly disappeared into her hair. "Yes, well, now that we've all had a lovely dose of testosterone, why don't we continue with the matter actually at hand?"

Emer stood up from where she was sitting with Grady and a few other familiars and said, "We familiars have something to add, and now seems like a good time for a change of subject." Several chuckles were heard but quickly quieted. "I think, with the combination of hit-and-run portaling and aerial attacks, our skin bonding technique could substantially increase our advantage. We didn't really get into too many details when we first described the process, but suffice it to say, it is possible for one Aos Sí to carry multiple familiars into battle with them. This means an Air Fae could lift multiple combatants while only needing to account for the single Fae's weight. We would need to do a bit of training with both the familiars and the Aos Sí to ensure the process works smoothly, but it's definitely possible and could give us yet another promising tactic in our arsenal."

Everyone seemed to be contemplating the ramifications of that revelation. Shay took a deep breath and responded, "Thank you, Emer. I think we've thrown quite a bit at the wall, so now we need to discern what sticks."

Fintan raised two fingers again, and Shay nodded at him to relinquish the floor. "All right you lot. We've all got a lot to think about now. I say we sleep on it and meet back here tomorrow, ready to discuss the best way to begin. You members of the Fianna, I especially want you to come up with strategies on how to divide and conquer the tasks in front of us. I'd suggest you iron that out before our meeting tomorrow. We don't expect perfection from you, but we do expect progress."

He pinned each of member of the Fianna briefly with his sharp gaze and received a determined nod from every one of them.

Deirdre added, "One last thing. Expanded Council members, please inform your Clans that in order for some of our tactics to be successful, we will be dividing the Aos Sí up more than normal. I know you are all used to the Clans being fairly insular, but that is not our best option in this case. Just let them know to expect it, so we have a minimum of complaining when the time comes to divide Fae into their respective combat groups."

Fintan and the others nodded, albeit with somewhat grim expressions. They were all too aware this would not be a popular decree, and they were not exactly excited about relaying the news.

Liam said, "Fianna members, I vote we meet at my mam's manor. Aoife's visiting and she will undoubtedly be excited to feed us all."

Conor piped up with, "He's not kidding. She really does love to cook."

The rest of them all nodded their agreement, and everyone began filing out of the Council Hall.

🔯🔯🔯

"Hot day-um Aoife can cook! I can barely move!" Keegan exclaimed, using a bit of a roll to mop up the last of the gravy from the pot roast they had all just finished. Then she sat back in her chair and looked around the Ó Faoláin manor gardens, where the Fianna and most of their extended family and friends were finishing up the feast Aoife had produced on demand, seemingly without effort. *How she just bustles around the kitchen and makes culinary masterpieces appear, I will never understand. I'd have burnt the place down trying to make a grilled cheese.*

Calder leaned close and whispered in her ear, "I know this is an important gathering, and we need to focus. And we will. But I want you to remember that after everyone goes home, I am going to take you to my room and do very naughty things to you. Just keep that in mind, Aibhleog."

He gently nipped her neck, causing her to gasp. He chuckled darkly and said, "Careful, love. Or everyone will know you're getting worked up."

Keegan couldn't help but snort at that as she replied, "By now I doubt there's a single Aos Sí who is unaware of how horny you make me. I mean, maybe there's a blind and deaf homebound Fae on one of the other islands who doesn't know, but I kind of doubt it."

Unfortunately, she said that a bit louder than she intended and Conor, without looking up from the last of his dinner, barked out, "No boinking on the table! For some reason, that seems to be my brothers' favorite place to get busy, and there are quite literally a dozen better places I can think of, starting with loverboy's bedroom."

Niamh and Siobhán simultaneously raised an eyebrow, causing Cara to say, "Everyone knock it off! Now we've got eyebrows in stereo!" That elicited more than a few laughs, even from the mothers.

"All right, before we get too far off the rails, I think we should begin discussing our next steps. From what we discussed with the expanded Council, we need to come up with a plan for implementing tactics regarding cavalry, portaling, aquatic battle, basic healer training, Earth rotations, aerial battle, and skin bonding," Liam summarized. "Am I missing anything?"

"Feck, I hope not. That's more than enough," Riley muttered, for once beating Conor to the snarky punch.

His mother replied, "Indeed. So, let's begin with what we're most familiar. I propose we continue the cavalry training as we were during the Fianna Trials. We will increase each individual's skill level to the fullest extent possible. Once the kinks are ironed out of the portaling and aerial assault tactics, we will work with them as needed."

"Brilliant. Deirdre is working on portaling. I have no idea what that means, but I trust her implicitly. As for aquatic battle plans, I believe the Shadow Weavers should take point there," Liam said, nodding to where Lorcan and his family were seated. The young Fomori/Water Fae glanced at Fergal, who shrugged and said, "Feel free, lad. I'll follow your lead."

Lorcan said, "Seems to me the best way to proceed with all of this is to create a schedule rotating different groups through the various tactics. It would be similar to the way you all trained for the Fianna Trials and that seemed to work fairly well. I can work with Fergal and Nora to organize teams of the Shadow Weavers so we can activate the Fomori blood in your people in a timely manner. Once everyone has been able to transform successfully, we will work on underwater battle strategies. We'll repeat that for each group. I will also make sure the Shadow Weavers rotate through the other tactics as well."

Liam said, "Perfect. What about basic healer training?" Morgan nodded to Muireann, who was sitting with Lorcan and his family.

"I've spoken with Da and Sláine about the best way to organize this training. We agree that Lorcan's idea for rotating groups through each of the various battle tactics makes the most sense. All of the senior healers will be responsible for a different aspect of the training, which will include everything from basic first aid to the more advanced field medic level for those who show an affinity for healing."

Sláine added, "Now that we're aware of the aquatic portion of the battle plans, we will make sure to address the best ways to treat wounds underwater."

Liam smiled at her and said, "Thank you, a stór, that will be most helpful."

Keegan raised her hand and the oldest Ó Faoláin brother nodded for her to speak. "Cara, Mom, and I will work with your family to make arrangements for rotating the teams to Earth. Since we don't have a great deal of time, I'd suggest keeping as many Fae as possible on Earth as long as we can. We'll need all the power boost we can manage to handle what's coming for us."

"We will have our contacts on Earth begin obtaining properties suitable for our needs immediately," Calder commented. Máire said, "And our family will begin creating the artifacts needed to create the perpetual glamours. It shouldn't take long, but we will need to get some idea of the amount of area we want to cover, as soon as you have those numbers."

"I'd be happy to work with Shay and Cara to come up with some functional aerial tactics," Niall volunteered. Grady added, "I will send you some of the air familiars. They may be helpful to you."

"We'll take all the help we can get," he replied, Shay and Cara nodding their agreement.

Emer stalked to an open area where she could be seen by everyone and said, "Grady and I will take charge of the skin bonding portion of our plans. More and more familiars have been gathering since we put out the call, so be prepared to chauffeur quite a few passengers during the training. It will take a bit of practice to get the hang of the mental aspects of skin bonding."

Keegan interrupted with, "Wait, what? Explain that, please."

"When we demonstrated the skin bonding process, you may recall we mentioned the ability for the Fae and familiar to speak telepathically while bonded. Since we will be dealing with potentially more than a dozen familiars bonding with each Fae, well, that's a lot of voices. This is new territory for us as well, but Grady and I have been discussing the best way to handle that particular difficulty. We've agreed the best course of action is to appoint one of the familiars as the speaker. All the other familiars will speak directly to the speaker, as little as possible to keep the noise manageable, and the speaker will relay any messages to the Fae. There are still some obstacles to navigate, but we're confident we can make it work."

"Whew, that's a crap ton of details, to steal one of Áine's phrases. My brain is overflowing," Conor said.

"Your brain overflows any time someone uses a word with more than three syllables," Riley responded, evidently eager to help pick up the snark slack at his twin's expense. Liam levitated a couple of small sticks and used them to smack his brothers on the back of the head.

Siobhán stood and announced, "I believe we've made enough progress for one day. Before this devolves into a full-blown circus, I suggest we get some sleep."

Everyone began heading out, while Siobhán and her boys started clearing the table and cleaning up. Keegan gave her mom and dad a kiss and explained she was going to spend the night, then she began to help the others. Calder came up behind her and whispered in her ear, "We'll handle this, love. I want you to go to my room and undress. Then pick out a paddle from the toy chest. Make sure it's one you like because I plan to use it for quite some time tonight. Leave it on the bedside table, put your silky blindfold on, then get on your hands and knees at the end of the bed and wait for me. Understand?"

Keegan's cheeks flushed and her heart began racing. She nodded, but he replied, "You know better than that, love. Say the words."

"I understand."

"That's my good girl."

☙❦❧

Calder was the last one in the kitchen, wiping off the last counter and draping the dish towel over the edge of the sink to dry. He enjoyed drawing out the anticipation for both of them, but damn, if his prick got much harder, he wasn't sure he'd be able to walk. *Time to go spank my girlfriend. I love my life.*

He walked down the hallway, stopping just outside his door. She had turned on some music to try and cover up her moans. *Nice try, love, but I want everyone to hear you scream. Maybe that makes me an arsehole, but I can live with that.*

He quietly opened the door and stepped inside. He paused for a moment and took in the scene before him. His love was on her hands and knees at the foot of his bed, naked and trembling. She was wearing her blindfold, and the music was loud, so she had no idea he was in the room. It made his cock twitch and spurred him to move.

He slipped his clothes off, the cool breeze from the overhead fan causing gooseflesh to ripple across his skin. Moving silently, he made his way to his bedside table, picking up a small bottle of massage oil he kept there, as well as the paddle Keegan had chosen (it was heart-shaped, so the marks left behind would be adorable).

He also turned the music down, very slowly, so it took her a moment to figure out he was there. He knew the moment she realized it, since her body stiffened slightly, and she began turning her head from side to side, trying to locate him by sound.

"Calder? That's you, right?" she asked, a slight hesitation in her voice because she was not one hundred percent sure it was her boyfriend in the room with her. He only let her worry about it for a few seconds, then he tossed the massage oil beside her, sat on the bed, leaned close to her head, and whispered, "Yes, it's me, love. And I have a challenge for you tonight. Are you up for it?"

"I, I think so," she replied, not feeling extremely confident in her current vulnerable state. He gripped her hair, tilting her head back slightly, then claiming her mouth hungrily. His tongue demanded entrance, and she happily complied. She was really beginning to settle into the kiss when he pulled her head away from his and said, "You'll have to be more certain than 'I think so.'"

He stood up and moved to stand behind her at the foot of the bed. He ran his hands lightly over her backside, kneading and massaging her back and glutes. "Would you like to try again? Are you up for my challenge?"

She nodded and immediately a sharp whack sounded, followed by the sting of the heart-shaped paddle landing firmly on the meatiest part of her ass. "We've talked about this, love. Use. Your. Words." He punctuated the last three words with sharp slaps of the paddle.

Keegan gasped with each smack, but Calder quickly began rubbing some of the sting from her skin, his fingers brushing against her slick folds ever so lightly, never quite touching as thoroughly or as long as she wished.

"Yes," she responded, "I'm up for the challenge. Will you tell me what it is?"

"Soon enough, love. And relax, if you don't enjoy it, I will not force you. You are in charge, Aibhleog. Always."

That made her moan and push back against him, hoping to move things along. He chuckled and said, "You're a needy ember tonight, aren't you?" He gave her another slap with the paddle while sliding two fingers inside her, finding the sweet spot and very slowly increasing his speed, causing the tension to build deep in her belly. At irregular intervals, he would give her a sharp smack with the paddle, lightly rubbing the paddle over the area afterwards to soothe the sting.

Before long, he felt her shivering with desire. Calder replaced his fingers with his cock, letting out a low moan as he seated himself deep within her. He did have the presence of mind to separate them with a water condom.

While he was buried there, he picked up the massage oil and drizzled a little between her ass cheeks, eliciting a loud gasp from his love. He chuckled softly and began rubbing his thumb up and down her crevice, swirling the oil around her tightest hole. He slowly eased his thumb inside the opening, allowing her time to adjust as he went. Then he began moving, slowly sliding both his cock and his thumb in and out of both openings.

Judging by the sounds Keegan was making, she did not object. "Ready for the challenge, anamchara? Because I'd love to use my water power to fill your ass and really make you scream. Can you take it, love?"

She was gasping and moaning loudly now. "Yes, please!" Calder slowed everything down and replied, "Tell me what you want, lass. Please, what?"

"Please fill me up!" she nearly yelled.

"Yes, ma'am," he replied with a chuckle, withdrawing his thumb and drawing some water from the air. He fashioned it into a bullet shape, slightly wider than his thumb, and solidified the outer layer, so it would hold its form. He slowly pushed it forward, little by little, pausing several times as he told her, "Relax, love. Just breathe and let me in. Oh yes, that's a good girl."

Finally, he was fully buried in her with his water bullet inside her ass. As he felt her beginning to relax a bit, he gathered a little more water from the air and sent it straight to Keegan's clit. He started spinning both of his aquatic sex toys, slowly at first, as he began withdrawing his cock then thrusting back in, his hands around her hips pulling her back against him hard. As the rhythm of his pumping increased, so did the water's spinning speed.

Soon he could feel Keegan begin to clench around him and said, "Not yet, lass. Wait for me." He increased his efforts and after a few moments said, "Come for me, love. Now, please."

She screamed like nobody could hear them and clamped down on his cock so tightly he instantly reached his climax, joining her in a loud moan as he buried himself deep inside her, coming incredibly hard.

They froze after that, panting heavily for a few heartbeats, then he withdrew from her, sending all the water into the bathroom and down the drain. Then, they both collapsed onto the bed. She pulled her blindfold off, looked at him, and said, "You need to challenge me more often."

They both laughed and he pulled her into his arms, giving her a kiss on the temple, and replied, "My pleasure, lass."

🔯🔯🔯

Family

is life

3

Lir and Áine stepped through the portal onto Murias, the Water Clan island, and turned back to wave at their bonded. The shimmering door currently connected to the World Tree snapped shut with a loud pop.

The two of them took in the scenery while they got their bearings. The home of the Water Fae was dotted with lakes and inlets, narrow strips of land weaving around and amongst them. There were a few trees here and there, as well as a plethora of aquatic vegetation in vibrant hues blooming in and around the water.

The fresh scent of the ocean wafted lightly on the breeze, adding an energizing aura to the area. Lily pads, some the size of a carriage, floated serenely atop the ponds, providing landing pads for colorful frogs and small birds. The chorus the fauna created was loud but incredibly lyrical.

The phoenix fluttered up to perch on Lir's back and asked, "So where to now, Goat Boy? You're the one with the map."

"We looked at it five minutes ago, right before we left. We need to head to the main village, which is west and slightly south of the tree."

The púca began heading in that direction, with Áine nervously pacing back and forth along his muscular, midnight-black back. He glanced back at her and commented, "Feeling a little anxious?"

"Pfft! I don't get anxious. I'm just high energy, that's all." She continued pacing for a few moments, then paused and said softly, "But when we talk to the Water Clan Fae, you'll help me explain how important this is, right? This is too important for me to screw it up."

He stopped, looked back at her again, and reassured her. "Of course I'll help, Áine. We're in this together. Don't worry, you won't screw it up."

The phoenix nodded, then sniffed, and replied, "Of course I won't. Don't mind me; I'm just feeling a little emotional since the fate of the world is literally in my hands. But I'm up for the challenge. Now, I think I need to work out some of this energy. How about dropping a house music beat so I can work out that tricky bit of choreography I've been working on?"

Lir gave a soft chuckle and said, "Happy to help, a stór." Then he gave her an up-tempo mmm-tss-mmm-tss-mmm-tss-mmm-tss, letting her dance out her excess energy while he carried them toward their meeting with the Water Clan.

It wasn't long before they could see the main village stretched out before them. At first, it appeared that all the buildings, and even the benches and paths that meandered throughout, had been painted in gorgeous tones of turquoise, cerulean, and every other shade of blue imaginable. But as they drew nearer, it became apparent that most of the color came from actual water running over, under, around, and through almost everything. The Water Fae did paint a lot of their surroundings, but they tended to choose shades of red, pink, yellow, and green, which then blended with the blue hues to create gorgeous tints of purples and teals, adding harmonious depth to the visual aspects of their environment. And when the sun hit all that water, the sparkling effect was truly dazzling.

Áine took in all of this while shading her eyes with one of her flaming wings. "I guess it's kinda pretty if you're into water. I still prefer fire, though," she offered, flaring her flames with that last sentence for dramatic effect.

Lir gave a noncommittal "mm-hmm" sound in the back of his throat, somewhat distracted by the magnificence of the aquatic sculptures and artwork dotted throughout the landscape. Swirling, rolling, dipping, and diving—the fluidity was mesmerizing as it constantly moved, never remaining still. The Water Fae artisans had created intricate patterns of Celtic knotwork through which their favored element flowed. The scene was, in a word—stunning.

As they drew closer to the village, a small delegation of Fae appeared to be making their way toward the familiars. Áine stage whispered, "Showtime, Goat Boy."

She launched herself off Lir's back and moved to hover in front of the group of Water Fae, all of whom were wearing quizzical looks, uncertain why a phoenix and a púca approached them in a very determined manner.

"Hello!" Áine bellowed, quite a bit louder than necessary. "We come in peace! Take us to your leader!"

Lir shook his head and said, "They aren't aliens, and

they certainly speak our language. Why are you yelling at them?"

The delegation members were watching this exchange with more than a little humor. They were still unsure what was happening, but as with most things concerning Áine, it was entertaining.

Áine looked back at the púca and said, "I was being diplomatic. But fine, you talk to them." Lir shifted to the chimpanzee form he preferred when thumbs were needed and held his hand out. The phoenix dropped the bag she was carrying into his hand and landed on the ground.

Lir opened the bag and withdrew the letter Deirdre had prepared for them. Hopefully, it would grease the wheels and make their task easier.

One of the Water Fae, presumably their chosen leader, took the letter, read it, and passed it to another Fae. The missive made its way around the group until everyone had a chance to peruse it.

The leader then stepped forward and said, "Well, this is not how I expected my day to go. And I'm sorry to hear things have devolved to the extent that your journey was deemed necessary. But I trust High Druid Deirdre and will do everything I can to make your journey progress as smoothly as possible. Now, please, follow me, and I will take you to the Druid responsible for watching over the relic you seek."

He led the way toward the Water Clan's Druidic Enclave, the familiars and the rest of the delegation following. After a short while, he said, "I'm sorry, it seems your unexpected arrival has robbed me of my wits and manners. My name is Brennan, and I am the elected leader of the Water Clan here in Murias. Deirdre mentioned your names, so I assume you must be Áine," pointing at the phoenix, "and you are surely Lir."

Both familiars nodded, and he continued. "It's my great pleasure to meet you both. And I want to thank you for your selflessness in volunteering to undergo this pilgrimage. We all owe you a great debt."

The phoenix practically preened under this effusive praise. "Oh, it's nothing. I'm sure anyone would have been willing to go, but we were chosen, so we'll gladly do our best to live up to your gratitude."

Lir managed to keep from grinning, barely. "Yes, thank you. We will certainly do our best."

They turned a corner and saw the Druid's Enclave of the Water Clan. It was even more beautiful, and impressive, than their first glimpse of the village had been. Ribbons of water twirled and swirled all around the buildings, creating fascinating, gorgeous sculptures and works of art.

Before they had truly had a chance to take it all in, a dark-haired elder Fae came out to greet them. She had warm brown eyes, and a sprinkle of freckles covered her nose and cheeks. She nodded to the Water Clan leader and said, "Fáilte, Brennan. Who might our visitors be? I wasn't expecting anyone today."

"Dia duit, Quinn. This is Áine and Lir from Tíonol. They have come with a letter from High Druid Deirdre, asking us to relinquish our relic to aid them in their quest. Apparently, it's been decided that the familiars will seek out their gods in the hope of obtaining their help in the impending battle."

Quinn's eyes widened slightly, but she recovered quickly. "I see. May I have a look at the letter?"

"Of course."

She skimmed the letter, let out a sigh, and replied, "I

had hoped the news we've been hearing was exaggerated, but it appears that was a foolish hope. Follow me, and we'll take a look at the torque."

She led them into the enclave, which was filled with little streams trickling by and moving water sculptures decorating every nook and cranny. It was a cool and calming environment, and the constant susurration of the babbling brooks was delightful.

After winding around a bit, they emerged into a chamber filled with several pools, all interconnected by streams and small waterfalls. A fresh, ocean-scented breeze wafted through, and several candles flickered on small tables and stands throughout. There were walking bridges spanning the water in several places to allow access to the room's central area.

In the middle of all this stood a low altar decorated with more aquatic sculptures and Celtic knotwork filled with constantly moving water. Surrounded by candles, a headless marble bust of a female form displayed the stunning torque of the familiars' water god.

Intricately woven strands of silver formed waves and water droplets, with Celtic knots and designs interspersed seamlessly throughout. The horseshoe-shaped torque was dripping with dark blue and teal sapphires, shimmering sky-blue aquamarines, vividly veined turquoise, and rich blue diamonds. Dumortierite and tanzanite in shades of violet-blue to purple were sprinkled in as well, adding depth and setting off the other shades beautifully.

Áine gasped at the stunning design, leaning forward as if drawn to the bling like metal to a magnet. Quinn grinned at her response, obviously proud of the gorgeous relic entrusted to her Clan. "Lovely, isn't it?"

The phoenix looked at her in disbelief and replied,

"That's the understatement of the century. It's breathtaking!"

"Agreed," Quinn responded. "So, how do you plan to transport it?" Áine pointed to the black bag held by Lir, who was still in chimp form. "It's bigger on the inside than the outside, and it'll keep stuff safe from harm."

The Water Druid nodded and reached toward the torque, intending to give it to the familiars and let them be on their way.

"Wait a moment, please," Brennan said, stepping forward and placing himself between Quinn and the torque. She pulled back in surprise, and he continued, "Tá brón orm, Druid, but I was hoping we might hold a céilí so we could present the questers with the torque and allow our people the opportunity to see them and wish them well.

"If I'm being honest, our Clan, or what's left of it with the majority of us in Tíonol right now, has been struggling with depression. Giving them something to look forward to, something positive, would be a gift. It would only take a few days to prepare, and it would mean the world to them."

Lir drew breath to politely decline, but Áine put her wing on his shoulder and said, "Sometimes people need a reason to celebrate when things look bleak, Goat Boy." He looked thoughtful for a moment, then nodded at her.

"We'd be honored," the phoenix said to Brennan. The Water Clan leader smiled at that and gave them a nod. "Excellent. Thank you for your kindness. I will get the planning started. Quinn, will the Druids be able to provide lodging for our travelers?"

She put her hands on her hips and scoffed, "You're lucky I don't take that as an insult, Brennan. Of course, we'll put them up."

He laughed and held his hands up in a placating manner, "No offense, lass. I just didn't want to assume anything."

"Well, they're welcome here as long as they'd like to stay," she said. "You just get started planning that party. Let's not keep them from their task any longer than necessary."

Brennan nodded and said, "I'll get started immediately. Áine, Lir, it was a pleasure to meet you. I'm sure we'll talk soon." He gave a brief wave and took his leave.

"Shall I show you to your rooms?" Quinn asked. The familiars both nodded, and the druid led them away.

☙❧

In his fainting goat form, Lir made his way out of the enclave. Áine had been gone a while, and while he was an optimist and tried to be positive, it was better to check on things sooner rather than later where the bird was concerned.

He rounded a corner, and out of the corner of his eye, he saw a flicker of flame. He turned toward it and saw the phoenix stretched out on an elevated patch of ground, eyes closed, basking in the late afternoon sun.

"Good afternoon, Áine," he said. She cracked one eye open and said, "It's getting there. Don't tell Quinn, but I'm tired of being surrounded by water. Everything feels damp. I just needed to soak up some sun for a bit."

"I understand. The sun does feel good." He glanced over toward a central courtyard, where several Fae were busy decorating for the céilí scheduled for that evening. In addition to all of the water sculptures and knotwork floating throughout the grounds, there were also floral arrangements and faery lights.

"It's about time to go meet Brennan. Shall we head on over there?" Lir asked. Áine stretched, gave a huge yawn, and replied, "Why not? Let's get this party started!" They ambled in that direction, and as they drew near, they spotted Brennan, who waved them over.

"Áine, Lir, I'm glad you're here! We've just about finished the preparations. People should begin arriving shortly. Help yourself to some food and drinks. I need to go take care of some last-minute details, but I'll find you when we're ready to begin the ceremony."

The familiars watched him bustle over to where some Fae were decorating so he could reposition the flowers slightly. "Dude needs to unclench his butthole. He's a bit too micro-managery for me," Áine commented. Lir snorted despite himself.

A haunting melody drifted toward them, causing Áine's head to perk up as she searched for the source of the music. She began flying in the direction of the sound, or her best guess at any rate, with Lir following.

Before long, they turned a corner and came upon a small choir of Water Fae, beautiful harmonies reverberating through the air around them. The phoenix settled onto Lir's back, tilted her head back, and closed her eyes, completely immersing herself in that song, in that moment.

Finally, the song ended on a long, low chord. Once silence settled in, Áine let out a satisfied sigh and exclaimed, "That. Was. Amazeballs." Then she launched herself into the air and fluttered around the singers, asking all kinds of questions about the song and the composer.

Lir wasn't exactly sure how it happened, but Áine had

talked herself into a solo before he realized it. And she wasn't even a member of the choir.

He was finally able to pull her away when Quinn showed up with the relic, resting on an intricately carved wooden display. They followed the Druid to the table in the center of the space, where she placed the torque and its stand in a prominent place.

Áine fluttered over to hover in front of the gorgeous relic. "So pretty," she mumbled to herself as she gazed longingly at the bling. Quinn did an admirable job of keeping a straight face as the familiar made goo-goo eyes at the jewels.

Brennan wandered over to them and said, "If you're ready, we'll get started." Áine and Lir nodded. The Water Fae picked up a small artifact and held it to his throat. When he began speaking, they realized it enhanced the volume of his voice.

"Everyone! Can I have your attention, please?" He waited a few moments for everyone to give him their attention, then continued, "Céad míle fáilte! As I'm sure you've all heard by now, we have a couple of visitors from Tíonol, Áine and Lir. We all know the threat we're currently facing, but these two have volunteered to undertake a pilgrimage to ask their gods for help in our battle. Their courage and selflessness should be applauded." Everyone clapped politely, and Áine made her best attempt at looking humble.

He turned toward Quinn, who was standing to his right side, and handed her the artifact. She held it to her throat, then said, "Áine and Lir, would you please join me?" The two familiars walked over to her right side and looked at her expectantly.

"We have read the letter High Druid Deirdre wrote,

introducing the two of you and explaining your need to gather all four of the gods' relics in the hope they will aid us against our enemy." Quinn leaned forward slightly, narrowed her eyes, and declared, "I think you two have good hearts. And I am very proud of you both for being willing to undertake this journey. However. I also want you to understand how important your quest is. To all of us. We are counting on you. I know that isn't fair, but it is the truth. Guard this relic, and those you'll gather, with your lives. We will be praying to your gods for success on your journey. Go n-éirí leat!"

More well wishes were shouted from the crowd as Quinn faced forward, setting down the voice amplification artifact and gently lifting the giant torque from its display stand. She raised the relic up above her head to display it to the crowd, letting them appreciate its beauty, perhaps for the last time.

After a few moments, she began lowering the torque, and once it drew near the level of her head, it began to shrink until it was of an appropriate size for her to wear. Lir didn't need to glance at Áine to know that her eyes were wide and her wheels were turning. *She will be wearing all four of those torques before we ever make it to the gods—guaranteed.* He gave a little goat shrug and decided there were worse things than loving bling, so he would cut her some slack.

Quinn took the black bag from Áine's talon when she held it out. Then she slipped the bag over the torque, tied it shut, and slipped it over Lir's head. The Druid picked up the artifact again and called out, "Now, let's send them off with a night to remember!"

The moon was high in the sky the next time Lir had a moment to stop and take a breath. Áine was completely pickled and had already talked the Water Fae into half a dozen conga lines. She did not appear to be slowing down any time soon. He was just grateful they had successfully finished their first task. Now, if the rest of them all went that smoothly, they might just stand a chance.

Family

is life

4

The newly risen sun created a field of diamonds as it caused the dew-soaked grasses and flowers to sparkle like gems. The nine members of the Fianna were gathered at the World Tree, ready to depart for Earth. They were responsible for setting up the facilities needed to house and train all the Fae who were preparing to move to the human world for the next few months.

Keegan was finishing her morning tea, and the frown lines on her forehead were finally beginning to soften. Calder, who was halfway listening to his brother, Liam, go on and on about the semantics of acquiring the properties and meetings with lawyers...blah, blah, blah. He knew he should be paying attention, and he would, but he was allowing himself just a tiny moment of rebellion. His beloved was far more captivating than his bossy older brother, even though she was perpetually cranky until she'd had at least one cup of his tea, preferably two.

I would gladly make my Aibhleog tea every day for eternity if she asked it of me.

"Deartháir beag, did you hear what I just said? Are you

even listening to me?" Liam sniped, irritation settling into his features like an old, comfortable hat.

Calder gave himself a mental shake and said, "Sorry, my mind wandered. Won't happen again."

To Liam's credit, he simply nodded, saying no more about the subject. "Yes, well, here are the main things you need to know. You, Keegan, Cara, and Riley will meet with our Kansas City attorneys and our realtor this morning at nine local time. They have already been briefed on the situation and should have a list of properties that will suit our needs. You'll spend the rest of the day checking them out. Unless they have a serious limitation, buy them all. The attorneys and realtor will handle all the paperwork and push things through quickly. Once they have it finalized, we will get them set up, swiftly I hope, and then we can start moving the troops in."

He glanced at Máire and Keegan and added, "Thank you two, and your family, for producing these larger camouflaging artifacts. They will be loads of help." The cousins nodded at him, like it was really nothing. Their family was talented enough; it really was a minor thing for them, but they were happy to help.

Emer, Grady, Laoise, and Saoirse were seated nearby, everyone but Grady wearing their tiaras. Bling was a hell of a drug. The leopard let out a low growl—her way of clearing her throat for attention. Liam looked at her and said, "Yes, Emer?"

"Will there be a way we can observe the properties as well?" she asked. The oldest Ó Faoláin brother thought about it, then said, "Máire, I think you carrying Laoise around like a little princess would go unnoticed around Dublin. Saoirse could come as well, if she were to shift into another small dog. And the only thing I can think of for the

KC group would be if Grady would consent to shifting into a dog and Emer could go as a house cat. Grady growled and Emer hissed simultaneously at the thought of changing their forms.

Cara shrugged and said, "It's up to you, but otherwise you'll have to stay inside at Calder's house. I thought you might prefer to see the properties." The big cat grumbled a bit, but she shifted into a pitch-black Maine Coon. She was a bit larger than normal cats of that breed, but close enough it wouldn't attract too much attention.

"What about you, lad?" Riley asked Grady. The wolf looked thoroughly disgusted, but he shifted into a jet black, enormous husky. Again, larger than normal, but not out of the realm of possibility.

Saoirse shifted into a little fluffy Pomeranian and stood up against Máire's leg. The Fire Fae scooped her up to join Laoise in her arms. Corley snickered and said, "You lasses look way too high maintenance."

Máire and the two familiars all sniffed and turned away from him simultaneously, causing more than a few laughs.

"All right everyone, let's get to work. Time is not on our side." The World Tree Druids opened a portal to Ireland and that group quickly crossed over. Once they were all through and the portal closed, Keegan and Calder looked at Cara, Riley, and their two slightly cranky familiars.

"Cheer up you two. You only need to use these forms when we go out in public. Most of the time you'll be hidden from humans and can assume your normal form," Keegan said in her best cheerful voice.

Emer rolled her eyes and scoffed a little. Keegan looked at Cara and said, "What the fuck? I expect that from Áine, but not from this one." Her cousin shrugged and said, "I think she misses the bird. She won't admit it, but she's been acting more and more like Miss Thang."

This time Emer scoffed more than a little and said, "I refuse to even dignify that with a response."

Keegan raised an eyebrow and said, "Uh huh. Whatever, girl, just retract the claws next time, 'kay?"

The leopard looked at her for a moment, then nodded, and said, "Fair enough."

Calder and Keegan stepped forward, each calling both of their elements, and brought their hands together. A bright white light burst from their fingertips as they drew their hands apart, creating a shimmering circular portal between them. They stepped back another pace, stretching the portal to an appropriate height for them to pass through, then flipped it on its side, letting it hover a few inches above the ground. Cara and Riley went first, followed by their familiars in their Earth disguises.

Calder looked at his love, grinned, and said, "Shall we?"

She grinned back, nodded, then jumped on him, sending them both tumbling through the portal.

☙☙☙

Keegan's chin slipped off her hand, causing her to jerk back to alertness. They were currently sitting in a conference room in an office building filled with attorneys. It had been almost an hour and the group's patience was wearing thin.

The sharp click, click, click of stilettos on the tile floor could be heard coming down the hall as one of the legal assistants appeared, her arms laden with more paperwork than anyone should have to complete. Riley was closest to the door, so he hopped up and held it open for her. She gave him a grateful smile, then dropped the forms and contracts on the table. She looked at the two brothers and asked, "So who is Riley and who is Calder?"

They identified themselves, and she separated the paperwork into two piles. She handed each a pen and said, "To save time we put half the properties in Riley's name and half in Calder's. It's all coming out of your family's funds and you're both signatories, so we figured it didn't really matter who the official owner was. Is that satisfactory?"

They both nodded and got started signing the various contracts and paperwork to make everything nice and legal. Finally, they came to the end and were able to leave.

Husky-shaped Grady gave a big stretch and commented, "Well, that was mind-numbing. I can't believe I'm going to say this, but I almost miss Áine's antics. At least the silly bird keeps things interesting."

Keegan sighed and said, "I miss her. It's hard to stay sad or nervous with her around." She looked at the others and suggested, "How about some food? We'll go back to Calder's and have something delivered."

Calder said, "I can always call Shannon and have her cook something. She doesn't mind. It's her job, but she likes cooking."

"Nope, I'm going to take advantage of being back in KC. The food on Tír na nÓg is fabulous, but I'm craving something you just don't find on the homeworld."

She gave Cara a mischievous look, and they both grinned and exclaimed, in unison, "Barbecue!"

※ ※ ※

A few days later, they were all hard at work getting the various locations ready for the soldiers who were due to arrive tomorrow. The furnishings were basic, but the Fae who would be joining them were all capable of helping to put the finishing touches on their living quarters.

All of the Fianna, as well as most of their families, were at the Kansas City location, helping them get up and running. Once they had the soldiers settled in there, most of them would go to the Ireland locations and offer their assistance at those sites. They might be under a deadline, but the expanded Council had organized everything so they could take full advantage of their available time.

Máire and Keegan, along with their mothers, were busy setting up the camouflaging artifacts responsible for hiding their activities from the humans. Once positioned and activated, they would cast a glamour over the area and maintain it indefinitely. Normally, self-charging artifacts would draw magic out of the air to slowly replenish their magical batteries. Because the ambient magic on Earth was significantly diminished compared to the Fae homeworld, Máire had suggested they rely on solar power to recharge the artifacts. She made the necessary modifications, and they were good to go.

Keegan looked over the artifact she was helping her cousin to place. "How did you get so good at creating these things?" she asked. Máire shrugged and said, "I don't know, I guess at first I was trying to impress my da. Waste of time, that."

"Yeah, guess so. I'm sorry you had to be the one to, uh—"

"Light him up? I'm not. He was a bloody menace. Turning him into a torch was the best thing I could've done." She finished positioning the artifact and activated it. She pretended the conversation didn't affect her, but the furrow between her brows told a different story.

Keegan gently placed her hand on Máire's shoulder and said, "Hun, he may have been a waste of air, but he was still your dad. I'm not saying you didn't do the right thing; I just wish you didn't have to, that's all."

Her cousin's sympathy caused Máire's stiff upper lip to tremble. As her eyes welled up, Keegan hugged her, rubbing her back and making comforting shushing noises. The tears continued for a couple of minutes, then the ever-independent Fire Fae pulled back and said, "Thank you. I thought I was over that, but I guess not."

"Oh, girl, even the TSA couldn't process that much baggage so quickly."

Máire gave her a blank stare and Keegan laughed, saying, "Sorry, I guess that's an Earth joke. My point is it takes a while to work through trauma like that. And it's not really linear. I'd be happy to talk things over with you, any time you need it. Or maybe there's someone else you could speak to?"

"Muireann helped me with some issues before. She was a good listener. Maybe I'll see if she would mind talking with me. And I might take you up on your offer as well, if that's all right?"

"Of course. If you'd like her input, Cara's a good listener, too. She has a lot of experience talking me down from the ledge. Usually right after Áine talked me onto it." They both chuckled at that. "Maybe we can find time for a girls' night soon?"

"I'd like that. Now let's go make sure our moms don't need any help." They wandered off in search of their mothers.

△△△

Family

is life

5

Shadows were thick in the kitchen pantry—thicker than they should be. Rónán huddled there, one eye on the bit of kitchen he could see through the gap between the dusky blue curtain concealing the pantry and the doorframe. He gnawed on a couple of dry bread crusts he'd found, but it barely took the edge off of the ravenous hunger clawing at his belly.

A few days ago, he'd attempted a foray into the gardens, hoping to snag some food. He'd waited until the wee hours of the morning, but when he snuck into the area, he noticed sensors placed across the entry way. He was lucky he noticed them or who knows what he might've summoned by tripping them.

The faint sound of approaching footsteps caused him to shrink back from the doorframe. He double-checked his shadows, making sure none of them spilled out into the kitchen.

"You bloody well know there aren't enough of us! How are we supposed to keep this up?" a deep voice complained, accompanied by the sound of baskets or containers of some kind being set down on the island countertop.

"We will keep this up because we must. It's not as if there's a choice in the matter," a higher-pitched voice, *maybe a female?*, responded dejectedly. Both voices sounded bone tired and at their wits' end.

"We need a way to keep tabs on the bastard. Then maybe we could formulate some kind of plan. We have to do something," the first voice cried, desperation evident in his tone.

The wheels in Rónán's head began spinning. *Wait, they sound familiar. Are these Shadow Faction members? Can I trust them?*

He leaned forward slightly, eager to hear more, and brushed against a broom leaning against the wall. The resulting crack when it hit the tile floor might as well have been thunder following a lightning strike.

Within mere seconds the curtain was ripped aside, and two fellow Shadow Weavers were scowling down at him.

"Rónán?" the female, a friend of his mother's named Orla, exclaimed in surprise. She and her husband, Brian, the other voice, had gone missing shortly before everyone disappeared.

"Aye, it's me," he answered. They helped him up from where he was crouched on the floor and led him into the kitchen proper.

"What in the world are you doing, lad?" Brian asked. "I know you weren't captured, or we would have seen you. Why are you here?"

"I don't know! I don't know what happened to everybody! I was hiding from my sisters, and I fell asleep. Then I heard an awful scream, in my head and out loud, and it woke me up. I wandered around, but everyone was gone."

The stress of the past several days finally caught up to him, and tears began trickling down his face.

Orla gathered him in her arms and just held him while he let out all that fear and uncertainty. When the tears began to slow, he pulled back, wiped his eyes on his shirt sleeve, and took a deep shuddering breath.

"Sorry," he mumbled, a bit embarrassed by his emotional outburst. His mother's friend gently but firmly gripped his chin and said, "None of that, lad. I know grown Fae who would not have handled what you've been through nearly as well as you have." She released his chin and tousled his hair. "And crying is nothing to be embarrassed by, at any rate. Brian here cries all the time, isn't that right?"

Her large, muscular, tattooed, and bearded husband nodded solemnly and said, "It's true. I'm a huge crybaby." That reply earned a soft chuckle from Rónán.

"Now then, what are we to do with you?" Orla began pacing, her mind working through various possibilities. "If we take you back with us, there's a chance Balor could surprise us, and I don't know how he would respond. He might not even realize you weren't always with us. But I'm not sure that's a chance we should take."

Rónán cleared his throat and asked, "Did I hear Brian say you need some way to keep tabs on Balor? Maybe I could do that."

"Absolutely not! That's far too dangerous!" Orla immediately objected.

Rónán shrugged and said, "It's been dangerous this whole time. At least now I'll have someone to help me. And feed me. Please say you've got food."

"Yes, yes, grab something from the baskets." She

studied him as he found a couple of carrots and an apple and began chowing down at once.

"Oh, for mercy's sake! At least rinse the dirt off the carrots!" She grabbed the carrots and took them to the sink to scrub them clean. Rónán dug into the apple while he waited for the carrots.

Brian joined Orla at the sink and whispered in her ear, "You know, love, you just got done telling him how well he's handled himself. Maybe we should see what the lad can do?"

"How can you even think that?" she scolded, her brow furrowing at the thought.

He took his wife by the arms and turned her to face him. "Because if we don't figure something out, and soon, he won't survive any longer than the rest of us. We will watch out for him. But we have to do something, and I think this is our best option."

She glared at him for a moment longer, but in the end, she couldn't come up with a better alternative. She sighed deeply and looked at the floor. Brian put his arm around her and turned them both to face Rónán.

"Very well, lad. But we will have regular check-ins and rules about how much risk is acceptable, understood?" she grudgingly conceded.

He nodded and smiled, happy to have a purpose, and companionship, at last.

༺༻༼༽

Balor grunted, pushing his mental coercion through the minds of the current group of Titans he was working with. Howls and screeches echoed through the chamber where the monsters were housed. He held it a couple of heartbeats longer than necessary, just to enjoy the chaotic pain he inflicted.

When he released them, they all gasped with relief. The faint buzzing that signaled the use of chaos magic began almost immediately, none of the Titans wishing to risk another painful warning. As much as they hated what he was doing to them, they all knew it was too late for them, there was no coming back from the effects of that warped power. And truth be told, the majority of them no longer had enough sanity left to really care all that much.

Balor made his way through the cavern, spurring the Titans to wield the dangerous, transformative magic. It didn't take long before all the mad, deformed monsters began wielding the magic. They all knew refusing to comply was pointless. Their master would get what he wanted, one way or another. Giving him an excuse to torture them only brightened his day.

☙❧❧

Orla and Brian heard the cacophony of the Titans being urged to begin their use of the chaos magic. They hastened to gather the food up and return to their fellow captives.

Before they left, she handed Rónán a small basket with enough food in it to last a couple of days. "Now, love, I need you to hide and skulk like your life depends on it, because it likely does. We will meet back here at midday day after tomorrow. Bring the basket and I'll refill it. If you happen to overhear or see anything helpful, you can report it then. But you better promise me you will be careful! Please!"

The adolescent gave her a bear hug in response. "I will. I'm just so glad to know I'm not really alone anymore." She patted his back and kissed the top of his head.

"All right, lad. We need to get back before Balor notices we're gone. Even though he knows somebody has to gather food from the garden, it still irritates him for some reason." She shrugged and turned to pick up her portion of the food.

The couple started to leave, but Brian stopped as he passed Rónán, putting a hand on his shoulder. "Stay quiet, stay safe. Practice your mental exercises and keep your shadows close. We'll make it through this."

The teen nodded and gave them what he hoped was a reassuring smile. He would've been disappointed to learn he looked more than a little nauseated.

Family

is life

6

"Listen up, ye dossers," Fintan bellowed, gathering the Fianna members' attention in his own endearing way. "The Council has divided all the Fae into nine regiments, and each of you will need to find it in you to lead one of them. At Deirdre's request, the elements are split evenly in each regiment. Your first job will be to figure out the best way of dividing the lot of them. Apparently, they're tinkering with the idea that each group of four, or quad as we've taken to calling them, will be able to portal around at will. I bloody well hope they know what they're doing. It all sounds like shite to me, but what the feck do I know?"

The nine Fianna warriors did an admirable job of keeping straight faces as the elder rambled a bit. After a moment, Fintan seemed to realize he had wandered off there.

"At any rate, once you've got them in their quads, we'll begin moving through the different strategies we're focusing on. Horses are being brought over as we speak, so cavalry training is where we'll start. That and just general conditioning. So, until all the horses arrive, which should take about three days, I charge you with devising some sort of activity that will not only hone our soldiers' bodies but will begin to build a sense of community and family within the quads. Because if we are to stand a chance against the creatures coming for us, we need to use every advantage we can. Dismissed."

That grim reminder of their circumstance quelled any remaining mirth. They all nodded grimly and gathered in a circle to discuss ideas.

"So, any suggestions?" Liam asked, crossing his arms and looking around at the others. Máire raised her hand, and the eldest Ó Faoláin brother nodded at her. "I think some kind of team sport would be good. Hurling?"

"Or we could teach them baseball," Cara added. "Learning something new together can build a sense of community."

"What about a relay? That involves teamwork," Niall commented. Corley gave him a light shove and said, "Should've known you'd want to run." The Air Fae grinned and said, "Well, of course. Why do you think the lass suggested hurling? Because she can kick our arse, and she knows it!"

Máire blushed but shrugged with a grin as the rest of them laughed.

Liam looked thoughtful, then commented, "As much as we might enjoy it, I don't think we should compete individually. We'd be better served by encouraging our quads and helping them develop that sense of community, and family, that will help us in the coming battle."

"Wait, I've got it!" Keegan exclaimed. She looked at Cara and said, "The Olympics!" Her cousin gasped, then nearly squealed with excitement. "It's perfect!"

"We'll give points for each medal, gold is three points, silver is two, and bronze is one. For the subjectively scored events, we could ask the Council to be the judges." Keegan had begun pacing as she fleshed out her idea.

"We need a grand prize," Calder added. "Something new to them."

Cara actually began jumping up and down, "Worlds. Of. Fun!" Keegan laughed and said, "Perfect."

Dillon cleared her throat and said, "While I'm thrilled you lot are excited by this, could you translate for those of us not familiar with Earth? Or Kansas City?"

"Okay, okay. So, the Olympics are this worldwide competition where the best of the best athletes compete in different sporting events. The top three contestants win medals—gold for first place, silver for second, and bronze for third."

Cara continued, "We can devise several different events and focus on team activities. Each quad can enter as many events as they want, kind of like a field day. As I mentioned earlier, we'll award points for each medal, and whichever group has the most points at the end will get to go to an amusement park with the Fianna."

"What exactly is an amusement park?" Niall asked.

"Oh, I know this one," Riley replied. "Calder took me to Worlds of Fun for my birthday last year. There are games and all these different rides. Roller coasters are brilliant!"

"Okay, you two lasses need to tell us how we can help," Calder commented. "Provided everyone agrees?" He looked around, getting nods from the rest of the group.

Cara picked up her bag and pulled out a notepad and sparkly purple gel pen. Across the top of the page, she wrote 'Faelympics,' then pointed her pen at her cousin. "Keegan, you start throwing out things we need to do, and I'll take notes. Then we can assign tasks."

The redhead nodded at her and said, "Great. We'll get this lined out; then we can figure out how to divide our regiments up into quads. I mean, how do we even start?"

Máire shrugged and said, "Since we don't know anything about the Fae who will make up our regiments, I say we just randomly assign them into quads. Aside from Tíonol, all the other Clans are still very insular, so there's little chance they have friends outside their own element. The way I see it, a big part of our job is to facilitate the building of those relationships."

Keegan looked thoughtful, then replied, "Good point. Okay, we'll just separate them randomly and hope they don't hate each other on sight.

Liam looked them over with a slight grin and said, "Brilliant. Now, let's organize our Faelympics. Do you cailíní have some sort of timeline in mind?"

Cara, who had begun to jot down notes and ideas, looked up and commented, "I think we should be able to organize everything this morning. Then, this afternoon, we'll all meet with our regiments and divide everybody up. Tomorrow we'll set everything up—we'll need various areas for the different events and a place to have the awards ceremony. The quads can use tomorrow to decide which event they'll enter. The Faelympics can take place the day after that, and we can go to Worlds of Fun the third day. Easy peasy."

Riley, who looked on with more than a hint of pride, teased, "Easy peasy, eh? I guess we should leave the organization to the cailíní. I'm feeling a little redundant at the moment."

Cara laughed and said, "If more things were left to us, I

have a feeling we wouldn't be preparing to fight literal monsters."

He came up behind her and said, "I've no doubt of that, love." He gave her a quick squeeze and a peck on the cheek.

"Enough, you two. You Ó Faoláin lads boink like bunnies, and we don't have time for that," Niall snarked.

"Considering you're dating my trollop of a brother, I'd say you would know first-hand," Riley replied, snarking right back with a grin.

Liam began, "All right, as much as we'd all love to debate my family's sexual prowess," at which point Keegan snorted, then quickly looked around to see if Siobhán was within earshot. She didn't need another quirked eyebrow on her record.

"I'd suggest we get started planning," he continued with a smile.

࿘࿘࿘

Siobhán looked around at the preparations for the Faelympics. The area most closely resembled an ant hill that had been kicked over. She couldn't help but smile to herself at the way Keegan and Cara had so quickly insinuated themselves into Aos Sí society, working hard to help prepare for the storm that was coming for them, even after some Fae had been less than kind to the two of them.

She looked over to where Niamh, Shay, and Spéir were busy directing traffic to help their daughters realize their vision. She turned to Morgan, who was standing next to her, and commented, "For a couple of lasses who grew up on Earth, they have certainly managed to embrace the Tír na nÓg penchant for extravagance."

He chuckled and replied, "The extra is in their DNA."

"Indeed."

The day of the first-ever Faelympics dawned hot and humid. Summer in Kansas City was settling in earlier than normal, but a nice breeze was blowing through the branches of flowering trees and ruffling grass in the distance.

Various areas had been delineated, and signs were placed designating which events would take place in each location and what time each would begin.

The Fianna were all busy giving their regiments pep talks as the first events were about to begin. They had decided a little side bet would add incentive to the games, so everyone was extra encouraging to their teams.

Muireann, Lorcan, his little sister, Ailáine, and several other Shadow Weavers had journeyed from the homeworld to watch the games and get a glimpse of what Earth was like. Declan had accompanied Ailáine, they were nearly inseparable, so he sat directly in front of the presentation area, allowing his bonded to sit in front of him and use his soft black belly as a comfy backrest.

Laoise, Saoirse, Emer, and Grady had gathered a large group of familiars, bonded and unbonded alike, to watch the games. Truth be told, they were missing Áine and her exuberant enthusiasm. Cara had even talked Emer into leading the familiars in a song to celebrate the opening ceremony, which was about to begin.

The Fianna led their regiments out to the central area, but with this many Fae, several groups were, by necessity, spread throughout the fields and pitches that had been marked off for the games.

Shay walked out to the presentation area, a slightly raised plateau and also the location they had chosen to bestow the medals after the games. "Céad mile fáilte! I'm delighted to welcome you all to the first-ever Faelympics! These games were designed to help build camaraderie amongst our quads, provide both magical and physical conditioning, and let us all enjoy the entertainment of the friendly competition. I'm sure you're all aware of the grand prize—a trip for the winning quad to visit Worlds of Fun with the Fianna. I'm told the roller coasters are brilliant!"

Cara grinned and gave Riley a squeeze while the rest of the Fianna chuckled. He blushed slightly and mumbled, "Well, they are."

Shay continued, "Now before we begin the games, I'm told the familiars would like to sing a song. Emer, I'll turn things over to you."

The inky black leopard prowled her way onto the plateau, followed by the rest of the familiars. Even Declan made his way up there, much to Ailáine's delight. Corley joined them off to the side, placing his gorgeous mosaic guitar around his neck and looking to Emer for her cue to begin.

The leopard looked to Cara, who amplified her voice with a twist of her hand, then nodded at the musician and softly began singing the opening lines of a song heard at many sporting events. After the first few words, Corley joined her, playing a melodic accompaniment. When the chorus came around, all the familiars joined in, Declan's booming bass blending seamlessly with Laoise's sweet soprano and the full range of voices in between. Another verse followed, and when the chorus began for the second time, even the Fianna and several other bystanders added their voices to the catchy Queen tune.

"We are the champions, we are the champions…"

Keegan got a little teary-eyed at the thought of Áine missing this performance. This was just the kind of thing the phoenix lived for. Out of the corner of her eye, she saw her mom filming everything with her cell phone and felt a little better at the thought of being able to share it with her bonded later. *She'll insist on making this an annual event and turning the opening ceremonies into a spectacle.* That thought brought a wide smile to her face.

Once the song ended, applause erupted, including a familiar sharp whistle from the Ó Faoláin matriarch, and the familiars resumed their places in the crowd. Declan accepted Ailáine, who gushed over him with hugs and kisses, telling him what a good job he did.

Shay resumed his spot on the plateau and said, "That was fantastic! All quads should have been informed by their Fianna commander of the schedule of events and when and where they need to be. So, without further delay—let the games begin!"

All of the competing teams quickly made their way to the first event for which they were scheduled. The Fianna and other spectators wandered among the various fields and pitches, some stopping to watch one of the games for an extended period, others pausing only briefly before moving on.

As the competitions continued, the atmosphere became more and more charged and excited. Calder saw his beloved cheering on one of her quads, and he couldn't resist wrapping her up in a quick embrace.

"Nicely done, lass. This is exactly the type of thing we needed to get our regiments on the right path," he whispered in her ear. She glanced over her shoulder at him, gave him a grateful grin, and then returned her attention to one of her quads. They were currently dominating the obstacle course competition, and she was making sure they knew she was proud.

"Yeah, baby!" she praised, clapping and yelling her support. Calder chuckled at her competitive nature, gave her a quick kiss on the cheek, then wandered over to where one of his quads was about to begin their next event.

Lorcan and Muireann were strolling along behind Nora and Fergal, who were trying to keep Declan and Ailáine in sight. The girl was so excited, though, that she bounced on her bonded's back, laughing and pointing at the various games, urging him to quicken his pace so they could see even more.

Muireann smiled at her excitement, but she was also tickled by Lorcan's reaction. He seemed truly confused, and a little amazed, by the variety of sports and games taking place. Finally, she asked him, "You seem confused, lad. Do you have a question about something you're seeing?"

He started slightly at her observation, then turned toward her and replied, "All of this is just so far outside of my realm of experience, I suppose I'm unsure what to make of it."

"You didn't have sports growing up?" she inquired, surprised. He shook his head, "Not like this. All of our physical activities were related to fighting or defending oneself, whether with traditional weapons, shadow weapons, or without weapons. We didn't really have much use for games, especially those involving teams."

Muireann cocked her head at him and replied, "I think that's a little sad. But no matter, this is something we can remedy. The next time a game of hurling happens, I'm teaching you how to play."

Her no-nonsense approach made him chuckle. "Yes,

ma'am." He pulled her close to him, leaned in to nuzzle her neck, and whispered, "Speaking of teaching, I think it's time for another lesson, love. So far, we've only touched on the basics. But perhaps a more in-depth approach is called for now."

He felt her shiver with excitement at the thought of all that might entail. "I can't wait," she responded, turning toward him. He stopped her and turned her back so she was facing away from him, continuing to nuzzle, kiss, and bite her neck. "Ah, ah, ah, not yet. I will let you know when it's time for that, understand?"

She nodded, but he gave her a sharp nip just under her ear and reprimanded, "We've already talked about this part, love. Say the words. Now, please."

"Yes," she said.

"Yes, what?"

She couldn't help but roll her eyes as she replied, "Yes, sir." She pulled away slightly, looked back at him, and said, "You know that's really irritating, right?"

He gave her an evil grin and said, "Of course I know. That's part of the appeal."

She sniffed and responded pertly, "I suppose I can deal with it occasionally. But just while we're playing, don't expect me to call you sir all the time."

"I wouldn't think of it, love. That would diminish its effectiveness at any rate, at least in my opinion. But don't fret; before long, I will have you begging to call me sir."

She cocked an eyebrow at him and said, "Is that so, lad?"

"Absolutely. Consider it a promise."

The sun was low in the sky, painting everything with a golden glow as the last of the quads made their way back to the central presentation area. The expanded Council had been diligently tallying results as the scores came in, so it was only a matter of a few minutes to finalize the winners.

Once everything was tabulated, Shay acted as emcee once again. They went through each event, awarding the gold, silver, and bronze medals to the top three quads and plying the winners with applause and praise.

After the final medals were given, Keegan's brow was furrowed as she mentally did the math. Her father had barely opened his mouth to announce the overall winning quad, when she completed her calculations and let out a loud, "Hell, yeah!"

Everyone laughed, and Shay said, "As my daughter has already discerned, our grand champions of today's games are the members of quad number thirty-three. Which also means that the Fianna leader with the most points in today's games is none other than Keegan Doran."

She broke out into a short happy dance, then joined her dad and the winning quad on the plateau. He placed larger gold medals around their necks and the crowd happily clapped and shouted, several more of those whistles joining the cacophony.

Then Shay gave one to his daughter, kissed her on the cheek, and said, "I'm so proud of you, a stór!"

"Thank you, Dad!" she responded. "And while this medal is fabulous, I'm even more excited about winning the Fianna's side bet."

He chuckled and said, "Oh really? And what did you win."

"I don't have to do any chores around this place for two weeks. Woo hoo!"

The spectators laughed and applauded, her excitement and exuberance infectious.

Shay motioned for everyone to quiet down and continued, "I'm very happy for you, love. Now, in addition to the medals, adulations, and chore reprieve, there's one more prize for the winning quad. You four will be joining the members of the Fianna at Worlds of Fun tomorrow. Enjoy!"

Family

is life

7

A line of Ubers pulled up to the amusement park entrance, and all the Fae who had chosen to attend piled out. The group had grown since yesterday, several of the Fianna's family members had decided they wanted to see what all the fuss was about.

Máire was wearing a bit of a scowl, so Cara hooked their arms together, and asked, "Why the long face, cuz?" Technically, only Keegan was cousin to both Fae, but the three of them had grown close over the past few months, so the Fire Fae felt like true family to her.

She took a deep breath and said, "Sorry. I'm trying to relax and enjoy myself, but it feels like we're wasting time. I just have a bad feeling I can't seem to shake."

Cara gave her arm a squeeze and said, "Hun, with all you've been through, I'd be amazed if you weren't a bit unsettled. But I think Fintan knows what he's doing. Acquaintances and casual friends might fight well together, but they won't go above and beyond the way they would for family. So, we need to create a family. After all…"

Máire giggled and said, "I know, I know, family is life."

"Yes, it is. And this is the way we create that family. Making memories and forming bonds by spending time together, doing things that are entertaining."

"Okay, I'll try to lighten up," she conceded with a smile.

"Good. Now come on, Keegan and I are dying to show you how much fun a roller coaster is!"

※※※

Ailáine could not stop giggling at her older brother's distasteful expression. She had just convinced him to try some of her bright pink cotton candy and he was apparently not a fan.

"Blech! What the hell was that?" he exclaimed, reaching for her drink to get the taste out of his mouth. He was disappointed to find that it was not water but syrupy lemonade, which made him gasp and suck some of the liquid down into his lungs. This resulted in an extended bout of coughing as he tried to rid himself of the offensive drink.

"I won't have to wait for Balor and his Titans; this place is going to kill me long before they get here," he bemoaned, throwing a nasty look at the cotton candy and lemonade.

Muireann, Sláine, and Liam were sitting with them, admirably attempting to keep from laughing at the Shadow Weaver.

Muireann gave him a dose of side-eye and snarked, "Feeling a touch dramatic today, aren't we?"

He plucked off a healthy chunk of the sticky pink substance and said, "Open your mouth. We'll see how you like it."

She obliged and he deposited the cotton candy on her tongue, where it melted immediately. She smacked her lips a few times and said, "Actually, I think it's lovely. Then again, I have a bit of a sweet tooth."

He looked mildly horrified that she found the sweet candy floss even remotely appealing. That was more than the rest of them could take, and they began laughing in earnest at his discomfort.

"Just when I think I've figured some things out, I realize I understand absolutely nothing about this place," he said, shaking his head.

Liam took pity on him and suggested, "I know of something that might be more to your tastes. Let's get some pizza."

"Does it have some sort of nutritional value, or is it more of this sickening sweetness?" he asked with a bit of trepidation.

Liam laughed, slapped him on the shoulder, and said, "It's not sweet. I think you'll like it. Come on." He pulled him to his feet, and the girls joined them, ready to get some lunch.

Ailáine reached for the rest of her lemonade and cotton candy, but Lorcan said, "Nope, that's enough of that. You won't sleep for a week as it is. Let's try some of this pizza. Maybe it will be remotely edible."

She pouted for a moment but was quickly distracted by the sights and sounds as they went in search of pizza.

⛦⛦⛦

Keegan and Calder were showing several of the other Fae the ins and outs of Worlds of Fun, including the winning group. Quad thirty-three consisted of the petite, red-haired Earth Fae, Rowan, the tall and muscular, dark-haired Air Fae named Bran; Desmond, a stocky male Fire Fae of medium height with long dark curls; and the Water Fae, Brona, who was a curvy blonde with a plethora of freckles. They were experiencing a bit of culture shock but were quickly coming to enjoy their outing.

Brona took in the behemoth roller coaster they were approaching with widened eyes. "That's a wee bit tall, don't ya think?" she asked Rowan, a bit of fear showing in her expression. Desmond draped an arm over each of the females and replied, "Come now, lass, think of it as an adventure! We'll all be right there with you."

She squared her shoulders and gave him a nod, but she did reach for his arm, needing a little reassurance. He crooked his arm and patted her hand encouragingly.

A long line of Fae disguised as humans made their way into the roller coaster cars. Those familiar with amusement parks were excited, and the newcomers were also excited, albeit with a slightly more tempered feeling, unsure exactly what they should expect.

There was a loud clanking as the coaster slowly climbed the first hill, the sound ratcheting up the tension and sense of anticipation. Once it reached the apex, the machine seemed to hover for an unusually long moment, teetering on the edge of fulfillment. Finally, the tipping point was reached, sending the coaster careening along the track at breakneck speed. Every Fae let out an ear-splitting shriek, reveling in the sheer joy of speeding along at an intense velocity.

The ride didn't last more than a few minutes, but by the time it ended, newbies and experienced adrenaline junkies alike were all laughing and smiling, thrilled with the experience and ready for more.

"Let's do it again!" Brona shrieked once the cars made it back to the loading area. The rest of them laughed, and

Keegan replied, "We'll come back later. Let's explore some more of the rides first. There's a lot of other cool stuff!"

The freckled Water Fae looked disappointed for a moment, but she said, "Fine, but I'm coming back to this one later. That was bloody brilliant!"

Riley mumbled under his breath, "I tried to tell them that!" Cara gave him a squeeze and conciliatory pat on the chest. "I know, love. I know," she responded.

⁂

"That's eight!" Ailáine remarked excitedly.

"How many more pieces do you think he can eat?" Sláine quietly asked Muireann as they watched the Shadow Weaver devour yet another piece of pepperoni pizza. His sister overheard and said, "Oh, he can keep going for a while. Mam says he has a high mebatolism." The two females chuckled, and Muireann gently corrected, "That's metabolism. But you were really close."

Ailáine nodded, brow furrowed as she attempted to commit the difficult word to memory.

Lorcan finally wiped his mouth and hands on a napkin, then leaned back and pushed his plate away from him. "Now *that* was worth the trip," he commented, a satisfied expression on his face. "But I had better start moving, or I'm going to need a nap."

Liam stood up and said, "Come on, let's head over to the next roller coaster. Then maybe we'll hit the Ripcord." The rest of the group got to their feet, stretching slightly after the somewhat lengthy lunch break.

"What's a Ripcord?" Lorcan asked.

"Bungee jumping," Liam replied. The Shadow Weaver just stared at him blankly, so he explained. "They strap you into a harness, then lift you up really high and let you swing down, swooping close to the water beneath."

"And humans do this for *fun?*" he asked, truly confused.

"Don't worry, you'll enjoy it. It's more fun than it sounds," Liam said.

"It would have to be. It sounds like a bloody nightmare," Lorcan sniped. Muireann broke out the side-eye again, then said "We'll catch up to you. Give us a minute?" Sláine and Liam nodded, walking ahead with Lorcan's sister.

"You are awfully testy today, a stór. Is something bothering you?"

Lorcan ran his hands through his long, silky hair in frustration. "I'm sorry, love. I'm just worried about what's coming. I don't think the Aos Sí truly understand the danger. I feel like we should be doing more."

She turned him toward her, placing one hand on his cheek. "I know you have no reason to trust us, but I promise you, we are taking this seriously. I personally think the idea of forming stronger bonds with each other is a wise move in light of the battle we're facing. We take family seriously and we will do anything to protect our own. And you and yours are now our own, love. So, try to relax and enjoy today. These moves will pay dividends later, I'm sure of it."

He covered her hand on his cheek with his own. "I truly hope you're right."

☖☖☖

On the way to the Ripcord, they ran into Keegan's group, heading in the same direction. Calder looked at Liam and said, "Ripcord?" His brother just smiled and said, "Mm-hmm."

"Excellent. Let's show them how it's done," the youngest Ó Faoláin suggested, receiving an affirmative nod in return.

Once they reached the ride, the first group ready to try it got strapped in. Then, a thick cable began tightening, pulling Cara, Riley, Keegan, and Calder higher and higher. When they reached the top, the cable was released, allowing them to freefall back toward the water beneath the ride. All four of them screamed like little girls. Things slowly wound down from there, the foursome swinging back and forth above their fellow Fae, who were looking on with a touch of awe.

"That looks ridiculously dangerous," Lorcan mumbled grumpily. Muireann gave the hand she was holding a squeeze and replied, "As my friend Sláine is fond of saying, 'Suck it up, Buttercup.' You'll be fine."

The Shadow Weaver cocked an eyebrow at her and said, "You'll pay for that later."

She simply shrugged and said, "Then we'll both have fun, won't we?"

He couldn't help but chuckle at that response. "Fine. I guess I'm being a little prickly."

"Like a cactus. A big one," she responded, completely straight-faced.

He wrapped her thick braid around his hand, tugged none too gently, and kissed her roughly. "You've made your point, love. Now, let's go try this insane pastime."

Family

is life

8

In his púca form, Lir walked briskly through the sparkly portal, a mildly hungover phoenix on his back, squinting grumpily at the sun. As the doorway snapped shut with a loud pop, Áine startled and turned back to glare at the offending portal, which was no longer there.

"Damn, Goat Boy, how much did I drink last night?" she asked, massaging her temples with her wings. He chuckled and said, "Apparently, a little too much."

"Very funny. That was actually a rhetorical question."

The púca shrugged, as much as he was able, and said, "Just trying to be helpful." He continued trekking through the heavily wooded landscape of the Earth Clan island, Falias. He had been here a few times with Calder, visiting the extended Ó Faoláin family, and was very much at home in the blooming woodlands of this place. The gardens around the World Tree had been modeled after this island, and while they were beautiful, they paled in comparison to the home of the Earth Clan. Lush and colorful, with flowers and foliage in a multitude of colors and textures, it would take a very long time to run out of breathtaking scenery to behold.

Even his irritable companion seemed to be enamored of the countryside, or at least she had stopped complaining. Hopefully, her taciturn mood would last until she recovered from her overindulgence.

Before long, Lir noticed Áine squirming strangely on his back. He slowed down and turned his head to look at her. She had opened the black bag and carefully withdrew the Water Clan relic.

The púca stopped and said, "Why are you taking that out of the bag?" She looked around, anywhere but directly in Lir's eyes, and mumbled, "No reason, just checking on things." She paused a moment, then continued, "But you know, I'd feel better if I could keep an eye on it. I mean, anything could happen to it in that bag,"

Lir chuckled softly and said, "You don't have to make up a reason, Áine. Just put it on. I know you'll keep it safe." Her eyes lit up, and she said, "Well, if you insist. I'll make sure it's secure." She slipped the relic around her neck, which had shrunk to the appropriate size, softly stroking the jewels a couple of times before cinching the bag shut.

"So, how far to the village?" she asked.

"Not too far, but we're stopping somewhere else first."

She cocked her head and replied, "Oh yeah? Where?"

He said, "You'll see. I promise you'll enjoy the stop."

She shrugged and settled down on his back, somewhat distracted by the gorgeousness of her borrowed bling.

After a while, they came upon a large house and stable, with several horses grazing contentedly in the adjacent meadow. Lir whinnied in delighted greeting and began trotting toward the house.

When they drew near, a short, curvy Fae with her

silvery blonde hair tucked back in a thick braid opened the back door and stepped out onto the porch. She dried her hands on a dish towel and tossed it onto her shoulder.

"Lir, my love! It's bloody wonderful to see you!" Her deep green eyes twinkled with pleasure as she held her arms out in welcome.

"Gram! It's been too long; I'm so happy to see you!" He trotted right up to her, and she put one hand on each side of his long face, cupping his cheeks like he was the most precious thing she'd ever seen. Then she wrapped her arms around his neck and gave him a bear hug.

After a good squeeze, she pulled back and said, "And this must be Áine. My daughter has told me all about you, lass."

"Your daughter?"

"Yes, Siobhán is my child. And those wild boys of hers are my grandsons." Understanding dawned as the phoenix finally caught up. She was hungover, after all, so the pieces were coming together a bit slower than usual. "I believe she told me you are bonded to Calder's lass, Keegan. Isn't that right?"

Áine nodded and replied, "Yeah, I've been keeping her out of trouble since before she was born." Lir couldn't help but snort at the idea of the phoenix keeping anyone out of trouble, ever. Trouble might as well be her middle name.

Calder's grandmother cocked an eyebrow in an eerily similar manner to her daughter, causing the púca to clear his throat and look away.

"I wish I could do that. You and Siobhán stop folks in their tracks with just an eyebrow. It's awesome." She attempted to raise just one of her eyebrows (or rather the flames in the general vicinity of where her eyebrows should be), but she couldn't isolate just one, so she ended up just looking startled.

"Yes, well, I'm sure you have your own set of gifts, love. Now, it's nearing time for the midday meal. Lir, choose a smaller form, please. The horses don't get to come inside, and neither does your púca form. You'd be knocking things over left and right, and nobody has time for that nonsense." She turned around and headed back inside, clearly expecting immediate compliance. Which, of course, she got. Lir shifted to his fainting goat form and followed her into the house, Áine still comfortably settled on his back.

The three of them passed through a mudroom and into a large kitchen with a dining table rivaling Siobhán's in size and intricacy of decoration. There was a fire in the large hearth, and a pot of something delicious-smelling bubbled on the stove. The aroma of freshly baked bread arose from a loaf pan covered with a dish towel.

Seated at the table was an elder Fae with wavy, salt-and-pepper hair and pale green eyes. He was hurriedly eating a piece of the potato bread that was presumably resting in the loaf pan under the towel. Calder's gram pulled up short, rested both fists on her hips, and scolded, "Brady Nolan, are you spoiling your dinner with my potato bread?"

He quickly swallowed the last of the evidence, then stood and approached his wife, making sure to flash her a beaming smile, complete with a couple of strangely familiar dimples. "Now, now, mo chroí, you know you were just about to serve us that bread. What's the harm in me taking a wee sample aforehand?"

"That's not the point, ye old thief. Dinner is not yours until I give it to you. You're after fouling up my whole presentation!" As he drew near, she swatted him with her dish towel, but he caught her around the waist, planted a kiss on her neck, and lifted her up to sit on the end of the table so he could plant a proper kiss on her lips. She attempted to stay annoyed but was only able to maintain her pique for a moment before she returned his kiss.

Áine watched with fascination before mumbling to Lir, "So many things just fell into place." Goat Boy chuckled softly in agreement.

"Yes, well, we can continue this conversation later," the grandmother said, slightly embarrassed by allowing herself to be distracted like that. She started to wiggle out of her husband's grasp, but he tightened his grip on her waist, gave her one more thorough kiss, then lifted her off the table and back to her feet, whispering, "We will indeed continue this *conversation* later, Treasa."

The phoenix couldn't help herself. "Boom chicka wah wah," she stage whispered to Lir. Brady looked over at her and barked a laugh. "I like this one!" he exclaimed, dimples on display once again.

Siobhán's mother, whose cheeks were still slightly pink, couldn't help but chuckle quietly to herself. "Why am I not surprised?" she mumbled. Then she looked at the phoenix and said, "But I like her too." Then she replaced the dish towel on her shoulder and announced, "Dinner is served. Brady, if you make a plate for Lir, I'll get Áine's ready."

"Um, are there mushrooms? I hate mushrooms," the phoenix asked.

"Don't worry, lass," Brady assured her. "I hate the slimy suckers, too. There are no mushrooms in this house."

Áine glanced at Lir and said, "I think I'm gonna like it here."

Once they had eaten and cleaned up after the meal, Treasa said, "Love, would you fetch a couple of horses? I thought we could escort these two down to the village so they can meet with the Druids about their task."

"Of course, won't take but a moment," he replied, heading out to the stable.

"I appreciate it, Gram, but we don't want to disturb you any more than we already have," Lir started. But Treasa was having none of that.

"Nonsense! You're family, and..."

"Oh, oh, oh, I know this one," Áine interrupted. "Family is life."

That brought a smile to the Earth Fae's face, and she said, "Just so, lass. Now, let's be on our way. Sooner begun, sooner done."

⁂

As they headed toward the village proper, Treasa cleared her throat and said, "May I ask you a question, lass?"

"Mm-hmm," Áine said, feeling rather sleepy after the delicious lunch and being rocked back and forth on Lir's púca back.

"Is that the Water Clan relic you're wearing?" she asked in such a tone that suggested genuine curiosity, not judgement.

"Well, I thought it would be safer if I kept an eye on it," she started to justify self-consciously.

"No worries, love. I've only seen the Earth Clan relic, so I thought maybe I could take a look at that one."

The phoenix straightened up and replied, "I suppose you could take a look. Goat Boy, scoot over so Gram can check out the torque, please."

Lir obliged, moving closer to Treasa's mount. Áine leaned toward her and said, "Go ahead, take it and look it over."

The Earth Fae hesitated, saying, "Oh, I didn't mean I need to touch it, I don't want to presume…"

Brady broke in with, "For crying out loud, mo chroí, you know you want to wear it. Just try the bloody thing on! When are you going to have a chance like this again?"

"Well, if you think it's all right, I guess it would be nice," she said.

"Come on, Gram, knock yourself out," the phoenix urged, stretching her neck out so the Earth Fae could easily reach the relic.

Treasa tentatively grasped the torque, lifting it from Áine's neck. She brought the now tiny heirloom close to her face to see the details and watched in fascination as it increased in size until it was large enough to fit around her own neck.

"I knew it would magically adjust itself, but that is still fascinating to watch," she observed, gently placing it around her neck and inspecting the intricate and beautiful craftsmanship with a feather-soft touch.

"Stunning," Brady commented. "I know, the torque is gorgeous, isn't it?" Treasa replied. "There's a torque?" he quipped, unleashing the dimples again. His wife gently slapped him on the leg, "You old flatterer," she scolded, but her smile betrayed her pleasure at the compliment.

"I'm telling you, Goat Boy, Conor makes so much more sense now," Áine whispered, causing Lir to snort again. Thankfully, Gram was preoccupied, so no eyebrows were unleashed.

After a few more minutes of enjoying the bling, Treasa ran her fingers over the torque one final time, lifted it over her head, and after it had shrunk to an appropriate size, replaced it around Áine's neck.

Then she turned her attention to the familiars and said, "We're almost to the village, but I wanted to mention something to you both before we get there. Brady has taken on the role of Clan leader while the rest of our Clan is in Tíonol, so he will do his best to grease the wheels and help you to accomplish your objective and be on your way, quickly. But, since most of our Druids have joined the battle preparations, I'm afraid the only ones left are a few of the youngest acolytes and a very old, very cranky wanker who may well try to obstruct your journey. He abhors change and tends to act like the relic is his own personal possession. I just wanted to warn you in case we're not around at some point, and he tries to act like a pox bottle."

"I like her," Áine stage whispered to Lir. "Me, too," he replied.

"At any rate, if you're having trouble with him and we're not around, just mention my name. That should be enough to whip him into shape," Treasa informed them.

Brady piped up with, "He's scared of her." She laughed and tried to qualify his statement, "I don't know if I'd go that far."

"Bloody terrified," her husband asserted. "Half of the village is, truth be told. My love is a force to be reckoned with." Treasa blushed but didn't disagree. "Well, somebody has to get things done," she mumbled.

A lush canopy comprised of interlaced flowering tree branches and vines caused dappled sunlight to filter throughout the Earth Clan Druid's Enclave. As the group approached, one of the young acolytes walked toward them and offered to tend to the horses. Treasa and Brady dismounted and handed him the reins to their mounts.

Their feet had barely touched the ground when an elder Druid walked toward them, scowling, grumbling under his breath, and leaning heavily on his cane as he shuffled their way. His wild white hair and rheumy pale blue eyes added to his air of thinly veiled hostility.

"Well, now, these must be the thieves I've heard so much about," he snarled at them. "Come to steal away our most precious relic for who knows what nefarious purpose!"

Brady said, "Now, Osgar, there's no call to speak to our visitors that way. They have a letter from High Druid Deirdre explaining their journey and requesting our assistance."

"Like as not, that letter is forged. Surely, our High Druid wouldn't be so foolish as to entrust our priceless heirloom to these two...familiars." That last word was spoken with extreme distaste.

Áine looked around at her companions, then asked, "Is this fuck knuckle for real?" Treasa fought to keep a straight face; Brady didn't even try. The phoenix turned her attention to the crotchety elder Fae.

"Listen, I don't know what crawled up your ass and died, but I have been insulted by far better Fae than you. And nobody suggests our High Druid is foolish, or misguided, or any other negative word you can come up with, at least not in front of me. So, you can either trot that sparkly torque out here now, or I can turn you into a pile of ash, and we'll discuss the matter with the next Druid up." She punctuated the end of her speech by flaring her flames impressively, causing the Earth Druid to take an involuntary step back.

Treasa turned her back to the Druid, stepped close to the phoenix, and whispered, "Nicely done, lass. You've terrified him more than I ever could. This presents an excellent opportunity, if we may take it from here?"

Áine nodded at her, never taking her eyes off of Osgar and keeping her flames at an elevated level.

The grandmother glanced at her husband with a knowing look. He returned it with an almost imperceptible nod. "Well, Osgar, what will it be? Would you prefer to be a pile of ash or help us help these familiars on their pilgrimage?"

He stuttered briefly, beads of sweat breaking out on his forehead. "I, I, I..."

Brady picked it up from there with, "Now, elder Osgar, I have personally inspected the High Druid's letter, and I can assure you it is most certainly authentic. She has requested our assistance, and it is our duty as Fae and your duty as a Druid, I might add, to provide said assistance at once."

As the Druid considered his circumstance, the Nolan patriarch stepped closer to him, wrapping an arm around his thin, bony shoulders, and said conspiratorially, "You know, I don't think you've considered the positive aspects of this request."

When Osgar looked confused, Brady clarified. "It is my understanding that when the Water Clan graciously allowed the loan of their relic, they held a céilí. There was food and drink, singing and dancing, and their Druid-in-Charge presented the torque to our traveling friends in a lovely ceremony. Just imagine, if you were to do the same, when these torques and this journey make the difference in the battle we are facing...why you'd be hailed as a hero!"

The Druid was obviously intrigued by that possibility, so Treasa brought it home with, "They might even go so far as to say you were primarily responsible for our victory."

Osgar cleared his throat and conceded, "Well, if you're certain the letter is genuine, I suppose we must obey our High Druid. And if doing our duty helps to win the battle, so be it. Far be it from me to stand in the way."

Brady gave the Druid a healthy smack on the back, causing him to stagger forward slightly, unprepared for such a strong gesture. "Brilliant, lad! Leave the boring details to Treasa and me; you'd better start working on your speech. Everyone will be hanging on your every word, so you'd best make it a good one!"

The elder appeared to be already developing his talking points, eyes glazing slightly. He said, "Yes, yes, that's excellent. I'll begin developing my message immediately. When should I plan for it?

Treasa replied, "Just a few days. Brady and I will get started immediately and let you know as soon as the details are finalized. Thank you so much for your support."

Osgar nodded distractedly, his mind already absorbed by the speech he was mentally writing. He turned and began hobbling back into the enclave.

Lir grinned at the Nolans and asserted, "You two have done that before."

Treasa cocked an eyebrow and said coyly, "Perhaps. Effective, isn't it?" That drew a laugh from all of them.

❖❖❖

A glowing crimson disk hung low in the sky as the Earth Clan members made their way to the gardens outside the Druid's Enclave. Swaths of gold and copper light glanced off the flowers and trees, painting the Fae who were gathering in rich, vibrant color.

Áine and Lir stood with Siobhán's parents in the center of the gardens beside a small table. In the middle of that table was a roundish item beneath a silky forest green cloth. Once most Fae were present, Osgar approached them, moving slowly, doing his best impression of royalty.

He stopped on the other side of the small table, lifted a small artifact to his throat, and said, "Fáilte. Thank you all for coming. Recently, I received a missive from High Druid Deirdre, asking for my personal help with a plan to help win the coming battle. In order to beseech the gods of the familiars for help, we must help these two envoys by loaning them our most precious relic."

He grasped the silky green covering and removed it with a flourish. Sitting on a headless male marble bust was the Earth god's torque, resplendent in shades from forest to sea foam to a rich, shimmering copper. Leaves and vines carved from emeralds and jade were woven amongst flowers created from Madeira citrine and amber. Diamonds sparkled from the center of the dark orange flowers. Intricate Celtic knotwork, crafted from thin strands of copper, nestled amongst the gems, tying it all together.

Áine let out a low whistle in appreciation. "That is fab-u-lous." Osgar shot her an irritated look, but Brady only smiled.

The Druid regained his composure and asked, "How will you carry the torque?" Áine stuck her talon up in a high kick, the black expando-bag dangling from it. Treasa took it from her, opened it up, and held it out toward Osgar.

The elder Earth Fae lifted the relic from the marble bust and brought it over to the bag, where it shrunk down to the size of the bag's opening. Then he gently lowered it inside, and Gram cinched the bag shut, handing it back to the phoenix.

The crowd responded with polite applause. Then, the sound of musicians tuning their instruments could be heard, drawing Áine like a moth to a flame. The rest of the Fae followed her, ready to relax and enjoy themselves.

As they followed Áine, Brady threw an arm around Lir's neck and said, "So, lad, how is the family? Is everyone preparing?" He shook his head. "It's so hard being away from you all. Treasa feels such a duty to our Clan, and she has a point about us being in the best position to help the younglings and the elders who can no longer manage on their own. But damn, do I miss my Bháni and her boys."

Lir leaned into Siobhan's dad and gave him a nuzzle of support. "We miss you, too, Gramps," he said.

Brady patted the púca's neck with a sigh and said, "Once this is over, I think it's time for a change. I'll have to work on Treasa to get her to agree, but I can handle it. Come on, lad. Let's get something to eat. And a pint." The grandfather walked ahead, seeking sustenance.

Lir watched him and thought, *I don't think it will take much convincing to get Gram excited about being with her family.*

"Goat Boy! Come over here and check out the musicians!" Áine bellowed at him from across the enclave grounds. He trotted toward her, knowing she would only get louder the longer she was ignored.

The area sectioned off for the players had a stage demarcated by small trees and bushes, and the ground had been raised and leveled. There were low tables and benches, as well as faery lights and small bonfires scattered throughout.

Áine and Treasa were front and center—prime entertainment viewing. If he joined them, he would be blocking the view of several others, so he decided to shift into the form of a chimp, since that also had the added benefit of opposable thumbs. He settled on the other end of the bench Treasa was seated at, with Áine wiggling excitedly between them, ready to break out her dance moves at the first opportunity.

The music started with some traditional reels and jigs, and before long, everyone was humming along or tapping their feet in time with the song. Brady soon joined them and was followed by a couple floating trays laden with food and drink choices.

They all chose a few treats and grabbed a pint, settling in to watch the performance. After a few more songs, one of the musicians made a sweeping gesture, and the top layer of the stage's soil rippled and smoothed, solidifying into a hard surface resembling a tile or stone floor. Soon, a group of several young Earth Fae filed onto the makeshift stage. They all wore their Earth Clan tartan, along with white, fluffy poodle socks and shiny black shoes that made a distinctive click as they walked along the stage.

Once they were in place, the musicians began an up-tempo treble reel. The young Fae paused for just a moment, and then their feet began tapping out the rhythm of the dance. The speed of the song was impressive, and their steps were even more so. As they bobbed and weaved, making their way through the progression of the dance, their feet moved so fast they were almost a blur.

Áine was utterly entranced. She'd seen hard shoe step dancing before but always found it fascinating. She couldn't help but want to recreate it, so she hopped down from the bench and began working out the steps. It didn't take long before she could do a fair job mimicking the dancers' movements. Since she was right in front of the stage, she was in full view of the dancers, musicians, and most of the Fae present.

When the song ended and the dancers finished their steps, everyone broke into raucous applause. The young Fae took a bow and motioned to the musicians, showing their appreciation. Then, both the dancers and musicians motioned to Áine, in recognition of her dancing skills.

The gesture seemed to truly surprise the phoenix. She was just entertaining herself, so the recognition was unexpected. But she quickly recovered her composure, taking a dramatic, sweeping bow to the delight of the crowd, who responded with cheers, applause, and a rather eardrum-shattering whistle that seemed familiar, coming from Gram's general direction.

Áine returned to the bench where her companions were seated, trying to remain modest, but her expression radiated pride. Brady gave her a look and said, "Nicely done, lass."

"Oh, it was nothing. I just enjoy dancing," she demurred.

"Well, it was some impressive footwork. You'll have to teach me," he said with a grin.

She narrowed her eyes at him and said, "Don't joke about dancing. It's sacred to me, you know."

He shrugged and said, "Who said I was joking? I love to dance."

The phoenix considered for a moment, then said, "Deal. After our pilgrimage is done and we've kicked some monster ass, we'll start your lessons."

Brady's dimples were on full display as he said, "Looking forward to it, lass. Now, I'd say it's high time we got to celebrating."

He waved one of the floating trays over, whispered directions to it, and watched it zip away. It returned shortly, carrying four pints, four shot glasses, and a bottle of whiskey.

Treasa looked at her husband, then at the phoenix, and said, "Well, now you've done it. He's gone and broken out the whiskey."

She cackled in response and said, "Bring it on!"

They spent the next few hours talking, laughing, and drinking. They listened to talented musicians and watched some more dancing from the younglings. Áine convinced Lir and Brady to join her in a lovely rendition of "Girls Just Wanna Have Fun," complete with some questionable but well-intentioned choreography.

By the time Treasa decided it was high time to head home, she was the only one not completely soused, and she wasn't exactly sober. Thankfully, the Druids were happy to give them a ride home in one of their carriages. They could pick up their horses later.

As they were piling into the carriage, Áine looked at a very drunk Lir, who was gripping the nearly empty whisky bottle in his little chimp hands and said, "Hey, I want some more. Give it to me."

Lir just snorted and said, "That's what she said."

△△△

Family

is life

9

Silky ribbons of shadow flowed from Lorcan's palms to wrap around Muireann's form, creating a simple shift-like garment. She then removed her regular clothing and took his hand, letting him draw her deeper into the ocean until the water reached her collarbones.

She felt anxious and excited as she stood there with nothing but a diaphanous shadowy slip flowing around her, swaying back and forth with the waves. Lorcan grasped her other hand and held both of them, giving a gentle squeeze.

"Deep breaths, love. This will be uncomfortable but brief, and you will be brilliant; I know it. Ready?" he asked.

She exhaled loudly, then nodded.

Lorcan gave her a sly smile and said, "Use your words now."

That made her giggle, and she said, "Yes, I'm ready."

"Good girl. Here we go." He released his Fomori magic, sending it into Muireann, urging it to seek out similar specks of magic within her blood. Once it detected something familiar, he sent what he thought of as a surge, waking up the Fomori particles inside her.

She gasped as his power rushed through her, feeling like tiny zaps of lightning pricking her from the inside. Her breathing came hard and fast as she managed the pain of the transformation, but as promised, the feeling was fleeting. After only a few moments, it had passed.

As Lorcan allowed his shadows to dissipate, she could see the effects of the change. Her legs seemed to be wrapped up in deep teal-colored metallic scales, iridescent and shimmering, forming a powerful tail. Similar scales had erupted over her breasts and along the length of her spine, and gills had opened up on both sides of her neck. She lifted one hand and spread her fingers, revealing a thin membrane between them.

The Shadow Weaver had also triggered his own transformation and was treading water in front of her, still holding one hand, allowing her a moment to adjust to her new form.

A look of awe came over Muireann's face, and she exclaimed, "This is fecking amazing!"

He chuckled and said, "It is pretty impressive, isn't it?"

"It's incredible!"

A little otter's head could be seen heading toward them as her familiar, Ula, swam out to join her bonded. Muireann waved to her and said, "Isn't this fantastic?"

The otter bobbed her head in affirmation, excited to finally enjoy the sea with her favorite Fae.

Lorcan pulled her close briefly, gave her a sensual kiss, and said, "I need to keep activating the Fomori blood in others. Why don't you go try your fins out with Ula? Don't go too far, though. There are dangers in the ocean you're unfamiliar with, love."

Ula, who had reached them by this point, said, "I'll watch over her. Come on, a stór, there's so much I want to show you!"

The healer let her familiar pull her away, giving Lorcan a brief wave before turning her attention back to the otter, giggling excitedly at the new world she was about to explore.

☙❧

A giant black and white orca gleefully leaped from the water, a tiny, cackling Fomori with dark red hair and a shiny, sparkling, sapphire tail clinging to his dorsal fin. Ailáine had been swimming with Declan for hours, enjoying his powerful sea form as he towed her around, tossing her in the air and generally having a great time.

Lorcan had been transforming the Aos Sí for those same hours, and he was exhausted. Muireann and Ula swam up to him, the former tucking herself against his side, twining her tail with his briefly, a sort of merrow embrace.

He gave her a tired grin, gripped her chin, and planted a slow, sensual kiss on her lips. She let herself melt into him, her fingers brushing against his waist, where the skin of his torso melded into the metallic bronze scales of his tale. With one hand on the small of her back and the other tangled in her lengthy, wet tresses, he roughly pulled her against him. His kiss turned forceful as his tongue demanded entrance to her mouth, which she gladly granted.

Lorcan was considering shifting back to his Fae form and continuing this in a more private location when his little sister and her killer whale familiar swam right up next to them. Declan shot a blast of air through his blowhole, startling everyone and causing Ailáine to begin cackling again.

Her brother narrowed his eyes and said, “Hilarious, Little Bug.” Then, he used his water power to splash her in the face. She sputtered, then kept laughing, enjoying herself immensely.

Nora, and Fergal swam up to them, the Weapons Master looking just as tired as Lorcan. “All right, lass, it’s time for some dinner. It’s been a long day,” their mother instructed. “And you two, will you be joining us?”

He looked at Muireann, who nodded and said, “We’d love to. My da is on Earth with Siobhán, and I’m starving!”

Nora grinned at her and replied, “Good. Fergal made an outstanding shepherd’s pie yesterday. It’s even better the next day, so you’re in luck.”

“That sounds brilliant,” she commented.

Lorcan finally pushed his plate away after his third helping of shepherd’s pie. And that was after a huge green salad and half a dozen hot rolls. Ailáine elbowed Muireann gently and said, “I told you he had a high metabolism.”

The healer smiled and replied, “Yes, you were right about that. And good job getting the word right.” The young girl grinned, pleased with the praise.

Her mother also grinned and said, “My two favorite lads both eat like a horse,” nodding to where Fergal was using a roll to sop up the last of his third helping. “Although it’s hardly surprising since triggering the transformation in others requires a great deal of energy.”

“Swimming also uses a lot,” Declan’s deep voice

rumbled. "Little Bug always eats like a baby horse when she goes swimming."

That evoked a gasp from Ailáine, who was newly fascinated by horses, having never been around them before arriving in Tíonol. "I want to see a baby horse! I bet they're adorable," she mused.

Muireann responded, "My brother's family raises horses. We can ask him if there are currently any babies you could see." The youngling nodded excitedly.

Everyone stood and began clearing the table when a sharp knock sounded at the door. Nora nodded to Lorcan, who went to answer the door.

Before it was even open completely, he found himself smothered by two sobbing blondes. The twins, Iseult and Imogen, clung to him as they babbled incoherently.

Muireann quickly joined him, assessing whether or not the two Shadow Weavers were injured. Once she was assured their pain was not physical, she gestured toward the sofa, and Lorcan guided them over to sit down.

By this time, Nora and Fergal had made their way over to them. Nora knelt in front of her son and gently put a hand on each of the twins' knees. "What's wrong, cailíní? How can we help?"

The twins took deep breaths and took turns explaining their situation.

"It's our little brother, Rónán."

"He didn't come over with the rest of us."

"We think he was hiding from us and missed the message that we were all leaving."

"We thought maybe he came over with someone else."

"But we've looked everywhere and asked everyone."

And then, in unison, "We have to find him!"

Nora squeezed their knees, then stood and began

pacing as she reviewed their options. "And what about your parents?"

"Mam is out of her mind with worry, and Da just keeps searching."

"But we've looked everywhere. We even swam back to the sea caves to see if he got hurt and needed help, but we found nothing."

"That's where they are now, swimming back and forth along the route from the caves, just hoping they'll find him or some sign of him at least."

Lorcan had an arm around each twin and was rubbing his hands up and down their arms, offering what comfort he could.

Muireann looked at the sisters with sympathy. She'd only recently been able to acknowledge her brother, but she knew how heartbroken she'd be if he were missing.

Fergal gave Nora a look and then pinned his gaze on Lorcan, saying, "Are you thinking what I'm thinking?"

He nodded and said, "Aye. We need to go back."

His mother's eyes widened, and she replied, "Hold your bloody horses, lad. I agree that something must be done, but we're not there yet. Let's discuss this with Deirdre first. She might have some insight that could be useful."

The two males looked at each other, and Fergal said, "I trust your mam, lad. And I trust your Aintín Dee. I think it's worth getting her input, don't you?"

Lorcan nodded and said, "Fine. We'll talk to her and then settle on a plan. But we need to move quickly. Rónán is the same age as Ailáine. We can't leave him with those monsters."

"Agreed," Fergal and Nora said together. Then she took hold of each twin's hand and said, "We're going to help you, loves. Just let us speak with Deirdre and formulate a plan. Why don't you two find your parents and explain the situation to them? Dee may want to speak to them, so ask them to return to the island and stay close. We'll work as quickly as we can."

The sisters nodded, then gave Lorcan a final squeeze, which he returned.

"Thank you all for your help."

"We really appreciate it."

"Of course! We'll talk to Deirdre right away. Get your parents home, and hopefully, we'll be in contact very soon," Nora assured them.

Lorcan walked them to the door, shut it behind them, and turned to face the others, wearing an obviously distressed expression. "I was afraid this might happen. If I hadn't killed Cathal when I did, we could've been more organized when we left, and the boy might be with us now."

Nora started to disagree, but Muireann was quicker. She crossed the room, gripped his chin in her hand, and said, "If you hadn't killed that monster when you did, Máire would be dead now. You did the right thing, love. Second-guessing yourself now serves no purpose but to undermine your confidence, and that's the last thing we need."

She held his gaze for a moment more until he finally nodded his agreement. Nora looked at her with increased respect and said, "Nicely done, lass." To her son, she said, "She's a keeper, love. Don't feck things up, eh?"

Lorcan rolled his eyes, and everyone else chuckled at his expense. Nora continued, "Now, let's finish clearing the table and visit Dee. Hopefully, she'll know how to proceed with a minimum of danger."

The High Druid walked among the acolytes spread out among the enclave's garden, each with their eyes closed, attempting to connect with each other. All acolytes underwent training and rituals that allowed them to tap into their environment on a deeper level. As the High Druid, Deirdre was able to gather the resulting strands of consciousness and funnel their natural gifts through her. This process created something more significant than the sum of its parts. She could then use that power to help protect her people. Or at least that was the hope.

She stopped when she reached the garden's center, took a deep breath, closed her eyes, and began centering herself. Once she reached a state of equilibrium, she gently began seeking out the shimmering tendrils of power emanating from the acolytes. Each time she found one, she would tug it toward her center, plaiting them together as she went.

Finally, once she had gathered each strand and woven them into a glowing power nexus being fed by every acolyte in the enclave, she could focus that energy and direct it in any way she chose.

She gently grasped the life force of the nearby trees and plants and fed power into them. New blooms and leaves erupted, and vines doubled and tripled in length, giving even the lush gardens of Tíonol more vibrance and vitality.

She opened her eyes to observe her handiwork. As she perused the new and improved gardens, she thought, *I can work with this.*

She gently released the strands, sending them back to their respective sources. The acolytes slowly opened their eyes, looking around in awe at Deirdre's handiwork.

"Nicely done, everyone. That was a rousing success. It's getting late; enjoy the rest of your evening. We will work on this again tomorrow."

Deirdre noticed her best friend and her family approaching the gardens as the acolytes wandered off to their own devices.

"What a lovely surprise!" she exclaimed with a smile. Then she noticed their serious expressions and continued, "What is it? What's wrong?"

Nora quickly brought her up to speed, Deirdre's expression growing more concerned by the minute. "Bloody hell," she cursed. "Fecking Balor and his fecking chaos magic. I am so over the whole bloody mess!" She took a couple of deep breaths and calmed herself.

"I'm sorry, loves. This whole situation is on my last nerve." She considered her options momentarily, then said, "Well, we've got two choices, I believe. I can try to contact Rónán psychically. I should be able to make contact, but there's a chance that Balor could detect the communication, which could put the lad at even greater risk. The other option is to send someone physically."

Fergal commented, "The lad and I have already begun discussing how best to infiltrate the stronghold. Just give us the word, and we'll go."

Deirdre held up a hand and said, "I would really prefer to keep that as plan B. I am sure Balor would love nothing more than to get his hands on Lorcan. It doesn't take much imagination to realize he must feel betrayed by a son who killed his pet psychopath, however much the animal deserved it."

She cocked an eyebrow and pursed her lips as she considered the best path forward. "Very well. Let's give it a go, shall we?"

The High Druid seated herself on a nearby bench, gesturing for the others to stay close. She closed her eyes and calmed her breathing, trying to find the elusive mental stillness that allowed her to reach out telepathically. Once she felt herself slip into that pool of calm, she sent out a tiny filament, searching for the young Shadow Weaver.

As she felt herself approaching the Fomori stronghold, she proceeded slowly and cautiously. She could discern the Titans in their cages, and their sheer number was disheartening. *Never mind that, worry about it later.*

Surprisingly, she felt the presence of several others who did not appear to be suffering from the effects of chaos magic. They all felt like adults, so she didn't risk contact with any of them.

She continued moving slowly throughout the empty rooms and corridors, seeking anything that seemed like it might be their errant young Shadow Weaver. She finally ventured into the kitchens and caught a flicker of something promising. As she honed in on it, she realized she had found him.

Rónán? Is that you?

She immediately felt the walls in his mind slam shut as he panicked at the unknown intrusion. *His defenses are strong—that's good. But let's see if I can wiggle my way in.*

She ever-so-gently began picking at the edges of his mental shields, sending feelings of safety and friendship as she did so to encourage his trust. After a while, she was able to pry up the edge of his wall and slip beneath it.

Wait, wait, wait, I'm not here to hurt you, lad! she quickly sent to him. *This is High Druid Deirdre with the Aos Sí. Your parents and sisters are safe with us, but they're very worried about you. Are you okay, Rónán?*

Yes, I'm fine for now. I met Orla and Brian, they're friends of my folks. The Chaos Faction took them; we thought they'd been turned into Titans. But since somebody killed Cathal, Balor needed help with things, so he postponed their transition. Now

I'm trying to spy on him and find out anything we can use to save ourselves and get the feck out of here. Sorry for the language; I'm a little frazzled.

Deirdre couldn't help but smile at the young Fomori. She was relieved to find he was uninjured and had found some help. *No worries, lad. I'm just glad you're doing okay. Now, since it's a little dangerous for us to keep communicating for very long, I'm going to let you go, and I will discuss our options with your parents and my friends. Can you be ready for a message tomorrow at the same time?*

The youngling answered affirmatively and agreed to share everything with Orla and Brian.

Stay safe, lad. We'll speak further tomorrow. Deirdre broke contact with him, took a deep breath, and said, "Well, that was interesting."

⁂

Ula waved at Muireann as she left to meet Laoise and Saoirse for a girls' night. *I wonder what they do,* the healer thought.

Lorcan reached out and grasped her hand as they walked through a wooded area on the way to Muireann's house. The waxing gibbous moon bathed the area in soft white light, and the stars overhead twinkled like pearlescent sand strewn across the inky night sky. She had always loved the night. The cool darkness felt soothing, and the sounds of night, crickets and small nocturnal animals going about their business, relaxed her as few other things could.

She let out a sigh of contentment, and Lorcan inquired, "Feeling at ease, lass?"

"As much as one can be with a battle looming. But

being outdoors at night always calms me. It's my happy place."

"Good to know. But if you wanted a little darkness, all you had to do was ask, love," he replied, his voice dropping to a purr as his shadows twined their way up her arm from their clasped hands. They dipped and swirled up to her shoulder, then branched out, gliding smoothly across her skin like silk. One branch crawled up her neck, twirled around her ear, and spread out across her scalp. Another dove down, sliding over her collarbone and across her sternum. There it split, curving under and around her breasts, trailing its way over her nipples before joining again just below her navel.

Lorcan paused there and said, "I want you, love. And I will eventually take you—every last bit of you. But tonight, I want to make your toes curl while you scream my name. Can I do that, Muireann?"

His shadows began moving downward again, very, very slowly, as he awaited her permission. She gasped at the sensation and said, "Yes. Please."

He chuckled darkly and replied, "Begging already? You're going to be so much fun." He put his hands on her waist and shoved her roughly against the tree at her back. His hands were quickly buried in her long dark brown tresses, which he used to pull her head back and expose her throat.

He licked, kissed, and nipped his way up and down her neck, sucking hard to mark her as his. His shadows were still moving south, but far too slowly for the healer's liking. She let out a moan and said, "Please!"

Lorcan slowed the shadows and said, "Please, what? Tell me what you want, love. Ask me nicely."

"Please touch me. Down there. With your shadows. Or your hands."

"Hmm. No, I don't think I will. Now lift your skirt above your waist." She shuddered at his command and lifted her skirt as requested.

Lorcan knelt in front of her, hooked his fingers in the sides of her silky underwear, and pulled them down so she could step out of them. He placed his hands on her inner thighs and said, "Spread your legs for me, love. Now, please."

She complied, opening herself to him completely. He began kissing the top of her thigh, nuzzling his way to the top of her slit. He blew gently across her core, causing another shudder. Then he ran his tongue along her clit, making tiny circles and occasionally biting the nub of her sex gently.

As her moans increased, he began speeding up his efforts. Then he slid two fingers inside her and curled them slightly back toward himself, rhythmically rubbing that special spot deep inside her.

He lifted his mouth long enough to say, "Don't you dare come yet, lass. I'll tell you when." Then he went right back to tormenting her.

She whimpered slightly and said, "Please!" He ignored her for a few minutes, alternating the rhythm of his thrusts to keep her teetering right on the edge.

He raised up again and said, "Please what?"

"Please let me come!"

"And who am I?"

Muireann paused, irritated that he was making her do this but way too excited to refuse. "Please, let me come, sir!"

"Look at me, love. Watch me as I make you come." He continued his efforts, his eyes never leaving hers, and was quickly rewarded with her clenching around his fingers, drenching him with her fluids, as she called out his name loudly enough that her neighbors most likely heard.

Once she relaxed a bit, he removed his fingers, licking the taste of her from them with relish. Then, he licked every bit of slickness from between her thighs.

After he was done, he stood and smoothed her skirt down her legs. Then he ground his hips against hers, letting her feel how incredibly hard he was for her. He crushed his lips to hers, thrusting his tongue into her mouth, forcing her to taste herself on his tongue.

Finally, he pulls himself away from her and says, "You're so fecking desirable, love. I've got to stop, or I will take you right here. And I have plans, so we need to quit."

She whined softly in disappointment. "But I want you, Lorcan. Inside of me."

"Soon enough, lass." He gave her a chaste peck on the cheek and said, "Take me home. I need a cold shower."

☙❧☙

Family

is life

10

Once Deirdre released their telepathic contact, Rónán just sat there for a moment, stunned. *If the Aos Sí are working on a plan to help us, maybe everything really will be okay! I've gotta tell Orla and Brian!*

The young Shadow Weaver was energized and excited, but he knew better than to go tearing through the halls of the Fomori stronghold. He crept quietly from the kitchen, cloaked in shadows and doing his very best to remain silent.

He had almost reached the Titans holding area, where the other Shadow Weavers were being held, when he heard shuffling footsteps and strangely heavy breathing, thick and wet. Thankfully, an alcove was nearby, so he quickly ducked in there, thickened his shadows as much as he dared, and threw up his best mental shields. He barely dared to breathe as he waited for the unwelcome visitor to pass.

Instead of continuing his journey, the leader of the Chaos Faction, for it could be no one else, slowed his steps as he neared the alcove. Rónán thought he heard Balor sniffing, as if he had caught a whiff of his scent and was trying to find it again.

Can he fecking smell me? the adolescent thought in alarm. *Never mind, I need to stay calm. Relax, just relax.* He began calming his breathing as best he could, saying a silent prayer to any god who would listen, begging for the monster to continue on his way.

Luck was in his favor this day, as Balor soon appeared to lose interest and continued into the cavern. Rónán slowly and carefully backed down the hallway and around the corner. He found a spot behind a giant, ugly statue of the original Balor, a vantage that allowed him to see when the current Balor returned to his rooms. He got comfortable and prepared to wait.

He practiced the mental exercises his sisters had taught him to keep his mind occupied. He was so thankful they had done that for him! His eyes welled a bit as he thought about them and his parents. If he made it through this, he vowed to never complain about his family ever again! But getting upset would help no one, so he calmed his breathing again and resumed practicing his defensive skills.

Thankfully, this visit was on the shorter side, and it wasn't long before he heard the leader of the Chaos Faction approaching. He held so still, he thought he might freeze that way and turn into a statue just like this hideous thing next to him. Once again, Balor paused when he neared the youngling's location, tilting his grossly misshapen head and appearing to sniff the air.

I have seriously got to take a shower. It would be bloody ridiculous if I got caught because I'm overly ripe.

But the beast quickly moved on, apparently eager to return to his rooms. Rónán waited a full ten minutes before moving from his hiding place, then he quickly flitted from one pool of shadow to the next, adding his own darkness to the mix as he went. He finally slipped inside the door of the Titans' cavern and made his way to the rooms where the captive Shadow Weavers could usually be found.

When he quietly entered the outer room, Brian was in the process of turning toward the door. The big Shadow Weaver was so surprised by the boy's appearance that he let out a high-pitched yelp. When he realized it was Rónán, he clutched his chest and said, "Bollocks, lad, you nearly gave me bleeding heart palpitations!"

The adolescent looked slightly abashed and said, "I'm sorry, Brian. I didn't mean to startle you."

Orla approached him and said, "You're not due to report in until tomorrow, lad. What's going on?"

"I know, but I have news and didn't want to wait. I just spoke telepathically with the Aos Sí High Druid, Deirdre. My parents and sisters were worried about me, so she risked the contact. She said they will discuss our options for getting us out of here. They're going to get us out of here!" The boy nearly tripped over his tongue, relaying all that in a rush.

Orla put her hands on his shoulders to help steady him and replied, "Now then, lad, calm yourself. Did she say anything else?"

"Yes, she'll contact me again tomorrow night at the same time and let me know what they figured out."

"Perfect," she responded. "We're going to make sure that Brian and I, and maybe a few others, are with you when she reaches out tomorrow." She pulled him in for a hug. "We can't get too far ahead of ourselves, but this is very good news, lad!"

The rest of the group all wore hopeful expressions for the first time in a very long time.

⚛⚛⚛

The next evening, Rónán waited nervously with the other Shadow Weavers for Deirdre to reach out to him. Finally, he felt a tentative touch in his mind and eagerly let her in.

Is it safe for us to speak now, lad?

"It's her!" *Yes, we can talk. I'm with the other Shadow Weavers.*

Perfect, that was very good thinking. The Aos Sí leaders have been discussing your situation, and of course, we want to bring you to Tíonol. The only question is how and when. We must plot our course carefully; there can be no missteps if we are to succeed.

The young Shadow Weaver relayed the information to the others.

"Is there anything we can do from our end?" Orla asked, and he dutifully repeated her question to Deirdre.

Just tell them to stay vigilant. Once we have organized our plan, we will let you know what part you will play. Until then, we will check in nightly. Stay safe, and know that we are coming.

⚛⚛⚛

Balor turned as he reached the far wall and continued pacing back in the other direction. He was unsettled, and he was unsure why.

Something is afoot. And without my pet to gather information, I am blind.

He paced a bit more, then stopped suddenly as he came to a decision.

I know someone was spying on me today. I must find out who they are and crush them. Then, I can focus on my Titans and unleash them upon our enemies. The Aos Sí will be dust beneath my heel.

HALLOWED ELEMENTS

Family

is life

11

Lir sat at Gram's kitchen table with a bag of frozen peas on his head and a strong cup of tea in his hand. He was in his chimp form because—thumbs. Treasa was putting the finishing touches on a traditional Irish breakfast, minus the mushrooms, of course. He just hoped it was as good a hangover cure as she claimed.

He looked out the half-open window and smiled despite his aching head. Áine and Brady had decided to get a jump on those dance lessons, so they were currently working on step ball changes and high kicks out in the yard. The phoenix had chosen "Love Shack" by The B52s to accompany their first lesson. She was also serenading everyone, and she wasn't half bad.

"No, it's step with your left on 'love' and kick with your right on 'shack.' Let's take it from the top." She was surprisingly patient with Brady. Although, to be fair, he was quite a decent dancer.

Gram came over to the table, glanced outside with a smile of her own, and asked, "Feeling any better, love?"

"Maybe a bit." He took another sip of tea and commented, with a nod toward the window, "They seem to be enjoying themselves."

"Well, Brady never meets a stranger, you know that. And Áine, well, she's quite the little fireball. He loves the snarky ones, so they're a perfect match."

She walked to the window and called out, "Breakfast is ready. Come wash up."

The two dancers let out a moan at the same time. "Ahhh!"

Treasa was having none of it. "Don't sass me! Step to it! Áine and Lir must get on the road."

"Come on, before she really gets cranky," Brady said to the bird. He picked up her iPod and speaker, put them back in her expando-bag, and dropped it around her neck. Then they headed inside.

Áine fluttered to her chair and said, "That smells yummo. No mushrooms, right?"

Gram smiled and said, "No mushrooms. Although you don't know what you're missing."

"I absolutely do, and no freaking thank you. Slimy little dirt-flavored blobs. Blech!" She made a few gagging noises to illustrate her point.

That earned her a cocked eyebrow. "Yes, well, we'll have to agree to disagree." She placed the last of the food on the table. "Tuck in, everyone."

The four of them ate in companionable silence for the next little while. Once they'd sated their hunger, Treasa said, "Well, I suppose you two had best be on your way. I have enjoyed having you here so very much. Now, pay attention, please." She pinned each of them with her dark green-eyed gaze. "I'll have your promise to watch out for each other. We're family, and—"

"Family is life," the other three finished. Lir, whose headache had receded somewhat, stood and returned the peas to the Fae-freezer. "We promise, Gram. We already promised our bonded."

"And we would've done it anyway," Áine added, with only a slight roll of her eyes.

"Good, then," she said with a nod. Brady came up behind her chair and began rubbing her shoulders. "She's trying to say, 'We love you,'" he explained.

"We love you, too," they responded in unison.

🔯🔯🔯

When Áine and Lir stepped through the portal into Findias, they were immediately hit with a blast of warm air. The phoenix stretched her wings wide and let out a deep sigh. "Oh, that's nice," she almost purred.

Lir chuckled. "I thought you might like that. We should head toward the village. It's a little further from their tree than the first two islands."

"Cool. I think I'm going to fly for a while. The air feels so *good!*" She launched herself into the air and let herself spiral higher and higher, riding the thermals. He could faintly hear her singing "Love Shack," obviously in her happy place.

He decided that he might as well enjoy himself, too, so he sprang into a gallop, zigging and zagging around any obstacles he could find. A few maniacal laughs could be heard as he let his wild side show.

🔯🔯🔯

When they started to see a few houses along the outside edge of the village, they calmed down a bit. No need to scare anyone running into the village like their tales were on fire.

Áine did one last aerial display before landing gently on Lir's rump. A small group of adolescent Fire Fae was nearby, and they all oohed and aahed over her performance. She grinned and gave them a grandiose bow. They ran ahead, presumably to let some adults know visitors were arriving.

It was only a few moments before a group of Fire Druids came out to meet them. An elder with a ginger and white beard and hair that appeared to be attempting to escape his head shuffled slowly toward them, surrounded by several very young acolytes.

The old-timer finally stopped a few paces away, squinted his rheumy pale grey eyes, and demanded, "Who the bloody hell are you two dossers, and what the feck do you want?"

Áine was so surprised, and delighted, that she couldn't help but let out a cackle. "You have got to be related to Fintan," she declared once her laughter died down.

"And how do you know me son?" the elder asked.

Lir chuckled as well, "I see it now."

"I asked how you know me bloody son!" the old Fae said, his irritation escalating quickly.

The phoenix narrowed her eyes at him and replied, "Calm your tits, ancient dude. Our bonded completed training for the Fianna under Fintan. I thought he was old and crotchety, but damned if you don't make him look like a babe-in-fucking-arms."

The aforementioned ancient dude scowled at them for another moment, but then his lip twitched, and he finally gave in to the grin he'd been trying to suppress.

"My name is Aidan Hayes. And you can be none other than Lir and Áine. Fintan told me about you lot. He also told me the fireball is a damned fine limerick composer."

Her eyes widened, and she said, "Do you know any good limericks?"

"I've been composing limericks for far longer than you've been alive, lass," he said with an air of superiority.

"Don't bet on it," she mumbled.

"Eh? What was that?" the old Fae asked.

"Oh, nothing. Hey, one of you kids come get this black bag from my neck."

One of the adolescent acolytes stepped forward and removed the bag from her neck.

"Okay, reach in, and you should feel a sheet of parchment at the top. Pull that out and let old Medusa there read it."

The acolyte reached in and pulled out Deirdre's letter, then started to hand it to Aidan, but the elder said, "Read it to me, won't you, lad? My eyesight's not what it used to be."

The young Fae dutifully read the missive aloud. When he was done, he returned it to the bag, cinched it closed, and replaced it around her neck.

"Right, well, we may have a slight issue," Aidan admitted.

Now, it was Lir's turn to narrow his eyes. "What sort of issue?"

"Yes, well, you see..." Aidan hemmed and hawed until finally, Lir had reached the limits of his tolerance.

"Bloody hell, man, spit it out! What is the issue?"

The elder sighed and said, "It's just me and all these young acolytes. I have been trying to keep up with all the duties, but these weans don't know how to do half of what is required. So, I was showing one of them how to polish the relic, and, well, he was acting the maggot and rammed it against the marble bust we use for displaying it. The torque's endpiece was severely bent, and we had to get it repaired."

"You *broke* it?! You broke the bloody relic of a *god*?! What the actual fuck are you douche canoes *doing* up in this motherfucker?!" Áine was a bit heated.

"Normally, I'm the peacemaker, but I'm afraid I agree with the bird," Lir commented.

"Now, now, I know we fecked things up, but we had a plan to fix it! There's an old hedge witch that lives on the other end of the island. She's a cantankerous old wagon, but she's the only one on the island who could fix the torque, since it required not just smithing but also repairing the magical elements. I sent the acolyte who broke it and his little brother to take it to her."

"And? Do you expect them back soon?" Áine asked.

"Well, that's where the slight issue arises. We expected them back yesterday," Aiden explained, running his hands through his hair and tugging on his beard as his anxiety mounted.

Lir studied him for a moment, then asked, "Is there a reason why you didn't make the journey? One would think the Druid-in-charge should handle something of this magnitude."

"Yeah, that wouldn't have gone well," the Druid responded enigmatically.

"Could you stop with the vague half-answers and just give us all the details? Who is this hedge witch, and why does she hate you?" Áine's tiny amount of patience had left the building.

"Fine. She's my wife. And she may have threatened to turn my bollocks into a handbag if she ever saw me again.

So, no, it would not have been a good idea for me to go," Aidan replied curtly.

"Freaking brilliant. Okay, so I guess Goat Boy and I get to experience our first side quest. Yippee!"

Lir sighed and said, "Do you have a map we could use?"

Aidan whispered to one of the acolytes, who ran into the Enclave, and quickly returned with a parchment scroll. The phoenix grasped the expando-bag, wiggled it over her head, then extended it toward the young Fae in a trademark Áine high kick. "Put it in here. He'll turn into a chimp later to unroll and read it."

Once it was tucked safely in the bag and back around her neck, she continued, "It's too late to start today. Let's get some dinner and get on the road tomorrow morning."

Lir nodded and asked Aidan, "I assume you have somewhere we can stay?"

He nodded and said, "Of course. Follow me."

As they followed the old Druid into the Enclave, Áine whispered to Lir, "I have a bad feeling about this. I hope we don't get permanently turned into frogs or some other freaky shit."

❀❀❀

It took them a day and a half to get close to the area marked on the Fire Druid's map. On the first day, they made it back to the portal tree and camped beneath it for the night. Áine begged Lir to tell ghost stories around the fire, but when he relented and told one, it scared her, and she made him stop before he was done. She tried to act like it was no big deal, but Lir could tell it bothered her, so he asked if she would sleep close to him, ostensibly to keep him warm. She agreed and curled up next to him, but only, as she put it, because she was so good at keeping others cozy.

Now, they had just finished the midday meal and were approaching a forest of blackened, petrified-looking lava trees created during a previous eruption from the small volcano located in the northeast section of the island.

Lir had shifted into his chimp form to take a look at the map. "It looks like the hedge witch's cabin is almost at the volcano's base on the far north side. We need to navigate through this forest of lava trees, and we should find it, no problem."

Áine, who's misgivings had not dissipated during the journey, mumbled, "Sounds like some famous last words to me."

The chimp put the map away and shifted back into his púca form. "Try to be positive, a stór. The sooner we find her, the sooner we can be on our way."

"It's like you don't even know me. *You* are the optimist. *I* am the sarcastic realist. Try to keep up."

They headed into the dark forest of tree-shaped lava molds, a mixture of smoke and ash making everything hazy and indistinct. The closer they got to the volcano, the more they noticed the air quality deteriorating.

They were currently skirting the edge of the dead forest, a large hot spring forcing them to delve further into the lava trees where the gloom was deeper.

"Stick close, Goat Boy. I don't trust this place. Don't want you to wander off and get spooked."

"I'll try to manage," he replied with a grin.

They had just rounded the hot spring and could see the northeast shore of the island. As they were turning to wind their way north to the hedge witch's cabin, they heard what sounded like giggling.

They shared a concerned glance and continued at a slower, more cautious pace. They took not more than a dozen or so paces when they came upon a perplexing scene. Two young Fae, undoubtedly those sent by Aidan to get the torque repaired, were sitting amidst all manner of little sticks and rocks, arrayed as if they were fighting a great battle. The younger of the two appeared to be in charge of the monsters as he had a larger stick figure in each hand, and he was using them to stomp amongst the smaller sticks and rocks, roaring and growling with the occasional giggle thrown in.

The older brother had difficulty mounting a defense as his laughter became increasingly boisterous. Before long, they were both sitting in the middle of the battlefield, cackling like loons.

"Uhm, excuse me, crazy Fae, but what the actual fuck are you two doing?" Áine interrupted with her usual flair.

The younglings were startled into silence, but when they looked at the two familiars, their eyes were glazed and distant, as if unable to make sense of their surroundings.

"I don't think they know what they're doing," Lir observed. "They are under the influence of something, but I'm not certain what."

"That would be my mam's doing," said a voice from the shadows behind the two lads. The familiars jumped, taking their turn at being startled unexpectedly. A female Fire Fae with long ginger hair, freckles, and light blue eyes stepped out of the shadows, hands raised to show her peaceful intentions.

"Hold it right there, sneaky sneakster. Who are you, and why are you spying on these two kids stoned out of their gourds?" Áine demanded, flaring her flames a bit for emphasis.

"I am Flannery, daughter of Kenna and Aidan," she answered.

"Your da is the ancient dude?" the phoenix clarified. The Fae smiled at the description and nodded. "Then that means your Fintan's sister?"

"Aye, Fintan is my older brother," she replied.

"Holy shitturds batman. I was not expecting a Hayes family reunion," she commented to Lir, who couldn't help but smile.

The púca turned his attention to the Fae. "You said this," he pointed a hoof at the still giggling adolescents, "was your mam's doing. What did you mean?"

She sighed and said, "'twould be easiest to let her explain. She means no harm." She gestured to the young Fae. "She just needed some time, and quiet, to work on repairing the relic. So, she slipped a tonic into the stew she offered them and charged me with keeping an eye on the lads. It's taken her longer than she'd hoped to make the repairs, but she should be finished soon. The tonic makes them happy and a bit scattered, but it will wear off soon, and we'll send them back to the village. Any other questions I will let her answer."

The familiars conferred briefly, but it wasn't as if they had many choices. So, they decided to follow Flannery back to her mother's cottage. She stopped to round up the younglings first, then the group headed around the base of the volcano for a short distance until they reached Kenna's home. They were lucky they had a guide as there was a glamour on the cabin that made one's eyes slip away from the structure. Without Flannery's help, they would have had difficulty finding it.

"Let me speak to her first. She isn't overly fond of surprises," The Fire Fae cautioned. She reached for the door, but it opened right before she could grasp the handle, startling her into stepping back. Then, there was a whooshing sound, followed by a dark red mist that flew through the air, painting the two familiars and two younglings with a burgundy powder. Áine had time to say, "What fuckery is this?" before she and the other three collapsed to the ground in a deep, dreamless sleep.

"Bloody hell, Mam, not again."

The golden hour was upon them by the time the two familiars began stirring, coppery rays of light illuminating their pink faces. The phoenix blinked twice, then quickly sat up and looked around. Her companion was also awake, shaking his head to clear it. The two young Fae slumbered on peacefully.

Seated in a rocking chair nearby was a stout woman with white-streaked ginger hair nearly as wild as her husband's. She had a pipe lit and was blowing smoke rings that wafted through the air unnaturally, morphing into amusing shapes that danced and flew, seemingly of their own volition.

"Who the fuck do you think you are, you withered, decrepit, bumbling, Sabrina-the-teenage-witch wannabe!" The phoenix stood up as she spoke, giving herself a shake and flaring her flames to remove the offensive powder. She could hear Lir standing and shaking as well to clean himself up.

Kenna took another leisurely puff from her pipe and sent a phoenix-shaped smoke ring to dance around Áine's head. "Withered and decrepit? Perhaps, although I'd offer I'm still a damn sight better to look at than my no-good lump of a husband. Bumbling? Hate to disagree with you, love, but I did give you a nice little unplanned nap, so I'm not certain how you came to that conclusion. Besides, there was no harm done."

The phoenix just stared at her in disbelief before stating, "No harm done? Then why did we wake up with our faces looking like a baboon's ass?"

Kenna shrugged one shoulder and said, "But you did wake up, eh? I'd say that qualifies as no harm done."

As Áine drew breath to continue the argument, Lir stepped up beside her and said, "Perhaps we could start over? My name is Lir, and this is Áine. We are on a critical mission and were tasked with coming to retrieve the Fire Fae relic. It's our understanding these lads," he nodded to the still sleeping adolescents, "were sent to bring it to you for repair. When they did not return in the expected time frame, Aidan," Kenna hissed at that name. "Yes, well, he asked us to check on them and hopefully pick up the now-mended torque. Can you help us with that?" He was pulling out every ounce of diplomacy he could muster, hoping to keep things from spiraling even further out of control.

Unfortunately, his companion was not done being angry. "Wait just a motherfucking minute! I'm not finished with this Glinda-the-Good-Witch bitch. If she thinks she can just—"

Flannery had heard the commotion from inside the cottage and joined them outside. "Look, there's no need for further name-calling. My mam is sorry for—"

"Don't speak for me, lass. I'm not sorry for one fecking thing! How do we know that pox bottle Aidan didn't send these two to spy on us?"

"Oh, for the love of—" Flannery began.

Lir made one more attempt. "Look, this is getting us

nowhere!" he bellowed, stunning them into silence briefly. "We're just here for the torque. We don't want to spy on you, we just want to take the relic, well and the younglings, back to the village. That's all. Now, will you help us with that or no?"

Flannery moved next to her mother's rocker and rested a hand on her shoulder. "Mam, I think we can help them, can't we?"

Kenna looked up at her daughter, sighed loudly, and responded, "Fine. But I'm keeping my eye on you."

"Right back at you, bee-atch," Áine snarked, pointing a wing at her eyes and then at the hedge witch.

Just then, the two brothers began stirring, so Flannery went to check and ensure they were all right. Once they seemed awake and finally alert, she made a quick circular motion in front of their faces, burning the remainder of the powder away without singeing so much as an eyelash.

"Well, I suppose you might as well come inside. The cottage doesn't look very large on the outside, but that's just an illusion. It's bigger on the inside." The old Fae stood up and entered her home, everyone else following behind her.

※ ※ ※

Flannery agreed to take the brothers back to the village the following day. It had been a while since she had seen her father, so they left shortly after breakfast.

Lir, who was now in his fainting goat form, was curled up by the hearth, content to wait for Kenna to finish repairing the torque.

Áine, however, had been completely captivated since the moment she saw the relic. Laid out on the hedge witch's worktable, it was truly stunning. Rubies, garnets, fire opals, orange tourmaline, and red jasper had been cut and placed to create ribbons and swirls of fire. Gold and copper were woven between and amongst the gems, shaping the tongues of flame. Celtic knotwork was intertwined, tying it all together beautifully. At the outer edges of each individual flickering fire, tiny white diamonds and bright blue sapphires mimicked sparks of the hottest flames.

The phoenix, perched on the worktable as close as Kenna would allow to the relic, gave a deep sigh. "I can't believe how stunning this is. It's just magnificent!"

The elder Fire Fae grunted in response, all her attention required for the delicate magical repairs. Áine watched for a while, admiring the beauty of the torque, but after a while, she grew impatient.

She made a valiant effort to stay quiet, and eventually, she began to pace back and forth at the end of the worktable. Kenna glared at her, which did absolutely nothing.

Finally, the phoenix stopped and, unfortunately, chose a delicate moment in the process to ask, "How much longer?"

Kenna sighed in frustration and testily replied, "Well, since you just ruined the past two hours' worth of work, we can add another two hours now."

"Sheesh, testy much?" she snarked, fluttering off the worktable to see what Lir was up to. "How's it hangin', Goat Boy?" she asked as he stood up to stretch his legs.

He gave one more big stretch, then just as he was about to answer, Kenna slammed her hand down on the worktable and yelled, "Feck!" This startled Lir, causing him to faint and fall over on his side.

Both Kenna and Áine couldn't help but snicker briefly at

the sight. The phoenix looked at the hedge witch and said, "I know it's mean, but that's just so hilarious." Then she leaned over and rubbed his side gently for the few seconds he was locked up.

Once over the fainting spell, he stood up and glared at the two females. "Glad I could entertain you two wankers." Then he curled back up in front of the fireplace with a loud huff.

Kenna looked somewhat chastened and replied, "Beg pardon, lad. I may be a cranky old witch, but that was uncalled for, and I apologize."

Lir, who was incapable of holding a grudge, nodded at her in acceptance of her apology. Then he looked expectantly at Áine.

"Oh fine. I'm sorry, Goat Boy. You know I love you, right?" Then she gently head-butted him in apology.

The next three days passed quietly as Kenna finalized the repairs on the torque, and Lir did his best to keep Áine entertained and away from the Fire Fae's work.

Around noon on the fourth day, Kenna stood up from her work and declared, "Done. Finally."

The little goat mumbled, "Thank goodness." Áine fluttered back up to the worktable to gaze upon the beauty of the relic once again. "So pretty," she said, reaching the tip of her wing toward the torque.

Kenna smacked the wingtip and said, "Do you ever learn? I just fixed the blood thing!"

The phoenix was about to retort when the cottage door opened, and Flannery walked in. "I'm back," she called out in a singsong voice, a smile on her face. The visit with her dad and the long walk to and from the village seemed to have put her in a good mood.

"Come give us a kiss, a stór," Kenna requested, and Flannery happily complied. "You're just in time. Despite the bird's attempts to sabotage my work," Áine rolled her eyes and scoffed, "I have finally finished the repairs."

"Brilliant!" Flannery replied. "Now, I know we've kept you longer than you'd have liked, but if I can request a wee bit more of your time, it'd mean the world to me."

"I suppose we can wait a little longer. But why, if I may ask?" Lir responded.

"Well, my brother's birthday is coming up soon, and he absolutely loves my shortbread biscuits. I thought perhaps I could make a batch, and you could deliver them to him when you get back from your journey. I would, of course, make some extra for you two as well."

Both familiars had a bit of a sweet tooth, so it didn't take much convincing for them to agree. As Flannery began making the treats, Áine decided to work on some choreography to pass the time. She even managed to talk Kenna into helping with the iPod and eventually got her to dance a bit as well.

"Five, six, seven, eight," she counted off, leading them in her routine. The sounds of various gangsta rap legends echoed throughout the cottage as Áine, Lir, in chimp form, and a Fire Fae elder perfected their crip walk. Flannery also joined in while the shortbread was cooling and enjoyed herself immensely.

As the last notes faded away, they all started laughing from sheer enjoyment. Flannery brought the mostly cooled shortbread to the table, where they all gathered for a sweet treat before the familiars continued their journey.

Once they were finished, Áine sighed in satisfaction. "You know, you're not half bad, old woman."

Kenna chuckled and said, "Right back at you, bee-atch," which made the phoenix cackle.

Flannery smiled; it had been a long time since she saw her mother so relaxed and enjoying herself. She placed a wrapped package of shortbread into the expando-bag, and placed it around Lir's neck.

Then Kenna took the torque from the worktable and placed it around Áine's neck. The relic resized itself to fit the phoenix perfectly. The familiar gently touched the gems, being extremely careful with the newly repaired item. "Thank you," she said simply.

"You're welcome, lass. Now, you'd best be on your way. I have a feeling your trials are far from over," Kenna replied.

The two companions bid the hedge witch and her daughter farewell and headed back toward the Fire Fae Faery Tree to continue their quest.

☘☘☘

Family

is life

12

Muireann gently traced the lines of the rather phallic-looking forced scarification on Lorcan's left bicep with her fingertips. Even though it was fully healed, it looked so painful that she couldn't help but lean in and kiss the area.

The Shadow Weaver put his right index finger under her chin and tilted her face up until she was looking him in the eye. "Not that I ever mind kisses from you, but what was that for," he asked, a curious smile on his face.

She shrugged and said, "I don't know, it just looks so painful. I hate to think of you going through that."

He chuckled softly and said, "Oh, love, it was incredibly painful. But it's over now. We've both had painful experiences in the past. Dwelling on them is rarely useful."

"Yes, but that doesn't mean I can't empathize. As a healer, that's sort of my thing," she replied with a wry grin. "So, what shall we cover up this monstrosity with? I could put a lovely image of Balor there, maybe with his third eye open and oozing a swampy green light. What do you think?" she teased.

"Oh sure, that would be brilliant," Lorcan said, his words dripping sarcasm. He looked at her intently for a moment, then seemed to come to a decision. "Tell you what, lass. Why don't you choose? Anything except a portrait of my hideous father. I don't need any reminders that I'm related to that."

She paused her inspection of the area and replied, "Are you sure? It's not often I'm given free rein. What if I choose something you hate?"

"I trust you, Muireann," he replied with a surprising depth of sincerity. "Besides, it can hardly look worse than it already does."

"Point taken. So, most of your other tattoos are of the Celtic tribal variety. Any objections to a different style?"

"None at all. Just make it something I won't shudder to look at."

"I think I can handle that," she replied, smiling at him as the perfect design occurred to her.

She got her supplies in order, choosing just the right colors. Then, she cleaned and prepared the area. Once everything was ready, she splayed her gloved hand over the area, closed her eyes, and let her water power sink into Lorcan's bloodstream. She identified the nerves that controlled the area to be tattooed and made a sort of tourniquet around them, blocking their signal to his brain.

When she was done, she opened her eyes and poked the area rather forcefully with one of the tattooing needles. "Do you feel anything?" she asked.

"Huh? Feel what?" he replied, unaware she had even touched him with the needle.

"Perfect. Let's get started."

Muireann added the final touches to Lorcan's newest tattoo, then wiped the excess ink and blood from his arm. She looked over her work, quite pleased with the end result. She handed him a mirror to view the finished product.

A gasp escaped his lips when he beheld her artwork. Shades of teal and aquamarine formed an aquatic background, complete with bubbles and a sense of movement reminiscent of the ocean. A few small, colorful fish and a bright pink jellyfish decorated the edges of the design. The main subject was a widely grinning Ailáine in her merrow form, long dark red hair floating about her head, sapphire scales adorning her powerful tail and covering her small, budding pre-pubescent breasts. Her sparkling eyes exactly matched the color of her scales, and Muireann perfectly captured her infectious joy. Small gills open along her neck could even be seen. It was utterly breathtaking.

The image entranced Lorcan, and his eyes even welled a bit. "That is the most gorgeous tattoo I have ever seen, love. And Ailáine will be over the moon. You've turned a hideous scar into a beautiful work of art. Thank you."

He gave it one last look, then put the mirror down and buried his hand in her hair, pulling her in close for a long, sensual kiss.

When he finally pulled back, she gave a low whistle and said, "I could get used to that kind of thank you."

"Happy to oblige, lass. Anytime. Day or night. Or day and night, whatever works," he replied with a smartass grin.

She grinned back at him and said, "As much as I'd like to continue this thank you, I need to prepare for the healer training session. Da and Sláine should be here shortly, and we're scheduled to begin with the first group right after lunch."

Lorcan nodded and said, "I'll leave you to it, then. Can I attend the session? Maybe we could include the other Shadow Weavers in it since we also have water affinity."

"Brilliant. I'll speak with you after the session and get your feedback on whether or not we should adjust the training in any way for the Fomori."

He stood and pulled her up as well. "It's a date," he replied, pulling her in for one more deep kiss. "And after you're done for the day, I will take you back to my room, feed you, bathe you, and spend a great deal of time and effort showing exactly how much I appreciate this artwork now gracing my arm."

"I can't wait," she said, eyes glazed slightly with desire at the thought of what he had in store for her.

"Excellent. Oh, the plans I have for you. Think about what those might be today. I want you wet and ready for me tonight, understand?"

She nodded, and he replied, "I'll let your silence slide for now. But plan to put that tongue of yours to good use tonight. And yes, you will call me sir this evening. However, I promise it will be worth it, love."

He gave her one final rough kiss, then left her, panting and breathless.

※ ※ ※

The Fianna and a few other interested individuals were waiting for the healer training to begin. For the past couple of weeks, the Fianna had all been diligently working with their regiments on Earth, either in Ireland or Kansas City. During this initial phase, they had decided to concentrate on general fitness, both physical and magical.

As expected, some rough edges needed smoothing over.

It was impossible to take Fae with diverse backgrounds and experiences and expect them to meld immediately into a cohesive fighting force. So, they had decided that in the evenings, they would play games or cards, really anything that cemented them into a familial unit. And the quads spent nearly every waking moment together, hoping to achieve a singular focus that would serve them well during battle.

"It's nice to finally start implementing some of the other elements of our battle plan," Keegan commented to Cara, who nodded in reply.

"Yeah, I feel like we have so much to do and so little time. It's beginning to stress me out," her cousin said.

Riley came up behind her, wrapped his arms around her waist, and whispered something in her ear that made her giggle.

Calder elbowed him and said, "They're starting. No snogging during training."

Morgan, the Chief Healer, took his place at the front of the room, flanked by Muireann and Sláine. "Let's get started. We've decided to go over the healer training with you lot first, not only so you can learn the information for yourself but also so you can assist members of your regiment where possible. You are always welcome to seek assistance from experienced healers, of course, but hopefully, you being able to answer minor questions that might come up will allow the seasoned healers to focus on training as many Fae as we can with our limited time frame."

He proceeded, with the help of his two assistants, to go over everything from basic first aid, which required no magic, to the more advanced elements of battlefield triage that only a few of them were even able to grasp.

Once he was finished, he looked over the assembled Fae, most of whom looked a bit lost. He smiled and said, "I know that was a lot of information, but you did well for your first lesson. I know this all seems overwhelming, but we will repeat this information over the next several weeks."

After they were dismissed, the Fianna left to return to their regiments for the final training session of the day. Morgan, Sláine, and Muireann were cleaning up when Deirdre, Nora, Fergal, and Lorcan approached them.

"Dia Duit," Morgan greeted them. "What can we help you with?"

"We need your input, Morgan," Deirdre began. "And yours as well," she said, including the two Water Fae. "We've just learned that the younger brother of some Shadow Weavers, as well as a group of adult Fomori, are stranded at the stronghold. None of them have been corrupted with chaos magic yet, and it appears that Balor has been using them to take care of his Chaos Titans. We can do nothing for those already warped by the chaos magic, but we can try to save this small group. I wanted to find out if there are any healers you might suggest accompanying us on this incursion in case medical help is needed."

Sláine and Muireann shared a glance, and then the older healer said, "Begging your pardon, but I think we may be able to help at least a few of those already corrupted as well."

More than one gasp sounded with that revelation. Deirdre recovered quickly, saying, "Explain, please, lass."

The Water Fae said, "You may not know, but I have been studying head injuries for over a decade now. I can't be one hundred percent certain, but from what I've uncovered about how chaos magic works, I think there's at least a chance we can reverse a great deal of the corruption."

Muireann chimed in, adding, "We may not be able to restore them completely, but if we can mitigate the majority of the damage, shouldn't we at least try?"

"Indeed," Deirdre replied, turning her attention to Morgan. "And what say you, Chief Healer? Is this truly possible?"

Morgan momentarily considered, then said, "Based on what I know of Sláine's research and our limited knowledge of chaos magic, I can give you a definite maybe." He shrugged and continued, "I wish I could say for sure. But her approach is quite ingenious. There's a good chance it could help."

The High Druid looked the group over and said, "Very well. Lorcan, you will lead a small group back to the Fomori stronghold to attempt to rescue the captive Shadow Weavers. I want you to confer with your mam, Fergal, and the healers to determine what recourse might be possible regarding the Titans. Please let me know what you decide."

"Aye, Aintín Dee. It will be done," he agreed.

For the next hour, Lorcan asked the healers every question he could think of to assess what might be possible and what would be required to complete an undertaking such as this successfully.

After several precise questions about the process of reversing the chaos magic, he finally said, "I think I've got the beginnings of a plan. But I need to speak with Máire."

Morgan and Sláine looked confused momentarily, but Muireann grasped the idea immediately. "Brilliant! That might make all the difference."

The other two healers caught up but a moment later. Morgan nodded vigorously as he played through the possibilities in his mind, and Sláine said, "It's certainly possible. The process would probably take a good twenty minutes, so keep that in mind when planning your trip. And please know that some will be just too far gone. Unfortunately, we cannot save them all. In fact, it will likely be a small number compared to how many there are. But saving a few is far better than saving none. If Máire thinks she can do this, send her to me, and we will discuss the options."

༺༻༺༻༺༻

To save time, Lorcan and Muireann gathered all members of the Fianna and brought them to Sláine's workshop on Earth. The healer was surprised when all of them showed up, but the Shadow Weaver explained that to save the captive Fomori, as well as the maximum number of Titans, would require more than just a few people. He figured the Fianna stood the best chance of getting in and out with the least collateral damage.

He laid out his plan and asked for feedback from Máire since she was the lynchpin of the whole affair. She rose from her seat and began pacing. She always thought better when she was moving. After mulling over the details for a few minutes, she said, "Well, it's got potential. I believe I can create an artifact that will accomplish what you need. And I think my mam, Aintín Niamh, and Keegan can also help produce them. Which is a good thing because the process will not be quick, and it sounds like we'll need a great deal of them."

Keegan added, "If it would help, I can ask my dad to see if any of the visiting Clans have artificers capable of this level of work."

Máire nodded and said, "Yes, we need all the help we

can get." She turned her attention back to Lorcan and said, "I think the best way to proceed is to give ourselves a time frame and produce as many artifacts as possible. Once our time is up, we will take all we've made, and that's what we have to work with."

Lorcan nodded and replied, "Very well. You work on the artifacts, and we will all continue our battle preparations. I will speak to Aintín Dee and determine our time frame. Then we strike."

Sláine added, "I hope you plan on Muireann and I joining you. We may be able to save a few more if we're there. And this will be dangerous—you might need healers along."

Liam and Lorcan both sputtered as they tried to think of logical reasons for their beloveds to stay behind in safety. Ultimately, they knew it was a losing battle and admitted defeat after only a brief conversation.

With a sigh, Lorcan said, "Very well. We all know our roles. Let's get to work."

❈❈❈

After the meeting, everyone wandered off to find something for dinner. Lorcan tugged Muireann over behind some trees, grabbed her by the hair, and kissed her soundly. When they came up for air, he said, "Would you do me a favor and fill your da in on what we decided? I need to do the same for Aintín Dee and set up a few things for our evening together. Give me an hour, lass, eh?"

"I'll be there. Is there anything in particular you'd like me to wear?" she asked.

"Whatever you think will look good on my floor," he

commented with a smirk. That elicited a giggle, and she hurried off to find her father.

⊛⊛⊛

She arrived at his door almost precisely one hour later and had to take several deep breaths to settle her nerves. Unsure what to expect, she was excited to find out what Lorcan had in store.

Once she had calmed herself, she knocked on the door. Only a few moments passed before he opened the door with a sensual smile, wiping his hands on a dish towel and tossing it over his shoulder. He leaned against the doorframe, crossed his arms over his chest, and ran his eyes hungrily up and down her body.

Since the weather was warm, she had worn a short, breezy teal sundress that was low cut on top, with wide straps and a wispy skirt. Her long, dark brown hair was down, falling in soft waves nearly to her waist.

After he was finished drinking her in, he took her by the hand, pulled her in close, and kissed her so softly and tenderly that she nearly melted. When he was finished with that, he nuzzled her neck, breathing deeply, captivated by her lilac and lemongrass scent.

"You smell divine, love," he said, pulling her inside and closing the door behind her. "But I need to distance myself for a bit, or this will be over far too soon, and I am not having that. As I said before, I have plans for you, my dear."

He led her to a small table, where several of her favorite foods lay. Somebody had been talking to her da—definite bonus points awarded for effort. Instead of sitting across from her as they ate, he pulled his chair right up next to her and pulled the strawberry cheesecake over to them. He picked up a fork and began feeding her little bites from all the different plates, starting with cheesecake. For the next half hour, he slowly and sensually fed her by hand.

When she declared she was full, he stood, pulled her chair out, and offered her a hand up. He led her over into his bedroom, which had been slightly redecorated since she had last seen it. In the corner, strips of shadow had been attached to the ceiling. There was what looked somewhat like a wide weight bench, but it was almost at table height. On a bedside table were several different items—a thick, thuddy shadow flogger, a soft, satin blindfold, and a small cup of ice, to name a few.

He positioned Muireann about two feet from the end of his bed, then took a seat on his deep red silk sheets. "Okay, love. It's time to see what that pretty little dress looks like on the floor."

She laughed softly, and a bit nervously, and began taking off her sundress. "Ah, ah, ah. Slowly, lass. I want to savor this."

She slowed down and inched the straps off her shoulder. Then she tugged it down over her breasts, and her waist, finally letting it fall to the floor. Underneath, she had on a copper-colored demi bra with teal, lacy trim and matching panties.

She was nearly as tall as Lorcan, with full breasts, wide hips, and legs for days. His eyes drank her in, hardening his cock and making his breath come quick and shallow. "You are magnificent, mo chroí. It is taking every bit of self-control I can muster not to throw you on this bed and fuck you until you scream my name. But that will come later. Right now, I want you naked." He leaned over and nudged the music playing softly in the background up a couple of levels.

She finally began feeling more comfortable and started to play to her very eager audience. She hooked her index fingers through the sides of her silky underwear and slowly slid them down her legs, letting them drop the last few inches to the floor and stepping out of them. Then she turned her back to him, unhooked her bra, threw it over her shoulder, and onto his lap.

"Turn around, love. As much as I adore that ass, I want to see all of you."

She turned around, breasts covered with her arm, biting her lip. "Drop your arm. Now, please."

She put her arm down and clasped her hands behind her back. "Come here and straddle me on the bed. I want to feel that silky soft skin."

She placed one knee on either side of his hips, sitting back on his legs and feeling his rock-hard length nestled in between her labia. He placed his hands on her ass, kneading and exploring, slowly moving them up to nestle deep in her hair.

He lowered his lips to her nipple, sucking and nipping, making it stand up while she gasped and softly moaned. Once he had thoroughly lavished it with attention, he moved to the other breast and repeated the process, fisting his hands in her hair hard enough to make her eyes water.

Moving one hand from her hair to her waist, he swiftly switched their positions, lowering her back onto the soft sheets. He spread her thighs apart with his legs, taking the opportunity to grind his hard cock against her core, causing a louder moan to escape her lips. He smothered it with his mouth, slowly deepening the kiss. His tongue demanded access and then invaded her mouth, tasting her hungrily.

The sounds she was making made it clear she was getting close to finishing, so he ended the kiss and lifted his hips away from hers. "I decide when you come tonight. Agreed?"

She pouted slightly, arching her back and trying to resume contact. He tightened his fist in her hair and said, "I asked you a question, lass. I expect an answer. And if you want to finish at all tonight, you will call me sir. Understood?"

"Yes, sir."

"And do you agree that you only come when I allow it?"

"Yes, sir."

"That's my good girl." He stood up and pulled her up as well. "Now, go kneel by the shadow rig and face the corner."

She did as instructed while he grabbed the satin blindfold from the table. He came up behind her and slid the blindfold over her eyes, kneeling at her back. He softly trailed his fingers over her shoulders and down her arms, then he began tying. He willed ropes into existence, draping and dragging the soft silky shadows across her skin. He tied her calves to her thighs and her arms behind her back. He made a harness, then attached her arms to her ankles, making her back arch and throwing her breasts forward.

He lifted her into the air using the shadow ropes attached to the ceiling until they were head to head. He kissed her roughly, then trailed over to her ear and down her neck. Very soon, her nipples were being teased and tormented once more, and her moans were growing louder and louder.

He raised his head from her breast and said, "Let's see how wet you are, eh? Are you ready for me to fuck you yet?"

"Yes!" she said emphatically.

He leaned down to her neck and nipped her hard, making her gasp.

"Who am I?" He whispered, heat in his voice.

"Sir. Yes, sir," she whimpered, straining forward, trying to make contact with his body.

He grabbed her around the waist, his other hand sliding through her slick folds, feeling how dripping wet she was.

He leaned in to whisper in her ear. "Oh, my. Such a good girl. Would you like a reward?"

"Yes, sir. Please!"

"Better get used to begging, love. You'll be doing that a lot tonight."

He slid two fingers into her dripping core, his thumb rubbing quick circles on her clit as he began curling his fingers against the sensitive spot inside her. He kissed her again, hard. Teeth clicking, tongues twirling, causing her breath to come faster and faster.

He began to slow his thrusts, and she whimpered again. He chuckled darkly and said, "Needy, needy girl. You don't get to come yet. I haven't even tasted you."

He knelt on the floor and buried his face between her thighs, licking and nibbling, using his fingers and occasionally blowing gently on her clit.

When she started clenching against his fingers, he immediately slowed his rhythm again. This time she complained loudly, which drew a sharp slap to her ass.

"You agreed that I am in charge of your orgasms tonight, love. And I'm not done playing with you yet. So, as your friend is fond of saying, suck it up, buttercup. Now, it's time for something new."

He lowered her to the ground but left her tied. Then he removed his clothing and walked over to stand in front of her. "Open your mouth, love. Let's see if you can take all of me."

She complied, and he slid his substantial length and girth slowly into her mouth. "Relax your throat, love. That's my good girl," he cooed, sliding another inch down her throat. He buried both hands in her hair and said, "Last bit, a stór. That's it, mo chroí. Take it all." He thrust the rest of his cock down her throat, holding her head there for a few seconds, relishing the feeling of fucking her mouth so deeply.

When he felt her begin to tense up, he pulled back enough that she could catch her breath, leaving two-thirds of his length in her mouth. "Breathe, love. Take a breath. Good? Good. Let's go again." He repeated this process a few more times until he began to doubt his control.

He released the shadow shibari and helped her to her feet, kissing her deeply to taste himself on her tongue. He turned her toward the bed, led her over to it, and had her lay face down, spread eagle. He quickly tied her ankles and wrists to the bedframe, then he went to the end table and brought over the thick flogger and half-melted cup of large cubes of ice.

He began running the cool strands of shadow all along her body, trailing it up and down, left and right. Then he lifted it and almost gently brought it down against her round ass. It felt almost like the kneading of a massage with only a slight sting at the end. He continued this for quite a while, and then he slid two fingers inside of her, finding things slick and slippery. "You like the flogger, don't you, lass?"

He played with her for a few minutes, then said, "My control is waning, love. Are you ready for me to fuck you now?"

"Gods, yes! Please, sir!" she panted, nearing the end of her control as well.

He lengthened the shadow ropes on her ankles and lifted her ass into the air, putting her knees under her hips. He gathered moisture from the air and formed a condom, covering his cock with a thin layer of water made impermeable. Then he picked up a piece of ice slightly larger than his thumb and held it above her ass, letting it drip into her tightest hole while he positioned himself below that, letting the tip slip just slightly inside her core.

"Do you want it, lass? Beg me for it. Now, please."

"Please fuck me, sir!" she was almost beyond herself now.

He thrust his length deep inside her and simultaneously pressed the ice cube into her ass, relishing the screech of pleasure that caused. She pushed back, grinding herself against him and encouraging movement as forcefully as she dared.

Lorcan began fucking her deeply, keeping the ice cube inside her as well. When he felt her clenching again, he said, "Would you like to come, love?"

"Yes, sir!"

He increased his rhythm and said, "Be a good girl and come for me, Muireann. Let me hear you scream."

She obliged him wholeheartedly, arching her back and screaming his name as her orgasm ripped through her. The pulsating walls clenching against him were more than he could take, and he joined in her scream.

Once their breathing slowed a bit, he released her bindings, pulled out of her, and cradled her back against his chest as they lay on their sides. He sent the water condom into the bathroom and disposed of it.

"Ready for your bath, love?"

She moaned sleepily, and said, "Mhmm."

"Give me a moment, then we'll take a bath together. After our bath, I'll even let you choose how we play next. Do you want to try breath play? Or maybe figging? I could take your ass in the bath with the nice, slippery bubbles? The options are nearly endless. And after I have taken you over and over and over again, maybe I'll let you get a little sleep. Maybe."

Family

is life

13

The sound of a scuffed footstep and a wet, raspy inhale saved him. It was past midnight, and the shadowy, silent hallways of the Fomori stronghold felt like a menacing labyrinth straight out of a nightmare. The quiet had allowed him to hear the danger stalking the empty halls, but it was also beginning to drive him mad.

The Chaos Faction leader had begun patrolling the stronghold hallways, his overgrown, warped countenance continually scanning every nook and cranny he encountered. Sometimes the only thing that warned the adolescent of the menace was the gurgling, wet breathing announcing Balor's approach. That and the sniffing. What was with the constant sniffing?

Rónán ducked back into a deep closet near the kitchen, held his breath, and gathered his shadows close to his body, as he waited for Balor to move beyond his hiding place. He focused all his mental strength on making his thoughts a blank slate.

As the monstrous Fomori continued past him, he

slowly let out his breath and tried to slow his pounding heart. However, he didn't dare make a sound or lower his mental defenses. He might be young, but he wasn't stupid.

This was not the first close call the young Shadow Weaver had experienced in the past few weeks, and the tension was beginning to take its toll. He needed a better plan.

Once he decided the coast was likely clear, he quietly eased himself out of the closet, moving ever so slowly. Then he worked his way back to the Shadow Faction rooms in the Titan's cavern, slipping from one pool of shadows to the next as stealthily as he could manage. Balor had been heading toward his rooms, so he felt reasonably safe approaching the cavern.

He slipped through the large steel door, taking care to close it behind him, and headed straight for the rooms that housed the captive Shadow Weavers. When he entered, Orla looked up from the book she was reading and, seeing his tense expression, immediately stood and crossed the room to his side.

"What is it, lad?" she asked. "Are you hurt?"

"No, I'm fine. Or, well, not fine, but not injured. Balor has stepped up his patrols. I feel like I'm being hunted constantly, and sooner or later, I will get caught. It's just a matter of time." He took a shuddering breath, the stress of his environment overcoming him for a moment.

Orla put an arm around his shoulders. Even strong, capable young Fomori needed comforting sometimes.

"Keep your chin up, lad. We will discuss this with Deirdre when she makes contact tomorrow evening. We'll figure something out, I promise."

"I hope you're right," he replied.

"I have some good news and some bad news," Deirdre began at her next check-in. "Our healers believe they may have a way to reverse the damage done by the chaos magic, at least for those still in the earlier stages of metamorphosis."

Several gasps sounded as the Shadow Weavers absorbed that knowledge.

"And we think we can utilize artifacts to help as many Fomori as possible in a short time."

"How short a time?" Brian asked, his wheels turning as he began going over possible scenarios.

"Twenty minutes, I'm told," the High Druid replied.

"That's fantastic," Orla commented. "And now the bad news?"

"It will take time to produce a substantial number of artifacts. We believe we have about six weeks left before Balor launches his invasion. So, we plan to give ourselves one month to churn out as many artifacts as possible. Then we will come for you. And hopefully, we'll also be able to free some Titans."

When he heard the timeline, Rónán couldn't help the mental sigh that escaped him.

Deirdre noticed and said, "What's the problem, lad?"

"It's just that Balor has begun more extensive patrols more often, and I'm having a harder and harder time avoiding them. I'm worried I won't be able to avoid him much longer."

"Well, that simply won't do," the High Druid replied. There was a pause as she considered the options. "Does Balor ever check in the Shadow Weavers rooms at night?"

The young Fomori relayed the question to the others

and replied, "They say he hasn't so far. He might pop in during the day, but they think he doesn't want to get the Titans riled up at night. It takes a while to calm them down."

"Excellent. Then, I propose you begin sleeping in the Titans' cavern. You can wait until late in the evening to sneak in and sneak out early in the morning. It would be best if you also started taking one of the others with you during the day. There's safety in numbers, after all. Ask Orla to come up with some cover story as to why the two of you would be out and about during the day.

"But most importantly, lad, I need you to stay on your toes for just a bit longer. We are coming for you. I promise. Keep your head down, be careful, and stay alive. Just a few more weeks, eh? You haven't been forgotten."

Rónán dropped his head and let out another shuddering breath. He relayed the message to the others, but Orla was already approaching and wrapping him in a hug. "I'm sorry, lad, we should've done this immediately. But I thought we'd be putting you in more danger, that on your own you could stay hidden, stay safe."

Brian added, "We had good intentions, but that doesn't really matter now. From here on out, you won't be alone. Aye?"

"Aye," the youngling agreed with a relieved smile.

☘☘☘

After breaking contact with the young Shadow Weaver, Deirdre sat back in her chair and pinched the bridge of her nose. *I wish I had more to offer the lad. I'll have to trust he can stay safe.*

She began to stand when suddenly, a vision struck her

so forcefully that her knees buckled. Luckily, she landed back in her chair. Her eyes rolled back so only the sclera showed, and her breathing increased rapidly.

Smoke, dark and hazy, drifted across the images in her mind. A flash of brilliantly colored scales. Huge, gnashing teeth and oversized, malformed arms swinging clubs made from large tree branches. Giant marine creatures writhing in battle through blood-filled seas. Explosions of fire, water, and earth whipped into a turbulent tempest. And through it all, a feeling of both joyful reunion and anxious dread.

Eventually, the chaotic images receded, and her eyes and breathing returned to normal. She sipped a bit of lukewarm tea from the cup beside her table, replaying what she'd seen over and over in her mind. *Well, that's clear as much,* she thought, chuckling inwardly at borrowing a phrase from her former mentor.

The images of the battle were disturbing but not wholly unexpected. However, the odd combination of joy and dread was more confusing. *Ah, well. We will soon find out what it all means. For now, we soldier on and hope we've made good choices. No use dwelling on what we don't know.*

Now, if she could convince herself to believe that everything would be brilliant.

Family

is life

14

The two questors stumbled out of the portal from Findias, quickly catching their balance once they'd taken a few steps onto Gorias, the Air Clan island.

"I feel like we're getting the hang of that," Áine said.

"That's good because I have no clue how many more times we're going to have to portal before this is all said and done," Lir responded.

"At least once more, I would guess," answered a voice to their left, startling both familiars soundly.

The voice belonged to an ancient-looking Fae, seated in a soft, cushy chair that was completely out of place next to the Faery Tree on the desert-like island of Gorias. She had a thick silver braid draped over her left shoulder, wispy tendrils curling around her temples where a few strands had escaped. Her skin was wrinkled, and her knees weren't what they once were, but her eyes were still a bright blue, her wit and humor shining forth clearly. A black raven was perched on her shoulder, with two others watching from the tree branches.

"Crap on a cracker, you scared the shit out of me!" Áine complained, fluttering over to perch on a small rock near her chair. "And why is there a La-Z-Boy in the middle of the Air Clan's desert?"

The elder Fae cackled at that and said, "If you were as old as I am and had the power to move things with air, you'd bring your favorite chair along with you, too."

The phoenix cocked her head and replied, "How do you know I'm not as old as you?"

"Because I clearly remember when you were born, lass. And I wasn't a youngling then, either."

Áine gasped slightly and said, "Who are you?"

Lir interrupted, saying, "I think I know. You must be Aisling."

"Smart, lad," the former Banduri said. "Yes, the former Head Ovate at your service."

The phoenix, feeling slightly intimidated by the presence of the elder, asked, "No disrespect, but why are you here? It's not bad news, is it?"

The Druid replied, "No, no, love. I just had a bit of a vision and thought I might be able to help you two with the last part of your journey." She paused a moment, gathering her thoughts.

"It won't be long before you will meet your gods. They will challenge you, but you mustn't back down. They respect courage and determination. They also love snark and bling, so they'll love you, little bird."

"They sound like my kind of gods," Áine remarked.

"Aye, they are. But keep in mind, they are immortal. So, while they may be willing to help, you will need to work at keeping them on task. Which is where you come in, lad," she said, turning to Lir. "It will be like herding cats, but I know you are capable. You must be. Our world depends on you."

The púca nodded solemnly, respectful of the gravity of his task.

"And you must help him, lass. This is not your strong suit, but they will be enamored of you. They are bored, having spent millennia trying to entertain themselves. They now create games and wagers about anything and everything. Use that. Keep them interested, whatever you do. Otherwise, your quest will fail. I believe they will have good intentions, but it's been so long since they've had to do anything in a hurry they may have forgotten how. Light a fire under their arse, literally if necessary."

The phoenix nodded thoughtfully, aware of the magnitude of what they were about to undertake.

"Very good. Now, I have one last piece of advice before you pick up your final bauble. The village leaders are good Fae, and they will help you. But the Air Clan likes a spectacle. So, if you want to accomplish your goal with minimal hassle, resign yourself to a ceremony during the Litha celebration. It's only a few days away, and they won't be able to resist making a big fuss. Oh, and lad, if you really want to make a good impression, grow some wings. If you hadn't noticed, the Air Clan are very fond of flying, and they respect those who can," she ended with a grin.

Lir grinned in response, reared back on his hind legs, gave a little shudder, and two huge, ebony-feathered wings sprang forth along his spine, right at the base of his mane. "How's this?"

"What. The. Fuck. Goat Boy! Why aren't you always in Pegasus form? The aerial routines we could have been performing!" Áine couldn't decide if she was excited or dismayed at not knowing her companion's capabilities.

Lir said, "I love flying, but running as a púca is amazing, too. You should try it sometime."

"Hmm. Maybe. We will see." The phoenix turned to face Aisling. "Thank you for your insight. We really appreciate it."

"My pleasure, love," she replied. "If you would do me a favor and tell Deirdre I'm so proud of her. And that I miss her, and she needs to visit me when things calm down. Now, go save the world."

※ ※ ※

The journey to the village went much faster in their phoenix and Pegasus forms, but there was still time for Áine to throw a little something together. As they approached, she called out, "Five, six, seven, eight!" Then they broke into a small aerial routine she had thrown together on the fly. Swooping and twirling, diving and climbing, it didn't take long for them to attract quite a crowd. With a final loop de loop, the two familiars landed gracefully in the center of the gathered Fae. Spontaneous applause broke out, and both of the performers took a bow.

"Céad míle fáilte! That was wonderful!" an elder Fae said, stepping forward from the crowd. "I'm Anfa, and I'm responsible for the Air Clan while most of our Fae are helping prepare for the battle. To what do we owe the pleasure of your visit," she asked politely.

Lir folded his wings tight to his sides and bowed his head respectfully at her. "We've been sent by the expanded Council, the Fianna and High Druid Deirdre, at the request of the familiars. In trying to give ourselves every advantage against the Chaos Titans, we have decided to make a pilgrimage to petition our gods for support in this battle."

Anfa nodded, "You're here for the relic, then?"

Áine fluttered up to Lir's rump, wiggled the expando-bag off her neck with her talon, extended it in a high kick, and replied, "Yep, you'll find a letter from Deirdre in there."

The Air Clan leader chuckled and fished the letter out of the bag. After looking it over, she said, "Everything looks to be in order. And, of course, we will give you the relic." She paused, twisting one of her silvery blonde curls around her finger, and appeared to consider something. "But, with Litha just a few days away, perhaps you could stay for the mid-summer celebration and allow us to present the torque to you in front of everyone?" She raised her eyebrows as she asked the question.

Lir replied, "Of course, we'd be honored."

The familiars passed their days crisscrossing the island, performing routine after routine that Áine would choreograph on the spot. She was almost manic with pleasure at taking her love of dancing and adding a third dimension.

"I think I like this island even better than the Fire one," Áine mused as she swung around in loops, riding the thermals in lazy circles. Lir was right there, making slightly larger circles and basking in the summer sun. "It's not bad," he agreed, barely cracking an eyelid as he soaked up the rays.

Aisling occasionally accompanied them on their flights, the elder's command over her element exquisite. Her gracefulness and finesse enhanced Áine's choreography, adding to the blissfulness of the phoenix.

Finally, the day before Litha arrived. There were bonfires sprinkled throughout the gardens outside their

Druids' Enclave. Faery lights floated through the air, and Fae were dressed in their finest clothing and draped with gold jewelry, paying homage to the sun on this shortest night and longest day of the year.

Various beverages—beer, wine, whiskey, cocktails, and mocktails—drifted throughout the gardens on floating trays. Food ranging from appetizers to entrees also made the rounds, occasionally receiving verbal instructions and rushing off to fetch a custom request.

Aisling was resplendent in a deep blue gown, accentuating her sparkling blue eyes and silver curls. She wore a gold tiara laden with sapphires and aquamarines, and her wrists and neck sparkled with golden bracelets and chains.

Áine wore her tiara, of course, but she also decided to don the Fire goddess's torque. She was dripping in bling, and it made her seriously happy. Lir, after much pestering, finally agreed to wear the Earth god's torque. The shining copper and sparkling emeralds looked magnificent against his midnight black coat. Aisling had also insisted on braiding some metallic gold ribbons throughout his mane.

Once everyone had arrived and had a chance to eat and drink a bit, Anfa stepped to a raised area before a bonfire at the center of the gardens, amplified her voice, and said, "Fáilte! We are here to celebrate the sun on the eve of Litha, the summer solstice. Tonight, we also have the privilege of presenting these two familiars with our Clan's relic to assist them on their pilgrimage as they seek assistance from their gods!"

Lir bowed his head, and she removed the expando-bag from around his neck. Then she lifted the Air god's torque from its carved wooden stand and held it aloft for a moment to let everyone view the artifact.

It was dripping with citrine, tourmaline, yellow

diamonds, and topaz, all shaped into swirls and gusts of air. Various shades of white and yellow gold Celtic knotwork twisted among the gems, adding dimension and a luminous metallic sheen. Tiny white diamonds and pearls outlined and enhanced the swirls of air, adding the perfect finer details.

After the crowd had viewed the relic, she slipped it into the bag, cinched it closed tight, and replaced it around Lir's neck.

"Go n-éirí leat! We wish you success on the next leg of your journey! But for tonight, let's celebrate!" Anfa exclaimed, and the crowd cheered and clapped in response.

Aisling, who was now seated in her favorite comfy chair in the middle of the gardens, having fetched it with her air power after getting a bit tired, caught Áine's eye and made a small motion with her head, asking the phoenix to join her.

"Excitable, aren't they?" the Air Fae whispered in her ear, a grin on her face. Áine returned the grin and said, "Hey, if they need an excuse to have a party, I am not complaining."

Over the course of the evening, the three of them sampled as many different types of food and drink as they could manage. The phoenix finally called it quits when she began nodding off and startled herself awake with an enormous belch.

She looked around and saw that Aisling had already floated herself home, and Lir was also beginning to fall asleep. "Come on, Goat Boy. Time for some shut-eye."

Áine fluttered up to his back, and he began slowly walking back to Aisling's cottage. Right before the rhythmic motion of Lir's steps lulled her to sleep, she had the fleeting thought, *Now, it's time to meet the gods.*

M.A. KILPATRICK

Family

is life

15

Calder was sitting on the end of his bed, brushing his still-damp hair. Fintan had informed the Fianna that the familiars had requested all Fae to wear either shorter skirts or kilts to the Litha celebration. And, in fact, from now on, while preparing for the impending battle. A more in-depth explanation had been promised at the festivities this evening, but he had an inkling of why that might be important. They would find out soon enough.

From the bathroom came the sounds of rustling and clacking, followed by a frustrated, "Fuck!" He took a deep breath and went to see if he could help his beloved out of her foul mood.

When he poked his head into the open doorway of the bathroom, he was dismayed to find Keegan in a silky sage green robe, dark red curls dripping wet, standing in front of the mirror with tears streaming down her face.

He immediately went to her, wrapped his arms around her waist, and nuzzled his face against her neck. "What is it, my ember? Why the tears?" he whispered against her neck.

She took a shuddering breath and said, "I can't find my mascara."

"I see," he replied seriously, lifting his head to look at her in the mirror. "Do you always cry when your makeup goes missing? Just want to know if I should plan to keep a supply handy for future emergencies." He let a wry grin break over his face.

Keegan elbowed him gently and said, "It's not nice to make fun of your girlfriend." Her lips were twitching slightly as she said it, however.

"I'm being serious, love," he responded. "If I can do something to calm any anxious moments you might have, consider it done. Having extra mascara on hand seems a small price to pay to keep you smiling, Aibhleog."

He grabbed her hairbrush, then grasped her hand, and gently tugged on it, leading her back to his bedroom. He sat on the corner of the bed, pulling her to sit between his legs. He gathered the excess moisture from her hair and sent it down the drain in the sink. Now that her hair was just damp, but not dripping, he began gently running the brush through her curls over and over again. He hummed softly while he worked, letting her breathe and work through what was bothering her.

Once her hair was well-brushed, he used his hands to scrunch it several times, then removed the rest of the water, leaving her with gorgeous, smooth curls. He wrapped his arms around her again and said, "So, should I ask Cara to help me figure out what kind of mascara to order, or is there perhaps something else bothering you?"

She leaned back against him and sighed. "What if I can't do this? I'm terrified I'm screwing up, and people are going to die because of me." Her eyes welled with tears again, and he gripped her chin, turning her toward him, and said, "It's perfectly normal to have doubts, lass. All of us are wondering the same thing. I don't know if we'll win this battle, but I do know that I am proud to fight beside you. And from what I've seen, you are giving this your best effort, eh?"

She nodded and sighed again. "That's all you can do, mo chrói. That's all any of us can do." He rested his forehead against hers, gently cupping her face with both his hands. He slowly leaned in to kiss her deeply.

When he finally pulled back, her breathing and heart rate had quickened. "Now then, we have a bit of time. Let me help you relax, love," he said, scooping her up and placing her higher on the bed.

He laid down on his side next to her and tugged on the belt of her robe, slowly opening it to reveal her soft, clean skin, still slightly pink from the hot shower she'd recently taken. He began kissing her again, tilting his head to deepen the kiss as he trailed his other hand across her body. He paid special attention to each breast, tweaking her nipples before moving his hand down to the red curls between her legs.

He pulled back from their kiss long enough to say, "Open your legs for me. Now, please." She grinned slightly at his demand. He would do anything for her but expected to be obeyed when they were intimate. She found his commands made her wet every time.

She spread her legs wide, and he wasted no time sliding his middle finger through her folds and deep inside of her. "Ah, love, you're always so wet for me. Always my good girl, ready for me to play with you."

She reached for him, trying to pull him on top of her. He

just grinned at her and lay there, very much in the same spot, saying, "I'm playing with you right now, lass. I may fuck you later, but not right now. Just relax and enjoy; I promise you won't be disappointed."

She narrowed her eyes and said, "Do I have a choice?"

He added another finger inside her, curling them in a manner that made her gasp. "You always have a choice, my love. Your choice is to let me pleasure you," he withdrew his fingers, causing another gasp, this time from disappointment, "or to have me stop."

"Now, now, don't be hasty," she said, reaching for his hand and guiding it back between her thighs. He chuckled darkly, resumed his pleasuring, and said, "That's my needy ember."

He began to kiss her again, more forcefully, and added his thumb circling her clit to the two fingers thrusting inside her core. As he increased his tempo, she began moaning against his mouth and clenching against his fingers.

He broke their kiss, nipped her on the neck, and said, "Are you ready to come for me, love?" She nodded, causing him to slow his rhythm slightly and nip her again, harder, and say, "You know better than that. I'll ask again. Are you ready to come for me?"

"Yes," she panted. He maintained things for a moment, then said, "Come for me, Keegan, and be loud. I want to hear you scream when you drench my hand."

He increased the speed of both his thrusts and his circling motion and was quickly rewarded with both a scream and a very wet hand as she clenched hard against his fingers in her pleasure.

He left his fingers inside her, slowing down but not stopping until he was sure she was spent. "Stay right here, love," he instructed, heading into the bathroom and returning quickly with a warm washcloth. He gently cleaned her up, gave her one last lingering kiss, and then helped her up, saying, "How are you feeling, lass?"

"Better, thanks."

"Oh, the pleasure was mine. Well, maybe not all the pleasure, but you take my meaning," he responded with another grin. "Now, unless you intend to wear that robe to the Litha celebration, you'd best get changed."

She began to gather her clothes for the evening when she remembered about the mascara. She turned to him, but he was already at the door, saying, "Cara is getting ready with Riley right now. Shall I ask her for some mascara?"

"Yes, please," she responded, then added, "And thank you, Calder. For everything."

"My pleasure, love. Truly." He gently closed the door and went to fetch some makeup for his beloved.

☙❈☙

Deirdre stood in front of her full-length mirror, putting the finishing touches on her outfit for tonight's celebration. An important part of Litha, the Fae's celebration of the summer solstice, was honoring the sun on the shortest night and longest day of the year. Their method of choice was to wear their finest clothing and as much gold as they could manage.

So, her reflection showed the High Druid in a metallic gold léine, a long tunic-like garment. Her skirt was pleated, billowing out when she turned from side to side a bit. The sleeves sat off her shoulders and were tight to the elbow, then draped almost to the ground. Dark green Celtic knotwork adorned the deep vee of her neckline and the long flowing sleeves. A tree of life decorated her stomach, its emerald branches splayed up to her chest and down to her hips, nearly joining roots to branches at her waist.

A dark green mantle flowed from just below her shoulders to the floor, the phases of the moon arched across the top in glittering gold. Beneath it, an identical tree of life rested, also in gold.

A golden torque rested upon her slim throat, sparkling as she lifted her chin, double-checking the little bit of makeup she applied. Fae her age usually appeared to be a bit more mature than Deirdre looked. She wasn't ashamed to say she was pleased with how she had aged.

Her long, blonde hair cascaded down her right side, the tiny strands of gold interwoven among the curls and little braids twinkling whenever she moved. She ran her fingertips over the shaved side of her head. It still felt odd, but she didn't mind how it looked.

She smoothed her hands down her skirt once more, then turned to leave the room. Before she had taken a step, a vision slammed into her so forcefully that she collapsed to her knees. Images of hazy green foliage with sunlight filtering through it interwoven with flashes of sparkling silvery-white flowers and the fuzzy-edged, bright, glowing circles of portals. As this movie played through her mind, she heard a soft, warm voice say, "Ask for what you need."

Then, just as suddenly as it began, it ended. Deirdre stayed on her knees for a few heartbeats taking deep breaths and processing what she'd seen. This vision was unlikely any she'd ever had before. It was somehow deeper and more resonant. As she began piecing things together, she thought she understood why.

She rose to her feet with the help of a nearby chair, smoothed her skirt once more, and walked toward the

Enclave's exit, considering the implications of what she'd seen. As she sat in the carriage on the way to the World Tree gardens, she mulled over the best way to proceed. She had been hoping something like this could be possible, but to have it offered was a good omen, in her mind.

By the time they reached the gardens, she thought she had devised a decent plan of action, provided the Fae she needed to help her agreed. *We will soon find out.*

Emer stalked back and forth restlessly, causing her tiara to wobble slightly as she turned to start back the other direction. She, and the rest of the familiars, were gathered not far from the World Tree, impatiently waiting for the last of the Fae to arrive and the Litha celebration to truly begin. Laoise, Saoirse, and Ula were also wearing their crowns—it was Litha, after all, and part of the fun was dressing up. Laoise had also added a tiny kilt in the Fire Clan tartan. Grady even participated, an understated, but very shiny, golden torque around his neck and a strip of the Earth Clan tartan draped diagonally across his chest, held together with a golden, leaf-shaped pin.

Less than half an hour later, as the crimson disk sank below the horizon, dressing the landscape in burning, gilded glory, it appeared as though the majority of Fae had appeared, and the festivities were about to begin.

Shay, dressed in a yellow Air Clan plaid kilt and crisp white shirt, stepped to the central area before the World Tree. He wore a golden torque, broach, and various other pins and jewelry, shimmering in the light cast by the sunset and the various bonfires sprinkled throughout the gardens. He held hands with Niamh, who was absolutely glowing in a léine made from a shimmery peach fabric. She had chosen a shorter style, and it was embellished with Celtic knotwork and flames in multiple shades of red, copper, and gold. She also wore a short mantle of copper with red and gold decorations.

A torque and a multitude of other gold jewelry were draped around her neck and limbs. Her blue eyes twinkled with excitement, and her strawberry blonde waves were twisted into an adorable updo, showing off the undercut on the sides.

Shay touched his throat and said, "Céad míle fáilte! Thank you for attending our mid-summer celebration of Litha! Everyone looks brilliant, and the familiars have promised to explain their request that we all begin showing a bit more skin."

No sooner had he mentioned the familiars than Emer and Grady appeared at the head of a very long line of their kindred. When they stopped directly in front of Shay and Niamh, the two leaders turned to face the gathered Fae, and the unbonded familiars began moving among the crowd. As everyone took their place, Emer nodded at Cara, who was standing nearby, and she gestured toward her bonded, amplifying her voice.

"Thank you, everyone, for consenting to our request. I'm sure you all remember the skin-bonding demonstration from the Fianna Trials. With the decision to use portals to switch locations during the coming attack, the familiars have agreed to work together and form multiple skin bonds with you as a battle tactic. This will allow Air Fae, when flying their quads around, to lift dozens of familiars as well, with no added weight. Then, when they land, those familiars can rematerialize and fight. However, skin bonding is easiest and most effective when the familiar can see the skin to which they are bonding. That is the reason for our request. We need you to get comfortable fighting in very little clothing so your skin can be readily accessed if skin bonding is necessary.

"The cailíní from Fae Glam have been working on designing acceptable battle attire that will not only be appropriate for multiple skin bonds but also allow for ease of movement. With some help from the Doran family and their skill with artifacts, these clothes will also be able to be dismissed, like a glamour, when the Fae wishes to assume their aquatic form. Then the clothing can be recalled when the Fae resumes their land form."

Several salon members moved to the front, forming a line to showcase their designs. The top basically consisted of either a leather bikini top or a cropped tank, and the bottom resembled a leather kilt. They had also conscripted Conor and Collin to help model the male version of the outfit, which was the same on bottom, a leather kilt-like garment. Some wore on top a strip of leather diagonally across their chest, with several slots along it, presumably for those who might wish to carry a physical weapon in addition to their elemental powers. A few females also had a similar leather sash, implying it was an optional component. Everything was marked with various forms of metallic gold Celtic knotwork.

Keegan nudged her cousin, Cara, and said, a little louder than intended, "Xena, baby!" The Air Fae snorted, but was saved from being the recipient of one of Siobhan's eyebrows when Fae Glam's Ramona, who had also grown up on earth, laughed and said, "You know it, chica! That show was totally our inspiration for these outfits. I made all of them watch it with me."

Emer glanced at Grady, who was shaking his head. "I

thought things around here would be slightly more normal with Áine gone. It appears I no longer know the meaning of normal," he said quietly with a slight chuckle.

"For the past several weeks, many of the unbonded among us have been observing you all. The majority of the unbonded will stay that way, at least until after the battle, in order to easily skin bond with multiple different Fae if necessary. But many have decided to choose their bonded now. This is the most significant mass bonding event in centuries," Grady explained.

After that, a thrumming in the air began that everyone could feel. All across the World Tree gardens, familiars approached their chosen, and bonds began snapping into place in rapid-fire succession.

Emer, Grady, and the other already-bonded familiars watched it happen in awe. A silverback gorilla bonded with Liam, while a chimp chose Sláine beside him. Niall watched as a lithe cheetah wove his way toward him, and Conor was speechless when he became joined with an Irish wolfhound. Dillon was chosen by an eagle, while Croía bonded to a peregrine falcon.

Deirdre watched all of this with tears in her eyes, stunned at the moment's beauty. She stepped up beside Shay, wordlessly asking his leave to speak. He nodded at her and motioned her forward to take center stage. She touched her throat to increase her voice's volume, then said, "Please, everyone, take a moment to greet your newly bonded partners. But don't go far. There is something you won't want to miss coming soon."

She waited a few more minutes, then made her way, one at a time, to Siobhán, Niamh, and Nora and explained her idea. The three Fae apologized to their newly-bonded familiars, an Arctic wolf, a snowy owl, and a wolverine, respectively, and then joined Deirdre at the base of the World Tree.

The High Druid positioned Siobhán on the north side of the tree, Niamh to the south, Nora on the west side, and took her own place on the east. The other Druids had quietly taken positions around them but further back, encircling them in the center. The four Fae around the tree each placed their hands on the bark, quieting their mind to a state of receptiveness, as requested. Deirdre centered herself, sinking into the stillness deep within. She then began seeking out the threads of the other Druids, plucking each one as she came across it in her mind's eye and weaving them into a thick rope of energy and intent.

Once she had gathered the Druid's offerings and added the other three Fae attempting to connect, she freely offered all that vibrant energy to the World Tree, asking for what she needed. Everyone included in that shining energy rope felt it when the tree answered.

A deep rumbling could be felt in their bones as an awareness seemed to awaken. "Because the mothers have asked, it shall be granted," echoed through the minds of all within that interconnected web in a solemn but warm alto.

Everyone looked up as the branches overhead began to rustle and sway as if a stiff breeze blew, but the air was still. Then hundreds, if not thousands, of small, silvery-white flowers with five petals, a pale green pistil in the center, surrounded by several stamens with bright pink anthers at the end of each white filament fluttered to the ground. The blossoms were glowing and glittery, seeming to almost pulse with a life of their own.

"Use my gifts well, beloveds," the mellow, honeyed voice enjoined in farewell, the awareness fading back within the deep stillness of the World Tree.

The four Fae lifted their hands away from the tree and congregated around Deirdre. "Well, that was intense," Siobhán commented. "But I didn't know you had children," she said to the High Druid.

"I don't," she replied, a mildly confused expression on her face.

Nora suggested, "Perhaps the tree was referring to your position as High Druid? That could be seen as a form of parenting, being responsible for guiding the Aos Sí."

Deirdre nodded, then shook her head slightly, bringing herself back to the matter at hand. "Yes, well, we must gather the faery blossoms and determine how best to distribute and carry them. I will collect them all and send them with the Fae Glam cailíní. They seem well-suited to integrate them into some sort of carrying apparatus."

The four of them gathered in the central area of the gardens, and Deirdre amplified her voice again. "The World Tree has gifted the Aos Sí with its very own faery blossoms. When combined with active power from each element, one of these will allow your quads to portal to any other faery tree or blossom. Each of you will receive one once the cailíní of Fae Glam have designed some way to carry and protect it."

The Druid lifted all of the faery blossoms into the air, swirling them over to where the Fae Glam members were assembled. They were already discussing the best way to proceed with the flowers. As they descended toward the cailíní, Madi, another Air Fae, grasped the blossoms with her own air power, Deirdre releasing them into her care.

The High Druid nodded to Shay, relinquishing announcement duties back to him. The Taoiseach, who was currently somewhat overwhelmed by the beauty of the hawk who had chosen to bond with him, nevertheless pulled himself together long enough to dismiss the Fae to their celebrations.

"Well, now, that's a bit to process, eh? Help yourselves to food and drink, enjoy the music and bonfires, and for those lucky enough to be chosen tonight, take some time to get to know your new bonded. Bain sult as!"

Family

is life

16

Keegan and Cara were doing basic stretches, warming their muscles up before taking their turn at cavalry training. The mass bonding event at the Litha celebration took place about a week ago, and the newly bonded couples were still getting to know one another.

Keegan sighed as she looked around at the Fae and their new familiars. "What is it, hun?" Cara asked.

"I just miss her. I know she's a pain in the ass most of the time, but this is the longest we've ever been apart. And I miss Lir, too. He's such a sweetie."

"Yeah, I miss them, too. I'll be glad when they get back, so we can kick some monster ass and be done with all this tension," Cara replied. She nodded to where Croía and Dillon were chatting. "Those two are so adorable it's a little nauseating."

Keegan laughed and said, "Yeah, but they're both so freaking nice, it's hard to hold it against them."

Dillon's new familiar, a bald eagle named Crann, was chasing Gorm, Croía's bright blue peregrine falcon, but he was in no danger of catching the falcon, who was incredibly fast. The couple was stretching, warming up for the cavalry training about to start, but neither could take their eyes off the sky.

Siobhán led Morrígan out to the center of the corral area and let one of her ear-piercing whistles fly. "Gather your mounts and gather round! It's almost time to begin." Over near the fence sat Ré, a snow-white Arctic wolf who had chosen the Ó Faoláin matriarch as her bonded. The two of them were already inseparable.

The Fae participating in the cavalry training led their horses into the corral, mounted up, and awaited further instructions. Croía, Conor, and Collin joined Siobhán in the center, ready to demonstrate the techniques they were practicing today. The two males were also chosen in the mass bonding event. Conor's new familiar was a shaggy grey Irish wolfhound named Mian, and Collin's was named Ómra, a stunning black rottweiler with amber patches on her eyebrows, lower face, chest, and feet. The two enormous dogs were sunning themselves just outside the corral with Niall's newly bonded cheetah, Dáithí.

"Today's exercise will be a bit different than what we've done so far. Since many Fae now have new familiars, we've decided to work on fighting and, well, just staying together. So, to begin, we would like you to work on riding and running, or flying, together. Croìa and the lads will go first. Join in as soon as you're ready," Siobhán explained. "And if any of you are unbonded, familiar or Fae, pick someone and shadow them. One of our biggest challenges in this battle will be staying together so we're all on the same page. Practicing that can only help. Be back here in half an hour, and we'll work on some evasive maneuvers. Now off with you!"

The three younger Fae and their familiars took off like a

shot toward a forested area behind the corral, the rest of the Fae and their bonded close behind. Keegan shadowed Cara and Emer since she was currently without Áine. The woods they were traversing were fairly dense, so the obstacles were numerous and coming quickly. Luckily, the Aos Sí had reflexes much better than humans, so there was little danger.

The thick foliage did provide a bit more challenge for the winged familiars trying to keep pace at such a low altitude with so many branches and trunks to dodge, but they handled it well. Crann decided to land on the rump of Dillon's horse during the areas with the most congestion. She glanced back at him, and he shrugged and said, "Work smarter, not harder," which made her chuckle. *Whatever works,* she thought.

When the thirty minutes expired, they returned to the corral area. Niamh and Étaín had joined Siobhán, and they were waiting to begin the next portion of the training. The Doran sisters had also received new familiars at Litha; a snowy owl named Féirín had chosen Niamh, and Étaín was now bonded to an elephant called Angus. They, along with Siobhán's familiar, Ré, had joined their Fae in the center of the arena.

"Welcome back! For the rest of today's session, we will work on evading the enemy on horseback. Our familiars will assist us today by playing the part of the monsters."

The three instructors took turns demonstrating how to evade attacks from the various familiars at about half the normal speed. They then increased the tempo and began switching familiars, creating an environment where the attack might come from any direction. Angus did an excellent job of demonstrating somewhere near the level of strength that the Titans might be capable of.

When the rest of the group entered the corral, the familiars started slowly at Siobhán's direction to allow their bondeds time to acclimate. Then, they ramped things up to a quicker speed. Angus, Ré, and Féirín also participated, creating an environment that began approaching the level of chaos they might see on a battlefield. Not quite there, but getting closer.

By the end of the session, the Fae were winded and a bit subdued. Seeing the sheer pandemonium they would face was a bit sobering. But it was far better to adjust now than in a battle where a moment's distraction could mean life or death.

"That's it for today. Please practice this in your free time. And familiars, I'd consider it a favor if you would routinely ambush your Fae. Learning to keep their head on a swivel might keep them alive."

As the group wandered out of the corral, Keegan leaned over to Cara and said, "Thank goodness Áine wasn't here for that little directive. Can you imagine the ambushes she would have cooked up?" She shuddered at the thought. Emer overheard and snarked, "Oh now, don't worry. Grady and I will make sure to include you and Calder in our surprise attacks. We wouldn't want you to feel left out."

The redhead facepalmed and said, "Maybe someday I'll learn to keep my mouth shut." Her cousin snorted and replied, "I doubt it."

༺༻༺༻༺༻

Liam grunted for the third time in the last two minutes as Sláine braided his hair. She tied off the end, leaned forward, and nipped behind his ear. "I'm beginning to think you just like to complain, lad," she whispered in his ear, his whiskers tickling her cheek. He'd announced a few weeks ago that if he had to mess with this long hair, he would quit shaving and save himself that trouble, at least.

He reached up, captured her chin with his hand, and kissed her deeply. "I'm sorry, lass," he said when they finished. "I'm not myself before a cup of tea."

She nuzzled her face into his neck and said, "You're lucky you're pretty. But now we need to get to the healer training. I'm one of the teachers; I can't be tardy." She swatted his butt as he stood up, and he turned around to help her stand. He paused to make a quick cup of tea and pour it into a travel mug.

She twisted her long, chestnut waves into a messy bun atop her head and slipped her shoes on. Her bare midriff prickled in gooseflesh, unused to being exposed. Since she would be with the healers, it was unlikely she would need to skin bond for the battle. But the odds weren't zero, so it was best to prepare, just in case. As she watched her beloved move around shirtless, muscles rippling across his broad shoulders and cut abs, she smiled. *I certainly don't mind the view lately, though.*

Their new familiars, Liam's silverback gorilla named Carraig and the chimp who had chosen Sláine, Trasa, had decided to help the cavalry with their evasive training. So, as the two of them walked to the building used for the healing lesson, she laced her fingers through his, continuing to admire his muscular physique. He was built like a bull, broad and barrel-chested, and, combined with the new beard and bared torso; she needed to start reciting from memory the bones in the hand before she made herself all hot and bothered. *Now is not the time!*

When they arrived in the training room, he lifted their clasped hands and kissed the inside of her wrist. She smiled at the gesture as she joined Morgan and the other senior healers at the front of the room.

The Chief Healer welcomed them and quickly paired them off to work on the skills they'd been focusing on. Sláine's partner was Cordelia, the poet from the Fianna Trials. "Dia Duit, Delia. How are you feeling about your progress thus far?"

"Pretty well, I think. I'm beginning to be able to see inside the body more clearly each time I try."

"Brilliant, lass. Why don't you try scanning me?"

Sláine held out her hands, which Delia clasped, and both Fae closed their eyes. The student took a deep breath and allowed her awareness to sink into her teacher's bloodstream, riding it around her system and noting anything unusual. There wasn't much, but she noticed something that seemed slightly off when she was swept through Sláine's wrist. She hovered there momentarily, opened her eyes, and said, "Have you had an injury to your right wrist?"

The healer opened her eyes, smiled at Delia, and said, "Why yes, I fell out of a tree and broke it when I was a child. That is a very old injury; I'm surprised you were able to detect it."

The student blushed and said, "I'm trying to pay more attention. I figure it could save someone's life. I will do my best to notice the details, hoping it will help."

Sláine smiled again and said, "I understand completely. You're doing brilliantly. Keep up the good work." Delia nodded gratefully and moved to the next station to practice with a different healer.

Her next student, Calder, took his seat across from her. "Hello, lad. Are you ready to begin?" He nodded. She held her hands out, palms up, and he gently rested his hands on hers. They closed their eyes, and he began scanning the healer's system. He found the same old wrist injury that Delia had. *These Fae are picking this up faster than I expected,* Sláine thought.

Calder paused a little longer than Delia and appeared to be considering something. Finally, he opened his eyes and said, "Does this old injury ever cause you pain?"

Surprised, she replied, "A wee bit sometimes, especially since I've been here on Earth when the weather changes. Why?"

"Because I think I can fix it using earth power. I think I can see how to smooth the break a little better, which should eliminate most of your discomfort."

Sláine considered it for a moment and then decided to risk it. "Well then, let's see what you can do. I will observe your work internally, so please go slowly. If I see anything objectionable, I will stop you. Agreed?"

"Of course," he said. They closed their eyes again, and each sank their awareness into the healer's right wrist area. Calder very slowly began knitting together the break, smoothing and melding until the scar was unnoticeable. Sláine was incredibly impressed.

While they were both still absorbed in the area, he asked, "Is that good? Should I try to do more?" The healer replied, "Lad, that is some of the most impressive bone knitting I've ever seen. Your ability to combine water and earth power makes quite a difference. I'm going to suggest to your da that we train Earth Fae to help with skeletal injuries from now on. It's been used before, but not widely, and after watching you, I believe that's a mistake. Keep practicing, a stór. And I'm looking forward to finding out if you've solved the bit of achiness that comes with a weather change. I have a feeling I'll be thanking you when the next thunderstorm rolls through."

"My pleasure, lass. I look forward to learning more and improving my technique," he replied, smiling. He squeezed her hands and went to the next station.

She watched him go and thought, *We've been so bloody stuck in our ways for far too long. Let's hope the changes coming are all as positive as this one.*

Family

is life

17

Deirdre had just finished braiding her hair for the day. As she tied off the end, her muscles seized, and she was flung against the back of her chair, her eyes rolling up into her head.

Images similar to those from her last unusual vision began streaming through her mind rapidly: teeth and claws rending flesh, a flurry of fins and bodies thrashing in the ocean, followed by far too much blood in the water, metallic scales, and vivid, glowing eyes, which caused her stomach to flutter strangely. At one point, she saw herself holding her hands out and found them glowing.

Even more disturbing than the images were the concussive thuds felt deep in her chest, causing enough dread to make her palms sweat and her heart race. The vision ended with a whiff of acrid smoke and the taste of ash on her tongue.

Once her physical sight returned and her breathing slowed, she leaned forward, resting her elbows on her knees and her face in her palms. She sighed deeply and said aloud, "These visions raise more questions than they answer, and I'm getting bloody sick of it."

She sat a moment longer, replaying the vision and trying to make sense of it. *Ah well, hopefully, I'll gather enough clues to make heads or tails of it before the fecking monsters get here.*

⁂

The Fianna and their regiments had all been gathered in the largest Kansas City training area. They had discussed it and felt that while it was too crowded to maintain indefinitely, spending time as one unit occasionally was helpful. Deirdre had suggested this initial air and portal training would be a good place to start.

The warriors were fanned out in a sort of horseshoe shape, facing the High Druid. She touched her throat and said, "Fáilte! Today will be our first attempt at implementing our hit-and-run portaling tactics combined with aerial attack formations. Keegan, will you bring over some of the faery blossoms and explain what you lot have accomplished?"

The redhead carried a small basket and joined Deirdre before the group. She gestured at the basket, and a small orb floated into the air, containing a glowing, glittering, silvery-white flower suspended in a clear liquid. She left that one floating at about eye level beside her and sent several others to hover throughout the group, attempting to place them so everyone could see a flower reasonably clearly.

"We experimented and determined that keeping the flowers suspended in water was the easiest and most effective way to contain it without crushing or destroying it.

Máire created the design, and my family and a few other volunteers replicated it. The sphere is somewhat flexible so that it gives slightly to cushion the flower, but the outside is impermeable—"

"Like a water condom!" someone called out, eliciting a few chuckles from the crowd.

Keegan snorted and said, "Something like that. Now, the Fae Glam folks have designed a sheath. You can tie it around your wrist, foot, waist, or neck, wherever it will sit comfortably and not get in the way."

She took a small strip of leather from her back pocket and slid one of the faery blossoms into the little pocket meant to hold it. Then she tied it to her wrist and held her arm up for those in front to see.

She lifted herself into the air and did a quick aerial lap around the soldiers, letting them see how it worked. As she went, she demonstrated its stability by moving her arm forcefully to simulate battle conditions as best she could.

She returned to Deirdre's side, and the two of them quickly distributed the faery blossoms and the holders to the Fianna at the head of each regiment. They passed the flowers out to their soldiers, allowing them a moment to get the blossoms situated and ensure speed and agility weren't compromised.

"Brilliant. I believe it would be prudent to begin with a little simple flying. If you'll separate into your quads, please. You don't need to be touching, but it will help your Air Fae if you're relatively close together. Let them lift you a short distance from the ground and set you back down, repeating several times and increasing the distance each time. Finally, they will levitate and fly you around a bit, keeping the height very low. Baby steps. I don't want anyone falling and breaking their neck; we haven't had enough healing practice for that nonsense."

They spent the next half hour practicing flight, getting smoother and steadier with each repetition. When Deirdre was comfortable with their progress, she called for them to land and return their attention to the front.

She nodded to Keegan and Calder, who had just joined her at the front of the group. They put their palms together and called all four elements, one spinning around each wrist.

The top quad in Keegan's regiment, the Fae who had won the Faelympics, were near the front of the crowd as well. "We'll fly over to the center. When we get there, we will call a portal to one of your blossoms and transport back to you," Keegan called to them. Brona, the Water Fae and de facto leader of the quad, nodded in response.

"Come on, big guy. Let's go for a ride," she said with an evil grin. She lifted them into the air, spinning them slowly around as she pushed them forward toward the center of the group.

When they reached their destination, she flipped them upright and said, "Let me do this one, then we'll trade off." He nodded, and she willed a portal connected to Brona's blossom into existence.

A bright light poured out of the quad leader's flower, pooling until a glowing white portal formed beside her. A few seconds later, Keegan and Calder flew through it, landing in front of the quad.

All six Fae were grinning and high-fiving each other. They had practiced that a few times and were relieved it went smoothly.

"To begin, we will pair off and practice portaling back and forth." The Fianna quickly got them into teams, and they took turns transporting themselves from one faery blossom to another.

By the end of the training, all the quads had significantly improved their flying and portaling abilities. Deirdre dismissed them and reminded them that if the familiars hadn't begun ambushing them, it was only a matter of time.

Bran settled the other three members of his quad gently on the ground. With a big sigh, Desmond stretched his arms out and said, "Any of you lot up for a bit of hurling?"

"Mhmm," Rowan replied. "Brona?"

"Aye, sounds good," the Water Fae answered.

Desmond saw Máire and Corley nearby and asked them, too. He also grabbed Sláine and Muireann, who were walking with Liam and Lorcan. Before long, multiple matches were underway. Everyone living there regularly had equipment, so gathering enough gear and getting things started took almost no time.

Keegan insisted on being on the same team as Máire, because she was a badass, and Calder, because he was a decent player, and if he got protective again and tried to save her, she might torch his ass, and that would put a real damper on sexy fun time.

Conor, who had wandered over after the last cavalry training, also insisted on being on Keegan's team, saying it was better for his health. Calder rolled his eyes and mumbled, "It was one time." His brother replied, "Yes, well, you don't learn very quickly, so better safe than sorry."

They managed to figure out teams, and it turned out that Corley and Máire were on opposing teams. Judging by their evil grins, this didn't bother them, however. Their competitive streaks were strong, and they both loved a challenge.

The game began, and things got physical quickly. Keegan and Máire were the first to make a run at the other team's goal, passing the sliotar back and forth so quickly it was almost a blur. Corley made a beeline for his girlfriend, who promptly elbowed him in the diaphragm, leaving him sputtering and gasping for breath. She and her cousin laughed and scored the first goal for three points.

Lorcan had no experience with hurling, so Muireann was explaining things as they happened. His athleticism allowed him to get up to speed quickly, although his style of play was a bit more violent than normal. There would be more than one black eye in the morning.

Máire and Keegan quickly discovered that incorporating Lorcan into their runs made things even easier as he laid people out without hesitation. Corley's competitiveness couldn't let that stand, so he moved to take the sliotar away when the Shadow Weaver was about to pass it to Máire.

The Earth Fae shoved Lorcan and attempted to snag the sliotar from him. The Fomori responded by punching Corley in the jaw, causing him to stumble and fall away while he continued the last few paces and scored another three points.

Liam shouted, "Foul! That didn't count, and we get a free!"

Lorcan approached him and said, "How was that a foul? I was protecting the sliotar, and I'm allowed to do that." He wasn't combative about it. Yet.

Liam, who was also a bit ramped up, continued, "You've moved well beyond the contact allowed in the rules, lad. And you've been aggressive the entire game."

The Shadow Weaver, for some reason, had decided he

was itching for a fight. But not with Liam. He huffed out, "Fine. Take the points and take your free."

Muireann tried to talk to him, but he pulled away from her hand as she reached out, saying, "I'm fine. Let's just play."

Liam's team took control of the sliotar, and he and Corley began bringing it down the field. Lorcan had tried to calm his mind, but it was not working tonight. *Let the little bitch bring it,* he thought, clenching his fists and gritting his teeth.

Corley, looking for a little payback of his own, caught a pass from Liam a few steps away from the angry Shadow Weaver. He moved the hurley and sliotar to his left hand, which was farthest away from Lorcan, then lowered his shoulder and charged straight toward the Fomori.

Lorcan allowed an evil smile to spread across his face, then lowered his shoulder to meet Corley head-on.

The sound they made when they collided made more than one Fae suck air through their teeth. The Earth Fae dropped his hurley and the sliotar, also dropping all pretense at playing the game. The two of them wrestled around on the ground, throwing punches and elbows.

Liam, who was just trying to win the game, stopped running and bemoaned, "Bloody hell. You two are fecking ridiculous."

Muireann quickly pushed them apart with a harsh burst of water, drenching them in the process. "What the feck is going on!" she snapped.

Lorcan, breathing hard with a bloody lip and a quickly swelling eye, replied sharply, "I don't like losing. And I certainly don't like it when I don't even get a chance to put up a fight."

Máire dropped her face into her palm, and Muireann

gasped. "So, what," she said, "I'm some sort of consolation prize?"

It finally dawned on Lorcan that he was being an asshole and had let his own competitive nature override his mouth. He widened his eyes and stammered, "No, love, uh, that's not, not what I meant."

Her eyes were quickly filling, and her cheeks flamed in embarrassment. She blinked tears back and quickly turned away from him, saying, "Never mind, I'm sorry I asked." She ran off the field and headed to her room.

Of course, Lorcan tried to follow, but Calder put a hand on his chest and said, "Nah, lad, that's not a good idea. Trust me, the lass will need a minute. But if you truly care for my sister, I'd suggest you start thinking of ways to atone. You are going to need them. I'll go talk to her in a bit and see how upset she is by then. Tomorrow is the earliest I would suggest speaking to her."

Lorcan pinched the bridge of his nose and sighed. *Bloody hell. Liam was right; we are ridiculous.* He turned around when he heard laughter behind him. Corley was still on the ground with a bloody nose and black eye, laughing hard.

"What the feck are you cackling about?" the Fomori snapped.

"You don't even really want Máire; you just hate losing. And now you've lost Muireann, too. I'm not even mad anymore, lad. You've punished yourself more than I ever could." He hopped up, wiped his bloody nose on his sleeve, and said, "Look, you need to listen to Calder. Between Keegan and Áine, he's had more than a little experience getting back into the feminine good graces. If anyone can help, it's him. And just so you know, he punched me once, too. Good luck."

Corley went directly over to Máire, planted a deep kiss on her, and clasped her hand, pulling her swiftly toward his room. Sláine shrugged, grabbed Liam's hand, and said, "Works for me. Come now, mo chroí, I need a massage."

He raised an eyebrow and said, "Yes, ma'am," allowing her to pull him toward his room.

Everyone else decided the game was over and began dispersing.

Keegan looked hungrily at Calder, sighed, and said, "Go on, big guy. Let your sister cry on your shoulder. And remind her that males are generally dumbasses on a regular basis, but you can come back from it."

He smiled at her, pulled her roughly to his chest, and whispered in her ear, "You know how much I love pleasure deferred, my needy ember. Go back to your room and put on something sexy so I can tear it off you when I get back. Put your favorite blindfold on and wait for me."

He nipped her neck just below her ear and swatted her before he walked away. She shivered in anticipation and headed for her room.

Family

is life

18

Calder knocked on the door to Muireann's room. "Please go away!" she called, sniffling.

"It's Calder, lass. Please let me in, just for a bit." He heard her sigh and listened to her footsteps as she walked to the door and opened it.

Her eyes were puffy, and her cheeks tear-stained when she looked up at him. "What do you want, brother?" she asked.

"I was hoping maybe I could help. I have some experience with making an arse of myself recently, so perhaps I can shed some light on what just happened back there," he replied.

She laughed bitterly, turned around, and walked back into her room, gesturing for him to follow. He closed the door behind him and joined her and Ula on the sofa in the little sitting area.

"I think what just happened was pretty self-explanatory, lad," she spat out, embarrassment and disgust fighting for control of her features. "I let myself get played.

He obviously still has feelings for Máire; I was just someone to pass the time with."

"Hmm, do you think so, love? Because if you really listened to what he said and how he said it, I think there's something else at play," he explained. "Sometimes, when Fae of the male persuasion get lost in their feelings or their tendencies, good or bad, we tend to get tunnel vision. I nearly fecked things up with Keegan because I was trying to protect her. What I didn't realize is that by insisting that *I* should protect *her,* I gave the impression that I didn't believe she could take care of herself. That was not at all what I thought, but I let myself act the maggot because I was overwhelmed by my protective tendencies. Make sense, eh?"

She nodded and responded, "I can see how that might happen, but it's not the same thing. He wasn't trying to protect me, he didn't want to be with me!" Her eyes began welling with tears again, and Calder tentatively put an arm around her shoulders, rubbing her arm to offer comfort. Muireann let her head fall to his shoulder and gave herself permission to have a good cry.

He brought his other arm up to pat her back gently, making soothing shushing noises. Ula snuggled next to her other side, humming softly.

After a bit, Muireann sat back, wiped her eyes, and said, "Thank you for that. I obviously needed it."

He smiled and said, "My pleasure, lass. I wish I could've done that for you when we were weans. But better late than never, I suppose." She returned his smile and nodded while petting Ula.

"Now, I have a bit more to say, and then I'll leave you alone. I highly doubt that Lorcan has any feelings for Máire. I'm not sure he ever did, really. I think perhaps the heightened emotions from the trauma they both endured might have colored their feelings briefly. No, I think he just really hates to lose. He's hyper-competitive, so for him to feel like he lost at something, especially, as he said, without an opportunity to actually fight for it—it was just too much for his ego to take. It's been eating at him, and today, he gave in to that obsessive ambition of his and made an arse of himself."

Muireann rolled her eyes and replied, "My ego was wounded is hardly what I would call a valid excuse."

"Oh, agreed. He fecked up nicely, and you should make him pay for it. In my experience, understanding someone's motives tends to ease things on the way to reconciliation."

She snorted, "Reconciliation? Not only did he insult me tremendously, he did it in public. How can I ever trust him again? I don't know if there's any coming back from that level of disrespect, brother."

"And I can understand that viewpoint, lass. I'm just hoping to pay forward the kindness my mam did me and urge you to consider your next steps thoughtfully. I'm not saying he deserves a second chance. Then again, I probably didn't deserve one, either. Just be sure the relationship isn't worth the effort, that's all. Because you've looked very happy lately."

"I have been," she admitted with a sigh. "That's why this hurts so much. I thought we were both happy. And now I don't know what to think."

"My suggestion is to give yourself whatever time you need. If you need to leave him twisting in the wind—and believe me, he is twisting—do what's right for you, love. If he's worth having, he'll be there when you're ready."

He stood up, kissed the top of her head, and said to Ula, "Take care of her, eh?" The raccoon nodded her agreement.

He squeezed Muireann's shoulder and left her to her thoughts.

⁂

Tréan yawned widely, stretching like the big cat he was. *I wonder if Lorcan and Muireann will sleep here or in her room tonight. I guess I'll find out soon enough. I would think they'll either be by momentarily or send Ula over here to keep me company.*

The lion had just settled his enormous golden head back on his paws, content to snooze a bit longer, when the door flew open so hard it smacked loudly against the wall and rebounded back into Lorcan, making him even angrier as he slammed it shut.

"Dare I ask?" the familiar drawled. Lorcan nearly snarled at him, "Not if you're wise."

"Hmm, that sounds like a value judgement to me. Good thing I value my own judgement. What did you feck up? You wouldn't be this angry if it weren't your fault."

The Shadow Weaver was one moment breathing hard, clenching and unclenching his fists, obviously furious, and the next moment, it seemed he deflated and collapsed into a chair.

"I may have destroyed the best thing that's ever happened to me. Over my idiotic ego. I'm such a fecking eejit." He buried his face in his hands with a mournful sigh.

"Well, spit it out. I can't help if I don't know the details."

Lorcan recited the painful details of what had happened. He didn't sugarcoat or omit any details.

When he was done, the lion gave a dry chuckle and said, "You certainly don't do anything halfway, eh?"

Lorcan sighed again and replied, "No, I don't know how."

"Well, lad, this knot you've created will take some time to unravel. Hopefully, the lass has a forgiving heart and a decidedly unvengeful nature. But you're still going to pay. Quite a lot, I would guess."

"I'd do whatever she asked if she'd forgive me. I'm just afraid I hurt her too badly. Gods, sometimes I'm as dim as they come."

"We all have our moments, Lorcan. True, yours was pretty spectacular, but I think the lass might surprise you. I'm afraid now all you can do is wait and see."

"Brilliant. Something else I suck at."

Someone knocked on the door, and the Fomori rose to answer it. Calder was on the other side and said, "Mind if I come in for a bit?" Lorcan gestured for him to enter, and they sat in a couple of chairs in his sitting area.

"I've just been to see Muireann, and you have got your work cut out for you, lad," Calder began.

"I know. I'm a fecking eejit."

"Join the club. I felt the same way not so long ago. I was able to redeem myself, and hopefully so will you."

"I don't even know where to start. Do I even stand a chance with your sister?"

"Well, probably not today. Or tomorrow. It's going to take time. You ripped her heart out. Publicly. And she is not at all happy about being disrespected like that. I have to say I'm not terribly happy about the state she's in right now, either."

"I know. I don't know why I get like this! The fact is, I don't even really—"

"Want Máire? I didn't think you did. The whole display

looked like a toddler throwing a temper tantrum because they didn't get their way."

"Ouch. Not saying it's not true, but still, ouch."

"Oh, lad, you're just lucky Áine isn't here. You'd already be missing your nipples."

Lorcan gulped. "That bird is unnerving."

Calder barked a laugh, "You have no idea. I've never spent so much time hunting for gold and jewels to stay on Her Majesty's good side. It's a good thing she is easily bribed."

"She can hold a grudge for a very, very long time. Her vengeance is legendary," Tréan added.

The Fomori gulped again. "Let's hope I can mend this before she's back, or I might not have to worry about the coming monsters."

Calder took a deep breath and said, "I wish you luck, lad. My sister has been hurt. Deeply. Healing from that, if it's possible, will take time. My advice is to be receptive and eager to do whatever she asks if it will earn her trust back. Right now, I'm not sure what she'll decide. But you might want to begin planning some epic apology, one that involves your public humiliation, preferably. You hurt and humiliated her publicly; I guarantee this doesn't improve without an equally public show of penance."

"I'll do anything she asks."

"That's a good start. Might I also suggest writing her a letter? I've discovered she is someone who needs time to process her emotions. Right now, she thinks you want to be with Máire and that she was nothing to you but a plaything. Letting her know how you really feel and what was going on in that thick head of yours will give her a chance to know what your true motivation was and have time to process the resulting feelings. Oh, and feel free to borrow that line; I'd suggest self-deprecation should be a large part of this letter."

The Shadow Weaver nodded and said, "I'll start right away. I'm sorry you got dragged into the middle of this, but thank you for helping us."

They both stood and clasped forearms. "Happy to help. Try to stay positive and give her the time she needs. She deserves that."

Lorcan nodded again and opened the door for Calder. After he was gone, the Fomori leaned against it and said, "Gods save me from myself. Tréan, I hope you're ready to help me with this letter. It's got to be perfect."

Family

is life

19

Aisling, Áine, and Lir landed gently on the northwest coast of Gorias, the rising sun casting long shadows before them. The seer turned to the familiars and said, "Remember what I said earlier, loves. The gods you will meet could make all the difference in the battle to come. Somehow, you must convince them to help. They will test you, but I know in my heart you are up to the challenge. Impress them, because all our lives depend on it. Then, keep them on task and get them back to Tíonol.

"I have packed some food for your journey. There is a small island, approximately three and a half days flight to the northwest. If you take turns riding in that marvelous little bag of yours, you should both arrive in good health. You can sleep in there, right?"

Lir nodded and said, "It's a strange environment, but we should be able to eat and sleep while riding in the expando-bag."

"Good enough then. Make haste and take care of each other."

They had already decided that Àine would fly the first leg of the journey, so Lir shifted to his fainting goat form and crawled inside the bag.

The phoenix took one last look at Aisling and said, "We will do our best." Then, she launched herself into the air and began winging her way toward the islands of the gods.

The ancient Air Fae whispered, "I know you will, a stór. I just hope it's enough."

⚭⚭⚭

She was less than two hours into her flight when Áine decided she was not cut out for solitude. She decided to test a theory and used her beak to jiggle open the neck of the expando-bag. Once it was slightly open, she bellowed into it, "Goat Boy! Can you hear me?"

A slightly muffled but audible reply could be heard, "Yes, can you hear me?"

"Yes! Oh, thank the gods, I thought I was going to lose my freaking mind! Now, we can talk during the flight." She paused for a bit, then said, "What should we talk about?"

Lir took a moment to consider and responded, "I, for one, am tired of worrying about this meeting with the gods. We know it's coming, and there's absolutely nothing we can do to prepare because we don't really know anything about them. So, I say feck it. Let's sing. You pick the first song, and we'll belt it out."

"Fine by me, lad. Let's start with Bohemian Rhapsody."

"Excellent choice."

The two familiars sang loudly as the phoenix flew at a steady clip toward the northwest, only adding the occasional dip and twirl to her flight. *Life without a sense style is hardly worth living, after all,* she thought with a mental grin.

They had decided to both fly for the last section of the trip to Clochán Island. Their journey had been tiring thus far, and they were looking forward to eating, and especially sleeping, on solid ground.

The tiny speck they had spotted on the horizon a few hours ago was quickly growing more prominent. The sky was full of puffy, pink and purple, cotton candy clouds, and above that, a swath of deep blue was sprinkled with a scattering of tiny, pinprick stars. A glowing orange disk bathed the water beneath them in shades ranging from honey gold to fiery copper as it descended to its nightly rest. There was a hazy pink area a little north of the setting sun, and the very tips of mountain tops could be seen through the thick cloud cover.

As they approached the island, they discovered it contained a multitude of flora, including several flowering trees in full bloom. The familiars landed next to one of the larger trees, its branches laden with a plethora of pink blossoms, and both dropped to the ground in exhaustion.

"Son of a bee-atch! I'm worn slick! We should've asked Máire for some kind of airplane artifact so we could ride the damn thing instead of using our wings like a couple of chumps!"

Lir chuckled and said, "We'll live, lass. We knew it would be a trying journey, but now we can rest a few days to regain our strength, then head on to the gods' islands."

"Yeah, yeah, I'm just saying we could've saved ourselves some effort. But whatevs, we're here now. Let's have some snacks," Áine suggested, removing the expando-bag from her neck and sitting beneath the big tree. Lir quickly joined her, shifted to chimp form, and dug out their provisions for the evening meal.

They ate the sandwiches Aisling had prepared for them as they watched the sun slip the rest of the way beneath the world's edge. "How do you think they're doing back home?" the phoenix asked.

Lir finished chewing the bite he'd just taken and responded, "I'm sure they're fine, love. They're smart, and strong, and capable."

She sighed and said, "I know. I didn't think I'd miss them quite this much."

He nudged her with his shoulder, offering his own form of comfort.

"Bah! Don't mind me, Goat Boy. I'm just tired and getting all mopey. Let's get some sleep."

Lir shifted back to his fainting goat form and curled into a ball. Áine snuggled up next to him, and soon they were sleeping deeply.

⁂

Lasair picked her long, needle-like teeth clean using a sharp splinter of bone. Cré and Ruaig had just finished gorging themselves and were curled up next to the fire pit, swiftly drifting off to sleep.

Tonn was busy licking the grease from her talons when the tell-tale signs of a vision struck out of nowhere. Her back arched, eyes rolling back into her head, breath coming shallow and fast. The others perked up a bit, anxious to hear what the water dragon had seen.

The images came so swiftly that it was difficult for her to make sense of them. She saw fiery and midnight black wings beating with desperation, teeth and claws rending flesh, the ocean (her precious ocean!) filled with writhing bodies and far too much blood. There were images of her and her fellow gods fighting amidst the chaos and carnage. And a brief glimpse of familiar blue eyes followed by the bitter taste of ash.

When her mind cleared and her body returned to normal, she looked at the others and let out a low whistle. "You know how I warned you all that shit was about to hit the fan? It's almost here. And we have a choice to make."

She described her vision the best she could and gave them her interpretation of the images. They went back and forth, discussing their options and the ramifications of each.

"Is it really almost over?" Lasair asked in disbelief.

Tonn shrugged, "You know how this goes. I see glimpses and shadows and piece things together as I'm able. But that is certainly how it looks at the moment."

"What are we going to do?" Cré asked.

Ruaig sighed and said, "The best we can."

Family

is life

20

Lorcan raised a hand to knock on the door to the office Deirdre used while on Earth, but she called out, "Come in, lad," before he had touched it. *How does she do that? I know she's a seer, but that's a wee bit creepy.*

He opened the door and took a seat in front of the desk she sat behind. She offered him a small smile as she put her elbow on the desk and dropped her chin into her hand. She gave him a piercing look, which he was embarrassed to say made him squirm a bit.

"How are preparations for the coming incursion?" she asked finally.

"Last I checked, things were going well. They are a bit ahead of where Máire thought they'd be at this point, so that's a good sign."

"Good to know," she replied, still giving him a look that made him a bit uncomfortable. "So, how do you think the mission will go with Muireann embarrassed and broken-hearted? Because that seems to me to be a complication we really do not need."

He sighed. *Bloody hell. I'd rather speak with my mam about this than Aintín Dee, and that's saying something.*

"I know, I know. I've been a fecking eejit. I don't know what's wrong with me sometimes."

"Yes, lad, you have. But I suspect that the impending battle's stress has you a bit more tightly wound than usual. And you're a wee bit intense on your best day," she explained with a slight grin. "Be that as it may, that's no excuse for the way you betrayed Muireann's trust and the public disrespect you've shown her is appalling, love." She pinned him beneath her gaze to drive the point home, and he found himself squirming again.

"I'm sorry, Aintín Dee, I really am. I know I fecked things up—badly. But I don't know how to fix it. And I genuinely want to fix it," he explained, his expression pained and his tone bordering on frantic. "Can you tell me how?"

Her expression softened, and she reached across her desk for his hand, squeezing it when he clasped hers. "Oh, lad, I wish I could solve this problem for you, but I'm afraid that's something only you can do. But I can give you a few suggestions. First, you are going to need to apologize profusely. And you are going to have to let her dictate the terms and speed of your reconciliation, if that's even possible. For both of your sakes, I hope it is because I think you two are a good match. But that will be entirely up to her, love. Lastly, don't hesitate to ask your friends and family for help. I know they will do whatever they can for you."

"Thanks for the advice. I'll take all the help I can get. Calder said much the same and suggested I write her a letter so I could apologize and give her time to process it without pressure. I've been working on it, but it's not quite right yet."

"I think that's a good idea, and Calder certainly has experience making amends," she responded with a wry grin. "Keep working on it, but don't let the search for perfection cost you the opportunity to begin the healing process. An earnest, well-intentioned message delivered promptly will always trump a perfect message drafted too late to be of any use."

He nodded, thankful for her guidance.

"Thank you for the update, a stór. I will check in on the captive Shadow Weavers and bring them up to date. Please get to at least a neutral state with Muireann. I know she's a professional and would never jeopardize the mission on purpose, but sometimes, it's hard to see past a broken heart. Can you do that for me?" She gave his hand another squeeze and released it.

Lorcan stood and nodded again. "I will do my best, Aintín Dee. I fecked things up and will try my damndest to make things right again."

"Good lad."

Later that evening, at the agreed-upon time, Deirdre was alone in her office; she took a few centering breaths to calm her breathing and heart rate. Once she felt grounded, she reached for Rónán, finding it easier to connect with him the more often she did it.

Lad, is that you? she asked, even though she was confident it was.

Yes, we're all here together, he replied.

Excellent. I just got an update, and the artifacts are being produced even faster than we'd hoped, so that's good news. Have there been any new developments on your end?

Not really. I feel a lot better now that someone always comes with me when I go out. And I'm finally able to sleep better with the other Shadow Weavers. He paused slightly, gathering his thoughts.

What is it, lad?

Well, Brian and Orla want me to tell you that Balor is becoming more unstable. They think he's losing his grip on his sanity.

Thank you for letting me know. I want all of you to be extra cautious. You need to hold on for a couple more weeks. We're coming, I promise you.

I know you are. We'll be careful.

Deirdre severed the contact, sat back in her seat, and pinched the bridge of her nose. *I need a bloody pint. Lorcan isn't the only one tightly wound with all this stress.*

She took a deep breath, then gasped as an image flickered through her mind. She was seated on the edge of a bed, and someone was behind her, rubbing her shoulders. Their hands were warm and strong, and a feeling of longing washed over her so intensely that it brought tears to her eyes. She tried to turn her head and see who it was, but the image slipped from her mind like water trickling through her fingers. The loss she felt was so sharp that she let out a soft whimper.

She took a moment to calm her breathing and regain her equilibrium. Then she rose from her chair and crossed the room to a cabinet where she kept her best whiskey. *Feck the pint, something stronger is called for this evening.* She poured herself a stiff drink, swirling the amber liquid in the cut crystal glass before taking a sip and letting it warm its way down her throat to her stomach. *And someday soon, I better bloody well figure out what these odd visions mean. I'm sick and tired of not knowing what I don't know.*

HALLOWED ELEMENTS

Family

is life

21

"Shake a leg, Dris! We need to get the training started, and if you were any more laid back, you'd be horizontal."

The old porcupine stopped ambling behind Fintan and sat down. "Feck off, ye old wanker! I'll get there when I get there. And now I feel the need to take a break." She looked away from him, lifted her head, and sniffed disdainfully, obviously offended.

"Bloody hell!" The elder said, then he closed his eyes, took a deep breath, and counted silently to ten. Afterward, he opened his eyes and said, "I'm sorry, lass. Being late makes me cranky, but I didn't mean to take it out on you. Can we please continue?"

The familiar considered for a moment, then replied, "I suppose." She stood up and, to her credit, attempted to move a bit faster than before.

When they arrived at the training area, the Fianna had their regiments spread out across the grounds with familiars, their own and unbonded, winding throughout the group. Emer and Grady waited at the front for them.

Fintan and Dris stepped up beside them and looked at Keegan, who activated her air power to amplify his voice with a twisting hand gesture. "Well now, ye dossers! It's time to learn all the details of skin bonding. The leopard and wolf will lead you through it all."

Emer snorted and said, "The leopard thanks you, Fintan." She turned her attention to the crowd of warriors and said, "The old man was correct; Grady and I will show you everything you need to know about skin bonding. I'm assuming most, if not all, of you saw the original demonstration done with Calder and Lir. So, today, I would like to demonstrate skin bonding with multiple familiars."

She nodded to Cara and Riley, standing nearby, and they joined the group at the front. Grady nodded at a small group of unbonded familiars, who also joined them.

"If you are a bonded Fae, your familiar should be the first to skin bond, if at all possible. The first connection made is the strongest mental connection. Now, I am going to skin bond with Cara, and then three of these unbonded familiars will also connect with her. She can then describe what she's feeling and hearing during the process so you'll better understand what to expect."

Emer and the unbonded familiars walked a few paces away from Cara. The leopard loped a few steps and leaped toward her. She seemed to disintegrate in mid-air and reform on the Air Fae's stomach as a tattoo.

Cara's eyes widened as she heard her familiar's voice in her mind. "She wants me to tell the unbonded familiars to go one at a time so I can adjust between each bonding. Oh, and I'm supposed to tell you what I'm feeling and hearing. When she bonded to my stomach, I felt a tingling sensation, but it wasn't painful or anything. And when she speaks to me, it's like I'm hearing my own thoughts, but they're in her voice, and I can tell it's separate from me." She paused a moment, obviously receiving instructions from Emer. "Okay, the others can start now, one at a time, please."

A coyote stepped forward, took a couple of trotting steps then launched himself at her thigh. The same dissolving and reforming as a tattoo process happened again. Her brain seemed chaotic for a moment, but then she heard Emer saying, "That was successful, love. The other familiars will try not to speak directly to your mind, so they don't distract you. They will speak to me, and I will relay their messages." Cara mentally nodded and said, "Two down, two to go. It was an odd sensation at first, but Emer quickly managed things. I'm being told that the first familiar to bond will be the speaker for all of them. The other familiars can speak to the Fae they've skin bonded with, but that should only be done in an emergency. Otherwise, our brains will get very noisy, which could be a fatal distraction in battle. Oh, and she said to warn you that if the Fae gets wounded, all familiars should unbond immediately. Please remember that and give blanket permission if that happens! If a Fae dies, any familiars skin bonded with them also die."

It was so silent after that pronouncement, you could've heard a pin drop as the gravity of the situation sank in. Cara took a deep breath and nodded to the seagull who was next in line. They repeated the same process and then a young wolf skin bonded as well.

"Well, my brain feels very full, I guess is the best way to describe it. It's not unmanageable, but we will need to practice this. With a little work, this shouldn't be a distraction."

She closed her eyes to concentrate and said, "Emer

would like Grady and Riley to begin the process, so you all can see everything once more before you try it yourselves.

The wolf and Earth Fae skin bonded, then another three unbonded familiars repeated the action. Riley's eyes widened with each new connection, but after a few moments, he seemed to relax. He motioned for Cara to amplify his voice.

"That is certainly an odd sensation, but I believe she's right. Once we've practiced a bit, and provided the unbonded familiars don't all start talking at once, we should be able to function like this quite nicely."

Cara looked thoughtful again and explained, "Emer tells me that the individual familiars can unbond in any order, and they can do so singly or as a group. Now, she and Grady are going to unbond so they can go amongst you and answer any questions you might have as you try it for yourselves. The unbonded familiars will remain a bit longer so we can practice operating with multiple bonds. When the first familiar unbonds, the next one in line takes over as speaker for the others."

Cara and Riley closed their eyes and silently gave the signal for their familiars to unbond. The wolf and leopard tattoos seemed to dissolve and the familiars reformed a short distance away.

Emer and Grady began moving among them, encouraging and answering questions. Everyone had a chance to bond and unbond multiple times to become more comfortable with the process.

When the wolf approached the Shadow Weavers, he could hear one side of a tense conversation. Lorcan was staring at the giant lion tattoo intertwined on his chest with his numerous pre-existing Celtic knotwork tattoos, saying heatedly, "I know I need to finish it and give it to her, but it's not ready yet, Tréan! I can't feck this up, too!"

He couldn't help the dark chuckle that escaped his lips. The Fomori narrowed his eyes at the familiar, then sighed and said, "Great, someone else has come to laugh at me. Bloody hell, I'm a joke."

"I'm sorry, lad. It's just you reminded me so much of Riley when he made an arse of himself to Cara. He was entirely stuck in his head and so terrified he was going to make things worse that he made things worse. I hope you'll forgive me for saying it, but your situation seems incredibly similar."

"Well, do you have anything useful to add, or would you rather just make fun of me?"

Grady channeled Áine momentarily and replied, "Can't I do both?" Lorcan rolled his eyes and sighed again. "Sorry, lad, just doing my part to pick up the snark slack while the bird is gone. But I do have a suggestion. After this training, I will bring Riley and a few others who might be helpful to your room. We will help you hammer out this letter that has you paralyzed, and hopefully, you can move forward."

The Shadow Weaver took a deep breath and said, "Thank you. I've got to do something because I can't even stand to be around myself right now. My little sister told me this morning I needed to 'grow a pair' and make up with Muireann because I was getting on her nerves. And I can't say I blame her."

"We'll do our best to help, lad. Now, best get back to practicing."

◈◈◈

Muireann, who had found a spot as far as physically possible from Lorcan, was practicing the process with Sláine near Liam's regiment. The healers had decided that even though they were expecting to spend their time during the battle healing injuries rather than participating directly in combat, it was wise for them to have at least a basic understanding of how to skin bond. You never knew what might be helpful in a chaotic situation.

Sláine glanced at her fellow healer and commented, "So, love, have you spoken with Lorcan since that nonsense during the hurling match?"

Her friend's face went stony, and she snapped, "No, and I don't intend to. He can bloody well rot for all I care."

"Mhmm. If you say so."

Muireann narrowed her eyes and replied, "I'm not sure what you're implying, but I can guarantee I have moved on. I'm sorry I ever gave him the time of day."

Sláine shrugged and said, "You don't have to convince me. But it sounds like you might need to convince yourself." She looked at the heartbroken Water Fae and said, "I'm sorry, lass. I don't mean to upset you. I think it's not as cut and dried as you'd like to believe, but I will drop the subject for now."

"Thank you. I appreciate that."

"How about we go for a ride after training? That always helps to clear my head; maybe it'll do the same for you."

Muireann thought a moment, then said, "Why not? Thinking about something else would be a welcome distraction."

Lorcan finished signing his name with a flourish and sighed deeply. *I've done my best. The next step is up to her.*

Riley, along with Grady, Emer, and several other familiars and Fae, had all crowded into Lorcan's room to help him work through what he wanted to say in his letter. The Shadow Weaver felt like an imbecile since he'd always considered himself a gifted writer. But this was just too important.

So, he had taken all their advice and sifted through it until he could cobble together a message he felt captured the appropriate mixture of 'You're the best thing that's ever happened to me' and 'I've been a douche canoe.' That last bit was Riley's suggestion, claiming it was a phrase Áine especially enjoyed using when people annoyed her. If it helped repair this seriously smoldering bridge, he would use whatever derogatory term was necessary.

"When are you planning to give it to the lass?" Emer asked. Tréan snorted and said, "You just don't want to miss the show." The leopard scoffed and said, "Nonsense. But perhaps it would be good to lend the lad some moral support."

"Could I make a suggestion?" Riley asked. Lorcan nodded. "Tomorrow is an American holiday, their Independence Day. I've been told that when we're done with training, they're planning a barbecue, a game of their version of football, and after sunset, there will be fireworks. I would give it to her at dinner. If you're lucky, she might respond before the evening ends."

Another sigh escaped Lorcan's lips. "I won't get my hopes up for that, but I think it will be a relief to give it to her. If she never speaks to me again after that, at least I will know I tried."

Tréan laid his giant head in Lorcan's lap, offering moral

support. The Fomori absently ran his fingers through the lion's tawny mane, thankful for his friendship. They hadn't been bonded long, but imagining his life without the big cat was impossible.

"Tomorrow it is. Thank you all for your help. Here's hoping it makes a difference."

<hr />

Aoife and Tommy had portaled to Kansas City for the Fourth of July celebration. When she heard about the holiday and the plan to offer everyone barbecue, she declared she would be in charge of that and began educating herself on techniques purported to produce the best Kansas City-style barbecue.

As a result, there were rows of grills and smokers, all filled with delectable cuts of meat. Tables were filled with all the usual side dishes—baked beans, cheesy corn, cole slaw, potato salad—she had certainly done her homework.

The Ó Faoláin brood, and anyone even remotely related to them, were all pressed into service, helping the beloved elder create a feast. She conducted the preparations like the maestro she was, using her ever-present wooden spoon as part baton, part cudgel. She rarely followed through on her threats, but Conor stole so many tastes that he would probably have bruises on the back of his hands tomorrow.

When everything was ready, Aoife called to Siobhán, "Would you mind, a stór?" A piercing whistle called them all to the rows of picnic tables laid out for the meal.

Shay amplified his voice and said, "Could I have your attention for a moment, please?" Everyone quieted down, and he continued, "Fáilte! I just wanted to take a moment and thank Aoife Ó Faoláin for her work in preparing this feast for us today." He paused and led a round of applause for her, which flustered her so much her cheeks turned bright pink. But she couldn't stop smiling.

"Brilliant! Since there are so many of us, we have set up several rows of tables to help us get through the lines more quickly. We will start at the front, and as soon as the table in front of you has almost made it through, please take your place in line.

"After dinner, several Fae who are familiar with American football have proposed a friendly game. If you're interested, feel free to join in.

"And finally, the highlight of the American Independence Day celebration is fireworks! How they manage to create those light displays without magic is a mystery. That will begin just after sunset. Now, let's eat!"

The Fae filed through the lines, picking out the food that appealed to them and finding a spot at the picnic tables. All four Ó Faoláin brothers and their beloveds, as well as Muireann, Croía, Dillon, and Collin, were seated at one of the tables closest to the food, which was convenient since they put a healthy dent in the food.

Conor, who had just finished his fourth helping of cheesy corn after downing a plate full of ribs, brisket, potato salad, and cole slaw, said, "Bloody hell that was good!"

Keegan glanced at him and asked, "What do they normally serve at a barbecue in Ireland?"

"Rain and alcohol," he replied with a straight face. She had the misfortune to be taking a drink at the time and nearly sprayed it out of her nose. Calder rolled his eyes at his brother while rubbing and patting her back as she sputtered and coughed.

Conor flashed his dimples and said, "Where's the lie,

deartháir beag?" Collin and Croía snorted, which made the rest of the table join in the laughter. Even Muireann smiled, though she looked as though she'd rather be anywhere else.

"Speaking of alcohol, who has a big bag of cans? A mighty thirst is upon me," Liam asked. Sláine elbowed him and said, "There's a whole bloody bar in the corner, go help yourself." He got up and began to head that way, and she called after him, "And bring me a pint!"

Several others called after him to get them drinks as well, so Niall and Collin hopped up to help him carry everything back.

Suddenly, Muireann tensed up, her shoulders bunching up around her ears. Sitting across from her, Calder noticed the change and looked over his shoulder at Lorcan approaching the table. He had a somber but determined look on his face as he came around to her side of the table, stopping at a respectful distance behind her.

Her brother took her hand and gently squeezed it for moral support. She glanced at him, relaxing just a bit.

Lorcan cleared his throat and said, "I don't mean to bother you, Muireann. I just wanted to give you this. I'd appreciate it if you would read it. That's all I ask." He dropped an envelope in front of her, her name written in beautiful, flowing script across the front.

She picked it up and nodded, still not looking at him. He sighed softly, then went back the way he came.

Calder looked at her questioningly and asked, "Do you want some company while you read it? I could go with you, or maybe Sláine—"

"Of course, I will. If you want me to," the other healer replied.

Muireann looked between them and said, "Thank you

both, but I'd like to read it alone first. I may want to talk about it later, but I'll need to collect my thoughts."

She stood and walked calmly toward her room; the envelope clasped tightly in her shaking hand. She didn't see it, but a pair of green-flecked, amber

eyes followed her every move until she was out of sight.

⟁⟁⟁

Once everyone had finished eating, Keegan lifted herself a few paces into the air and amplified her voice, saying, "If any of you would like to learn how to play American football, please meet over in the meadow beside the corral."

Several Fae had gathered when she and the rest of the Fianna headed over there. Some wanted to learn to play, but more were interested in watching first. Keegan and Cara, along with Calder and Liam, who had developed an appreciation for the sport while visiting Kansas City, tooks turns explaining the rules and demonstrating the basic moves.

Tréan bumped Lorcan and said, "Are you sure you want to do this? The last time you played a game, it didn't end well."

The Shadow Weaver gave him a dose of side eye and said, "Very funny. Yes, I'm sure. I'm a nervous wreck knowing she's reading my letter. I need to hit something. This seems like a perfect opportunity."

"Just don't hurt anyone, lad. Especially Corley. I feel like that would make the situation worse, not better."

"I'm not going to hurt him. Or anyone. Much. Besides, I believe it has finally sunk into my thick skull that I was not mad at him; I was letting my ego rule me. I've decided I'm not fond of that at all. But I still want to hit something."

Lorcan joined the other Fae being divided into teams. Calder raised an eyebrow at him, and the Fomori said, "Don't worry. I need to do something physical. I can't abide just standing around waiting."

The Dúbailte considered that, then nodded, and went back to helping decide who to put where. Keegan whispered to him, "Are you sure that's okay?" as she nodded toward Lorcan. Calder shrugged and said, "He says it's fine. I think he doesn't know what to do with himself. And he probably needs to hit something."

She shook her head and mumbled, "Guys and hitting stuff."

Fintan had volunteered to be the referee. He had visited America a few decades ago and fell in love with the game.

"Listen up ye dossers! I'll be flipping a coin to see who kicks off and who receives. If you have no idea what I'm talking about, you'll figure it out soon enough." The old Fire Fae flipped a coin, and the game got underway.

With their natural athletic ability, the Fae picked up the idea pretty quickly. Before long, it was hard to tell they hadn't been playing it their whole lives.

Máire, of course, was a badass. She, Keegan, and Cara were a force to be reckoned with, and the others on their team enjoyed every minute of it. Máire was playing quarterback and she threw a long pass to Keegan as Corley was coming to sack her. She got the throw off in time, barely, but was planted by her love the next second.

"Oof!" The air gushed from her lungs as, even though he attempted to keep from fully crushing her, his not-insubstantial weight landed on her torso. "Oi, I'm sorry, lass! Didn't mean to squish you like a bug! But now that I'm down here—" He leaned forward to nuzzle her neck, but she punched him in the ribs and said, "Get the feck off of me, Corley! You are not getting laid in the middle of a football game!"

He laughed and rolled off her just as Calder plowed into Keegan downfield, causing the ball to pop high into the air. Lorcan happened to be standing nearby, caught the ball as it descended, and immediately took off toward the opposite goal.

He did a decent job of evading pursuit until the only thing standing between him and the goal was Liam. The Fomori was a few inches taller, but the Earth Fae was wider. When the two of them collided, the resulting crunch made everyone wince. As they both lay there on the ground, Lorcan started laughing.

"What the bleeding hells are you laughing at?" Liam managed to wheeze out.

Through his continued laughter, the Shadow Weaver sputtered, "I needed that!"

Sláine stomped onto the field and yelled, "Fecking eejits, the lot of you!" She knelt by Lorcan first and extended her senses into his bloodstream, riding it around his body, sensing the various injuries.

"You've got two cracked ribs and more bruises than I care to count. I'll fix the ribs, but you'll live with the bruises."

His cackling had finally slowed down to an occasional chuckle. "That's fine. Totally worth it."

She turned her attention to Liam. After scanning him, she said, "You're just badly bruised. And you will also live with them."

She stood up and said, "Sorry, you're going to have to find some other way to maim yourselves. Football is over for today."

She turned back to her love and said, "You and I need to

talk." She reached her hand down to help him stand up. Then she turned on her heel and headed toward her room, expecting Liam to follow. Which he did.

She reached her room, Liam close behind, and opened the door, gesturing for him to go first. She came after him, softly latching the door behind her. As he turned around, she tackled him onto the bed and said, "Stop fecking scaring me! I'm anxious enough as it is."

"I'm sorry, love. I was just surprised and couldn't get out of the way. But I'm fine, lass," he murmured, wrapping his arms around her, nuzzling her neck.

She sighed and let herself melt into his embrace. Liam kissed his way up her neck to her lips, slowly and softly, but she was in no mood for soft. She deepened the kiss, nipping his bottom lip, pressing herself against his body, her hips grinding against his.

He let out a moan, burying one hand in her long, silky hair and using the other to grip her ass, pressing her even harder against his stiffened length. He broke the kiss and said, "Can I taste you?"

She gasped, then nodded, and began climbing up his torso until her knees were on either side of his face. He hooked one finger around the silky deep blue panties she wore, sliding the material to the side. Gripping her ass with both hands, he lowered her onto his face, his tongue finding her slit, and he began lapping at her clit, occasionally pausing to worry it between his teeth gently.

Moaning loudly now, Sláine rocked back and forth, grinding herself against his tongue. Liam moved his right hand forward and slid two fingers deep into her core. She gasped again and started really riding his face as he began pumping his fingers in and out, his tongue and teeth working her clit a bit harder. A few moments later, she clenched hard against his fingers and drenched his face.

Once her heartbeat and breathing calmed, she crawled back down Liam until they were face to face again. He pressed his lips to hers, letting her taste herself on his lips and tongue. She could feel his rock-hard cock pressing against her through their battle clothing. She reached down and freed it, stroking up and down, teasing and taunting him for a bit.

She called a water condom to coat his length, then straddled him, lowering herself until he was buried deep inside her. She rotated her hips, moaning as he pressed against the most sensitive area inside her.

Liam may have whimpered slightly, which caused an evil grin to break over her face. "Do you like that, love?" she whispered, circling her hips again. Her speed slowly increased until she felt herself about to tumble over the edge, then she growled in his ear, "Come with me, a chuisle mo chroí. I want to hear you scream."

That sent them both to their climax, and Liam didn't scream alone. She collapsed on top of him, and he cradled her there for a long time. Finally, she rolled off of him, sent the water condom to the bathroom, and said, "That was amazing, love. But now I want to see the fireworks!"

She began straightening her clothes and pulling her hair up into a messy bun on top of her head.

"Are you sure you don't want to go for round two?" Liam asked, puppy dog eyes in full effect.

"Nope, I want to see fireworks. We can play some more after.

He gave a soft sigh, then stood and straightened his own clothing. She came up behind him and redid the warrior's knot tied at the base of his skull. Then they headed out to see some fireworks.

⁂

Lorcan still hadn't moved from where he'd landed after colliding with Liam. A heavy load of stress had been lifted from his shoulders when he'd felt the impact. He'd given Muireann the letter and maybe he'd knocked some sense into himself. He wasn't sure, but it was an improvement.

Everyone else had long since abandoned him, and he'd even sent Tréan with the other familiars to watch the fireworks. They had just started, and he could see and hear them just fine where he was. He was also a little afraid that if he stood up, this sense of peace would dissipate. Better not to risk it.

He turned his head at the sound of soft footsteps approaching from the side of the corral. Muireann walked toward him, but he couldn't tell from her expression if the news was good or bad. *Guess I'll find out soon enough.*

She knelt down beside him, sitting back on her knees seiza-style. She looked at the ground while she collected her thoughts, then raised her eyes to his and said, "Thank you for the letter. I appreciated the respectful tone."

"You're welcome, lass."

She paused again, then continued, "I'm not sure what to say, Lorcan. I understand what happened, I think. I know that sometimes we react without thinking, and our baser nature can take over. But just because I understand doesn't mean I can get past how you made me feel. In front of everyone. Do you have any idea how embarrassing that was? How blatantly disrespectful?" She found herself getting worked up and stopped to calm herself. She hated confrontation, but sometimes it was necessary.

Lorcan said softly, "Would you like me to answer?"

"I don't know. I, I guess so."

"I've thought of almost nothing else but how badly I treated you since it happened. I know that just because it wasn't intentional doesn't make it hurt any less. But I can promise I will do anything if it means I can have another chance with you."

"I just don't know, lad. I have to think about this some more."

Lorcan was disappointed, but he took some comfort in her speaking to him again.

He met her eyes and said, "Take all the time you need, lass. I'm not going anywhere."

She nodded, then looked up at the fireworks going off above them. "Do you mind if I watch the fireworks here?"

He smiled and patted the ground beside him, but not too close. She lay down next to him, lacing her fingers behind her head.

That was more than I expected, he thought, his smile widening slightly at the encouraging sign.

Family

is life

22

Áine and Lir stood on the northwest shore of Clochán Island, the rising sun at their backs, throwing long shadows out in front of them, as they watched the sky beginning to lighten.

The phoenix looked at the púca turned Pegasus and said, "You ready for this, Goat Boy?"

Lir took a deep breath and nodded at her. "Let's get started. Time to meet the gods."

☖☖☖

Cré rushed forward to tap the pickleball gently over the net, leaving no time for Ruaig or Tonn to return it. As the plastic ball bounced a second time, Lasair threw her paddle down, gave a shriek of victory, and jumped on her teammate's back, her crazy curls in various shades of red and orange bouncing wildly. She hugged her arms around his thick neck, careful not to take an eye out on his spiky green hair. He threw his paddle down as well and raised his arms in a vee shape, pumping his fist in the air a few times and spinning the two of them around as they celebrated their victory.

"Bloody hell! Careful with the paddles! It's a pain in the arse to replace those, you know," Ruaig complained. He gathered the abused paddles and gave the offenders a healthy dose of side-eye, tossing his long blond curls over his shoulder in irritation.

Lasair snorted, removed a ring from her finger with a giant ruby in its center, and threw it at him, saying, "We've been collecting bling for centuries. I'm certain you'll manage." The Air Dragon in Fae form caught the ring in midair and scoffed, "Just because we can replace it doesn't mean we need to be wasteful."

The winning team had already stopped listening and were busy bellowing "We Are the Champions" at the top of their lungs. Tonn, who was mildly amused and playing with her long blue dreadlocks while watching her companions' antics, suddenly threw her head back, eyes rolling up in her head, and her heart and breathing began to race.

Thankfully, Ruaig was right beside her to lower her to the ground as her legs gave out. She twitched for just a moment, and then her eyes, breathing, and heart rate all returned to normal.

She sat up, quickly looked around at the others, and said simply, "They're almost here."

The familiars had flown most of the day before they entered the edge of the mists covering the gods' islands. The sun was low in the sky, painting the clouds and haze a vivid, tawny copper shade.

Lir looked at Áine and said, "Stay nearby, lass. I don't

want to lose you in these mists." She moved a bit closer and said, "These clouds give me the heebie jeebies. I hope they don't last too long."

Wingbeats could be heard approaching them, but they sounded enormous. Both familiars looked all around them, unable to find the source of the sound.

Suddenly, a giant gust of air rushed toward them from the left, blowing them off their course for a moment before they righted and reoriented themselves.

"What the actual fuck was that?" Áine exclaimed, mildly alarmed.

"I don't know, but I think we should keep going," Lir responded. They had barely resumed flying when an even larger gust of air hit them again, this time from their right.

"Okay, that's beginning to piss me off," the phoenix declared. The two of them were hovering, trying to get their bearings, when a monstrous roar split the air. It sounded like it was coming from all around them.

Before they could decide how to proceed, a flash of red scales passed so close above them it felt like they could have reached out and touched them. Suddenly, they were being bombarded by flickers and streaks of green, blue, red, and golden wings, glimmering metallic scales glinting briefly where the setting sun occasionally broke through the clouds. The attacks came from above and below, left and right; there was nowhere to hide from the bombardment.

When a jet of water drenched the disoriented and battered familiars, Áine decided enough was enough. She let out a roar and released a blast of flame that burned off the nearby cloud cover, revealing the four elemental dragon gods.

"Fuck me sideways, that was annoying!" she yelled, glaring at the slightly amused-looking deities.

The giant blue water dragon smiled, which was a bit alarming on a dragon, and said, "I like her. She's spicy!"

The red fire dragon said, "Of course you do, she's one of mine."

"And mine," the yellow serpentine air god added as he undulated around the others.

"I want to know more about the Pegasus," the stout green and coppery earth dragon said, moving closer to Lir than was completely comfortable and looking him over with a critical eye.

"Look, while we're very flattered you find us so fascinating, and really, who could blame you, we are on the clock here," the phoenix explained.

Lir, moving a bit closer to Áine and putting some distance between himself and the overly curious Cré, said, "We have come seeking your help. We've brought your relics and beg an audience with you."

"Ooh, we haven't seen our blingy torques in forever," Lasair said. "Where are they?"

"We've got them in the expando-bag," Áine replied, tucking her chin to indicate the black bag around her neck. "Yo, can we please land somewhere? We've been flying all day, and this conversation would be much easier on the ground."

The gods glanced at each other, and then Tonn said, "Very well. Follow me."

The dragons headed due west, and the familiars stayed close so they didn't lose them in the mists, which were still fairly thick the closer they got to the gods' homes.

After a brief flight, the familiars followed their hosts as they began descending toward a large blob. Once they dove beneath the cloud cover, the blob became a grassy island covered with various kinds of livestock and other fauna.

They were guided to a slightly elevated area with a large firepit where benches and smooth, flat spots provided a place for the gods to rest and congregate in whatever shape they chose to take. Once on land, the dragons all shifted to their smaller, but no less flamboyant, Fae forms.

The fire goddes, with her flame-colored ringlets, crimson eyes, and warm, honey-colored skin, cleared her throat and said, "My name is Lasair and this is Tonn." She gestured toward her companion with mocha skin, long dreadlocks in shades of turquoise, blue, and purple, and glowing teal eyes, who nodded at them.

"The blond is Ruaig." The air god, who had ivory skin, incandescent golden eyes, and long, blond curls, gave them a little wave. "And the walking mountain is Cré." The hulking earth deity grunted and crossed his thick arms across his chest. His skin was a few shades darker than Tonn's, his hair was short, spiky, and neon green, and his chartreuse eyes twinkled with amusement despite his gruff mannerisms.

Lir nodded at each of them respectfully and replied, "I am Lir, and my companion is Áine." The phoenix was a bit starstruck and stared blankly at the four gods. "Lass, why don't you hand them the bag so they can get their relics out?"

She blinked at him several times, then said, "Oh. Yeah, okay." She wiggled the bag over her head and presented it to Lasair with her signature high kick. The fire god smiled at the show and said, "Thank you, love." She opened the bag and, one at a time, pulled forth the various torques belonging to her and her companions.

Each god slipped their torque on, the relics automatically adjusting as needed to fit around their neck, and sighed softly as it settled into place. They might be gods, but they were also dragons, and being reunited with a piece of their hoard was a welcome feeling.

Lasair began to hand the bag back to Áine, but the phoenix said, "Dig around in there some more. There should be a letter explaining our situation. Oh, and if you feel some shortbread in there, that's Fintan's birthday present, so leave that alone."

The fire goddess grinned at the thought of the phoenix ordering her around but did as the bird asked. She found the letter and read it aloud for the others to hear.

When she was done, Lir commented, "So, you can see why we're here. Both the Aos Sí and the familiars are in tremendous danger. Will you help?"

Tonn took a seat on one of the benches and said, "We will have to discuss this before we make a decision. There is more at stake than you know, and we need to weigh the ramifications carefully."

Áine appeared to be ready to argue with the dragon shifter gods, but Lir said, "We understand, of course." She glared at him and said, "Goat Boy, ain't nobody got time for—"

"I know, love. But it's not unreasonable for them to discuss it before making such a huge decision."

She sighed and said, "I guess."

In his deep, rumbling bass voice, Cré said, "We understand the urgency, lass." And Ruaig added, "But as Tonn said, you don't have all the information yet. We will move as quickly as we can."

Lasair continued, "In the meantime, Tonn and Ruaig

will find you something to eat while Cré and I create somewhere comfortable for you to sleep."

Lir and Áine nodded, content to wait for now.

Family

is life

23

The early morning sunlight filtered through the waves above her, creating a twinkling turquoise oasis, filled with brightly colored fish and other sea creatures. Muireann had decided to go for a swim before the aquatic battle training began, hoping it would clear her mind.

The last few days had been some of the most confusing of her life. Lorcan's idiotic display during the hurling match had crushed her. But then he'd given her that letter, pouring his soul into it, telling her that in the short time they'd known one another, she had captured his heart. She didn't know what to think.

She swam for a while, pausing to smile at Ula in her otter form, playing with some other familiars a short distance away. Laoise had chosen a seal, and Saoirse was a dolphin, the three chasing each other around. Occasionally, a madly cackling Ailáine and Declan, in his orca form, would crash into them, and they'd all laugh and race to catch them.

As she was watching their antics, she saw Máire and

Corley nearby, the Fire Fae wrapping her tail around his and kissing him soundly. Then, he ran the back of his hand down her cheek and swam over to join some other members of the Fianna.

Máire swam her way and motioned for them to surface. Muireann nodded, and they broke the surface.

"Good morning, lass. I know you probably don't want to talk to me—"

"No, I don't mind. I know you had nothing to do with Lorcan making an arse of himself."

Máire smiled and said, "He certainly did a brilliant job of that, eh?"

"An outstanding job."

"Well, I just wanted to perhaps shed a little light on the situation from my perspective. You helped me not so long ago, and I'd like to return the favor."

Muireann nodded. Máire collected her thoughts momentarily, then continued, "I was intrigued by Lorcan for about five minutes. He's obviously gorgeous, and his confidence is also very attractive. While I was trapped in the Fomori stronghold, he saved my life, and that tends to bring up some confusing feelings, too."

She paused again, then said, "Look, I'm not very good at this, but I'm trying to tell you that neither Lorcan nor I ever had serious feelings for the other. Corley may be a wanker at times, but he understands me. And he has stood by me at my worst. That is worth far more to me than any temporary physical attraction brought on by some sort of fecked up transference."

Muireann considered her words, nodded, and replied, "Thank you, lass. I appreciate you speaking with me."

"Of course. I hope it helps," she moved to go, but stopped and turned around, saying, "Oh, and if you decide to give him another chance, make sure to tell him how lucky he is you're even speaking to him. He really was an arrogant arse."

The healer smiled at her and responded, "If he hasn't figured that out by now, there's no hope for him. But a little reminder wouldn't hurt, I suppose."

"Good lass. Take care. I hope it works out for you, whatever you decide." She swam over to join Corley, who pulled her tightly to his side.

Muireann sighed, a little jealous at their display of affection. She turned away and came face to face with the object of her confusion.

Lorcan smiled slightly and said, "Might I have a word, lass?"

"I suppose," she replied.

"I've been thinking about what will happen to Ailáine when the battle begins. My máthair thinks that she and Fergal will be able to protect her, but I'm afraid Balor may seek out my sister and me. I was hoping perhaps she could stay with you and the other healers? I know you have no reason to help me, but for her sake—"

Muireann's eyes flashed as she said, "Don't insult me, lad. I would never endanger the lass because I might be angry with you. Of course she can stay with us. We will keep her as far from the fighting as we can manage."

He sighed in relief and said, "Thank you, Muireann. You don't know how much that means to me."

"I think I might have an inkling. No matter how much of an eejit you may have been, I have never seen you be anything but protective and loving to your little sister. I know what she means to you."

Lorcan smiled at her, shrugged, and said, "She's my Little Bug. I'd do anything for her. Even though she did tell me to 'grow a pair' the other day. Still not sure where she picked up that little nugget."

Muireann couldn't contain the laughter that bubbled up at the thought of the sweet, adolescent Shadow Weaver snarking at her brother. "Dare I ask why she said that?"

He dropped his gaze and said, "Because I was moping around like the sky had fallen."

"I see."

"Yes, well, I may not be back in your good graces, but I feel like I've at least made a bit of progress," he said, daring to lift his eyes to meet hers.

Now it was the healer's turn to look away. "I'd say that's a fair assessment." She looked back at him and narrowed her eyes, "But, if you're wise, you won't let that go to your head. I'm still not entirely certain how I feel. And until I am certain, you are firmly on my shit list, lad. Best get comfortable."

He couldn't keep a slight smirk from his lips as he replied, "Yes, ma'am."

She quirked an eyebrow at him and said, "Watch yourself. You're nowhere near as charming as you think you are."

His smirk widened a bit more, and he said, "If you say so."

An orca with a giggling Shadow Weaver hanging from his fin surfaced beside them and blew a shot of air out of his blowhole.

"Why do you keep doing that, Little Bug? You know it annoys me."

"Well, duh. You just answered your own question," she said with more giggling. Ailáine turned her attention to Muireann. "So, did he grow a pair, yet, and make up with you?"

The healer couldn't help the snort that elicited. Lorcan pinched the bridge of his nose and said, "I'm working on it. By the way, where did you hear that phrase?"

"What phrase?" she said with a grin.

"You know exactly what I'm asking. Why did you suddenly start telling me to 'grow a pair'?"

Her giggle turned into a cackle. "Conor taught me that while we were working on horseback riding. He's funny!"

"Oh yeah, he's hysterical. I can see I need to have a word with the lad," Lorcan replied.

"Don't embarrass me! Besides, can you really say you didn't deserve what I said?" she asked with far too much logic for her brother's liking.

"Fine, I won't say anything to him. But please stop using that phrase. Deal?"

She pouted a bit, but finally agreed. "Deal."

They saw Nora and Fergal moving toward them, probably to let Lorcan know they were ready to begin the training. His sister yelled out, "Mam! Da! Declan and I've been practicing our double flip. We're getting so good at it!"

Muireann watched the three adults stare at Ailáine in mild shock. She gathered it was the first time the lass had called Fergal her da. Nora leaned close and kissed her love on the cheek, who held out his arms to the youngling and said, "Come here and tell us all about it, Little Bug."

She joined them and explained how their double-flip practice had been going. Declan hung back for a moment and said, "She spent so long with very little joy in her life. I'm glad she's not wasting any time now that she's free to experience happiness with her loved ones. Just a little food for thought."

He swam over to join his bonded and her parents. Lorcan chuckled and said, "Subtle, eh?"

Muireann smiled and replied, "He means well."

"Aye, he does. I'm going to join my family so we can start the training. Thank you again, lass, for helping to keep my sister safe."

"My pleasure."

⁂

Fergal nodded to Deirdre, who made a twisting motion with her hand to amplify his voice. "Fáilte! The Shadow Weavers will lead the aquatic portion of our battle training since we've had more experience with underwater movement in our altered forms."

The Weapons Master asked everyone to transform and enter the ocean. Lorcan and several other Fomori demonstrated various technical maneuvers and underwater weapon strikes. During this aquatic portion of the battle, many of their elemental weapons would be significantly hampered, so regular physical knives and spears would be vitally important.

The Shadow Weavers had the advantage of being able to forge weapons from shadow, but the Fae would need to carry their weapons on their person. The Fae Glam cailíní had created various harnesses and holsters for the Aos Sí to strap their chosen elements of destruction firmly to their merrow bodies. They were using practice weapons while training, but the Earth Fae, with help from the Fire Clan, were busy forging a wealth of sharp and pointy implements for the coming battle.

It would take a bit of practice, but that's why they were working on it now. They had choreographed their battle strategy carefully, implementing each element, layer upon layer, to give them the best odds of a successful outcome.

Fire and Air Fae, whose elemental powers were the least effective underwater, were encouraged to stick to the shallower areas to bring their magic to bear when the Titans ascended from the ocean. As the monsters rose from the waves, attacking their heads and torsos with gusts of extreme wind and gouts of flame, could potentially catch them off guard.

Once they'd had some time to practice the moves and techniques they were shown, the familiars began harassing the Fae to simulate a bit of the chaos they were likely to experience. With his large orca form, Declan was especially effective at mimicking the attacks a large Titan might use. Several of the other familiars also chose larger water creature forms—Emer was a tiger shark, and Grady chose an inky black octopus with bright blue rings all over. It wasn't exactly the same as being attacked by a true enemy without any pulled punches, but it still helped to mentally prepare them for the stressful atmosphere they would face.

By the end of the training, the Fae had begun working in tandem, slingshotting each other to gain extra momentum for their attacks and isolating select familiars to overwhelm them.

Lorcan swam up to where Fergal and Nora were discussing the Fae's progress. "They're adapting faster than I expected," he commented, receiving nods from both.

"I knew they were capable. Now, if everything goes well, we might stand a chance," Nora added. "It's almost time for the rescue mission. Do you feel prepared to return to that place, love?"

Lorcan shrugged and said, "There's not much we can do to prepare. An unsettling amount of luck will be needed for us to succeed. If you have a favorite god, now might be a good time to say a prayer."

"Oh, I'll say a prayer, make a voodoo doll, and perform a rain dance if it'll help. But I was asking if *you* are ready to go back there. And risk running into Balor." She gave her son a sympathetic look, knowing this couldn't be easy for him.

He shrugged again and said, "I'll be fine, Mam. I've lived under that monster forever. I'm used to that. I'm more worried about one of the Fae getting hurt and being unable to stop it. Or one of the Shadow Weavers currently imprisoned being caught. Who knows what would happen to them?"

She put her hand on his shoulder and said, "Don't sell them short, lad. We just got done saying how well they were adapting."

"There's a big difference between doing well where they are safe, and things are calm and maintaining their equilibrium when they are in the kind of intensely dangerous atmosphere of the stronghold," Fergal interjected, Lorcan nodding in agreement.

"Agreed. But I still believe they will rise to the occasion. And you can help them do that, lad," she replied.

"I will certainly try," he promised.

☘☘☘

Family

is life

24

Rónán snuck another handful of juicy, deep purple blackberries from the bucket he used to collect them. Brian pretended not to notice, figuring the lad had little enough enjoyment in his current situation. If a few stolen berries made him smile, it was a small price to pay.

They were gathering fruit and vegetables from the garden later in the day than usual. The Titans had been restless lately, and it was taking longer and longer to get them to settle down. Brian thought it was most likely a result of Balor's increasing paranoia. The Chaos Faction leader appeared to be unraveling, stalking the hallways at all times of the day and night. When he came to check on the Titans, he would mumble to himself, sometimes working himself up so much he would strike out at whatever unfortunate Titan was nearest. Fortunately, the Aos Sí would be arriving soon, as things were quickly becoming untenable.

"Lad, would you gather those bags of apples and

peaches we piled over there?" Brian asked, pointing off to the left side of the garden.

"Aye, I'll grab them," the young Shadow Weaver replied. He ran over between the fruit trees to pick up the produce they'd piled there earlier. He draped the straps of the bags over his shoulder and was about to rejoin Brian when he heard a shuffling sound, followed by a deep rasping breath. He immediately froze and dropped to the ground behind one of the thick berry bushes.

"What are you doing out of your cage, little mouse?" Balor's guttural speech made it difficult to understand his words, but there was no mistaking the malice in his tone.

From where he was hidden, Rónán couldn't see the monster, but he saw Brian's expression. The adult Shadow Weaver kept his gaze lowered and his body language passive and docile. His voice, when he answered, was calm and placating.

"I'm just out here gathering some food. Normally, a whole group does this, but today the Titans are restless, so it's just me."

A low, vicious chuckle came from Balor. "I don't think I believe you. I think you are spying on me. I know someone has been following me, trying to uncover my secrets to use them against me. Is that you, little mouse? Have you been stalking me, just waiting to pounce?" The Chaos Faction leader stepped closer until Brian could smell his rancid breath.

"No! As I said, I was gathering—"

A thick, gnarled hand wrapped around Brian's throat, cutting off his air supply. "Silence! I've heard enough of your lies. It's time to join your brethren and take your place as my newest Titan."

Rónán clapped his hand over his mouth to keep from

crying out as Brian was dragged from the garden. He gathered his shadows and crept behind them, carefully keeping his distance while still keeping them in sight.

Balor strode boldly down the corridors, dragging Brian along with him, allowing him just enough air to keep him conscious. He kicked the doors to the Titans' cavern open, letting them slam against the walls and hang there limply with the hinges bent. He proceeded further into the cavern, then bellowed for the Shadow Weavers to attend him.

During the commotion, Rónán sneaked through the doorway and hid in a small, shadowed indention in the roughly hewn stone walls.

The others all came running, and when Orla saw Brian, she wailed and lurched forward, trying to get to him. Three of her companions restrained her, likely saving her from a similar fate.

Balor shook Brian like a ragdoll at the other Shadow Weavers and shouted, "You thought I wouldn't find him, but I did! I may need some of you to maintain my Titans, but I can surely spare this one."

He wrenched open a nearby cage and tossed the big Fomori inside as if he were a child, slamming the bars shut after. Brian lay in a crumpled heap, taking deep breaths and trying not to make things any worse.

Balor gripped the cage bars and cracked open his third eye, a sickly, greenish-yellow light oozing forth and bathing the Shadow Weaver in its putrid gleam. When the light struck him, Brian screamed in agony, his body spasming almost like he was seizing.

That tri-tone voice slammed into the minds of everyone in the cavern, dropping several to their knees, although the words were directed at the big Fomori in the cage. Balor loved an audience and wanted to make sure everyone understood the consequences of spying on him.

I have begun the transformation process. You will soon begin to change, and before long, you will crave my chaotic light. Once you have transformed sufficiently, chaos magic will also be yours to wield. You will likely be insane by that point, but that's a small price to pay for the glory of the Fomori, eh?

He finally closed his third eye, allowing Brian to collapse into stillness. He looked at the other Shadow Weavers and said aloud, "Don't let me catch any of you outside this cavern again, or you will all be added to my Titans. And stay away from this one. He needs to marinate for a bit."

It was so silent after Balor stomped out of the cavern you could hear a pin drop. Then, Orla wailed again, shook off the hands holding her back, and ran to the cage containing her beloved.

Brian was still very shaky, but he managed to scoot along the ground until he could grasp his wife's trembling hands through the bars of his cage. She squeezed his hands, sobbing inconsolably.

"Oh now, shush, lass. I'm still here. And the Aos Sí will be here soon. All is not lost, not yet," he consoled, his thumbs rubbing circles on the backs of her hands.

Rónán quietly walked up behind her, knelt down, and said, "I'm so sorry! This is all my fault." His eyes were welling with tears, and he looked utterly defeated.

Orla released one of Brian's hands, reached behind her, and pulled the youngling close to her. "That's the most ridiculous thing I've ever heard, lad. That monster is responsible for this and no one else. You just happened to be nearby, that's all."

He nodded, not entirely convinced but wanting so badly to believe her. "So, what do we do now?"

Orla sniffed, took a few deep breaths, then said, "We let Deirdre know what's happened when she contacts you tonight. And pray that she can help us."

※ ※ ※

The High Druid was sitting down to prepare for her check-in with the captive Shadow Weavers when a vision struck her like a lightning bolt. It was short but powerful, and when the images stopped running through her mind, she let out a deep sigh and cursed. "Bloody hell! Fecking paranoid Balor and his impulse control issues!"

She stepped into the hallway outside her office and called to her assistant, "Get Máire Doran here as quickly as possible!"

Luckily, the Fire Fae wasn't far away, and she arrived quickly, poking her head inside the open doorway and saying, "You asked to see me?"

"Yes, lass, thank you for coming so quickly. I just had a vision and I'm afraid we've run out of time. I'll be talking to Lorcan and the others shortly to let them know."

Máire's eyes widened, and she swallowed hard. "How can I help?"

"I'm about to make contact with Rónán and the other captive Shadow Weavers, but a problem with our rescue plan occurred to me. You see, while you lot are reversing the damage done to the Titans, I believe Balor will be able to detect a disturbance. After seeing my latest vision, I realized he is connected to each of the Titans, because he inundates them with chaos magic to start the process of their transformation. It forges a kind of tether between them. So, we need a way to disguise what is happening. Thoughts?"

Máire's brow furrowed as she considered the options. "What about a kind of mirror artifact that reflects the energy? I think I could make that work. We'd have to choose one of the Titans that is too corrupted to reverse, and I'd need Sláine or Muireann to help me place it, but it should be possible."

"That sounds perfect, lass. How long will it take to get that ready?"

"Maybe a day? I'll start on it right away."

"Hurry all you can, love. Time is of the essence."

After Máire left to begin creating the mirror artifact, Deirdre once again started the process of centering herself to make contact with Rónán. Once she had calmed her mind and felt grounded, she reached out to the adolescent.

Deirdre! I have so much to tell you! he responded as soon as she made contact.

I know, lad. I had a vision a short time ago. How is Brian doing?

He seems okay for now, but we don't know how long that will last. When are you coming?

Soon, love. I've already got Máire creating an artifact to help us disguise our actions from Balor. Once I meet with those going, I should know more, but I wanted to reassure you that we know what has happened and will be on the way shortly.

Rónán paused to relay the information to the other Shadow Weavers. Orla received the news with grateful tears, and Brian, still holding his wife's hands through the bars of his cell, shuddered in relief.

I will contact you later this evening once I have conferred with the others. Stay strong, we're on the way.

⚜⚜⚜

All the rescue party members, except Máire, who was already hard at work on the mirror artifact, had gathered in the High Druid's office. Deirdre quickly got the group up to speed and asked Lorcan, "How long before you can leave? We're out of time, I'm afraid."

The Shadow Weaver nodded and said, "As soon as Máire is done, we'll be ready. I'd suggest going late at night. Even Balor has to sleep at some point, and our chances of disturbing him should be lessened then."

He turned his attention to the rest of his group. "Pack any physical weapons you want to bring in a bag. Any objections to leaving tomorrow night at midnight?"

Everyone nodded solemnly, the gravity of the situation sinking in.

Deirdre looked them all over and said, "Thank you all. Corley, please fill Máire in on the details.

"Now go and prepare yourselves. The captive Shadow Weavers and Titans are counting on you."

⚜⚜⚜

Family

is life

25

Lir shook his head as Áine and the dragons took another lap around the islands Ruaig claimed as his own. They were very similar to the Air Clan island, mostly desert and dunes with plenty of thermals to aid their aerial antics.

"Come on, Cré! Get the lead out, man!" she taunted. The stout earth dragon huffed and landed next to the púca in Pegasus form.

"She's a wee bit manic, eh?" he commented, eliciting a chuckle from Lir. "That's one word for it."

The other four continued flying briefly, then Tonn and Lasair joined the spectators. As they landed, the fire dragon whistled and said, "Whew! The bird's got stamina; I'll give her that."

Ruaig and Áine continued their game of tag, chasing each other and performing incredible feats of aerial prowess. Finally, they grew tired and landed near the others.

"Day-um, I needed that! I haven't had a good game of chase in forever."

Lir replied, "I'm glad you had fun." To the dragons, he

continued, "And I was happy to see each of your islands and collections of bling, even though it took several days. But we really, really need to discuss your help with the battle the Aos Sí are facing."

The four gods shared glances, then Tonn said, "Before we discuss the details, you both need to understand something. There is more at play than you know, and there could be very real consequences, for all the Aos Sí, if we return with you. I'm not exaggerating when I say the cure could turn out to be worse than the disease."

Lir said, "It's hard for the cure to be worse than the disease when, if left untreated, the disease is almost guaranteed to be fatal. If I get a vote, I say we risk it. Are you willing to explain what these consequences are?"

The giant blue dragon shook her head, the mane of tentacles around her head swaying gently. "I'm sorry, lad, but that's not our story to tell."

Áine fluttered up onto Lir's rump and said, "I vote one thing at a time. How the hell can we worry about some vague, ominous *consequences* in the future if the monsters kill us all first?"

Lasair looked at Tonn and shrugged, saying, "They've got a point. And who knows, maybe the Fae can help us think of a solution we haven't considered?"

The water dragon sighed and said, "I hope you're right. It sounds like there's not much choice if we want to have the chance to find out." She glanced at Cré and Ruaig, saying, "What about you two? What's your vote?"

They looked at each other, then Ruaig said, "I'm game. Wouldn't be much fun if the monsters wipe out the Fae."

Cré added, "Aye. We'll deal with the repercussions afterward."

Tonn nodded and Lasair said, "Very well then, we're

agreed. It will take a bit to get everything tidied up around here, and then we'll be on our way."

Lir mumbled, "Finally."

※※※

Lir and Áine spent most of the next two days running errands for the gods. They kept livestock and prey animals on the center island for food. They had automated feeding systems to set up, and each dragon had their hoard to secure before they would even consider leaving.

The dragon hoards had surprised the familiars a bit. They all had plenty of jewels and gold and bling in general. However, each dragon also had other, more surprising, items that were important to them.

Cré, the earth dragon built like a tank, collected kittens. There were more than a dozen of them in his lair, with all manner of toys and cat trees, scratching posts, and little miniature houses for them to play in.

When they'd first seen it, Áine had simply asked, "How?"

Ruaig chuckled and said, "He sneaks off to Earth all the time and finds strays. Truth be told, we think he's a bit touched."

The earth dragon god scowled, scratching the kitten in his arms behind the ears, and mumbled, "They don't have anybody to care for them. Why shouldn't I give them a better life?"

Tonn's hoard highlighted fine art, including paintings, sculptures, textiles, and even a stunning work of quilled paper. Áine had difficulty not touching the pieces until Tonn actually growled at her for getting too close to one.

Somehow, the fact that she was in her Fae form at the time made it scarier.

Ruaig's collection included a variety of motorcycles, mostly dirt bikes. The air god even demonstrated their stunt capabilities, which fascinated Lir's daredevil side.

Knives, swords, and other bladed objects were Lasair's obsession. The walls of her lair were covered with stunning weapons, and she had a particular fondness for jeweled and intricately designed hilts.

༺❈❈❈༻

By the end of day two, the gods had decided they were ready to go and made plans to depart first thing the following morning.

They had just finished dinner and were sitting around a big bonfire. Tonn had just finished a cup of tea and set it down beside her when her eyes rolled back, and she stiffened, breathing fast.

"What the actual fuck is wrong with her?" Áine exclaimed in surprise.

"She's having a vision," Lasair explained. "They don't usually last long, and she'll tell us what she saw when it's over."

A few moments later, the water goddess came back to herself. She turned to the familiars and said, "You will both face terrible trials before this battle is done."

The phoenix gulped and looked at Lir, saying, "Well, that's not ominous at all." He nodded in agreement.

Tonn looked at her and then the púca. "I'm sorry for both of you. This will be painful but necessary if we are to have any chance of success. Knowing this, do you still intend to proceed?"

They both nodded solemnly.

"Very well," she continued. "Let us enjoy each other's company this evening. Tomorrow, we leave for Tionól and a meeting with the monsters."

☙❦☙

Deirdre was washing her face before bed, and as she patted her skin dry with a plush, purple towel, a vision struck. She dropped to her knees, nearly clipping her temple on the edge of the vanity.

The images came hard and fast, ripping through her mind in an almost painful fashion. As quick as they were, she only caught flashes and glimpses, but it was similar to the other visions she'd had recently. She saw long blond curls and had the strongest suspicion someone was smirking at her. Blue and red scales flashed by at breakneck speed, weaving in and out of smoke and fog. The green and copper shell of the largest turtle she'd ever seen shimmered beneath the waves. And throughout it all, the most confusing sense of familiarity.

Once it ended, the seer crawled a few paces to the wall and turned around, putting her back to it and sighing in despair. She wouldn't stay there, but just for a moment, she let herself feel sorry for herself. She cried softly, and after a few moments, she dried her tears, took a deep breath, and pulled herself up off the floor.

They had monsters to kill. She could cry when they were dead.

☙❦☙

Family

is life

26

The moonlit waves lapped at the shore as the rescue party members gathered to begin their journey. The Fianna were all there, as well as Lorcan, Fergal, Sláine, and Muireann.

Máire and Keegan handed out expando-bags, like the one they'd sent with Áine and Lir, so that everyone would have access to the artifacts their family had been creating over the past month. They simply had to reach inside and they could pluck out a small device that would help reverse the effects of the chaos magic Balor inflicted on those he conscripted.

Máire also carried the special artifact she had just created to help mirror the link between the Titans and their master. That one was so vital to their plan that she decided to keep it on her person.

Lorcan instructed them to enter the water, dismiss their clothing, and then trigger their aquatic form. In short order, there were thirteen merrows bobbing in the waves, their brightly colored tails muted in the pale moonlight.

"The swim will take us about thirty minutes. Stay close,

there are dangers in the ocean you are not prepared to fight, and we don't have time to save your arse because you wandered off and attracted the attention of a shark. I will lead the way, and Fergal will bring up the rear."

The Fomori dove beneath the waves, and the rest followed, taking care to keep him in sight. Although the colors appeared faded without the warm golden sunlight to brighten them, the underwater world they moved through was softly beautiful. Aquatic flora swayed back and forth to the ocean's rhythm, small fish darting to and fro, exploring like the curious creatures they were.

The half-hour seemed to pass quickly, and soon, they were all standing inside the sea caves, dripping wet, having activated their clothes while still in the water. The Fomori and Water Fae quickly whisked all the water from everyone's hair and clothes, returning it to the ocean.

Lorcan and Fergal stood at the front of the group before a circular demarcation in the center of one of the cave walls. "As soon as we cross into the portal room, I need you all to maintain total silence. We don't know what we will find in the stronghold, so be ready for anything. Has everyone practiced their mental barrier and camouflage?" asked the Weapons Master.

They all nodded, and he continued, "Excellent. The lad will take the lead, and I will follow you all. We will hug the wall to our right, and the two of us will extend a hazy shadow around us. Do *not* wander off, and do *not* let your mental shields slip for even a moment. All our lives depend on it."

He glanced at Lorcan and gestured for him to activate the shadow portal. The younger Fomori touched the very center of the circular area, leaving behind a tiny dot of murky silver, which began to swirl and grow until the entire circle was filled. A wave of translucence rippled through the shadow portal, indicating the connection with the Fomori stronghold was intact.

Lorcan stepped through the portal and moved quickly out of the way so the others could follow. The portal room and nearby hallways were empty, so their incursion was still unnoticed for now.

He led the group down the hall, the fingers on his right hand trailing lightly along the wall as he moved as quickly as possible. It didn't take long before they neared the Titans' cavern. The doors were still hanging askew after Balor's last visit.

They crept into the cavern and around the corner to where the captive Shadow Weavers were huddled, waiting for them. As soon as Lorcan was visible, a young Shadow Weaver barreled into him, wrapping him in a desperate hug.

"I'm so glad you're here. I'm fecking sick of this place. I miss my parents and my sisters," he whispered, his words coming out in a rush.

"There now, lad. We're here. You're safe," Lorcan whispered back, rubbing the adolescent's back as he trembled. After a few moments, the trembling calmed, allowing the older Shadow Weaver to extricate himself.

He looked around for Máire and found her curled into Corley's side, shaking, her eyes wider than normal. *I was afraid of this,* he thought.

He approached them and said, "Lass, I know that the last time you were here, very bad things happened to you. But Cathal is dead. He can't hurt you anymore. And we need you to set up the mirroring artifact."

He looked at Corley, who was staring at his beloved helplessly. "She needs your strength, lad. Help her remember what she's capable of so we can do what we came here for."

The Earth Fae shook his head to clear it, then leaned close to Máire and began whispering affirming words in her ear, lending her strength until she could find her own. It didn't take long before her shaking stopped, and she seemed to regain her equilibrium. She took a deep breath and asked, "Can someone show me where the oldest Titans are? We'll need to leave this mirroring artifact in place while we make our escape, so it has to be set up on one of the victims who is too far gone to be saved."

As one of the other Shadow Weavers nodded and motioned for her to follow, Máire whispered to Corley, "Thank you, love," and softly kissed him on the cheek. As she passed Lorcan, she squeezed his arm and said, "And thank you, too, lad. I appreciate it."

She followed her guide into the shadows, anxious to get the artifact set. After they were gone, Fergal said, "As soon as they get back, we will begin setting the reversal artifacts. It's my understanding that you need to put it close to the cage and press the button on top to activate it. Move as quickly and as quietly as you can.

"Cara, Niall, and Keegan, can you set up a soundproof air shield? If the Titans begin making noise as the reversal happens, I don't want it to alert Balor." The three Fae with air power nodded and went to put it in place.

"Sláine and Muireann, I'll leave it to your discretion where you can be of most use. You'd know better than me." The healers nodded in response.

While they were waiting to begin, Muireann strolled over by Lorcan and said, "That was nicely done, you know. I'm impressed."

He smiled at her and replied, "I'm not always a complete arse."

She laughed at that. "Good to know." She turned to leave, and he caught her elbow, saying, "Muireann, I know now is not the ideal time, but I was wondering if, after the battle is over, we could maybe start over? We can take it as slow as you want. Would that be okay?"

She looked at him intently, then said, "Perhaps. No promises, but I'll consider it."

He nodded and said, "Thank you." She walked away to rejoin Sláine and Liam.

Máire and her Shadow Weaver guide returned, a slightly haunted expression on the Fire Fae's face. "The mirroring artifact is in place. I don't think there will be a problem with it. We chose one of the oldest Titans, and he was well beyond gone mentally."

She looked at all of them and said, "We have to save as many as we can. What he's done to them is truly monstrous. Nobody deserves that. If we can save them, brilliant. If we can't, we should put them out of their misery."

Fergal agreed, "We will, lass. Now, let's get to work."

᠅᠅᠅

They were shown how the cavern was laid out and where the newest Titans were, and they got started immediately. Sláine and Muireann began by working on Brian personally, although that didn't take long since he'd only begun the process the day before.

When they said he was good as new, Orla collapsed into his arms, sobbing her relief. He just held her, rocking back and forth, rubbing circles against her back.

The rest of them were practically running from cell to cell, quickly activating an artifact, dropping it by the cage's bars, and hurrying to the next. This went on for several hours until they finally ran out of artifacts. For the last half-hour of that time, Sláine and Muireann were pretty sure they had moved beyond reversible cases. But as long as there was a chance and they still had artifacts available, they would make an attempt.

The Titans who were successfully reversed were kept in their cells, but those with earth power had been busy destroying the locks on every one of their cages. Máire had made a special point to lead the young girl she had seen on her earlier visit, out of her cell and into the group of Fomori.

Like many others, her reversal wasn't perfect physically, but she now stood a chance at some semblance of a life. Many of the former Titans were still quite a bit larger than they'd been before their transformations, but most of the warped aspects of their appearance were at least minimized, if not completely reversed.

Fergal, Lorcan, and the other Shadow Weavers ensured all the former Titans knew what was expected when they were ready to leave. It was a simple concept. Run. Quietly and quickly, just run to the portal room and get the hell out of Dodge.

By the time they were finished and ready to depart, the majority of the rescuers had tear-streaked faces. The cruelty inflicted upon these Fomori was far greater than they had expected. And the victims were so grateful; it was heartbreaking.

As Lorcan and Fergal met to begin the departure, the younger Shadow Weaver said, "We should have destroyed that bastard a long time ago."

"Aye, lad. But better late than never. Now, let's get these

poor sods to their new home and prepare for the fight he'll bring to us."

Fergal left first, moving at a silent sprint so he could get to the portal room and open the way back to the sea caves. Lorcan had positioned the three Air Fae throughout the group to maintain the air shield they'd kept up during this whole process.

Once the Weapons Master had a head start of a few minutes, the rest followed. They moved as quickly and quietly as possible, but their group was now very large, which made things a bit more complicated. And it had taken longer than they expected; it was almost dawn, and they needed to get the hell out of there.

Lorcan finally rounded the corner and saw the entrance to the portal room. He encouraged them to begin running. "Go, go, go," he whispered. Fergal will have the portal open. Just run through it, dive into the ocean, and swim for home."

The line began moving faster, but it still took far longer than the Shadow Weaver liked. After what seemed like hours, he saw the remaining Fianna members bringing up the rear. He fell in behind them and entered the portal room, practically diving through the shadow portal and then into the ocean, finally breathing a small sigh of relief. They weren't home free yet, but they had all made it out of the stronghold alive, and that belonged firmly in the win column.

※ ※ ※

Balor stirred, roused from his restless sleep by some unknown disturbance. He rose, tilting his massive head to the side, trying to determine what had awakened him. Something was wrong.

He left his room and began making his way to the Titans' cavern. The closer he got, the more he was sure something was amiss.

When he finally stomped through the mangled doors into the cavern, he was greeted by the sight of row upon row of empty cages. Nearly a thousand of his Titans had somehow disappeared.

Rage washed over him so fiercely that the final thread of his sanity snapped. He bellowed his anger, smashing anything he could get his hands on, destroying several of the now empty cells.

Once his anger had abated slightly, he attempted to access his link to the remaining Titans but could not find it. He began searching, trying to narrow down where the issue was.

Finally, he found the small mirroring artifact outside the cage of one of the oldest Titans. He stomped on it, destroying it instantly, and found he could reestablish the link with the Titans who were left.

He gave them their new orders, causing the bars on every cell to swing open. They shuffled their way toward the large tunnel in the back of the cavern, which led to the sea.

Balor watched as all the Titans entered the ocean and transformed into warped and mangled sea creatures. He pointed them toward the Aos Sí and commanded, *Destroy them all.*

Family

is life

27

Deirdre had begun pacing back and forth along the beach quite a while ago. She had expected the members of the rescue party, and whomever they had managed to rescue, back a while ago, and she had a bad feeling. There was too much that could go wrong, too many things beyond her control, making her uneasy.

The family and friends of the Fae and Fomori who had journeyed to the stronghold were also near the shore, as well as the majority of Shadow Weavers. Rónán's sisters and parents stood with Nora and Ailáine, nervous but hopeful, awaiting the return of their loved ones.

Less than ten minutes ago, Dillon's newly bonded familiar, a bald eagle named Crann, had grown impatient and flown a bit further down the coast, hoping to catch sight of them. The High Druid froze when she saw him winging his way back, yelling at the top of his lungs, "They're coming! And they've brought company!"

Everyone surged toward the shore, anxious to see what was happening. Within moments, heads started popping above the waves as the rescue party approached the beach.

The Fianna, healers, and Fomori, including the recently liberated Shadow Weavers, were the first out of the water.

They stood in a couple of rows with Lorcan and Fergal in the center, Rónán between them. His parents and sisters pushed their way to the front, his mother dropping to her knees a few paces away from him. The young Shadow Weaver screamed, "Mam!" and ran directly into her outstretched arms. His father and sisters also knelt and hugged the youngling, tears of joy streaking everyone's cheeks.

Deirdre watched the reunion and had to blink back her own tears, ecstatic that the rescue mission had succeeded. She turned toward Lorcan and Fergal, about to ask for details when she saw what could only be former Titans walking up behind the rescue party. She couldn't help but gasp as more and more victims of Balor's chaos magic kept coming.

Most of them still had some physical signs of their transformation, the most common being an unusually large size. They continued emerging from the water, the rescue party being pushed forward and the crowd making room, until nearly a thousand former Titans stood on the shore.

Conor let out a low whistle and said, "Bloody hell, that's a lot of Titans. This island is getting crowded."

The High Druid watched Siobhán give him the eyebrow for that comment, but just as Deirdre was turning back to speak to the rescue party, another vision struck. She managed to stay on her feet for this one and it was thankfully brief.

Once it had passed, she said, "Fergal and Nora, can you organize the Shadow Weavers to help find clothing and food for our newly freed Titans?" They nodded their agreement.

"I will fill you in once I know more. I'm not sure what's coming, but something significant is about to happen at the World Tree." She turned to the rescue party and the other Fae spectators and said, "Anyone with air power, grab as many people as you can and meet at the World Tree. It feels like things are about to change drastically. I don't know if that's good or bad, but we're about to find out."

She and the other Air Fae divided up the rest of them and raced toward the World Tree. The trip didn't last long, one of the perks of flying. The different groups had barely landed when the World Tree's portal activated.

Those directly in front of the portal saw a determined-looking phoenix barreling toward them. As soon as she crossed over, she screamed, "Everyone move back! Give us some room!" She circled around and landed on Keegan's shoulder, giving her bonded a squeeze, and whispering, "You're gonna love this!"

Next came Lir, but instead of his normal púca form, he flew through the portal, tucking his wings slightly as he came through, then snapping them out to display the full glory of his Pegasus shape. He landed next to Calder, who stroked his silky mane and said, "Well, this is new, lad. I can't wait to hear your tale!" The familiar leaned into his bonded's side and chuckled but said no more.

Following Lir came a muscular dragon with metallic scales in all shades of red, orange, and burgundy. She had horns resembling corkscrews around her head, gleaming, razor-sharp ebony claws, and glowing crimson eyes. She made one pass over the crowd and landed gracefully a few paces in front of Deirdre.

Áine began to introduce her, "This is the fire goddess—"

"Lasair," Deirdre finished, a slightly dazed expression on her face.

Before the dragon or phoenix could reply a larger, stouter dragon with metallic scales in shades of green and bronze with spiky green horns all over his head burst through the portal, landing less gracefully next to the red dragon.

Lir said, "The earth god is—"

"Cré," the High Druid supplied again.

Next in line was a lithe serpentine dragon, with sparkling scales in shades of yellow, gold, copper, and white, his eyes exuding a golden glow. His head was covered with long, flowing, tentacle-like scales, and an unmistakable smirk could be seen on his face. He was extremely quick, taking two laps above the crowd, then practically floating to the ground on Lasair's other side.

Áine looked at Deirdre and said, "Do you want to do it, or should I?"

"This is Ruaig, the air god," the seer replied, eyes wide and a little wild.

The final goddess through the portal was somewhere in size between Lasair and Cré and covered with metallic scales ranging in color from sky blue to teal to sapphire to purple. She also had tentacle-like scales, creating a mane around her head. She did a lap above their heads and settled gracefully on Ruaig's other side, almost moving more like a cat than a dragon.

Lir didn't even attempt the introduction, he just nodded at Deirdre, who responded, "And this is Tonn, the water god."

She blinked several times, looking extremely confused, and said, "I don't know how I know any of that."

"But we do, love. All will become clear shortly," the

water dragon said gently. Then, the four gods all simultaneously bowed deeply before the seer.

That sight caused a mental avalanche to cascade through Deirdre's mind. Memories she didn't know she was missing began slamming into her brain, answering so many questions she didn't realize she had.

While she was processing what she'd just learned, Conor leaned over to Riley and said, "I'm so confused." His twin snorted and replied, "That's hardly new for you."

Deirdre took a deep breath, gave them all a weak smile, and said, "Sorry about that. I just had a brief vision, and I need to consult with the dragon gods to clarify a few points. I promise you, I will fill you all in just as soon as I can."

She turned to the gods and said, "If you'll all follow me, I think we should have our discussion in my office." They nodded, then followed her as she flew off in the direction of the Druids' Enclave.

Áine put her wings on her hips and said, "Does anyone else find it disturbing that our High Druid just lied to all of us?"

⸙⸙⸙

Deirdre landed in the gardens outside the Druid's Enclave, the dragons touching down right after her, shifting to their Fae forms. They followed her to her office, and she shut the door, then turned to face the gods. "I've missed you so much!" she cried, tears streaming down her face. The four of them surrounded her in a group hug, all tearful and joyous at once.

After they regained their composure, they all took seats in a rough circle. "So, I obviously regained my memories. That will take some getting used to. But won't they be coming for us now? We can't fight two enemies at the same time!"

"Calm yourself, matháir chríona," Lasair said gently. "Only your memories have returned, nothing else. They should still be unaware."

The seer sighed in relief, massaging her temples. Ruaig smiled wryly and commented, "Feeling a little more crowded in there now?"

She chuckled and said, "You could say that." She looked at each of them in turn, then asked, "So, what happens now? Do you know?"

Tonn responded, "I think first things first, we kick some monster arse. Balor has always been a megalomaniacal piece of horseshit, just like his namesake. We should have put him down ages ago."

"But what if I need to regain the rest to succeed? Out of the frying pan and into the fire seems less than ideal."

The usually stoic Cré covered her hand with his and said, "We will burn that bridge when we get to it."

"Perhaps not. I have some thoughts about that but haven't fully fleshed them out yet," Lasair mused.

"Well, flesh faster. It may be unavoidable, and we do not need anyone else bearing down on us right now," the High Druid grumbled, a bit off her game with all that had happened.

The fire dragon quirked an eyebrow at her, causing Deirdre to rethink her tone. "Sorry, love, it's been a trying day, but that's no excuse." She paused momentarily, gathering her thoughts. "Very well, we will put that worry aside for the moment. But what will we tell the Aos Sí? They know something unusual is going on."

"Do they trust you?" Tonn asked.

"Yes," the seer replied.

"Excellent. Tell them that we have determined your latest vision must be kept secret until after the battle, or we risk defeat. To fill them in on everything now would only cause confusion and chaos, a distraction we cannot afford."

Deirdre sighed and conceded, "Very well. But the moment it's safe to tell them, I will. I dislike lying to them. They deserve better than that." The gods nodded in agreement.

Family

is life

28

As the Fianna, members of the expanded Council, and delegations of Shadow Weavers and familiars entered the Council Hall, Deirdre, and the dragon gods, in their Fae forms, watched them take their seats.

Although no one but the High Druid had seen them as Fae before, it was easy to tell who was who. The earth god, Cré, was still built like a tank. He had dark brown skin with a bronze sheen, spiky neon green hair, and glowing chartreuse eyes. Lasair, the fire goddess, sported wild ringlets in the same shades of red, orange, and burgundy as her scales. She had honey-colored skin and luminescent crimson eyes. The lithe male with long blond curls and vibrant golden eyes could be none other than Ruaig, the air god. And the tall, curvy water goddess with beaming teal eyes, caramel-colored skin, and dreadlocks in all shades of blue and purple was obviously Tonn.

Based on their expressions, despite the seriousness of the situation, they were pretty amused by what they saw.

Not surprisingly, they seemed entertained the most by the queen of snark.

Áine was still excitedly telling Keegan, Calder, and anyone else who would listen, all about the trip she and Lir had just taken.

"When we got to the Earth Clan island, we met Siobhán's parents! Did I tell you that already? Well, her mom, her name is Treasa, but Lir called her Gram, anyway she is *so* much like Siobhán. Or I guess Siobhán is so much like her. And she can do that awesome whistle, I wish I could do that. But her *dad!* I'm telling you, Conor makes way more sense now. To be honest, I wondered if there was a blonde, dimpled mailman around here somewhere. But after meeting Brady, that's his name, Brady. After meeting him, I swear Conor is the spitting image, both in appearance and attitude! And Gramps even agreed to let me teach him to dance! Before we left, I had already taught him the basics of crip walking."

As the phoenix paused for breath, she caught sight of Fintan taking his seat. "Crap, I almost forgot! Goat Boy, I need the expando-bag." Lir, in his fainting goat form, stuck his head out in her direction so she could snag the bag with her talon. She turned back to Keegan, "BRB, I need to deliver a birthday present to Fintan from his sister. We met her on Findias, she was really sweet. His mom was a raging bee-atch at first, but she turned out to be okay in the end. Did I tell you she blew this knockout powder at us? Made us pass out and turned our faces as red as a baboon's ass! Well, my face is already red because—fire. Anyway, I'll finish that story in a minute. Fintan!"

She fluttered over to the crotchety elder Fire Fae, landed on the table in front of him, and extended the expando-bag in a high kick, saying, "Hey old dude! I've got a surprise for you!"

"What the bleeding hells are you blabbering about bird? Have you finally lost the little bit of mind ye had left?"

"Whatevs, butt nugget. Your sister gave us a birthday present for you. But if you don't want it, I'm happy to keep it for myself." She turned and gathered herself to fly back to Keegan.

"Flannery sent me something? Oh, I bet it's her shortbread! She knows how much I love that!"

Áine gave him a dose of side-eye, then stuck her talon back out so he could open the bag and dig out his present. "Fine, but only because I really like Flannery. You, on the other hand, remind me of your mother."

Fintan, the wrapped package of shortbread in his hands, let out a sharp bark of laughter at that comment. Unfortunately, it startled Lir and made him lock up in a faint. This made both Áine and Lasair snort, which earned them both an eyebrow from Siobhán, who was quite fond of the familiar and disliked it when anyone made fun of him.

"Brave lass to cock an eyebrow at a goddess," Tonn whispered to Deirdre. The seer chuckled and said, "You don't know Siobhán Ó Faoláin. I've never met a smarter, more protective mother."

"Really? Never?" the water goddess smirked. The High Druid's lips curled into a half-smile, and she gently nudged Tonn with an elbow.

"Áine! Stop laughing at sweet Lir, or I'll hide your tiara!" Keegan snapped at her familiar.

"Like you could! I never take it off."

"Fine, then I'll hide mushrooms in all your food," the redhead retorted, hands on her hips.

The phoenix gasped and said, "You wouldn't dare!"

"Try me." The familiar narrowed her eyes at her bonded as if weighing her options.

"You are no fun at all, you know that!" the bird complained, but she fluttered over to where the goat had already recovered, settled herself on his rump, and mumbled, "Sorry, Goat Boy."

Shay took that opportunity to welcome everyone and call the meeting to order. "Fáilte everyone! After the past hour's events, it appears we have a lot to catch up on, so I will be turning the floor over to Deirdre and her guests."

"Thank you, Shay," Deirdre said. Then she looked the gathered Fae over and said, "I know you all must have many questions, but I'm afraid I must beg your indulgence for a bit longer. I recently had a vision, and we have determined that disclosing its contents could seriously impede our chances of victory in the coming battle. Please, I beg you to trust me for now. I promise you I will explain everything once this war is won."

Siobhán raised two fingers, and Deirdre nodded at her. "We do trust you, Deirdre; I hope you know that. So, if you say withholding this information is in our best interest, that is good enough for me. But I do have a question. Might we know what part your companions intend to play in the battle?"

Tonn answered, "Of course, lass. We will fight alongside all of you. We wouldn't be here otherwise."

"Brilliant, thank you," she replied.

"Perhaps we could hear what you have planned," Lasair suggested.

For the next half-hour, the Fae leaders, with help from the Shadow Weavers and familiars, filled the gods in on what they had worked out. From their cavalry capabilities to the plans to portal in and out with quick hit-and-run strikes, they made sure to leave nothing out.

When they were finishing up, Lorcan raised his hand to speak. Deirdre said, "Yes, love. Go ahead."

"I wanted to update you all on the situation with the former Titans. Fergal and my mam have spoken with quite a few of them, and apparently, they have decided they want to fight. The reversal process has diminished their size and strength, but they still have much to offer. And frankly, they are furious with Balor and grateful to us for rescuing them. That makes for some powerful incentive."

"We would be fools to turn them away," Cré added.

"Agreed," Deirdre said. "I believe they would be most effective in the first line of defense. Their innate ability with water would serve us well by creating a blockade in the ocean, hopefully cutting down the number of Titans we will have to face on land. They can retreat with the Fianna's regiments once the battle moves inland. We will divide them up so they know where to go and to whom they should answer."

She looked over the Fianna and other leaders and said, "Any objections to that course of action?"

Morgan raised a hand, and Deirdre nodded at him. "I wonder if some could be spared to help the healers? Their strength and water powers could be beneficial to us."

"Of course, that's an excellent idea. Any other requests?"

When no other comments or questions were raised, she continued, "Very well. When I received the vision telling me the gods were about to portal in, I was also shown Balor's response to our incursion. I believe he has finally snapped. After he threw a bit of a temper tantrum upon discovering how many Titans we rescued, he released the rest of them into the ocean. They will have to come the long way, so I estimate they should reach us around midday the day after tomorrow."

Despite knowing this battle was inevitable, a few gasps and worried muttering could be heard. It's one thing to know something intellectually but quite another to face it head-on.

"We've trained. We've strategized. And we've developed a sound battle plan. We've done all we can to prepare. So, now we need to get some rest. I propose we send out air and water scouts tomorrow afternoon to ensure we aren't caught unaware." Nods of agreement were seen all around.

"Until then, do your best to relax and get some sleep. We will meet at the coast two hours after midday tomorrow. Slán."

The Aos Sí, Shadow Weavers, former Titans, familiars, and gods currently occupying Tionól spent their last peaceful day and night loving each other in whatever manner felt right to them.

For a time, the familiars all gathered around their newly-present gods, laughing as Áine and Ruaig wore themselves out trying to prove who was fastest or listening to Declan and Cré recite their poetry.

The Fianna made certain their regiments knew what was expected of them when the battle was joined, then dismissed them to enjoy their remaining time of peace before the chaos ensued.

As the sun set, painting the island in vibrant shades of gold and copper, the Ó Faoláin family, with all their friends and loved ones, sat in the gardens around the World Tree and enjoyed dinner together. Conor decided it would be funny to chase Áine around with a mushroom, threatening to make her eat it, and returned to the table, missing his eyebrows. As the phoenix fluttered into her seat next to Keegan, she huffed and said, "Be glad it wasn't your nipples!"

After dinner, everyone left to spend time with those closest to their heart.

Liam led Sláine back to his rooms with promises of a deep tissue massage. She chuckled and said, "It better be deep, lad," then allowed him to pull her along the path.

Cara and Riley had been kissing on a garden bench for a while, and the Air Fae decided she was tired of so many clothes between them, so she straddled him and lifted them both in the air, flying them back to his rooms.

Conor and Niall had already wandered off at some point, most likely enjoying the gardens in each other's arms.

Keegan and Calder watched their parents walk arm-in-arm back to their respective houses, kissing and touching along the way, unable to keep their hands to themselves.

Áine looked over at Lir and said, "Come on, Goat Boy. Let's go see if Fintan has any shortbread left that he might be willing to share." She flew up to his púca rump, and he headed toward the elder's place.

Keegan smiled as their familiars left the garden, then looked hungrily at Calder and said, "Come on, big guy. Let's go build another bed in the forest so you can have your way with me."

"As you command, my needy ember," he replied with an evil smile. He took her by the hand and led her to a more private section of the gardens. He used his gifts to create a makeshift mattress, then grabbed Keegan and pulled her to him. He kissed her roughly, his hands fisted in her hair, and pulled her head back so he could bite and kiss and suck his way along her jaw to her ear and down her neck to the hollow of her throat.

She gasped at the intensity of his affection but returned it just as strongly, her nails leaving marks down his back as he lavished his attention on her. Soon, he pulled back and said, "Get on your knees, love. I want to fill your throat."

She knelt before him, lifted the leather kilt he wore, and took most of his length into her mouth, running her tongue in circles along the underside. He let out a low moan, tangling his fingers once again in her hair.

"That feels amazing, mo aibhleog. Now, relax your throat, and let's see if we can go a little further." She did as he asked, allowing him to slide further down her throat until he was completely buried. He stayed there for a moment, relishing how warm and wet it felt, then he pulled out of her mouth and lifted her to her feet.

"Undress, lass. Now," he commanded. "Don't make me do it for you, or you'll likely find your clothes shredded." She hurried to comply, and once she was completely naked in front of him, he scooped her into his arms and tossed her onto the bed he'd just made for them.

"You are stunning, love. Sometimes I can't believe how lucky I am," he said, dropping to his knees in front of her. He put his hands on her thighs and said, "Open for me, Keegan. Now, please."

She shuddered at his demand and spread her legs wide for him. He slid his hands beneath her ass and lowered his face to nibble and lick the warm center of her core, which was slick with her desire. Occasionally, he would lift his face and slide two fingers inside of her, using his thumb to circle her clit. Then he would bring his tongue back to lick and tease her clit, driving her to the edge of madness.

"Please!" she moaned.

"Please what, love? Use your words," he teased, never stopping the attention he was lavishing on her sensitive center.

"Please, let me come!" she moaned again, louder this time.

He appeared to consider it for a long moment, then finally said, "Very well. Come for me, lass. Drench my face and scream for me."

She toppled over into a mind-blowing orgasm, yelling her pleasure to the stars as she wrapped her hands in his hair, grinding him against her core.

Once she calmed a bit, he lifted his face, and climbed up her, kissing her fiercely, his tongue demanding entrance to her mouth, swirling the slick desire coating his lips and tongue against hers, letting her taste herself.

She was quickly becoming aroused again, wrapping her legs around his waist to encourage him to move things along.

"Do you want me inside of you, love?" he asked, sliding the tip of his cock along her entrance. "Tell me what you want me to do to you."

"Fuck me, please. I can't take much more of this!"

"Oh yes, you can, lass. You'll take all I choose to give you. And beg me for more." He played with her a bit longer to prove his point until she was whimpering with need.

He finally took pity on her, covered his length with a water barrier, and buried himself deep inside her with a moan of pleasure. After a moment, he slipped an arm under one of her legs, placing it over his shoulder, and began grinding against her, pumping hard. The deeper angle threatened to undo him, but he managed to maintain control long enough to bring her trembling back to the precipice of release. Then he moaned deeply, saying, "Come with me, mo anamchara."

As they both felt intense waves of pleasure ripple through them, she called out, "A chuisle mo chroí!"

After the strongest sensations had passed, he collapsed beside her and said, "I love you, too, my fiery ember." She snuggled against him, wishing they could stay this way forever.

He ran the back of his hand affectionately down the side of her cheek, then grinned as he pulled a few twigs and leaves from her hair. "Let's go back to my room, love. We can take a shower, and I'll wash your hair. Then we'll do all this a few more times before we get some sleep, eh?"

"Sounds divine," she replied.

In Deirdre's room, while the seer took a shower and cried under the stream of water, thinking no one could hear, the four dragon gods took all the cushions, pillows, and blankets they could find and made a giant nest. When she came out, dressed in a soft, silky nightgown, her hair dripping wet, Tonn whisked the excess water away, and they guided her to their nest. The gods surrounded her and laid her down in the center, curling around her.

Finally, with her memories restored and friendships renewed, she let herself release the rest of her sorrow in the comfort of their arms, eventually drifting off to a cathartic sleep.

Family

is life

29

Fae, Fomori, and familiars lined the beach the following day at the appointed time. Deirdre and the dragon gods stood before them, ready to begin their preparations for the battle.

"Fáilte! We must discuss some vital details. First, Tonn will lead some of our fastest swimmers in a sweep of the area adjacent to the island. Ruaig will do the same with our flyers and air familiars. We will post sentries along the route, both in the ocean and the air.

"Lasair and Cré will station Fire and Earth Fae along the shore. As the Titans approach, we will attempt to lift them from the water enough that the Fire Clan on the beach can bring their powers to bear on the attackers. Likewise, the Earth Clan will use the aquatic flora to slow down and entangle the monsters as they go."

"Some of the Air Clan will also quickly transport wounded via portal from the sea to the triage area, currently being constructed around the World Tree gardens.

"The Fianna have been tasked with dividing their regiments up appropriately. Nora, Fergal, and Lorcan have done the same with the Shadow Weavers and former Titans.

"The familiars will fill in wherever they feel most needed. Once the battle moves onto the shore, and we must assume it will, we will proceed with our hit-and-run attacks, portaling in and out quickly." She paused momentarily, then continued, "Finally, I want to thank all of you for your willingness to defend our home and each other from the evil at our gates. I know you have questions, yet you are still willing to trust us and do what must be done to keep us all safe. For that, you have my undying love and gratitude. We are family. And, to borrow a phrase from the Ó Faoláin's—"

"Family is life," was the resounding reply. Even those not blood-related had certainly heard the family motto, and its meaning was never so universally felt and appreciated as it was at that moment.

Deirdre smiled and replied, "Just so. Go raibh maith agat, my friends. Now, let's go kick some monster arse."

△△△

Tonn waited for the last of the chosen swimmers to assemble, then said, "We will swim swiftly but carefully. Stay together and stay sharp. Keep your eyes on me, and if I start swimming back to the island—follow...quickly. If everything is clear, those chosen for the first round of sentries will assume your posts."

She turned away from them and let her silky dress, in shades that matched her hair, naturally, fade into her skin as if it never existed. She took a running start and dove into the ocean, morphing as soon as she hit the water into a giant octopus, sapphire-blue with shimmering shades of cornflower and teal, the suckers on her limbs a lovely violet. Her luminous teal eyes watched the others transform into their aquatic forms, the former Titans moving protectively to the front of the group in case they encountered the monsters sooner than expected.

Calder was one of the last Fae on the beach. Keegan was reluctant to let him go, but she knew he had to; his dual powers could be helpful. She gave him one last kiss and smacked his ass, saying, "Remember, I'll be close. Find a way to signal me if you need help, and we'll portal the fuck outta there. Stay alive, Ó Faoláin. That's an order."

"Yes, ma'am." He grinned at her, ran the back of his hand down her cheek, then ran toward the water.

He dove under and shifted into a merrow, deep emerald-green scales wrapping around his lower body and gills opening along his neck. He swam quickly toward the front as Tonn took off toward the Fomori stronghold.

The late afternoon sunlight streamed through the water, making everything glow vibrantly. Colorful fish scurried away, startled by the sudden influx of merrows and aquatic familiars. Declan, in his orca form, was close behind the water goddess, and he'd already spotted Emer, a tiger shark, and Grady, an inky black octopus with electric blue rings, not far behind.

Everything went smoothly for the first couple of hours when suddenly Keegan's head, surrounded by an air bubble, popped beneath the waves, upside down, about ten paces ahead of Calder.

He jolted to a stop, then swam forward more slowly and pointed toward the surface. When he reached her, they both rose above the waves.

"They're coming! Now! Not tomorrow!" she panted, short of breath from her rapid flight back to him.

"What? How far?" Calder asked, eyes narrowing as he began considering their next steps.

"About a thirty-minute flight. I can fly quite a bit faster than they can swim, but they're less than an hour from here."

"Bloody hell. I'll let Tonn know. You have to get word to Deirdre," he stated, preparing to dive back beneath the waves.

"The fuck I do! Cara is already halfway there or more. I'm staying with you," she protested, crossing her arms over her chest as she floated above him. "If I'm needed elsewhere, I'll go. Until then, we stay together. Besides, we only need the two of us to portal so we can move faster. I think that might be important."

He nodded at her and said, "Agreed. Let me talk to Tonn. I'll be right back, lass."

He dove down and quickly found the water goddess. After he explained the situation, she replied, "Fecking Balor! He must be driving them like a psychopath to be this close! Has Deirdre been informed?"

"Cara is on the way now."

"Very well. We are almost beyond the island. We will form a barricade around the island's southeast tip since I assume that's where they will attempt landfall. Send Keegan to catch one of the other Air Fae and have them relay the message back to Deirdre. This was the strategy we discussed, but we need to maintain contact to coordinate our attack. Then she should return in case we need other messages relayed."

Calder replied, "I have a faster suggestion. It only takes Keegan and I to portal back to the World Tree. If I go with her, we'll save a great deal of time."

"Brilliant. Join her and get Dee the message. Bring me back any response she might have."

He nodded and left to follow her instructions.

Tonn turned around and led everyone to the shore to their left, returning to her Fae form as she stood in the waves, head and shoulders above the water so she could speak. "We must form our barricade here, making them fight for every step forward. Ground forces will be here shortly to back us up, and I'm sure they'll also send a few healers. Everyone choose a spot and stay sharp."

As soon as Calder popped his head above water, he quickly explained the situation to Keegan, shifted back to his Fae form, and they activated a portal back to the World Tree. He gave Deirdre the update from Tonn. "Fecking Balor! Very well. We'll get everything set in motion. Tell Tonn I'm keeping Ruaig and Lasair in reserve, but I'll ask Cré to join her and bring some of the other Fae for backup. You two stay close to one of the gods and report back periodically."

"Aye," Calder replied, moving behind Keegan, wrapping his arms around her, clasping hands, and portaling back to Tonn.

They landed next to one of the former Titans, who was chest-deep in the ocean close to Tonn. After he delivered the message, she said, "Thank you, lad. Can you two please help Cré and the healers and ground soldiers who will be arriving soon? I need to get back in the ocean."

They nodded and walked up onto the beach, where several groups were landing. Áine and Lir were among the familiars in the group, and they quickly joined their bonded.

"Did you hear? They're almost here! I am so ready to

fuck up some monsters!" The phoenix flared her flames for emphasis.

"Cool your jets, Miss Thang," Keegan replied, crossing her arms and pinning her familiar with a warning glare. "We will not win this battle by going off half-cocked."

"I'm not half-cocked; I don't do half of anything. It's fully cocked all the way, baby!" She did a slightly manic loop-de-loop for emphasis.

Keegan pinched the bridge of her nose and said, "Lir, sweetheart, will you please keep an eye on the wild child?" Lir nodded and said, "Of course, love. I'll stay close."

"Everyone gather around," Cré called in his deep rumbly voice, bringing the group's attention to him. "We will soon face our enemy. You've all trained for this. You know your roles. Trust each other and yourselves. End of pep talk." The earth god was not the most verbose, but if he said something, you could trust that he meant it.

"Air Fae, station yourselves along the shore and be ready to lift the wounded from the water and join your quads to portal them back to the healers at the World Tree. Muireann and a few other healers are here to perform triage as needed to stabilize any critical injuries before they are portaled.

"Fire Fae, you will be our snipers. As the Water Fae engage the Titans beneath the water, they will attempt to lift the monsters' heads above the waves. If you see a Titan's head pop up—burn it off. But choose your targets carefully, we don't want any friendly fire accidents."

"Oh, oh, oh, like whack-a-mole!" Áine exclaimed, her anxiety-masked-as-excitement cranked well beyond anything Keegan had ever seen. She opened her mouth to try and calm the bird down, but Lir beat her to it.

"We talked about this, Áine. You will get plenty of

action, as you like to call it. But we need you to be smart. This will be dangerous enough, no unnecessary risks, eh?"

The phoenix landed on Lir's rump, took a couple of deep cleansing breaths, and seemed to rein herself in a bit. "You got it, Goat Boy. Sorry, I just want to get this over with."

The púca looked over his shoulder at her and replied, "We all do, love. You've just got to keep things at a low simmer, not a rolling boil, understand? That's how we keep mistakes from happening."

"Áine, Lir, can I see you, please?" Cré asked. The púca walked them over to the earth god. "I know we have some Air Fae and familiars keeping an eye on the approaching threat, but I was hoping you two would fly ahead and get an update."

The phoenix launched herself into the air and hovered before Cré. "Our pleasure," she replied. "Come on, Goat Boy, let's do a little recon!" Lir gave a whole-body shake, and a pair of large, ebony wings unfurled between his shoulders. "Right behind you, lass."

The two of them launched into the air, winging their way toward the Fomori stronghold.

"Be careful!" Keegan called after them. Lir tossed his head and called back, "Always!"

"Earth Fae! We are going to turn the area in front of our soldiers into an obstacle course. To do that, we need to assume our aquatic forms and use our element to hinder, stall, and annoy the monsters coming for us. Remember, Balor drives them, but they have very little mental capacity left. If we can distract and lead them away, we can pick them off individually."

When he was done speaking, he morphed into a giant sea turtle, his skin several shades of green with mottled copper and bronze covering his shell. "Follow me!" He slid into the ocean, swiftly moving to the front of the aquatic soldiers.

Calder gripped Keegan's chin and said, "I'm going to help where I can. You stay safe, and we will bring you some moles to whack. Or immolate, whatever works."

Keegan nodded solemnly and replied, "I'll be fine, you just make sure you're careful. There are plenty of us to protect the others; you don't have to do it all yourself, eh?"

"Aye, lass." He kissed her fiercely but briefly and strode into the ocean, dismissing his kilt as he dove beneath the waves. His metallic green merrow tail was the last piece of him to disappear into the water.

"Keeg! Where are Calder, Lir, and Miss Thang?" Cara called as she and Riley landed with their other two quad members.

"Áine and Lir are doing recon, and Calder just left with the other Earth Fae, led by Cré, to prepare underwater obstacles for the monsters."

Riley turned to the Water Fae of their quad and said, "Shall we give them a hand?"

"Aye, let's go," she said.

He turned to Cara, mashed their mouths together briefly, and said, "Be right back, love." Then he and the Water Fae strode toward the ocean.

"Stay safe!" Cara called, receiving a backward wave in reply.

☘☘☘

Tonn swam along the row of former Titans who had insisted on being the vanguard of their defenses. While she had no doubt that the Aos Sí were taking this battle seriously and would do everything in their power to protect their people, these Fomori had been through hell, and it showed in their eyes. Not only did they want to protect their rescuers, they wanted payback. And since most of them had believed they were as good as dead just a few short days ago, they were also willing to sacrifice themselves. Better to die in the service of protecting their allies than be used as a weapon against them. While she hoped the casualties would be minimal, she could appreciate and respect that level of commitment.

Cré swam up to Tonn, nodding at her and pointing with his flippers to indicate to the Earth Fae with him to begin filling in among the former Titans and other Fae near the front of the defenders. They quickly began multiplying the underwater flora, weaving it into lengths of rope-like material, ready to snag and harass their opponents at the first opportunity.

🔯🔯🔯

Groups of quads continued to arrive, leaving those Air and Fire Fae waiting on the shore to direct them. As the Water and Earth Fae joined the others in the water, the remaining Fae were busy placing themselves in optimal locations.

Cara looked at Keegan and said, "You know, there's no reason we need to wait for the Water Fae to lift the Titans above the water. I have an idea." She explained her plan to the Air and Fire Fae nearby. They discussed the pros and cons, deciding her plan had merit and was worth a try.

Suddenly, they saw Áine and Lir racing back toward them. "They're almost here!" the phoenix screeched, pulling up to hover in front of Keegan and Cara. "You have maybe ten minutes," Lir added, approaching at a slightly more sedate pace.

Corley and Máire's quad landed just then. "Corley, the Earth and Water Fae are all in the ocean. Find Cré and Tonn and tell them we'll have incoming in approximately ten minutes," Keegan explained.

"Aye," he replied, kissing his beloved, then running toward the water and diving beneath the waves to deliver the message.

Keegan quickly filled her cousin in on their slightly modified plan. Máire tilted her head, considering what she'd just heard. "Brilliant. Let's get into position."

Cara quickly paired up the Air and Fire Fae, then they lifted into the air and began flying toward the oncoming Titans, Áine, Lir, and a few other air familiars joining them.

They quickly moved beyond the rows of defenders visible beneath the cerulean blue waves. A few Air Fae and familiars could be seen a short distance beyond them, marking the head of the line of Titans being herded toward them.

"Shall we give my idea a shot?" Cara yelled to the others.

"Why the fuck not?" Keegan replied with a fist pump. She could perform the procedure alone, having both air and fire power, but the rest of them partnered up and spread out to find a Titan. They had decided to make their attempts at the same time, hoping it would sow confusion and allow the aquatic warriors beneath them to pick off more of the monsters in the chaos.

Cara counted down, "Three, two, one, go!" Each of the Air Fae sent a column of air swirling down around their chosen Titan, quickly lifting them at least partially above the waves. Their Fire Fae partner would then shoot a white-hot burst of flame directly at the monster's head, immediately eliminating them.

Áine was an especially good shot and was able to destroy almost a third of those taken out with only the help of Keegan to lift the Titans above the water. She, of course, had to provide a running commentary of her kills.

"Take that, bee-atch! You want a piece of me? Bam, no more head for you!" It was somehow more than a little unhinged and mildly entertaining at once.

They took out dozens of Titans this way, but Balor eventually caught onto the tactic and instructed the Titans to call upon their power over chaotic weather. Roiling clouds bubbled up, dark and ominous, wind howling and lightning sparking all around them.

Half of the Air Fae gathered all the Fire Fae and flew them back to the shore. The remaining Air Fae joined forces to push the weather system further out to sea. Once it had dissipated, they joined the others on land.

By this time, the Titans had reached the first line of aquatic defenders. The former Titans had an almost feral reaction once the monsters were within reach. They tore into Balor's puppets with a vengeance, wielding shadow weapons violently and ruthlessly. Now that they'd been given some semblance of life back, they would protect it at all costs. They might not all survive, but they were bound and determined to take every single Titan with them and give the others a chance to live.

The Water Fae behind the former Titans found themselves on cleanup duty, whisking the bloody water further out to sea and moving the bodies and body parts into a grisly pile on the beach.

They also moved any injured former Titans to the shore so they could get help. Muireann and her fellow healers quickly sealed bleeding wounds, assessed internal injuries, and stabilized broken bones before sending them back to the primary healing encampment at the World Tree. They saved all they could, but unfortunately, more than a few of them joined the pile of dead on the beach.

The healers were keeping up so far, but they were at their limits. Muireann called to Ula, who was helping nearby, and asked her to find Áine or Lir and have them fly back to the World Tree for reinforcements. The raccoon replied, "I'll grab one of the quads and portal back there. It'll be faster," and left to find one and deliver her message.

☙❦☙

On the front lines, the former Titans had made quite a dent in the oncoming tide of monsters, but they just kept coming. And the defenders were beginning to tire.

Tonn and Cré encouraged the remaining former Titans to retreat to the shore, and Water Fae, Shadow Weavers, and Earth Fae took their place. Calder, Riley, and Corley worked in tandem, using the underwater flora to trap the monsters in place, after which Lorcan, Fergal, and several other Shadow Weavers would slice through them.

Calder also filled in as a front-line healer when needed. So far, the injuries had been minor and easily repaired, keeping more Fae in the fight where they needed them.

Several Water Fae continued with the original plan of lifting the monsters for the Fire Fae to take them out. Even underwater, they could hear Áine cackling as she fried one monster head after another. Apparently, unhinged was her mood of the day.

The two gods also carved a path through the Titans, their body count mounting quickly, but even they were unable to keep up with the crush of monsters swimming toward them. They shared a look, and Cré swam to the surface, narrowly avoiding a gout of flame as the phoenix became a little overzealous.

"Bloody hell, bird, watch where you're aiming! We need you to sound the retreat up here. It's time to move the defenses onto the shore."

Meanwhile, Tonn had gotten the defenders underwater to begin an orderly retreat. The Earth Fae concentrated on tying down the Titans with aquatic plants and vines, giving everyone space to pull back to the shore.

The gods resumed their Fae forms and quickly began ushering everyone onto land. As Cré looked up, he saw Áine circling overhead and called her to him, Lir following close behind. She flew over and hovered in front of the god. "We need reinforcements! Find a quad and portal back to the World Tree. Send in the cavalry!"

She turned and spotted Keegan drifting down to land beside Calder, who had just trudged out of the water, looking tired but determined. "One Dúbailte Uber, please! We need to get help in here ASAP! Cré wants us to portal to the World Tree and bring back the cavalry!"

Calder wrapped his arms around Keegan, grasping her hands in front of them, and said to Áine, "Get over here if you're coming!" She quickly fluttered over to land on his shoulder, Lir trotting up and leaning against Keegan's shoulder as the portal burst to life before them. They stepped through on a mission to find reinforcements.

△△△

Family

is life

30

Lasair paced in a large circle around Deirdre, restless for the fighting to begin. "Are you sure we shouldn't go help? I feel like an eejit sitting here doing nothing," the fire goddess complained.

"Soon enough, love. We need to pace ourselves if we're to have any shot at outlasting Balor and his Titans. Tonn and Cré will let us know when they need help." The High Druid could sympathize with the dragon, but they needed to be smart.

Ruaig was currently floating above them, taking everything in. He'd chosen to stay in his Fae form so he could more easily stay close to Deirdre in the cramped area she currently occupied. There'd be time to let the dragons out later, he suspected.

The World Tree portal flared to life again, having just opened a few minutes ago for Ula and a quad. More healers were needed at the shore, so Sláine and her group were readying themselves to join those already at the front lines.

This time, Keegan, Calder, Áine, and Lir burst through

the portal, rushing directly toward Deirdre. "We need backup, stat!" the phoenix yelled. "Call in the cavalry! Round up reinforcements! Move your asses, people! This is not a drill!"

The High Druid couldn't quite keep the smile from her lips when she replied, "Thank you, Áine, we'll send word to begin gathering." She turned to where Sláine and the other healers prepared to head to the front lines. "Lass, continue your preparations, but hold off on portaling just yet. I need to put a few items in place first. It'll be quick, I promise."

She looked at Ula and the quad who'd been sent to bring the healers, then at Keegan and Calder's group, and motioned them all to join her. "We're going to set up a series of blockades. Ula, you and your group will portal back to the shore. Open a portal for those soldiers and healers to return here for a bit of rest. Then, I want you to fly back to the first barrier location discussed in your training. Keegan and Calder's bunch will head to the stables, open a portal to the first group, and funnel cavalry and additional foot soldiers to the first barrier. Afterward, they will portal back here, and you will head to the next barrier location so we can repeat the process. Understood?"

Both groups nodded and moved to carry out their orders. Ruaig and Lasair joined Deirdre, and she said, "Lass, since you're itching to fight, you go with the first group, and Ruaig, you can take the second. Once Tonn and Cré have caught their breath, they will rejoin the battle."

The fire goddess clapped her hands together sharply and exclaimed, "About time! Let's bring the pain!"

☙❦☙

Ula and her quad portaled back to Muireann and the others, who were beating a hasty retreat as the first of the Titans were just now peeking their heads above the waves, hoping not to get frickaseed.

The healer was a bit harried, having commandeered a few Air Fae to help transport the last few injured who hadn't been portaled back to the healers at the World Tree.

Lorcan walked with Tréan and Declan a few paces away, but his eyes rarely left Muireann, the fighting so far only serving to remind him how much she meant to him and how much of a wanker he'd been. He was now even more determined to win her back. He just had to keep them both alive in the meantime.

"Ula!" the healer cried when the familiar's group appeared. The raccoon ran to her bonded and hopped up into her outstretched arms. They squeezed each other, then Ula said, "We're to open a portal back to the World Tree for you all to use, then we fly to the first barrier location. Another group will send some cavalry and ground soldiers to that spot, and we'll fly to the second location and repeat the process. Then we'll set up the final barrier at the World Tree."

Muireann nodded and said, "Stay safe, love. I will be rotating into the field with Sláine and the others. Come find me when you're done transporting soldiers, eh?"

Ula nodded, gave her another squeeze, and the healer walked her back over to the quad she was helping. As she walked back, Lorcan moved a bit closer to the healer. She glanced at him from the corner of her eye and couldn't help the small smile that blossomed on her face.

The quad called their elements and opened an extra-large portal to the World Tree. Everyone who'd been fighting on the front lines hurried through the glowing, spherical doorway. On the other side, there were several Fae, Druids, and junior healers who showed them to an area where they could rest and get some food and drink.

※ ※ ※

After the portal closed, Ula said, "Let's go, they're waiting on us!" The Air Fae lifted everyone and took off like a shot, which was wise, considering the first line of Titans was getting a little too close for comfort.

They raced away from the shore, eager to distance themselves from the enemy. Soon, they found themselves in the middle of the Feis grounds.

Eventually, they made their way to the raised platform in the center of the grounds. This was the location of the first barrier and the reinforcements should be portaling in any time now.

Less than ten minutes later, the portal opened, stretching wider and taller than normal to allow the cavalry to ride through. Horse after horse, carrying Fae after Fae pounded through the portal, quickly veering to the left or right and circling around to either side of the doorway. There were over a hundred mounted soldiers by the time they were done, followed soon after by a couple regiments of quads. Liam and Dillon were in command of the ground forces, and Siobhán was leading these cavalry troops.

The portal had barely closed when the newly arrived soldiers heard the whoosh, whoosh, of very large wings. A flash of vermillion and burgundy scales sliced through the air as Lasair dove from high above, banking and circling back around to hover before them.

The fire dragon lifted her head and shot a fountain of white-hot flame high into the air. She followed that with an ear-shattering roar. "This is what happens when you piss off a dragon!"

She thrashed her tail a few times and roared again before she managed to calm herself enough to finish what Dee had asked of her. "Everyone get ready, I'm about to go put the fear of me into them. I may bite off a few heads, too, haven't decided yet."

She turned toward the monsters and flew that way. The healers were busy setting up a triage station in the Healer's Compound at the Feis grounds, a fairly short distance from the raised platform. Sláine had already conscripted some Air Fae to create a kind of relay system to transport the wounded to the triage station quickly.

The cavalry was in place and ready to engage. All the quads had begun flying around, practicing portaling from one location to another.

Everyone knew when Lasair engaged the Titans by the resounding roar she let loose. This was followed by the hiss of flames enveloping monsters and the resulting shrieks of pain and terror.

The goddess decimated hundreds of Titans, but this level of violence could not be sustained indefinitely. She began to move slower, and the Titans whipped up some nasty weather once again.

A winter squall bubbled up out of nowhere, complete with lightning, whipping winds, and freezing rain, which quickly coated Lasair's wings. She flared her flames to melt the thin layer of ice, but she decided a quick break was necessary.

She flew back toward the reinforcements, calling out, "Incoming!" She circled in the direction of the Healer's

Compound, touching down in front of it and shifting to her Fae form.

"I need some food," she called out as she landed, wobbling slightly until Sláine grasped her elbow to help steady her.

"This way," the healer instructed, leading her to a table with a few snacks. Lasair sat and quickly helped herself, replenishing her depleted energy stores.

They could tell when the Titans reached the other Fae. There was the sound of portals opening and closing, screams and thuds echoing around them.

Much sooner than the healer had hoped, injured Fae began arriving. As instructed, the Air Fae conscripted for transporting duty began floating those needing care into the makeshift triage center. Sláine quickly directed the other healers to assess and stabilize injuries, sending the worst wounds to Morgan and the other healers at the World Tree.

Lasair finished her impromptu meal and called out to the Water Fae, "I'm heading back out there. Remember our strategy—hit and run. That means you all need to be ready to portal out of here at a moment's notice. I will send someone back with an update."

Sláine nodded, thinking, *Let's hope we're making progress.*

△△△

When the fire dragon reached the battle, she was impressed. Her fighting style was of the straightforward and direct variety. *See enemy, burn enemy* was pretty much the extent of the strategizing her skills required.

But watching the Fae swarm the Titans, separating and isolating monsters whenever they could, then teaming up with other quads to overwhelm and destroy them one at a time was more effective than she had expected. The cavalry was especially helpful with confusing the monsters, making it easier to cut them down.

The only problem she could see, as she watched more and more of the warped and monstrous Titans, shuffle forward, continuously pushing those in front of them further into the fray, was that there were just so many of them. *Fecking Balor!* The sheer number of lives he'd ruined was unbelievable. *We should have destroyed him long ago. Yes, it might have drawn the wrong kind of attention, but it looks like we're facing that regardless.*

She shook her head, *No time for that now! Time to fry some monsters!* She chose a spot behind the front line, far enough back to avoid harming the Aos Sí, and bathed a huge swath of Titans with her hottest flames, immolating them almost immediately.

Lasair did not consider herself to be the most sentimental creature, but watching hundreds of Fomori be destroyed violently and painfully, through no fault of their own, was such an immense waste that it made a lump rise in her throat and tears gather in her eyes.

Since she despised crying, the whole situation ratcheted her anger up several more notches. She let out another mighty roar, then screamed, "Balor! Show yourself, you bleeding coward!" She began zig-zagging over the crowd of Titans, spraying her flames, but primarily looking for the leader of the Chaos Faction.

If we can cut the head off the snake, we can end this quickly and save lives. Now, where is that piece of shite!

She continued her search until she was almost back to the shore and could see what appeared to be the end of the line of Titans. Balor was nowhere to be found.

I don't like this at all. Time to regroup!

She headed back to the front line, intent on returning to Deirdre and her fellow gods to decide on their next steps in light of Balor's absence. She was approaching the main fighting area and began her descent to set down behind the Aos Sí vanguard.

If she had bothered to look behind her, she might have noticed the angry storm clouds gathering at the behest of several Titans. A resounding boom shook the land as a clap of thunder rang out, howling winds and driving rain adding to the chaos.

Lasair did look back now, just in time to see dozens of huge, needle-sharp icicles flying toward her. She dodged and accelerated her dive, but wasn't quite quick enough to evade all the projectiles. Her scales provided sufficient armor to protect the majority of her body, but three of the icicles sliced through the thinner membrane of her wings, tearing jagged holes and eliciting a scream of pain and frustration from the fire goddess.

Her landing was less than perfect, falling more into the category of a controlled crash. More of the dangerous icicles were headed her way, and she braced herself for their impact, when a shield of earth and rock arched itself over the frazzled and injured dragon.

She looked around and saw Liam several paces away with his hand up, controlling the shield, protecting her from further injury. She shifted into her Fae form, the wounds on her wings transferring to her shoulders in this wingless shape she'd chosen.

The Titans noticed that their attack had been thwarted, but it wasn't hard to determine who was responsible. Their focus shifted to Liam, who suddenly found himself the target of those wicked icicles. He quickly created a second shield to protect himself but could not avoid all the projectiles. One icicle sliced deeply along the left side of his ribs, and another pierced his right upper thigh, embedding half its length within his flesh.

He was able to maintain the shields, but a roar ripped from his throat as he struggled with the intense pain. Several quads rose into the air, and their Fire Fae shot controlled bursts of flame above the crowd, melting the icicle projectiles before they could land.

Siobhán, upon hearing her oldest bellow in pain, wheeled Morrígan around, intending to head to her son. Lasair noticed and said, "Wait! I'll go to him, you get Sláine!" Liam's mother hesitated briefly, then nodded and tore off toward the triage center.

"It's time to retreat! I need several quads to bombard the front line, and somebody open a bloody portal and get the healers and wounded out of here so the soldiers can follow," the fire goddess directed the Aos Sí as she ran to check out Liam.

The Earth Fae was not in immediate danger, but his blood loss could become concerning if not handled now. Fortunately, Siobhán and Sláine arrived just then, the healer nearly jumping from the horse before she stopped moving.

She quickly assessed his injuries and determined the slice along his ribs was probably painful but not life-threatening. His leg, however, was bleeding more than she liked. She let her magic sink into the wound, encouraging the blood to clot and slow the bleeding. Once that was done, she dug around in the small satchel she'd brought and quickly wrapped a bandage around his leg, letting it help stop the last of the bleeding.

Now that she was reasonably certain he would survive

the wound, she sat back on her heels, put her hands on her hips, and said, "I thought we had an agreement, lad. The fighting's barely begun, and you're already bleeding on the damn ground!"

Liam opened his mouth to respond, but Lasair beat him to it. "Don't be too hard on him, lass. He saved me from further injury, and I'm grateful for the help."

"He's always been protective, even to his own detriment," his mother added.

The dragon then pinned him with her glowing crimson gaze and said, "Listen to the females in your life, lad. Things will go so much smoother if you do."

Deciding that with his mother, his beloved, and an actual goddess in agreement, his chances of winning any argument were roughly zero. So, he nodded and smiled.

The whoosh of a portal opening was a welcome sound, as was the sight of healers and their patients quickly moving through the shimmering doorway. Next, the majority of fighters followed, with Sláine, Siobhán, and Liam bringing up the rear.

Lasair shifted back to her dragon form and said to the last few quads, "I'll hold them off while you make a run for the portal."

As soon as they broke off and flew for the portal, she bathed the front line of monsters with a wall of flame, causing momentary confusion and retreat from the Titans as they attempted to flee the fire.

This gave her, and the remaining quad holding the portal open, the few seconds needed to step through and rejoin those at the World Tree.

Lasair stumbled through the portal with the final quad and immediately made her way to Deirdre. The High Druid took her hand and led her to a nearby bench, sitting with her and sending an assistant to bring Cré and Tonn to meet them. Ruaig was already stationed at the second barrier, but they would fill him in after they received the update.

When they were all gathered, the fire goddess relayed what had happened at the battle of the first barrier. They all felt good about their troops' casualty-to-kill ratio. Nobody wanted any soldiers to die, but that was not the reality of war. All they could do was attempt to minimize their losses and end the battle as quickly as possible.

Far more concerning was their inability to locate Balor. Since it was unlikely he had decided to abandon his Titans and run away, the chances were excellent that he was planning something...unexpected.

"I think we need to proceed as planned. There's not much we can do until we find the bastard. But all of you must be extra careful. Keep your eyes and ears open, and we'll adjust our plans when we have more information," Deirdre commented.

The three gods nodded, and Tonn replied, "Very well. But we need to consider unbinding you, Dee. It may be our last resort. Do you have any ideas about how we could hide you once that happens?"

They needed to hide her. *That's it!*

"I do now!" she replied, anxious to find out if her idea would work. She looked around and saw Emer and Grady nearby, so she called them over to her.

"I need to get a message to Máire, but she's already at the second barrier. Could you portal over there and let her know she needs to see me as soon as she can break away?"

"Aye," Grady replied. "The fighting may already have begun, but we'll give her the message."

They walked over to Cara and Riley, who were with the other two members of their quad. They quickly opened a portal for them and the leopard and wolf hurried through it.

Deirdre and the dragons discussed different options, provided Máire could deliver the means to hide the High Druid, if necessary. *Lass, I hope you're as smart as I think you are.*

Emer and Grady quickly oriented themselves once they were through the portal. They didn't see the Fire Fae immediately, but they came across Conor, directing the cavalry to take their positions before the Titans arrived.

"Have you seen Máire, lad?" Emer asked, her eyes still scanning the crowd of soldiers. "We have a message for her from Deirdre."

"No, but give me just a bit, and I'll take a look around for her." He finished giving instructions to the last few riders, then nudged his horse into a quick trot to make a quick sweep of the perimeter in search of the Fire Fae.

While they waited, they watched the healers setting up a triage center. Cordelia, who had been eliminated from the Fianna Trials after breaking her arm, had proven to have a natural ability with healing and had quickly proven herself to be a worthy leader. So, she had been given the responsibility of leading the healers during this expected skirmish at the second barrier.

It didn't take long for Conor to find Máire, and she and

Corley soon approached the two familiars. "What do you need from me?" she asked.

"Deirdre has a very important question for you and has asked you to return to her at your earliest convenience," Grady replied.

Máire began to reply but was drowned out by the sound of a massive thunderclap, followed quickly by hurricane-force winds driving freezing rain and sleet sideways, making it impossible to see or hear.

The Titans followed the storm, taking advantage of the disoriented Fae and doing tremendous damage in a short time. Ruaig launched his dragon form into the air and quickly rallied the Aos Sí. They began implementing their hit-and-run strategy, but they were more than a little rattled by the vicious onslaught.

Máire's quad swiftly lifted into the air, attempting to get above the storm. Once they broke through the clouds, the Water Fae sucked the moisture from the system, and the Air Fae, with Ruaig's help, pushed the remaining disturbance further out toward the sea. The Fire Fae then sent burst after burst of flame down upon the heads of the Titans, and Corley ripped stone from the ground beneath the monsters, fashioned it into several razor-sharp spears, and began skewering Titans with them.

Meanwhile, the healers were quickly inundated with wounded after the Titans' blitz attack. The Air Fae who'd been tasked with transporting them were having a hard time keeping up, so Delia put another healer in charge of the triage and went out into the battlefield to help the wounded where they were.

Conor used the cavalry to help isolate individual Titans so the quads could take them out. He had just sent some riders to separate a couple of monsters, and he noticed they were having trouble, so he called Collin to help them out. The young Earth Fae joined the other riders, and they had almost separated the Titans, but one of them appeared to suffer some sort of breakdown. It began screaming and flailing the crude sword it carried wildly.

Collin found himself caught between the crazed monster and its slightly calmer companion. His horse attempted to bolt, tossing the Earth Fae from the saddle. His right arm got tangled in the reins as he fell, stretching it out, threatening to dislocate it from his shoulder. As the horse continued trying to get away, the berserk Titan brought his weapon down blindly, severing Collin's right arm just above the elbow.

Conor would never forget the sound the youth made as his arm was sliced from his body. The horse bolted, the arm still tangled in its reins as a grisly souvenir. His cousin made a mad dash to reach Collin, who had passed out from the trauma and was still very much in danger from the raving Titan. But Delia was closer. She reached him first, quickly slowed the bleeding, and signaled an Air Fae to help her get him back to the triage center.

The crazed Titan chose that moment to lose the last little bit of his mind, bellowing his pain and rage as he raised his jagged sword above his head. The new healer covered Collin's body with her own, desperate to save him at all costs.

The monster's sword sliced down where Delia's neck met her shoulder, wedging itself in her spine. Collin's eyes had just fluttered open in time to see her eyes go wide, then shut for the last time as her body collapsed on top of him.

Conor lifted a stone spear from the earth and pierced the lunatic Titan right through the heart, dropping him immediately. One of the other quads had taken care of the berserker's companion, and the Air Fae Delia had called for arrived. She lifted Collin and quickly carried him to the portal Ruaig had just ordered to be opened so they could retreat.

Conor dismounted and removed the sword from Delia's body, brushing her hair back from her face gently. Then he laid her across the horse in front of his saddle, remounted, and galloped through the portal.

△△△

Family

is life

31

"Collin!" Croía screamed as she watched the Air Fae float his unconscious, bloody form from the portal to the main triage center nearby. She leaped from her horse before it was actually stopped and ran over to him.

"What happened?" she cried, speaking to no one and everyone at once.

Conor, tears streaming down his face, answered, "I'm the fecking screw-up everyone thinks I am; that's what happened."

Siobhán rode up and said, "No, mo leanbh, you are *not*. And I'll hear no more of that, understand?"

The distraught Earth Fae just hung his head, one hand gently stroking Delia's back as if he could still somehow comfort her.

Siobhán let her shrill whistle fly and called out, "I need an Air Fae!" Cara was nearby, and she rushed over to help.

Conor's mother dismounted Morrígan, stopped at Croía's side, sending her to the triage center to wait for news of Collin, and approached her son. When she got close enough to determine it was Cordelia's body he was carrying, her own tears started. She hadn't known the lass well, but she didn't have to be familiar with her to understand her death was a horrible waste. And it appeared that Conor thought he was responsible.

Cara approached Conor as well, letting out a startled gasp when she saw Delia's wound. Through her tears, she said, "Let me take her, Conor. You brought her home; now let us have her, love."

His hand clenched around her waist, reluctant to let her go, as if that would somehow make it more real. But he let out a shuddering breath and lifted his hand off her, allowing Cara to gently lift her with air and float her over to a makeshift morgue area. They would mourn their dead later if any of them were left alive to do so.

Siobhán rested her hand on Conor's knee and said, "Do you want to tell me what happened?"

He lifted his eyes to meet her gaze, despair evident on his face. "We were doing fairly well, but a couple of Titans were being difficult, so I sent Collin over to help. One of the monsters went bloody nuts and Collin's horse reared and bolted, unseating him and tangling his right arm in the reins. As he was being dragged, the berserker slashes down and, and..." He paused a moment to collect himself. "After he cut off his arm, Delia ran over to stop the bleeding. I could've saved her if I'd only been a little closer, a little quicker. But the berserker was still berserking and it killed her as she tried to protect Collin. This is all my fault, Mam."

"Climb down, son. I need to have a word with you."

He sighed again but dismounted as she asked. "From what I understand, Delia was a natural healer. She would have to be for Morgan to allow her to lead a group of healers like that."

He shrugged and nodded. "And Collin has been begging to be part of the fighting. He wanted to protect our people, the same as the rest of us. I know you don't believe me right now but remember these words—You are not to blame for this, Conor. You did what you were trained to do. And Delia and Collin both knew this was dangerous, but they wanted to be a part of defending our home. Don't minimize their sacrifices by trying to take blame that isn't yours."

His eyes widened as he considered that. His mother squeezed his arm and continued, "Just keep that in the back of your mind, love. This will take time to process, but you need to know it's not your fault. This is a fight to the death, and neither side will escape unscathed."

Niall could be seen approaching, a worried expression on his face. "Go talk to the lad. I'll go check with Morgan and see if there's an update on Collin. And I hate to be unfeeling, but the monsters are still coming. Your head needs to be back in the game before they get here, eh?"

He nodded to her right before Niall caught him in a tight embrace. Conor buried his face in the crook of his beloved's neck, allowing himself one more moment of grief.

Siobhán patted Niall on the shoulder and said, "Let him mourn a bit, then help him get it together. I don't know how long we have before the Titans arrive." Niall nodded, one arm around Conor's waist, the other hand rubbing circles on his back.

She took a deep breath, then remounted Morrígan to find her beloved and check for news about Collin.

Working near the main triage center, Deirdre watched in horror as Collin was transported in. Then she saw Cordelia being floated over to the morgue area with that horrific wound. This was not the first serious injury or death they'd experienced today, but these two Fae were so young that it ripped her heart out to see such suffering.

Focus! There will be time to grieve later. I hope.

Ruaig joined her, and the other three gods, Cré and Tonn had recovered their strength from the first battle, and Lasair had just gotten the okay to return to the fight, her wings already healed from the earlier damage.

"What happened, lad?" Deirdre asked.

The air god sighed and said, "I'm still not entirely sure. Our tactics were working, we were cutting down their numbers, isolating and eliminating them, using our hit-and-run strategy. Then, it seemed like several of them lost what was left of their minds. The only thing I can think is that Balor must've nudged them mentally and caused several of them to melt down."

"Fecking Balor," Lasair complained, "He has really outstayed his welcome, don't you think?"

"Indeed," Deirdre replied. "Let's hope Máire can come through with what we require because our options are growing ever fewer."

"And what is that?" the Fire Fae asked as she approached the group.

"Ah, just the lass we need," the High Druid said. "I have a question for you. Could your mirroring artifact contain something, reflecting it back on itself, so to speak?"

The skilled artificer considered the question. "It's possible, I suppose. But what would it need to reflect? What are we trying to contain?"

The seer looked at the dragon gods as if asking them a question.

"I think it's time for full transparency, love. It seems unlikely we will prevail without unbinding you," Tonn said.

Deirdre turned her attention back to the Fire Fae and replied, "My power. We need to disguise it."

Máire looked extremely confused and said, "Your air power? Why would we need to hide that?"

"No, lass. My other power." The High Druid went on to explain the situation, the Fire Fae's eyes growing wider with each new revelation.

When all the secrets had been revealed, she said, "Bloody hell, Dee. Can I still call you that? Feck me, my brain is having a hard time with this." She shook her head and said, "I can freak out later. To answer your question, I believe I can hide your new, or rather very, very old, power. I'm not sure I can do it indefinitely, but long enough to come up with another, more long-term plan, should be feasible. But I need to go to my workshop. And I'll take Corley with me. I might need an extra pair of hands, and he'd probably follow me anyway." She shrugged in acceptance of her beloved's protective nature.

Deirdre nodded, then caught the eye of Rónán, who had been given the relatively safe job of running errands for the healers. She waved him over and instructed, "Lad, go find two horses and bring them back here." He ran off to complete his task.

She turned to Máire and said, "You find Corley and the two of you hand command of your regiments over to your seconds. Come back here and grab your horses, then make haste. I don't know how much time we have, lass." With a nod and a gulp, she was off to find her beloved. They would need to move fast.

Ruaig leapt into the air, immediately shifting to his dragon form and taking off to see how long they had before the Titans arrived.

Deirdre spotted Laoise and Saoirse nearby, apparently waiting for their Fae to return. She approached them and said, "Could you gather the familiars and let them know it's time for skin bonding? I'll get the Fae, and we'll have a quick chat before the monsters get here."

They scurried away, quickly gathering familiars and sending them to the World Tree to prepare for their next part in the battle plan. The High Druid amplified her voice and said, "Gather round everyone! We need to prepare for the next attack."

Once they were mostly together, sprawled throughout the gardens, she continued, "The Titans will be here shortly. I believe it is in our best interests to load up on skin bonds, so each quad will have its own miniature fighting force to take these bastards out. Isolate, separate, eliminate."

"And keep your head on a swivel!" Siobhán cried, earning a few chuckles.

"Indeed," Deirdre agreed. "Remember to begin with your bonded, then let as many unbonded familiars tag along as you can. The more, the better; we want the Titans surprised and confused when they unbond and swarm them."

Ruaig zipped overhead, calling out, "No time to be gentle, I'm afraid. We're about ten minutes from incoming."

"You heard the snaky gold dragon! Get your arses tatted up with as many familiars as you can!" Fintan added, his bellow reaching even those Fae on the far side of the gardens. His porcupine familiar, Dris, stood beside him, nodding in agreement.

What came next was oddly fascinating to watch. A bonded Fae's familiar formed the first skin bond, and then the unbonded thronged the soldiers. Anywhere a patch of skin was showing, a familiar could be found attaching themselves to it. The only exception was the facial area, since unbonding from that location could disorient the Fae and cause an accident in the midst of battle.

Áine chose to bond to Keegan along the top of her spine, wings stretched up, pointing to her skull. As soon as she was finished, she thought, *Did I do that right? Wow, this is weird. I can hear myself think, but I can hear you think, too. Bizarro!*

Thanks for the insight, girl, but it's time for the others to bond. They'll talk to you and you relay any messages to me, okay?

The phoenix scoffed mentally and said, *Yeah, yeah, I know how it works.*

More than a dozen additional familiars bonded to Keegan's skin, and by the time the last of them was finished, Áine was less dismissive.

For fuck's sake, quiet down! she bellowed internally, making Keegan squint in pain. She smacked the palm of her hand against the side of her temple a couple of times, thinking, *Got it under control in there?*

Getting there, the phoenix replied.

Well, get there faster. The monsters are almost here.

Somehow, Áine mentally nodded.

The Fianna arrayed their regiments in front of the World Tree and triage center, protecting their most vulnerable. Lorcan, Fergal, and Nora dispersed their Shadow

Weavers and former Titans among the Fae warriors, ready to use water and shadow to hamper and contain the monsters as best they could. Their familiars sprinkled themselves throughout, filling in any potential gaps. Siobhán had the cavalry stationed throughout the gardens, ready to cause confusion and relay messages and supplies wherever needed. Shay and Spéir coordinated Air Fae to help transport the wounded or whatever the healers required to be moved.

Deirdre spread her Druids throughout the area of the gardens in front of her. She connected with each of them and braided the power they funneled to her into a rope of energy, which she sent through the earth and into every Fae soldier participating in this battle. It wasn't much, but it might help them maintain their stamina throughout the fight.

They didn't have long to wait before they could hear the Titans approaching, their grunts and occasional screams seeming louder and more frantic than before. Their master was driving them hard.

When they were almost to the Aos Sí forces, the front several rows just disappeared, portaling out to the side. The monsters pulled up short, obviously confused and distressed by what they didn't understand.

While the creatures were disoriented, the quads who had portaled out flew around behind some of the Titans. The cavalry added to the chaos by racing between and around the monsters like a disgusting and dangerous barrel race, if the barrels were alive and warped beyond recognition. And insane.

Once they had isolated a few of the Titans, the quads landed and signaled their skin-bonded familiars to materialize. Suddenly the monsters were being ripped apart by familiars while the Fae brought their elements to bear. It was a chaotic and strangely fascinating sight.

Their tactics were extremely effective at first, whittling down the number of Titans substantially. So many died, in fact, that it began hindering both sides as they had to maneuver around the bodies. Deirdre called for several Air Fae to transport the dead to the morgue area, which was quickly outgrowing the allotted space.

In the confusion of the battle and the chaos of shuffling dead bodies around, a few of the creatures were able to slip through the vanguard and draw near the healers. Lorcan, Fergal, and Nora, along with their familiars and a very annoyed Declan in his bear form, were able to handle the odd breakthrough at first. Then, something changed.

The Titans began acting like an overturned hornets' nest. Their behavior became more erratic and violent, with self-preservation no longer of any importance to them. Several creatures screamed and charged straight ahead, mowing down anything and anyone in their path.

The Fae reinforced their lines, taking the monsters out as quickly as possible, but they were seriously close to being overwhelmed.

Deirdre broke contact with the Druids, releasing them to help where they could. Then, she and the dragon gods conferred quickly, while taking out the occasional stray monster that got too close. "I don't think we can wait any longer!" Cré rumbled, stomping the ground so hard a shockwave knocked the currently charging Titan onto her back. "We need to unbind you and bond. It's our only chance!"

"And what happens when the others show up while we're licking our wounds? We'd be decimated," the seer argued. Lasair sent a blast of flame to incinerate the downed creature's head, then replied. "In case you hadn't noticed, we're already being decimated! We need to act now!"

Deirdre resigned herself to choosing the lesser of two evils, when the thunder of hooves reached her ears. She turned to see Máire and Corley riding like their hair was on fire. The two pulled up their mounts and jumped down.

"I've got what I need, but it will take me a few minutes to put it all together," she explained.

"Do what you need to, lass, just do it quickly!" The Fire Fae set to work, making the needed adjustments to the artifact to turn it into the inward-facing mirror they required. Ruaig launched in the air for some quick aerial recon while Máire worked.

While she worked, the Aos Sí were quickly losing the battle. Titans stomped through quad after quad, leaving death and destruction behind them. There were hundreds of trampled Fae, many with familiars forever bonded to their skin. The strategies and tactics they had practiced and worked on were no longer effective against an enemy made up of kamikaze troops.

Keegan and Calder were running themselves ragged, trying to save as many lives as possible. The speed with which they could portal and attack was the only thing even remotely effective at this point. Calder also attempted to do very basic first aid when he could, saving more than a few Fae. Keegan used her air power to whisk the injured back to the triage center once he had them remotely stable.

Despite the best efforts of those two and the rest of the healers, the ground was still littered with broken and bleeding Fae and familiars. They were simply unable to keep up as their people were being slaughtered. Keegan's quad thirty-three, made up of Rowan, Bran, Desmond, and Brona worked so well together that they almost seemed to anticipate the others' reactions. But even they weren't immune to the insanity of the Titans. Keegan let out a sob as they came across the quad's broken bodies while headed toward the World Tree to regroup.

They landed close to Deirdre and the healers, hoping to protect them to the bitter end. Áine demanded to be freed, and Keegan gladly obliged her, grateful for the break since she could feel a migraine building behind her eyes after the constant running commentary she'd had in her head this whole time.

"We're losing this fucking fight!" the phoenix yelled once she finished materializing. She hovered for a moment, looking around. "We need to level the playing field. Where the hell is the big baddie? We haven't seen that douche-canoe Balor yet. If we take him out, the rest will fall."

Ruaig raced back toward the World Tree just then, bellowing, "I found Balor! He swam along the coast and is approaching from the south. That's why they're going crazy, he's close enough now to really crank up the mental compulsion."

Máire said, "Done!" and handed Deirdre a small artifact. It had a leather strap that she could wrap around her wrist to keep it secure.

"Turn it on now and do what you need to do. Hopefully, it will keep everything contained."

"Hopefully?" Lasair asked. "Are we sure we trust this lass?"

"Do you have a fecking choice?" Máire snarked at the fire goddess. "You lot came to me, and in less than an hour, I created a pretty fecking advanced artifact. If you don't trust me, do it yourself."

The red dragon shifter scowled at her briefly, then smiled and said, "I like her."

"Yes, yes, you can fangirl over the smart one later. Right now, we have bigger problems," Tonn said, anxiety taking its toll on the ordinarily mellow dragon. She looked at Deirdre and continued, "It's time to restore you, Danu."

Family

is life

32

"Wait, what?" Keegan said, her eyes going wide. "Did she just say Danu? As in the mother of the gods, Danu?"

"It would appear so, lass," Calder replied, a look of shock on his face as well.

Lir and Áine both inclined their heads in a show of respect. "I knew I liked her," the phoenix whispered to the Pegasus.

Danu smiled at them, returned the familiars' nods, and replied, "Yes, my loves. I promise I will explain everything, but not right now." She turned her piercing blue eyes on each of them in turn, then continued, "I need to let my companion gods unbind my power so that I can help defend my children and stop Balor. It's not fair to ask this of you, but I need some time. Will you four do your best to delay him? I will come to you as soon as I can."

Keegan and Calder looked at each other and their familiars. "We'll do it," the redhead replied. "Come on, guys. Time to save the world."

They all lifted into the air and sped away toward the leader of the monsters.

⸻ ⸻ ⸻

The four dragon gods surrounded Danu, and each called their element. Water droplets coalesced from thin air, swirling around Tonn's arms, crisscrossing her chest and waist, and twining around her legs. Ruaig called a mini cyclone into existence, the whirlwind spinning around his limbs and core. A flowering vine grew from the earth, crawling around Cré's legs, over his hips and waist, up his chest, and down his arms. Lasair just erupted in flame.

They raised their arms, took a step forward, and joined hands, palm to palm. Their heads rocked back, and a brilliant golden glow erupted in a sphere around them. The light surrounded Danu, lifting her up and slowly spinning her around. Her hair and kilt swayed gently, floating around her as if underwater. She began to glow softly as she reabsorbed her power.

⸻ ⸻ ⸻

The four defenders of the Aos Sí didn't have to fly far before they came upon the bane of their existence. They pulled up as soon as they came within sight of the rampaging monster.

"Blech! He's like Jabba the Hutt and a Cyclops had a baby. A very, very ugly baby." Áine was not impressed.

"I don't care what he looks like. We need to slow him down!" Keegan replied, stationing herself and Calder to float directly in the path of the Chaos Faction's leader. The familiars moved to flank him, attempting to keep his attention from settling on any one of them. They called their powers—the four elements for the two Fae, fire for Áine, and crackling electricity for Lir. They began circling, again each trying to draw his gaze from the others.

Balor roared in frustration at his continuously moving targets. He swept his head from side to side, opening his third eye to bathe his opponents in the sickly green light of his chaos magic.

They were able to dodge that easily enough, and they began sending a barrage of attacks his way. Calder hurled stone spears at him, then shaped water into thick needles and yelled, "Freeze them!" Keegan sucked the heat from the air around them and added a little extra air power to her love's projectiles, peppering the beast with a multitude of punctures and slices.

Balor called forth an electrical storm, sending several lightning bolts their way. Keegan quickly spun them away, barely avoiding the attacks.

Lir sent sizzling waves of electricity at the monster, momentarily stunning him and interrupting his assault. The chaos beam struck the Pegasus with a glancing blow, disorienting him slightly, but he recovered quickly and retreated, landing on the ground to regain his equilibrium.

"I'm setting you down by Lir. Check on him while Miss Thang and I flambé his ass!" Calder nodded, and she deposited him next to his familiar.

While that was happening, Áine began taunting the half-crazed creature. She flew nimbly around, calling him names and slinging insults he most likely did not understand.

"Hey, numb nuts! Yeah, you, shit-for-brains! You're so ugly, when you look in the mirror, your reflection looks away!"

She got carried away then and flew close enough that Balor could touch one of her flaming tail feathers. She immediately flared her flames and laughed as he howled in pain.

"You're not the brightest crayon in the box, are you?" She circled back around to join Keegan in front of the monster.

"What do you say, girl, time for a little barbecue?" Keegan asked.

"Oh ew, I'm not eating that pile of slug spooge. But I'll certainly help you cook him!"

"Then let's light him up!"

Both of them sent a wall of flame at the beast, Keegan ramping it up with her air power until it was white hot. Balor was able to pull water from the air and douse the fire, but it immediately vaporized the moisture, giving him a painful burst of steam to the face.

"Fuck! I forgot he has water powers, too!" the phoenix exclaimed. "Split up!"

Keegan dove toward Lir and Calder, and Áine whirled the other way. The Pegasus launched into the air, his bonded on his back. The Fae was unused to the wings, but he adjusted quickly.

The four circled and distracted the monster, throwing attacks at him and landing many of them. But he also inflicted his fair share of pain.

Lir and Calder got too close during one of their assaults, and Balor clipped them with a roundhouse punch. The Pegasus crashed into the ground, the attack having broken one of his wings. Calder also landed roughly, a few paces away, his right upper arm broken. Keegan quickly landed next to them, protecting them from attack while they were vulnerable.

Áine used the distraction to accomplish her ultimate goal in life. She flew over to one side of the monster, quite a way above his head. Then, she revved her flames up and focused them on one side into a tight beam. She let out a wild roar and dove, her path crossing directly in front of Balor. She extended her wing as she passed by, allowing that focused line of flame to carve a line across the monster's chest. She had finally burned someone's nipples off.

The creature discovered a new octave as the scream of pain ripped from his throat. The phoenix barely dodged the resulting backhand, but as soon as she was out of reach, she did an impressive series of aerial moves in celebration, letting out a shriek and a drawn-out, "Fuck, yeah!"

The wailing coming from the beast grew more and more crazed, the pain goading him into retaliation. But instead of going for Áine, he aimed at Lir and the two Fae on the ground.

He opened his third eye and let that swampy green light bathe the three of them with his chaos magic. The resulting disorientation and malaise left them moaning and weak, unable to escape the beam.

Áine loosed her flames at the monster, but he called up a storm and kept a steady stream of rain falling. She tried moving around to get at him from different angles, but he blocked her attacks no matter where they originated.

The phoenix let out a scream of frustration, hovering in the air, unable to help her family. Suddenly, a sense of calm descended over her. She turned to Calder's bonded, and said, "Lir. Take care of them for me." He nodded his agreement, unable to speak from the effects of the chaos magic.

Áine began spinning in place, her body moving faster

and faster; a hum, faint at first but quickly gaining volume, began as her body began to glow a coppery orange.

Keegan let out another moan that turned into a long, drawn-out "No!"

The glow surrounding the bird gradually deepened to a dark, vibrant ruby red, her body spinning unbelievably fast. Lir knew it was almost done and managed to gasp, "Calder! Earth shield, now!"

Calder raised a curved shield of thick earth before the three of them just in time. The hum, which was annoyingly high-pitched, erupted in a sonic boom, the red glow expanding outward as a shockwave of lava-hot flame.

The force of the blow hurled Balor backward like a rag doll. He hit the ground and lay still.

The cessation of the chaos magic beam left the three of them gasping in relief. Keegan sat up and peeked around the edge of the earth shield.

A giant crater, blackened and smoking, extended out concentrically from where Áine had been. The Fae looked around, but her familiar was simply gone.

A wail rose from the center of her body—heartbreak and despair given voice. She let it echo across the meadow until she no longer had breath to sustain it. Lir and Calder, both with their broken limbs tucked close to their sides, nestled her between their bodies, tears streaming down their faces as they held the sobbing, desolate girl.

Long before it felt right to move on, Balor's body twitched. Then it twitched again, this time moving a little longer. Finally, he stirred in earnest, not even having the grace to have perished in Áine's sacrificial flames.

"Why won't he fucking die!" Keegan screamed, ready to leap up and finish him off by herself. But Lir stopped her by saying, "Do that, and you make her sacrifice pointless.

Because you *will* die. I don't know how he's still alive, but if he can survive the death flames of a phoenix, he is beyond us, love. We'd better pray Deirdre, I mean Danu, is ready because we're done. It will take a god, or rather gods, to defeat this monster."

The glowing sphere surrounding Danu had just dissipated, lowering her body back to the ground. While the sphere had disappeared, the goddess herself was still glowing brightly. She had just opened her eyes and drew breath to speak when Áine's flames exploded across the field of flowers where they battled.

Lasair bowed her head, and the other four gods gasped. Then Danu shook her head and said, "We will mourn later. Right now, I have got to kill this son of a bitch."

"I think this is going to take all of us, love," Tonn said, her form instantly dissolving, traveling through the air, and imprinting in her blue dragon form as a tattoo curled around Danu's right arm. Lasair followed suit, her red dragon landing along the goddess's left arm. Cré was next, his stocky green dragon wrapped around her right leg. Ruaig was last; his yellow serpentine dragon form twined sinuously around her left leg.

Danu clenched her fists and flexed her arm and leg muscles, feeling the power of the dragon gods coursing through her. She rose into the air and flew the short distance to where the three companions sobbed in their grief.

"I'm so sorry! She was fearless, and she will be missed." She looked them over and noticed Balor stirring a short distance away.

"Now then, you three need to visit the healers. Let me take it from here." She lifted them and, with a flick of her wrist, sent them flying back to Morgan and his team.

Danu rose into the air and flew directly toward the still-stunned and smoldering monster. She settled to the ground a few paces in front of him and rested her hands on her hips.

Balor managed to struggle to his feet, his large frame towering over the goddess. He let out a wet, raspy chuckle, saying, "I see the neglectful mother finally got her memories back. Your own forgotten daughter has loved, protected, and prepared us for victory far better than you." She gasped, suddenly putting the pieces together. He scoffed at her in disgust.

What a bleeding wanker! Lasair commented. Tonn snapped, *Not now! She needs to concentrate!*

"My daughter was not forgotten! She chose to let envy and selfishness rule her and caused immense heartbreak and turmoil as a result." Danu called all four elements, each one spinning around the limb marked by the corresponding dragon god. "But never fear, lad. I will deal with my wayward spawn eventually. First, though, I will deal with you."

She began throwing various elemental attacks at the monster, assaulting him so quickly he could barely remain on his feet. With a roar, he opened his third eye, spewing his noxious green chaos magic onto the goddess.

Danu felt the sickly energy trying to seep into her, attempting to warp and shift her magic into something destructive and violent. She tapped into her innate power of creation to purify the energy and send it back toward Balor.

He screamed and immediately closed his eye, cutting

off the flow of the now pristine magic, which scalded and burned the monster's warped and gnarled energy pathways.

"Aw, what's wrong, love? Is grandma's magic too much for your little brain?" She pinned him with her gaze and asked, "Have you ever wondered why The Morrígan insists on gifting you with magic that corrupts your body and mind? Could it be perhaps that she is more interested in controlling you than helping you?"

"She only wants the best for us! Sometimes that requires sacrifice!" he screamed, shaking his head and breathing hard as he recovered from Danu's magic.

"Mhmm. Funny how you are the only ones doing the sacrificing, eh?"

He let out an earth-shattering roar, unable to cope with the logic the goddess presented, and charged forward. He blasted chaos magic at her and threw lightning from an impromptu storm he drew forth.

She deflected both attacks easily, then said, "Balor, you know you don't have to live this way, right? With the help of our healers, we could attempt to repair the damage the chaos magic has done to your body and mind."

What are you doing? He doesn't deserve your mercy, Danu! Ruaig complained. *Everyone deserves mercy,* the goddess replied.

That brought the Fomori up short, and he just blinked at her in surprise. After a moment, he narrowed his eyes and said, "You're just trying to poison me against her. But I won't let you. I will destroy you and your pathetic replacement children!"

He attacked again with the blight of his chaos magic and lightning, winds whipping around them and stinging sleet pelting them.

Danu just shook her head sadly and said, "So be it." She called the elements again, weaving them together in a long, thin whip-like weapon. The different strands pulsed and glowed, seeming almost alive in her upraised hand. She waited until Balor was just a couple of paces away and swung the lash rapidly sideways, slashing it across his throat.

The monster's huge, misshapen head landed at her feet, bouncing a few times before rolling to a stop. His body remained standing for a brief moment before crumpling like a marionette with the strings cut.

Danu released the elements, then closed her eyes, freeing the dragons from their skin bonds. The tattoos faded from her skin, particles of the gods traveling through the air, coalescing into the four gods in their Fae forms.

They quickly surrounded her, offering a brief supportive embrace. She pulled away from them and said, "Let's finish this."

The dragon gods shifted into their draconian forms, and all five gods lifted into the air, speeding quickly back toward the Aos Sí and the Titans they were still battling.

When they were within sight of the battle, it became evident that the monsters were very nearly defeated. The gods made quick work of the remaining enemies and landed near the triage center by the World Tree.

There were far too many dead and wounded. Lasair leaned close to Danu and whispered something. The mother goddess gasped and said, "Of course!" The fire goddess took flight, heading back toward the site of the final battle with Balor.

She landed near the center of the smoldering crater in the middle of the meadow. She leaned down, brushing aside some ashes and debris, picked something up, cradling it gently, and flew back to the triage center.

She searched through the patients, staying out of the way of healers running themselves ragged to keep up with the needs of the injured. She soon found the youngest Ó Faoláin brother sitting on a bench, his arm in a splint to allow it to finish healing, his familiar in goat form next to him, and Keegan cradled against his other side, crying quiet tears.

The fire goddess approached the group, her hands covering the object she had retrieved from the crater. She stopped in front of them and knelt down in front of Keegan.

"I think you left something back there," she said with a slight smile. She opened her hands to reveal what appeared to be a small egg-shaped chunk of lava rock and handed it to the redhead.

Keegan took it, looking first at the egg, then back to the goddess, a questioning expression on her face. "Feed her fire, love," Lasair replied.

The Dúbailte's eyes brightened, and she directed her hottest flames around the black egg-shaped item. Cracks began to appear throughout the object, a bright red glow emanating from inside.

After a few moments of this, a loud cracking sound was heard, and the top of the egg popped up slightly, wobbling just a bit. Keegan ceased her fire and gently lifted the jagged piece of shell. Underneath was a tiny, sparsely feathered phoenix blinking her wide eyes, looking up at her.

The phoenix then reached her wings up to touch the top of her head. Her little face scrunched up into a scowl and, in a high-pitched, squeaky little voice, she said, "Gods-dammit! I need a new crown!"

M.A. KILPATRICK

Family

is life

33

It would take a long time for the Aos Sí to recover from Balor's madness. Those survivors who were conscious and ambulatory quickly pitched in to help those who needed it. Siobhán, Niamh, Étaín, and Spéir took it upon themselves to organize the various Fae and set them to the work that needed doing.

The healers were most in need of help. They were exhausted from the immense energy they had expended. Siobhán steadied Morgan as he swayed on his feet, the Chief Healer having given more of his power to the injured than anyone else. But Sláine and Muireann were nearly as depleted, so Lorcan and several other Shadow Fae volunteered to help with the less seriously injured. It wasn't long before Tonn approached and made them all go sit down and rest a bit while she tended to the last of the wounded.

The healers were all escorted to a table with food and drink to help them regain strength. Sláine and Morgan collapsed against Liam and Siobhán, who fed them bits of fruit and cheese.

Lorcan didn't want to presume anything, so he gently

wrapped an arm around Muireann's shoulders, desperately trying to avoid crushing her in his arms. She looked at him with red eyes and tear-stained cheeks, and said, "I've lost patient after patient today. So much bloody death. I'm not wasting one more moment." She turned to him and buried her hands in his hair, pulling his face down to meet hers. He blinked just once before pulling her tight against him and deepening the kiss, wrapping her long braid around his wrist and tugging slightly.

She melted against him for a moment, letting him support most of her weight. He broke off the kiss and swept her off her feet, taking her to the table and placing her in his lap as he sat down. He fed her tidbits as well, her head nestled in the crook of his neck.

Shay and Spéir organized several other Air Fae to use their air power to transport patients from one section of the triage center to another. They also moved the casualties to the morgue area.

Earth Fae turned over the soil in areas coated with blood and viscera, relegating the remnants of battle to the dark earth, where it would be repurposed and recycled.

Máire, Niamh, and Étaín led a small team of artificers in creating several large cooling artifacts. Other Earth Fae created huge earthen domes to store the deceased. Once the artifacts were ready, they would keep the shelters cool enough to preserve the dead until they could be appropriately celebrated and remembered.

Once the immediate needs were met, Shay asked those who were able to gather near the World Tree for a much-anticipated explanation from their High Druid.

She stood before them, allowing the natural luminescence her power imbued her with to shine forth. As the Fae noticed her new glow, there was a fair amount of whispering and conjecture. She waited for the crowd to settle a bit, then amplified her voice, saying, "Fáilte, members of the Aos Sí! I believe it is time I reintroduced myself. I am Danu, mother of the Tuatha de Danann. Most of you know the story of my first children, or at least some version of it. I would like to briefly recount the actual history.

"My husband, Donn, and I created the pantheon of Irish gods. Our children were numerous and beloved, although there were some periods of strife, as is often the case with any family. My power is the essence of creation. After a time, it instilled a restlessness in me to create anew. I met the elemental dragon gods, and we agreed to form a new race. They combined the essence of their magic with my power of conception, and the Aos Sí were born.

"I was so delighted with my new children! They were curious and adventurous, and I loved them dearly.

"My husband was very supportive and would often join me to visit the first of the Aos Sí. Some of my older children, however, grew jealous and bitter. They viewed the time I spent creating and visiting my new children as a slight against them. The ringleader of this small but vocal faction was my triune daughter, The Morrígan. She could not accept the idea of sharing my affection with a new group of children.

"So, she and a few others gave me an ultimatum. Either I relinquish my power and memories and join the Aos Sí in Tír na nÓg, or she and her fellow malcontents would attack my new children and destroy them. Destroy you.

"They also insisted the dragon gods remain on their islands. They were allowed to retain their memories but were forbidden from contacting us. They complied but began creating the familiars to be our companions and guides."

This revelation caused more than a few gasps and murmuring. Danu held up her hands, waiting for the crowd to settle so she could resume her tale.

"I was backed into a corner. Unfortunately, while not actively plotting against me, the rest of my children were also not forthcoming with a lot of vocal support.

"So, we made our home here. There have been hiccups along the way, but I am very proud of how far we've come."

"But how do the Fomori fit in?" Lorcan asked.

"Well, my love, it turns out that The Morrigan decided to try creating her own children. Thus, the Fomori were born. You're my grandson, lad," she said with a beaming smile.

"If The Morrígan is evil, though, doesn't that make us —" the Shadow Weaver began.

"*No,* a stór. The creator does not imbue goodness or evil to their children. What those children choose throughout their lives decides the type of Fae they will be," Danu said somewhat sternly.

"However, in this case, The Morrigan stepped over the line by introducing chaos magic and corrupting Balor's mind."

Nora asked, "And what will happen now that you have both your memories and power back? Won't they be able to tell?"

Tonn spoke up, adding, "We don't think so. Máire adjusted a mirroring artifact to bend the aura of her magic back upon itself. That should keep any sign of her returned abilities from alerting the Tuatha de Danann."

"But, I won't lie to you—We will eventually have to deal with them. Whether in years, decades, or centuries is the question. To prevail, we must think long-term, devise strategies that enhance our strengths, and develop plans to mitigate our vulnerabilities.

"In the meantime, we will honor the sacrifice of our fallen soldiers and celebrate our victory at the upcoming Lughnasa observance. We will move forward as a family."

Siobhán mumbled something, and Danu smiled at her. "Louder, please, lass."

"Family is life," the petite blond repeated, returning the smile.

⧈⧈⧈

The next several days were spent cleaning up the aftermath of the battle. The large earthen domes created to contain the casualties were filled with Fae, Fomori, Titans, and familiars. They would be cremated together on pyres during Lughnasa.

The minor injuries all healed quickly, but the more seriously injured continued to recuperate, and the healers called on volunteers to help them care for the many patients currently convalescing. Lorcan and Liam seemed to spend a great deal of time helping around the Healer's Compound, as did Siobhán. Having seen so much death and destruction, none of them wanted to let their beloveds out of their sight.

Croía and Dillon also volunteered often, checking in on Collin and attempting to lift his spirits.

"Morning, Stumpy!" his sister called out cheerfully. The young Earth Fae rolled his eyes at her attempt at humor. "You're not as funny as you think you are," he replied, gingerly adjusting his position, careful not to jostle his wounded arm.

Croía kissed the top of his head, smirked at him, and replied, "Yes, I am."

She gave Ómra, a good scratch behind the ears, and sat next to her at the foot of his bed while Dillon took the chair off to the side. When he was first injured and brought to the healers, he regained consciousness enough to free her from the skin bond. She had been frantic when she rematerialized but had calmed down once the healers stabilized him. She had stationed herself at the foot of his bed ever since.

Collin looked at his sister, took a deep breath, and asked, "Has Danu said when we can start the reconstruction?"

"She said to let you regain your strength for another couple of days, then she'll begin if that's what you want." She paused a moment, then continued, "You know you don't have to go through that pain, right? Your family will love you whether you have both arms or not."

He nodded and said, "I know that. But I want to be able to dance with a lass or toss my weans in the air someday. Besides, there are plenty of people with an injury like mine who would give anything to regain their limb. I feel like not taking advantage of this opportunity somehow dishonors them. I can take the pain. It will be worth it."

She smiled at him and replied, "Very well, lad. I just wanted to make sure you knew you had a choice."

"And Muireann said she will help with the pain. She's become quite good with blocking the neural pathways to minimize discomfort," Dillon added encouragingly.

He nodded, looking slightly less anxious. He yawned, eyes watering slightly. His sister gave his foot a squeeze and said, "We'll let you get some more rest. You work on regaining your strength, and we will worry about getting you a new arm in a couple of days."

Collin laid back down, Ómra nestled at his feet, and was nearly asleep before the two of them left his room.

As they were leaving, they ran into Muireann and Lorcan, who were organizing supplies. "How's the lad feeling this morning?" the healer asked.

"Tired, but determined to go through with the procedure," Croía replied.

Muireann nodded and said, "Aye, I figured he would. I'll help him all I can. He'll be fine, lass, I promise."

🔱🔱🔱

The sun was a warm glowing vermillion disk as it hung low in the sky on the eve of Lughnasa. Faery lights floated throughout the World Tree gardens, twinkling in the late summer evening, illuminating the multitude of opulent floral garlands decorating the space.

Fae had begun congregating around the gardens, dressed in flowing summer dresses and kilts in the colors of their clans. Everyone wore floral crowns with vines and leaves trailing down into their hair. Of course, the familiars wore their jeweled crowns, but they also had the Fae Glam cailíní weave flowers and vines amongst the bling.

And, of course, Dana worked overtime to create an even more extravagant crown for Áine's tiny little nearly bald head. It would grow with her as she regained her size and strength, although that would take years, much to the familiar's dismay.

Shay greeted those assembled, "Fáilte! We gather this evening to honor the fallen and celebrate the future. We will begin with the funeral rites, led by Danu and the dragon gods."

The casualties of the battle had been placed upon pyres

in an open meadow adjacent to the gardens, and their allegiance before death was considered unimportant. Titans were laid beside Fae, Fomori were intermingled with familiars, acknowledging the sacrifice of all. The number of the dead was heartbreaking.

Danu and the four dragons rose high above the pyres, hovering in the air. The mother goddess tilted her head back, and a plaintive, mournful tune without words poured forth. The dragons began a beautiful aerial dance, diving and soaring, weaving among each other in a visual display of equal parts grief and hope.

After a few moments, as Danu's song reached a crescendo, Lasair passed over the pyres time after time, bathing them with her flames until the fires soared high above them.

The High Druid-turned-goddess let her melody fade into silence, tears streaming down her cheeks in her grief. She gazed out at the crowd, heartsick at the pain visible on her children's faces. She tilted her head back once more and let out a keening wail. She was quickly joined by the dragon gods, who roared their grief into the night.

The crowd began to participate, their howls and shrieks of pain creating a cacophony of mourning. The keening slowly began subsiding as, one by one, those gathered released their pain into the ether and let their wails and cries fade into silence.

Danu and the dragon gods, now in their Fae forms, drifted back to the ground, the bonfire of pyres flaming behind them.

"Let us now celebrate the memory of the fallen. Tell stories of their lives and laugh at the memories. Eat, drink, sing, dance—whatever calls to you this night. At dawn, I will perform a handfasting ceremony for any of you who care to join with another."

⟁⟁⟁

Groups congregated around small bonfires scattered throughout the World Tree gardens, eating, drinking, singing, and dancing, celebrating the lives of those fallen.

In honor of Delia, the Fianna, and their friends and families told stories about the poet and healer. Áine, her tiny body tucked into a pocket sewn on the front of Keegan's gauzy white sundress, insisted on another limerick competition in her memory. The others happily complied, coming up with the randiest and raunchiest poems they could manage. Cré, an enthusiastic poet himself, attempted to create a limerick and failed miserably. Fintan and Lasair, on the other hand, were able to match Áine's supreme level of filthiness, causing the phoenix to cackle with delight and say, "Fuck yeah, I've found my tribe!"

Collin, having endured the painful process of having Danu regrow his arm, was beaming as his friends and family congratulated him. The new limb had a silvery sheen, which Danu said would diminish somewhat but would likely never completely go away. The lad couldn't care less; he was simply delighted to have regained a fully functional arm.

⟁⟁⟁

Couples gathered throughout the gardens as the sky began to glow with the impending sunrise, surrounded by their friends and families. The recent losses they had all suffered left everyone feeling sentimental.

Danu and the dragon gods in Fae form rose into the air above them, and the mother goddess began, "From the ashes of grief, we rise together to begin anew. By standing before us today, you signify your desire to be joined, heart and soul, to one another. Please join hands."

As the couples complied, the four dragon gods called their elements, which swirled around them. Danu continued, "Do you each promise to love and cherish, serve and honor one another? To support each other through any trials that might come your way, so long as you both choose this union?"

"We do," echoed throughout the gardens.

Each dragon sent a thin filament of their element to wrap around each couple's intertwined hands, the strings plaiting together in a glowing knot.

"May these hands heal, protect, shelter, and guide each other. As this knot is tied, so your lives become bound together, one to the other."

Danu's ever-present luminescence began to increase, getting brighter and brighter until it burst forth to envelop everyone present. The recipients immediately felt a sense of joy and well-being unlike any they'd experienced before.

The elemental knots connecting each couple's hands glowed brightly, then sunk into their skin, leaving a tattoo of the braided elemental filaments behind.

"Congratulations, you are now joined and blessed by the mother goddess and the dragon gods! Kiss your beloveds!"

The couples each shared an intimate kiss as the sunrise peeked above the horizon, sending beams of golden light to illuminate the gardens and those celebrating within.

Keegan and Calder's kiss was cut short by a muffled, high-pitched, "You're squishing me!" They pulled back, and an affronted Àine popped her tiny head out of the pocket, saying, "Watch it! You'll have plenty of time to suck each others' faces off later."

Keegan rolled her eyes and replied, "You're incredibly high-maintenance, you know that?"

"Yeah, I love you, too," the phoenix replied. Now let's party before the boom chicka wah wah starts."

Family

is life

EPILOGUE
SIX WEEKS LATER

In celebration of Morgan's birthday, Siobhán threw a huge party and invited all their friends and family, which made for a rather large gathering. They had decorated the manor gardens with more flowers and foliage than normal, and Aoife and Tommy were visiting, so of course, the elder female insisted on cooking a feast.

Keegan and Cara were setting the table and bickering. Niamh and Siobhán were nearby and after several minutes of the cousins snarking back and forth, they both snapped, "Enough!"

All four females looked at each other and scowled. Muireann and Sláine, along with Lorcan and Liam, had the misfortune to enter the gardens at that moment, and the looks turned on them were less-than-friendly.

Danu and the dragon gods were right behind Muireann's group, so they saw the incident and were puzzled by the out-of-character behavior. But Siobhán recovered quickly, as did Niamh, and they both welcomed the newcomers, apologizing for their crankiness.

The rest of the guests arrived shortly after that, and

everyone found their seats. Croía, Dillon, and Collin helped Aoife and Tommy bring out the food, which consisted of several legs of lamb, scalloped potatoes, and green beans with tomatoes and mushrooms, much to Áine's dismay. As the aroma of the meal wafted through the gardens, Keegan and Máire jumped from their seats and ran to empty their stomachs into the nearby bushes. Several other Fae looked mildly nauseated as well.

Tonn looked around the group, then looked at Danu, and said, "I think your handfasting blessing was a bit too strong, *mother* goddess. Your power of creation has taken hold in the lasses, and they're busy creating."

Danu's eyes widened, and she said, "Oh, dear."

Everyone wore confused expresssions as they struggled to understand what was going on. Áine, who thankfully had hopped out of her pocket to sit on Lir's back before the vomiting began, piped up in her squeaky little voice and said, "Aww, I've seen this in the movies! You're all preggers!"

Emer looked at Grady and said, "Told you so."

The silence was deafening as comprehension spread throughout the group. Varying levels of terror and excitement were plain to see on the expressions around the table.

Tonn stood up and said, "Everyone stay calm, let me see what's actually going on for certain." She closed her eyes and sent her power around the table, letting it sink into all of the females to determine the truth of the situation. The azure glow of her energy quickly passed by some of the females, however it hovered over the abdomens of Keegan, Máire, Cara, Sláine, Muireann, Niamh, and Siobhán, glowing cheerily.

When she was finished, she opened her eyes and

declared, "Well, your family is about to increase by eight. Congratulations!"

The stunned expressions remained, and speech appeared to be beyond any of those directly affected by the news. Aoife was beaming, thrilled by the idea of a new batch of babies to adore. Lir took that opportunity to ask, "Um, it seems only seven lasses are affected, but you mentioned eight babies?"

The water goddess looked at the goat and replied, "That's because your bonded is apparently an over-achiever. Keegan is carrying twins."

That was too much for the redhead, who barked a sharp laugh and said, "Of course I am! Fuck me sideways."

Conor smirked and replied, "Well, I don't know about sideways, but obviously, the rest of that ship has sailed."

She grabbed a hot roll from the basket in front of her and pegged the dimpled smart-ass between the eyes. This only made him laugh harder as he snagged the rebounding roll from the air and bit it in half. Siobhán was too stunned to even cock an eyebrow at her son.

Conor, for once not responsible for the chaos, said, "I'm going to be a guncle, how exciting is that? You lot better dig in. I hear you're going to need loads of energy. Let's eat!"

The End

Afterword

Well, you made it through, mostly unscathed, I trust. I thoroughly enjoyed writing this story, and if you enjoyed reading it, I hope you'll consider leaving me a review. It's one of the easiest ways for you to help an author out. And it's free, so that's a plus.

Thank you to my alpha, beta, and ARC readers, as well as all the readers who consistently like my content and buy my books. You all mean the world to me, and I am so thankful for your support. If you'd like to connect, I am @makilpatrick.author on social media and my website is makilpatrick.com.

Also, I want to credit Reddit user u/Condenastier for the "rain and alcohol" comment. It was too funny not to borrow.

Thank you all for taking this journey with me.

Go raibh maith agat!

M.A. Kilpatrick

AFTERWORD

Milton Keynes UK
Ingram Content Group UK Ltd.
UKHW041945131124
451149UK00005B/522